Susan Stephens was a professional singer before meeting her husband on the Mediterranean island of Malta. In true Mills & Boon style, they met on Monday, became engaged on Friday and married three months later. Susan enjoys entertaining, travel, and going to the theatre. To relax she reads, cooks and plays the piano, and when she's had enough of relaxing she throws herself off mountains on skis or gallops through the countryside singing loudly.

USA TODAY bestseller **Lucy Monroe** lives and writes in the gorgeous Pacific Northwest. While she loves her home, she delights in experiencing different cultures and places on her travels, which she happily shares with her readers through her books. A lifelong devotee of the romance genre, Lucy can't imagine a more fulfilling career than writing the stories in her head for her readers to enjoy.

THE PLAYBOY PRINCE OF SCANDAL

SUSAN STEPHENS

AFTER THE BILLIONAIRE'S WEDDING VOWS...

LUCY MONROE

MILLS & BOON

First Published in Great Britain 2021
by Mills & Boon, an imprint of HarperCollins*Publishers*
1 London Bridge Street, London, SE1 9GF

The Playboy Prince of Scandal © 2021 Susan Stephens

After the Billionaire's Wedding Vows… © 2021 Lucy Monroe

ISBN: 978-0-263-28232-0

MIX
Paper from
responsible sources
FSC™ C007454

This book is produced from independently certified FSC™ paper
to ensure responsible forest management.
For more information visit www.harpercollins.co.uk/green.

Printed and bound in Spain
by CPI, Barcelona

THE PLAYBOY PRINCE OF SCANDAL

SUSAN STEPHENS

For my readers.

There's nothing better than reading and music to lift the mood. I hope you enjoy reading this book even more than I enjoyed writing it, and that the happy-ever-after ending gives you the type of happy feeling that stays with you until you pick up your next romance.

With my love to you,

Susan xx

CHAPTER ONE

The Winter Palace of Prince Cesar Romano di Sestieri Ardente, Isla Ardente

'Sofia Acosta? Are you serious?' Cesar speared a look at his long-suffering equerry, Domenico de Sufriente. Dom had been reading out the proposed guest list for Prince Cesar's annual banquet celebrating the start of the polo season, to be held at Cesar's *palazzo* in Rome.

'Signorina Acosta should be invited with her brothers,' Dom pointed out, 'or you risk insulting the entire Acosta family.'

Cesar frowned. That would not do. He planned to play exhibition matches in aid of charity with the Acosta brothers' Team Lobos in various locations across the world. Working out a way to exclude his least favourite woman without offending her brothers was impossible. It couldn't be done.

Dom cleared his throat to attract Cesar's attention. 'You expressed a wish to field a mixed team for your next charity event. Having grown up in competition with her brothers, Sofia Acosta is—'

'Don't mention that woman to me!'

'One of the finest riders of her generation,' Dom ventured.

'But not a professional rider like her brothers,' Cesar pointed out.

'True, but there are few who can match her on the field of play.'

After the furore she had created, Sofia would pull in the crowds, Cesar silently conceded. The exhibition matches would benefit all his charities. 'Her skill on horseback is undeniable, but I'll never forgive her for what she did.' Using his hand like a blade showed his feelings on the matter.

'The article?' Dom proposed mildly.

'Of course the article.' What Sofia had written was the most florid pack of lies, and with her by-line brazenly plastered over the rubbish in a newspaper belonging to Cesar's old adversary Howard Blake. He'd been at odds with the man since their schooldays, when Blake had stopped at nothing to get some innocent fellow student to take any blame directed at him—until he'd tried it on with Cesar. That hadn't gone too well for Blake, Cesar recalled.

What was the relationship between Blake and Sofia? Was she another innocent dupe, playing a role in some new tactic Howard had thought up to bring Cesar down to repay him for policing Blake during their years at school? Was it possible Sofia hadn't realised the harm the article could do to her family and to his? Why target him at all? They met in passing at polo matches, so why had she set out to destroy his reputation?

He only knew the woman through her brothers, though he'd registered Sofia's face and figure, as both were outstanding. Was she in cahoots with Blake? Without knowing the facts, he could rule nothing out. There was only one certainty, and that was that he refused to dignify her smut with a response.

'I will deal with Sofia Acosta in my own time.'

'Yes, sir.'

Dom bowed his head, but not before Cesar had caught sight of the expression on his equerry's face. 'Why are you looking so smug, almost as if this pleases you? You're lucky that you still have a job—that anyone in the palace has a job. Sofia Acosta tried to bring us all down, so please don't suggest she has any finer qualities. She's a typical over-achiever, dipping her snout into multiple troughs because she can't bring herself to keep it out. I applaud dynamism, but not when the only possible motive is profit.'

'She rides like a demon,' Dom reminded him.

'Perhaps you would too, if you'd grown up in a horse-mad family.'

'I doubt it,' Dom murmured beneath his breath as he straightened his perfectly straight tie.

'Regrettably, she would be an asset to the team,' Cesar added, musing out loud. 'She'd draw the crowds based on her scandalous nib-dipping alone.'

Money-grabbing siren, he raged inwardly. Sofia Acosta might have the face of an angel, and a body made for sin, but it seemed to him that she'd stop at nothing, even bringing down a country, if it stood in the way of her lining her pockets.

A warm breeze chose that moment to steal in through an open window. It went some way to softening his tension, by reminding him of what lay outside the palace. However luxurious—and Palazzo Ardente was exquisite—a palace was just a set of rooms, static and unchanging, while the ocean and the beach were fresh and new every day.

'Just don't put that woman anywhere near me,' he instructed as he left his desk.

'The banquet will be held at your *palazzo* in Rome where there is a very long dining table...'

'Excellent. I will sit at the head, while Sofia will be at the far end with my mother and sister.' The hint of a smile tugged his hard mouth. 'I'd like to see Signorina Nib-Scribbler lecture them on the error of my ways.'

Sofia Acosta, outstanding polo player, amateur artist and sometime journalist, had famously written an article about European royalty, mostly featuring Cesar, though she had also taken a passing swipe at her brothers. The headline banner had screamed, 'Is Royalty Necessary in Today's World?' The piece had caused a storm on social media. As an ex-Special Forces, polo-playing billionaire prince, Cesar had been put under the microscope—Sofia's fantasy microscope. His reported success with women, according to her, had made him sound more like a rampaging satyr than a dutiful prince.

She'd found numerous archive shots, showing him in every form of undress: playing polo bareback, barefoot, in banged-up jeans, topless, with a bandana tied around his head, making him look more like a kickboxer on vacation than a serious-minded working royal. There was even one of him naked beneath a waterfall, slicking back his hair as if he had nothing better to do than idle away his time in a tropical lagoon.

Granted, a few shots showed him in his official capacity, but always with an array of different women on his arm.

Had there really been so many?

The upshot of it was that a playboy billionaire, more intent on womanising and indulging in a hedonistic lifestyle than leading his country, was as far away from the man he was as it was possible to imagine. Duty came first. Now. Then. Always.

Not to say he had no appetite for pleasure, but that was then and this was now, and he always looked forward. Sofia Acosta had dredged up the past, embroidering the facts until they could only cast doubt in people's minds. What he found almost harder to believe was the way she'd dragged her brothers through the same mire. So much for family loyalty!

Why should he forgive Sofia Acosta for making him and his friends of many years the butt of her argument when she hadn't given him the courtesy of seeing her words before they had gone to print? The effect on his pride might have been fleeting, but the longer-lasting effect on his country, and on the trust of his people, was what he cared about. Had she thought of that before she had put pen to paper? He doubted Sofia Acosta had thought of anyone but herself.

And now he was expected to sit in the same room as this woman and make small talk with her?

'Sofia Acosta won't be the last unwanted guest you are forced to welcome,' Dom pointed out, reading Cesar's mind with his customary ease. 'Think of this as a trial run for the many unpleasant duties you'll face in the years to come.' Dom turned the page in his notebook. 'You requested a meeting with Sofia's brothers and your sister Olivia after the formal dinner?'

'Correct.' Anything to avoid dancing with the twittering princesses his mother and sister had no doubt seen fit to invite.

'And Sofia Acosta will be included as well?' Dom pressed diffidently.

'She will have to be included,' he reluctantly agreed. He frowned. 'That's supposing we can drag Signorina Acosta away from her hippy commune.'

'The facility is more of a retreat,' Don ventured as

he handed over a report, 'funded entirely by Signorina Acosta.'

'With money inherited from her parents?'

Don confirmed this.

'So, the demon rider has some redeeming features,' he murmured as he scanned the report Dom had offered for him to read.

'This is my decision,' he stated. Unfolding his athletic frame from the chair, he went to stand by the window. 'I will meet with the Acostas, including Sofia Acosta, and my sister Olivia, after the state dinner while the other guests are enjoying dancing to the orchestra.'

'A wise decision, sir.'

Dom had his head down, but why was he smiling? What was his equerry thinking? Recently, Cesar had begun to doubt Dom's advice, because something had changed in his manner. His equerry wasn't as open as he had used to be.

Before he could progress his thoughts, a pair of sparkling black eyes invaded his mind. They belonged to a voluptuous woman who could throw any man off his game. It was hard to avoid Sofia Acosta when they attended polo matches across the world, and when their paths crossed there was always fire between them.

There'd be no fire at his dinner. Sofia must learn that she could not profit from rumour and stolen, off-duty snaps. She knew nothing about him. He knew even less about her. If Dom handled arrangements for the dinner correctly, that was how it would remain.

Sofia Acosta's rustic rural retreat, deep in the heart of Spain, where Sofia's brother Xander is tired of sitting for his portrait

'If you could stop painting for a moment and speak to me!' exclaimed the magnificent brute on his towering black stallion. 'I should never have agreed to this!'

'If you would stop ranting for a moment and keep still,' Sofia soothed, 'maybe I could finish this...'

Paintbrush high, she checked her work, and silently admitted that it was nigh on impossible to capture the darkly glittering glamour of a man who overshadowed everything in his immediate vicinity, including the stallion he was mounted on. 'Against all the odds,' she declared as she laid down her brush, 'I've finished. Come and see, if you like—I'm sure you'll love to see yourself blazing like a comet, fiercer than your stallion Thor.'

'Which is exactly the impression you intended to convey, I imagine,' Xander commented in a husky drawl as he eased his neck. 'Why must everything be sensational in your world, Sofia? Why can't you settle for calm?'

'If that's a reference to the article—' She stopped speaking as hurt overtook Sofia's natural desire to defend herself. Xander was her eldest brother, and the only one of the four prepared to listen to her defence when it came to an article that had appeared in print under her name but had been written by someone else. As of now she had nothing to back up her claim.

'You're a talented woman,' her brother insisted as he dismounted. 'You have your retreat, your riding... And you're a passable artist,' he remarked grudgingly as he scanned the canvas she'd been working on. 'You don't need to add journalist to your quiver of accomplishments. Be content with what you've got. Settle down. Enjoy life.'

'Like you?'

Xander ignored this reference to his continuing bachelor state. Having had responsibility for the entire family thrust upon him when their parents had died, he'd never loosened up and allowed himself to live.

'Why this pressing urge to see yourself in print, Sofia? I'm guessing it must have paid well.'

That was what all her brothers thought—that she had sold her soul to the devil in return for a hefty pay-out. The truth was rather more complicated. She had never wanted to see her name in print, but the offer of lots of money to write 'something harmless' had proved irresistible. There were so many people she wanted to help at the retreat she had created. Without a constant flow of funds that was just impossible.

Since her mother's death, Sofia had lived her life as she believed her mother would have wanted her to, which included building a haven where others could escape for a while to recover from their difficult lives. Never in a million years had she imagined that once the article was written it would be changed, or that her brothers would be put under the same distorted spotlight.

Both they and Prince Cesar did so much good in the world, and yet some sleazy scribe had altered Sofia's words to make it seem that they and Cesar showed one face to the public, while living scandalous lives. If she didn't keep her mouth shut, there would be more articles, she had been promised, and these would be worse than the first. To protect her brothers she couldn't say anything, not even to Xander, though the article had done irreparable harm to their relationship.

Finding pony nuts in his pocket, Xander gave his stallion some treats before handing him over to a waiting groom. Turning around, he dipped his head to confront Sofia. 'Who wants to read everything in the garden of the super-rich is rosy? Was that your thinking? I don't understand you Sofia. Why didn't you come to me for money, instead of selling your cross-eyed opinions to that scurrilous rag?'

Because the damage had been done. The article she had written in good faith had already been changed.

'If you need money so badly I'll make you a loan right now—'

'No. Please!' Xander was always ready to save the day, but she had to do this to prove the article was a lie. The threat of a second article appearing under her by-line, mentioning trumped-up charges involving financial shenanigans between Cesar and her brothers, was enough to secure Sofia's silence.

'There's something you aren't telling me,' Xander stated with certainty.

This was the moment she should tell him the truth, but from the moment they had been orphaned, Xander had taken all the responsibility on his shoulders. She had to sort this out. 'I'm not a child any longer. I appreciate everything you've done for me, as we all do, but you must let me stand on my own two feet.'

'Your stubbornness will be the end of you,' Xander snapped as they left the barn. 'I can't understand why you picked out Cesar for special mention. He's done more good than you know, and yet you appear to have gone out of your way to undermine him. You put a country at risk with a few thoughtless words, making out that Cesar is a playboy prince when nothing could be further from the truth. I expected better of you, Sofia.'

She expected better of herself and, knowing she deserved every stinging word, she remained mute.

'Cesar would never discuss the good he does,' Xander continued, frowning, 'and I've no doubt some of the readers will believe your piece of smut. The way you dwelled on him, anyone would think you were half in love with him and jealous of the life he leads.'

'Which only shows how little you know me.' She sounded defiant, but she was broken inside. Xander thinking so little of her hurt like hell. The article had paid well, and every penny of the money had gone to her retreat. The demand for places had expanded so rapidly she'd desperately needed additional funds. Naively believing that what she wrote would be printed word for word, the chance to write an article for a national newspaper had seemed too good to be true. And guess what?

As for falling in love with Cesar... The little she'd seen of that magnificent monster had convinced her that she could never fall in love with such a hard-bitten individual. She'd tried love and had found it a pallid substitute for the romantic novels that had informed her teenage years. That had been when she had been unable to secure a date. Having four high-octane brothers, overlooking her every move, had hardly been an incentive for likely suitors. Rubbing paint-covered hands down her paint-covered, overall, she took Xander to task on the subject of Cesar. 'Every single time I've met the man he's seemed insufferably superior.'

'I think you're harking back to one time when I had to remind you to curtsey when Prince Cesar visited our family home to trial some ponies. You were sixteen years old. Cesar was twenty-four. You may have noticed that over the years that he's changed. You've both changed. He's a hard man because he's had to be.'

Cesar had almost had the throne snatched from under his nose, she remembered. According to the press, a self-seeking man who cared nothing for the Queen, her family or the country had somehow weaselled his way into court, where, with a great deal of flattery and false promises, he had set about making himself indispensable to the Queen—a polite way of reporting he had been her lover. Having uncovered the truth and banished the conman from the kingdom, Cesar had stayed on at court to support and comfort his mother. Sofia heaved a sigh. So he wasn't all bad, just autocratic, aloof and way beyond her reach.

'You will accept the Prince's invitation,' Xander stated firmly. 'His banquet will be your first step towards rehabilitation before you appear in the match.' She had to drag her mind back to the present as Xander continued, 'It's the least you can do. If the public sees you playing polo with the Prince, it will reassure them that things are back to normal.'

Whether it did or not, the thought of seeing Cesar again both chilled and excited her. As compelling as a human cyclone sweeping along on a wave of testosterone, Prince Cesar of Ardente was perfect hero material for susceptible females, but Sofia was neither susceptible nor was she in the mood for trembling in awe at a royal prince's feet. There was nothing more tiresome, in Sofia's opinion, than a six-foot-plus titan lording it over her, as she, with four self-opinionated brothers, was well placed to judge.

'We will attend Cesar's banquet as a family.' Xander stated in a tone that brooked no argument. 'He has requested a meeting with all of us, including his sister Olivia, after the banquet to discuss the upcoming charity polo matches, in which, I presume, you'll be playing.'

'Of course.' Sofia's retreat was one of the charities that would benefit. She could hardly refuse. Neither would she refuse the invitation to Cesar's banquet, though it meant confronting the man she had supposedly slammed in print. That was the best reason for attending she could think of. She'd see her brothers again, and if Cesar really thought so little of her, she had no further to fall.

CHAPTER TWO

HIS STAFF HAD outdone themselves. Never could he remember such a glittering scene. The dining table at his *palazzo* in Rome seated more than a hundred and each high-backed seat, sumptuously covered in night-blue velvet, was occupied tonight. Chandeliers sparkled like diamonds overhead, bouncing light off the jewels of those bound by wealth, power, pedigree, as well as an abiding passion for horses and polo. He was the only mongrel in the room.

His father's son by his mother's handmaid, Cesar had the Queen to thank for raising him as her own. She had plucked him from an uncertain future when Cesar's birth mother had abandoned him in favour of her latest lover. Romano born, he would now be Romano bred, the Queen had decreed. Though as soon as he was old enough to understand the implications of becoming heir to the throne, the Queen had insisted that Cesar must curb his wild streak. She was still working on that.

'Is everything to your liking, sir?' his equerry asked.

'I can't thank you enough, Dom. Please convey my appreciation to the staff.'

Staring through the forest of crystal and silver ablaze like fire on a ground of white damask, his attention fixed on one woman. Sofia Acosta seemed confident and happy and was certainly animated as she chatted easily to his sister Olivia and to his mother, the Queen. His plan to spike Sofia's journalistic guns by seating her with the two women in the room who were strongest and most loyal to him appeared to be foundering. They were clearly enjoying each other's company.

He couldn't have seated Sofia Acosta far enough away, he reluctantly accepted. Even in another room, she would claim his interest. Cesar wasn't the only man present to have noticed the most fascinating woman in the room. What made Sofia so intriguing was the way she chatted so easily with his mother, and achieved what he would have believed impossible at a formal banquet, which was to make his mother laugh.

'You seem distracted.'

Sofia's brother Xander was seated next to him.

'My sister has not done something else to upset you tonight, I hope?' Xander suggested with concern.

'I've moved past that article, and we avoid each other whenever possible.' He hadn't spoken more than a curt hello to Sofia since she'd arrived at the *palazzo*.

'How will this distance between you work when you're playing in the same mixed polo team?'

'The match is in aid of charity. We'll forget our differences and concentrate on that.'

'That's very generous of you,' Xander commented. 'I'm not sure I could be quite so understanding.'

They shared a look. Both men were warriors; neither was understanding.

Cesar shrugged. 'Sofia's your sister and you are my close friend. I won't sully our friendship by carrying on a public feud with your sister.'

Xander raised an amused black brow. 'And this distance you talk of will be enough for you?'

'There's the entire length of a table between us to-night. And when we play our matches, the length of a polo mallet will suffice.'

'Just don't hurt her—emotionally hurt her, I mean. Sofia acts tough but she's always ready to be hurt, and that makes her vulnerable.'

'What do you take me for? I've no interest in her in that respect.'

'Don't you?'

Beyond the fact that Sofia would play an important part in the matches, no, of course he didn't. Who was he trying to kid? Cesar asked himself grimly as Sofia, together with his mother and his sister, threw back their heads and laughed.

How had she won them over so easily? He recalled his mother saying that royal life could be much improved if only people had the courage to express an honest opinion. He imagined Sofia had no trouble doing that. It had become obvious to him tonight that she was a natural communicator. But was she also a natural snoop, using this occasion to fuel another article?

The way to his mother's heart had always been unconventional. Sofia personified quirky with her abundant black hair cascading down her back in a shimmering waterfall of natural waves. Some attempt to tame it had been made. She'd tied a band of brightly coloured flowers around her forehead. Who did that at a royal banquet? He had to admit that the coronet of fresh blooms teamed perfectly with the summery, ankle-length gown Sofia had chosen to wear. With its intricate embroidery, jingling trinkets and happy, summer colours of yellow and pink, the dress perfectly mirrored the smile on her face.

A mix of anger and lust flashed through him. Sofia

had the brass neck not only to outshine every other woman present but to sit amongst his guests as calm as you like. She'd clearly charmed the two people in the world who mattered most to him. Of course, his mother was notoriously tender-hearted, a thought that led him to study Sofia again. Was she as amusing and straight-forward as she appeared tonight, or was Sofia Acosta a wolf in a rather attractive sheep's clothing?

Decision made, he excused himself from the table. Sofia exclaimed with surprise when he reached her chair. Bowing to his mother, the Queen, he dipped his head to murmur in Sofia's ear, 'I need you to come with me right now.'

Her eyes turned wide and curious. 'Are you throwing me out?' A smile was hovering around her mouth.

'Just come with me, please.'

They had attracted the attention of his mother. He smiled quickly for her sake.

'Is it time for pudding?' Sofia addressed herself to the Queen. 'Do we have to change places?'

His mother was laughed warmly. 'No, we do not change places between courses here.' She spared a sharp look at him. 'I believe my son would like to speak to you alone. Am I right, Cesar?'

'Correct,' he rapped, though his mother had managed to make it sound like a romantic assignation when nothing could be further from the truth. He was determined to address the issues between him and Sofia before the business of the meeting began.

He caught a whiff of some delicate wildflower scent as Sofia left the table. With a pretty curtsey for his mother, she thanked the Queen for a wonderful evening.

'Come back to us,' his mother said, with a warning look to him.

'Don't we have a meeting after dinner with Sofia and her brothers?' his sister Olivia drawled with a knowing smile in his direction. Olivia was taunting him with the fact that, as she very well knew, more lay behind his desire to take Sofia from the table than business.

'Don't let us keep you, Sofia,' she added silkily. 'My brother appears to have something pressing on his mind.'

As well as on the placket of his evening trousers, he grimly recorded.

'A stroll in the garden?' he gritted out as soon as he and Sofia were out of earshot.

'You make it sound so appealing,' she murmured.

'Fresh air, and a chance to relive old times,' he proposed.

After what she'd done, he expected Sofia to at least have the good grace to pale at his challenge, but instead she firmed her jaw, inviting, 'Lead the way.'

'Life is more exciting when you say yes,' he remarked with irony.

'In some instances,' she countered.

'In all,' he insisted, striding on.

It was his eyes that made him irresistible, she decided as Cesar led her through the open glass doors and into the garden. Well, almost. *She* would resist, of course. Black sable in colour, they delivered a message no woman in charge of her senses could misinterpret. He had a particular mix of intensity and easy confidence that held the promise of sensational sex.

Brutally handsome, Cesar was savage on the polo field, which was why her brothers often fielded him on their team. And even before the infamous article the media had hinted at Cesar's extraordinary prowess in bed. Did every palace bedroom have a reporter sitting on the windowsill? Were there paparazzi in the bushes even now? she wondered as he led her deeper into the black, fragrant night.

What did Cesar want with her? Why was she here? Where sex was concerned, he was betting on a loser. She might be twenty-four, but her experience to date was incredibly limited, involving inept fumbles in a car, several lunges in the stable, subjecting her to an assortment of acne, halitosis, sloppy kisses and inept, searching hands. This was hardly the stuff of which dreams were made, and was definitely not sufficient preparation for a night-time encounter with Cesar.

'Sprigati!' Cesar urged as her footsteps lagged. 'Hurry up, Sofia!'

This was no romance, only impatience in his voice. So what was this about? Did he plan to rant about the article? He should. She deserved it. He'd probably warn her off ever writing about him again. She could handle that. She hadn't wanted to write about him in the first place.

'It's private enough here,' she stated firmly, refusing to take another step.

'Not private enough for me,' Cesar informed her curtly.

She sucked in an involuntary breath as he swung around to stare at her. Formidable by moonlight, and backlit by flickering torches, Cesar was an awesome sight. Sweet-smelling jonquil and delicate sprays of white star jasmine scrambling up a nearby wall, threatened to weaken her with their scent. Lifting her chin, she confronted him. Entirely by chance, she'd chosen the most romantic spot to stand her ground. Far beyond the palace walls the lights of the city provided a fitting backdrop for a man whose darkly glittering glamour rivalled even that of night-lit Rome.

Cesar's response was the lift of a brow. 'Well? Why have you stopped here?'

'I would like to know the purpose of this meeting.'

A humourless huff was her answer. 'You'll find out,' he called over his shoulder.

'Life is more exciting when you say yes.' Cesar's words banged in her brain. But what had she said yes to?

What was this woman doing to him? He could take his pick. Countless beauties vied for his attention. He wanted none of them because they were obvious and Sofia was not. She simmered with sexuality, yet retreated if he so much as looked at her a beat too long. Was she a virgin? Was that even possible at Sofia's age? Remembering her brothers, he thought it more likely than not. Which rubbished his thoughts on seducing her. The idea of bedding an innocent was inconceivable to him. He preferred older, more experienced women who knew the score, women who used him as he used them, for casual pleasure with no strings attached. His dealings with Sofia Acosta would, from this moment on, be solely restricted to business.

Things did not go entirely according to plan. Having led Sofia into a secluded, lamp-lit pavilion where they would be quite alone until the meeting with Sofia, his sister and her brothers began, she was immediately on guard. Angry and affronted as he was by what she'd done, he had no intention of terrorising her. To this end, he switched on the light and left the route to the door clear, while Sofia stood in the centre of the pavilion, staring at him with a multitude of questions in her eyes.

'What do you want of me, Cesar?'

He kept his distance, but her intoxicating scent had joined them by some invisible alchemy. Bringing the article to mind, he dismissed the magic with a cutting gesture of his hand. 'An explanation would be a start.'

'I'm so sorry, it was—'

'A mistake?' he queried, finding he couldn't contain his anger. 'A mistake that threatens to damage my reputation and that of your brothers?'

'How many times can I apologise?'

'I'm listening.'

'It wasn't what you think—'

'So it wasn't an appalling exposé?' When she didn't answer, he lost it completely. 'If you accepted my invitation to attend the banquet tonight so you could carry on "snooping" for another article, let me warn you that my legal team will take the newspaper down, and you with it.'

There was silence for a moment, only broken by the sound of the Acosta brothers laughing and joking as they approached. For a moment he saw surprise, even anger in Sofia's eyes, as if she'd forgotten the purpose of the meeting, and perhaps thought he'd orchestrated a confrontation with her brothers to get to the bottom of her reasons for writing the article.

Frowning, she confirmed these thoughts. 'I thought our meeting with my brothers and your sister Olivia was scheduled to start after the banquet?'

'It is,' he agreed. 'Can't you hear the orchestra? The dancing has already started.'

They stared at each other while electricity between them sparked like a living force. It was a force that would find no outlet tonight.

'You could help put out the agendas,' he suggested. 'Clipboards? Now?' he proposed when she continued to stare at him in bemusement. 'The charity matches?' he prompted. She lifted her chin with an expression so like his sister Olivia's he could have laughed. The two women shared many characteristics—combat being only one of them. Excellent. He loved a good fight. 'Well? What are you waiting for?'

'For you to say "please",' she suggested mildly.

'*Please* sort out the clipboards,' he ground out, to end the impasse.

Gathering up half of them, she thrust them into his hands. 'Two work faster than one,' she explained, braving his astonished glance coolly. 'Shall I pull these tables around so we can face each other at the meeting?'

He could think of nothing he'd like less than to sit facing Sofia Acosta. Concentrating on anything else would prove impossible. 'This is an informal gathering when friends, who are also teammates, can snatch time in their busy schedules to discuss our upcoming matches.'

'We need clipboards for that?' she queried.

'Are you going to question every decision I make?'

'Only if I think it necessary.'

That level stare into his eyes again, and yet she seemed so calm and logical. The urge to see her wild with lust would have to keep for another time.

'My schedule is cast in stone,' he intoned icily. 'I've laid out an agenda so there can be no unnecessary mistakes in dates or overlaps in commitments.'

She pulled a wry face. 'I'm sure my brothers will love that.'

'I've already checked to make sure our schedules are in synchrony, and they agree with my plans.' Why was he even telling her this? he wondered as a brief wistful look swept over her features. Of course, since the article, he was closer to her brothers than she was. Was that his fault too?

'I'm glad my brothers are happy,' she said at last, with obvious sincerity, 'but does that mean anyone involved in the matches must sacrifice previous appointments to accommodate you?'

'Are you're talking about yourself?'

Her face paled but her lips firmed. 'I was thinking about your sister.'

'Ah, Olivia.' He huffed an ironic laugh. 'She wouldn't allow anything to stand in the way of riding with your brothers. As for you...'

'Yes?' Sofia's eyes narrowed in unmistakable challenge.

'I imagine you'd do anything to heal the rift you've created in your family.'

Perhaps that was a little harsher than he'd intended.

Sofia lowered her gaze but rallied fast. 'I'll study your agenda and let you know.'

As he quirked a brow, she queried, 'Men rule and women obey in your world?'

'You've met my mother and sister. Do you think that possible in my family? But playing in a team is different. Someone has to be in charge or chaos will ensue.'

'And that someone is you?' she challenged. 'Sounds as if you mean to be more dictator than team leader.'

Right on cue, his friends and fellow players, the Acosta brothers and his sister Olivia, came into sight in arrow formation, with Xander spearheading the group.

'I look forward to hearing your explanation of why you felt it necessary to cause such trouble with that article,' he told Sofia before they arrived, leaving her in no doubt that it hadn't been forgotten but had merely been postponed.

CHAPTER THREE

THE CHANCE TO ride with Cesar and her brothers was a lure Sofia would always find impossible to resist. How much more so under present circumstances? Having brothers breathing over her shoulder used to annoy her, but now she missed the closeness more than she could say. The change in their relationship since the article seemed irreparable sometimes, and determination alone wouldn't heal that rift.

She had to find a way to make her brothers believe her, but without being able to tell them everything for fear of them hitting out at Howard Blake, and him hitting out even harder, she was uncharacteristically powerless. Loyal to a fault, her brothers would see the false rant printed in the newspaper about Cesar, with Sofia's by-line proudly displayed at the top, as a blow against all of them.

In trying to save her retreat, she had only succeeded in alienating those she loved most. The upcoming matches were the best chance she'd get to ride with her brothers on neutral territory. She hoped the physical demand of the matches would help to restore at least some of the camaraderie between them.

Her feelings where Cesar was concerned were conflicted. She was a moth drawn his very fierce flame.

Cesar was shrewd, sexy and keenly intelligent. His body kept her awake at night. Dreams were safe. Reality was far more complicated. If she were foolish to offer herself up, as a waiter might offer a canapé, Cesar would swallow her down, lick his lips and move on. Leaving her where, exactly?

Embarking on a voyage of sensual discovery with Cesar would be like casting a minnow into a shark pool. She'd be saved that embarrassment as he couldn't have made it clearer in the pavilion, before her brothers and Olivia arrived, that he would never forgive her for what she'd done.

As the meeting went on, Cesar didn't attempt to include her in the discussion, while her brothers gave her thin smiles when they looked at her at all. Only Olivia pressed her lips together in a reassuring smile, as if she, at least, wanted to believe better of Sofia.

'Are we done here?'

She jumped to attention as Olivia spoke.

'I have a rendezvous later,' the Princess revealed.

'A *rendezvous*?' Cesar demanded icily. 'With whom, exactly?'

'A friend.' That was as much as Olivia was prepared to divulge. This seemed to amuse Sofia's brothers, though for the sake of Cesar they confined their feelings to sideways glances. What were they hiding now? she wondered.

She didn't have to wait long to find out.

Xander was as heated as Cesar when it came to issuing instructions. 'Make sure you're never on your own. Don't do anything that might put you at risk.'

'Isn't that rather the point of a rendezvous?' Olivia drawled with amusement, sliding a conspiratorial glance Sofia's way.

This was one situation she didn't want any part of. Breaking the stand-off, she moved to the door. 'I should get back to my room to log all these dates in my calendar.'

'We can walk back together,' Olivia agreed, seeming as keen as Sofia to escape the mounting tension.

When five autocratic individuals thought they could manipulate the lives of two young women, they had another think coming. Both Sofia and Olivia had endured brotherly smothering as children, and neither of them was prepared to roll over and accept a command simply because one of the titans had uttered it.

'Not so fast.'

She stared at Cesar's hand on her arm.

'We haven't finished talking,' he informed her.

She moved away from the doorway to allow everyone else to leave. 'What do you want to talk about?'

'I think you know,' he insisted. 'You speak and I listen.'

'And then you judge me?' She was trembling inwardly, but that was something he didn't need to know. Could anyone be more attractive, while appearing so hard and autocratic, than Cesar Romano? Cesar was as huggable as an iceberg, and as distant as a faraway sun. 'In my world conversation flows back and forth.'

His stern expression didn't change by as much as a flicker. 'I will evaluate your excuses when I've heard them.'

'So I'm already guilty in your eyes?'

'I have the evidence in print.' He said this with an easy shrug. 'If you can have something that might reverse my conclusion that you are a cold-blooded, money-grabbing traitor to your kind, then please let me know.'

'My *kind*?' she repeated tensely. 'Do you think I imagine myself as lofty as you?'

'I have no idea what you think, but I do know I find it hard, if not impossible, to contemplate working with you on the team unless I have some understanding of what drove you to be so condemning in print. In case you're in any doubt, the only reason you're on the team is because of your prowess as a rider, and the attention your notoriety will bring to the match.'

She had no excuses to offer. Desperate to raise money for her retreat, she'd been tasked with providing details of life behind the glamorous polo scene, little realising she was going to be manipulated by a newspaper mogul called Howard Blake. There was no point now in wishing she hadn't taken that call. She'd been naïve, thinking the polo scene, with its royal connections and appeal to various celebrities, would be something people wanted to read about. She hadn't realised that in writing a harmless article she had inadvertently provided Blake with enough detail to flesh out, making his lies seem perfectly believable.

Now she wondered if Cesar had been his target all along. Prince Cesar certainly had the most to lose when it came to reputational damage. Her brothers could shrug it off. Though that wasn't what they'd told Sofia, of course. In truth, any attempt to tarnish their reputation only enhanced it, for with the exception of Dante, who was now a happily married man, her brothers prided themselves in being the bad boys of polo.

'What?' Cesar pressed, jolting her out of her reveries. 'Not a word of explanation?'

None that she could tell Cesar. First she must find a way to curb Howard Blake's bullying ways. His next victim might be more vulnerable than she was. Blake had already threatened to bring down her brothers if she went public with the fact that he'd changed her words and, goodness knew, there was enough rumour and scandal to damn them. With Sofia's relationship with her brothers already stretched to the limit, she couldn't risk it taking another blow.

'I have no excuse,' she said flatly. 'The invitation to write the article came at a time when I needed money badly, so I wrote a story I knew would sell.'

'*You* needed money?' Cesar demanded with incredulity, no doubt thinking about her brothers' massive combined wealth.

'I have no part in my brothers' tech empire. I launched the retreat with my own money. It grew to a point where I needed a much wider-ranging roster of staff, and that requires proper funding.'

'You couldn't ask your brothers for money?' Cesar exclaimed with disbelief.

'Of course not. I stand on my own two feet.'

'This one defamatory article will keep your retreat running for how long?' His stare pierced her. Cesar's mind was already made up. She was guilty as charged.

'You don't know me, yet you set yourself up as my judge and jury and, if you had your way, executioner.'

Cesar's expression turned as black as thunder. 'And you only know what you've read about me,' he fired back.

She couldn't deny it.

'Gutter journalism,' he derided. 'Aren't you ashamed, coming from a family as proud and as upstanding as yours'?'

Cesar was viciously opposed to everything she stood for. She had to keep her nerve. She could so easily make things worse with careless words, and that would mean losing that closeness with her brothers for ever.

'I imagine you made a pretty penny out of the rubbish that was printed.'

'It wasn't *my* rubbish. It was heavily edited—'

'Rubbish,' Cesar supplied. 'It's easy to deny you had any part in it now.'

'Believe me or not, that's your prerogative. I had no say in the finished article, and every penny I was paid went to support my retreat.'

Disbelief was written all over Cesar's face. 'I'm giving you a chance to clear your name,' he stated harshly. 'This may be your only chance. I suggest you think hard and long before you walk away from me tonight.'

'I don't think anything I say will make you change your mind, so I see no point in staying.'

'I'm sure not,' he agreed.

His short laugh chilled her. She glanced at the door. 'I should be getting back.'

'We both should. I will escort you. Far be it from me to see harm come to any woman, even you. I can only think you're a cuckoo in the family. Regardless of what you've done to them, I know your brothers would do anything to protect you, and I respect their wishes.'

A now familiar blaze of shame burned through Sofia's veins. But one thing was nagging. There had been detail in that finished article that even she hadn't known. So who had? She would have to find out to stand a chance of making peace with her brothers and Cesar.

'I thought you might have more pride,' Cesar remarked as they walked side by side through the gardens to the palace. He made it sound as if she'd disappointed him.

'I have no pride,' she said honestly. 'If I have to wash dishes to keep my retreat going, then that's what I'll do.'

'In between selling more stories on those you profess to help?' he bit out.

The calm she was fighting so hard to maintain was shattered. Trust was perhaps the most vital element in a sanctuary where people came to recover and rebuild their lives. The thought of disclosing even the smallest detail she'd been told by one of the guests was as shocking to Sofia as seeing her brothers and Cesar damned in print.

'At least you have the good sense to appear ashamed of your actions,' he commented as they slowed on their approach to the open doors to the banqueting hall.

Shame was the least of it. This was the first time that she had been faced by the fact that Howard Blake might target her retreat. He must be stopped, but to do that she'd need help. Powerful men like Cesar and her brothers were the only individuals she knew with sufficient clout to curb Blake's bullying, but the truth would have to come out.

Cesar gave her a brief sideways glance. 'You appear confused.'

'Not confused,' she assured him. Suddenly everything was crystal clear. 'I need your help,' she admitted.

'So you're every bit as self-seeking and as selfish as I thought? *You* cause the damage, and now *you* need help?'

She was determined not to show her feelings. Hiding how stung she felt had been second nature growing up. She'd soon learned not to blub in front of her brothers.

'I made a mistake,' she confessed. 'And now I want the chance to make things right.'

'Why don't you take some well-earned respite at your retreat?' he demanded sarcastically. Whirling on his heel, Cesar made to peel away. 'You can find your own way from here.'

She caught hold of his arm. 'Cesar, please...'

He didn't shake her off, and his expression was calculating. The punch to her senses was extraordinary. 'Are you sure it's rehabilitation you're looking for? Or do you have something else in mind?'

She sucked in a sharp breath, but desire never came first for Sofia. She squashed her feelings to concentrate on others, but now she must forget her pride, forget about being a cool-headed woman, and just this once risk everything for the chance to make things right.

He couldn't have been more surprised when Sofia stood on tiptoe to brush a kiss against his lips. 'I'm sorry,' she whispered.

Feelings rampaged inside him at the realisation that Sofia wanted more than to apologise. He knew the signals. This was unusual play for a woman who had betrayed him, and betrayed her brothers, yet for all her bravado there were shadows behind her eyes, and that set up doubt regarding her guilt. He had to know more before he took things further.

Did he care enough to find out?

'Aren't you in enough trouble?' he demanded harshly. 'Go back to the ballroom. There should be more than enough distractions there to keep you occupied.'

'Cesar, please...'

Tension swirled around them as she clutched his arm. Reluctantly, he admired her grit.

'I need to talk to you, Cesar, nothing else, I promise.'

He gave her a cynical look to find her eyes pleading and her lips tempting. He was no saint. She matched him like a tiger, kissing him fiercely as she thrust her body against his. It was as if some force beyond their control had taken them over, Sofia especially, until they were bound together in a dance as old as time.

But something was off kilter. Was desperation driving Sofia's passion or were her feelings for him genuine? Would he ever know? Concluding that deciphering her motives was beyond him right now, he pulled back.

'Did I do something wrong?' she asked, staring up with confusion in her eyes.

'You did nothing wrong.'

She had tasted of honey and innocence, so if anyone was at fault he was. Her mouth was swollen and red where his stubble had abraded it, and her eyes were bottomless pools of distress. *But was that an act too?*

'Why are you doing this?' she asked, rubbing the back of her hand across her mouth, as if to hide the evidence of how much each of them had invested in one single kiss. 'Why kiss me at all?' she demanded. 'Why not ignore me and wait for the evening to end? Then you wouldn't need to see me again until we ride in the matches.'

'I might ask you the same question,' he pointed out.

'You don't want this,' she said with sudden certainty, shaking her head. 'I forced myself on you.' Her face crumpled. 'How you must hate me.'

The idea of Sofia forcing herself on him made him want to laugh, but he couldn't be that cruel. 'Hate is a powerful word,' he commented mildly instead.

'But I can see fire burning in your eyes,' she claimed. 'So why kiss me, Cesar? *Why?*'

'I could say you started it.' He kept his hands loosely looped around Sofia's waist. She made no attempt to break free. 'And you kissed me back. So why did you do that?' he asked with genuine interest.

She was silent and then her eyes cleared as she admitted with faint surprise, 'I couldn't stop myself.'

Appearing seductive, as she most certainly did, yet vulnerable might be part of Sofia's script. She had caused more trouble than could be imagined. Proving he was worthy to rule was a lifelong task, and an article hinting at financial irregularities in his past, however fictitious, did him no favours. He'd embraced responsibility for his country gladly. His countrymen would always come first, and Sofia Acosta would not be allowed to distract him.

'Seems to me you were consumed by that same impulse to kiss me.' Growing embarrassment reddened her cheeks.

He shrugged off her suggestion. 'Everyone's entitled to a momentary lapse.'

'Even me?' she asked.

If he could forget all the doubts and half-truths and uncertainties currently swirling around them, Sofia was perfect, and he wanted her. His body was aroused to the point of pain, but it was the challenge in Sofia's eyes that made her irresistible. Her lustrous hair, tumbling in wild profusion to her waist, glinted like black diamonds in the muted light, making the temptation to fist a hank, so he could draw back her head to taste the soft skin of her neck, was overwhelming. But why give her that pleasure?

'Perhaps that stupid kiss was a lapse we should both accept and move on?' she suggested.

Sofia Acosta was beyond infuriating, yet he loved the way she could rally so fast and come back fighting. Her dark gaze brightened as she intuited his thoughts. Or was that a scheming light? Maybe her only reason for kissing him was to soften his mood in order to dig up more dirt to use in another article.

'Who are you, Sofia?' Holding her at arm's length, he dipped his head to stare into her eyes. 'I can't decide if you're a rogue member of the Acosta family, who cares nothing for your brothers' love or your family's reputation, or if you're under some form of duress?'

Was he imagining it, or did she flinch when he said that? 'If there's something on your mind, please, tell me.'

He was so certain she was about to say something revealing, but Sofia's hesitation suggested she thought him as dangerous as whatever was causing the shadows behind her eyes. *Dios!* Would he never find out the truth about this woman?

There was only one certainty here, and that was the heat rising between them.

'Is this what you want?' he demanded.

'Yes!' she exclaimed, eyes closing, lips parting as his hand found her.

'Then I suggest you find someone else to ease your frustration. I don't play games with dangerous little girls.'

CHAPTER FOUR

CESAR STALKED BACK towards the palace, leaving Sofia standing on her own. She couldn't catch her breath, let alone order her thoughts. Kissing him had been a huge mistake that had left her feeling embarrassed and humiliated. Giving in to wild impulses would only ever lead to trouble. Judging by his expression, she couldn't have sunk any lower in Cesar's opinion.

Not only did he believe her to be a gutter journalist but someone who held her body cheaply, like a counter to be played when it suited her. What irony that nothing could be further from the truth. Her body might ache for Cesar's touch, but not like this, furtively and wildly, but passionately, truthfully and openly. With a long, shaking sigh she dragged herself back into the moment. It was vital to clear her head before returning to the party.

She found it easier than expected to remain in the gardens, where the scent of blossom soothed her. It was quiet and removed from the upbeat atmosphere inside the brilliantly lit palace ballroom, which gave her chance to search her mind for a solution to keep her retreat afloat.

On top of that, she had to keep her brothers and Cesar and any future victims safe from a blackmailing tyrant. Cesar was the most obvious ally. No one wielded more power than he did, but she'd lost his trust. He couldn't have made it clearer that he despised what she'd done, and despised the person he believed she'd become. He wasn't alone in that. Right now she hated herself, but it was no use crying over spilt milk. She smoothed her hair. This was a time for action, not brooding. It would take too long to try to win back Cesar's trust by small increments. She had to be bold, and the only way she knew how to be bold was in the saddle.

The retreat she had created, on land left to her by her parents, was another gentle, contemplative setting, created specifically to house those who badly needed help to rebuild their lives. She could see now that her paintings had been her way of escaping reality, but what was needed going forward was Sofia in warrior mode. There could be no more missteps or hesitation. She had always looked out for herself, and her next task was to convince one of the most commanding men on earth to join forces and help her defeat a bully.

Well, that should be easy, Sofia reflected as she made her way back through the night-fragrant garden. Her body burned with arousal after the encounter with Cesar, while her mind was burning up with embarrassment. Cesar didn't trust her. He didn't like her. And though he needed her to ride in his charity polo matches, he almost certainly wouldn't shed a tear if he never saw her again. But since when had life been easy? There was always a new hurdle to jump. This one just happened to be higher than most.

Having studied Cesar's famous agenda, it was immediately clear that where anything was connected to him, money was no object. First-class travel arrangements had been made for all, including the horses. With influential contacts across the globe, Cesar naturally anticipated that everyone's path be as smooth as his. He could alter the destiny of a country at a stroke of his pen, for goodness' sake, and all she needed was for Cesar to help her end the bullying tactics of one wicked man.

· First she'd have to win back his trust and change his opinion of her. The feat loomed ahead of her like an insurmountable wall.

Then it was a wall she'd go around, or go through, Sofia determined.

She paused before entering the ballroom to allow her heartbeat to steady. She would need every bit of her composure to confront Cesar again. Most important of all was to hide her feelings for him. Attraction had no part to play in this. She had a job to do.

Dannazione! Where had she gone? Where was Sofia? Had she fled the party? Gut instinct said no. Sofia wasn't the type to run away from anything or anyone. She'd had to be gutsy to survive four hard-living brothers—and him, Cesar reflected as he unconsciously swiped the back of his hand across his mouth where her lips had touched his.

Only one Acosta brother had found love. He turned to look at the team's fitness trainer, Jess, whose husband was Dante Acosta. Jess was a down-to-earth farmer's daughter and a trained physiotherapist, who had helped to heal her husband when doctors had practically given up on Dante submitting to the months of treatment required. They somehow managed to combine Jess's career with Dante's business and polo-playing schedule, and quite obviously their love for each other was blooming, as Dante had confided that family life came first.

Dante had been lucky finding Jess, but lightning

never struck the same place twice, and neither Cesar nor Sofia's other brothers had even come close to finding a soul mate.

'Cesar...'

Sofia! He swung round. 'I thought you might have left the party.'

'Is seeing me a good surprise or a bad one?' she asked coolly.

It was impossible not to notice how beautiful she was, and how appealing only she could be with a coronet of fresh flowers in her hair. 'What do you want?' he asked, impatient with himself for feeling this way about her.

'Bad surprise, I take it,' she said.

He frowned.

'I'm here to apologise,' she explained. 'There's no mileage in you and me being enemies. We have to work together during the charity polo matches so we can raise as much money we can. Why not declare peace now?'

He shot her a cynical look. Sofia had many things to apologise for, but he didn't feel inclined to drive her away. 'Why don't you find somewhere to sit and enjoy the party while you can?'

'While I can?' she queried. 'Do you expect something to go wrong imminently?'

Ignoring that, he offered to find her a seat. He scanned the crowded ballroom.

'I can find my own place to sit down,' she assured him, 'but thank you.'

'I could deliver you back to my mother.'

'Like a missing parcel?' she suggested, starting to smile.

He shrugged. 'It would be the polite thing to do.'

'In that case, I accept.'

But she trembled at his touch. Her expression, however, remained carefully neutral.

'You're too kind,' she told him when he brought her in front of the Queen.

'I'm not kind at all,' he murmured in Sofia's ear, 'and you would do well to remember that.'

Then his mother took over, smiling at their approach. 'Ah, Cesar, I was wondering how long it would be before you asked Sofia to dance.'

'Dance with Sofia?' He couldn't hide his surprise.

His mother glossed over his lapse in good manners by drawing Sofia forward to kiss her on both cheeks.

'You've been far too kind,' she told his mother.

'Nonsense,' his mother insisted. 'I notice Olivia is dancing with one of your brothers. Well, Cesar,' his mother pressed, 'why are you keeping Sofia waiting?'

Why indeed?

'If Cesar doesn't feel like dancing—' Sofia began to protest, clearly not keen to feel his arms around her.

'Nonsense. Of course he does,' his mother the Queen insisted in a tone he'd never heard her use before. 'How can my son refuse to dance with such a beautiful guest?' This query was accompanied by a long, hard stare at him.

Sofia slid him a withering look. This was no puling princess touting for a crown, or some celebrity social climber with vaunting ambition, but a real woman with genuine feelings and a history that he could never forget. Any interaction between them was bound to be tense and awkward.

'Cesar?' his mother prompted.

'I can refuse you nothing,' he told his mother sincerely.

'Good!' the Queen exclaimed. 'I shall increase my demands in future.'

'I have no doubt of that,' he murmured, exchanging an amused look with a woman he held in the very highest regard.

'Well?' she urged. 'What are you waiting for? I'm sure Sofia is longing to dance with her Prince.'

If looks could kill he would be dead. His mother, usually keenly observant, had missed the opposition to this idea on Sofia's face. 'This is no easier for me than it is for you,' he assured Sofia once they were out of earshot. 'One dance and then we're done.'

'Until the matches, when we'll be thrown together again,' she reminded him with a rueful slant of her mouth.

'When that happens, you'll do your job and I'll do mine,' he stated firmly.

'To the very best of my ability,' Sofia promised with a long, fearless look into his eyes.

He gave a cynical huff, but it was hard not to believe her. No one could accuse Sofia Acosta of entering into anything in half-measures. When they reached the edge of the dance floor, in deference to his rank the other couples stopped dancing and stood back. If he refused to dance with Sofia, there would be food for gossipmongers the world over. The orchestra struck up a waltz in keeping with their splendid surroundings.

'I've heard of dancing with the devil,' Sofia murmured dryly.

'Are we taking it one step further?' he suggested.

'The demon on horseback dancing with the devil?' she remarked. 'At least we should march to the same beat.'

But they didn't march, they danced as closely as two people could. 'Relax,' he suggested. 'Unless you aim to cause comment.'

'More than I already have?' Sofia countered. 'Just by being here I've caused comment. No one has forgotten the article.'

'Including me,' he assured her, 'but I choose to rise above it, and this is a wonderful opportunity to stop the rumourmongers in their tracks.'

'Is that the only reason you agreed to dance with me?'

'Can you think of any other?'

Noticing how many people were covertly using their mobile phones to take pictures of them, he drew Sofia even closer. He might have expected her to pull away, but at least in that she had more sense. 'Let's play their game,' she said, surprising him.

'Why not?' he agreed, softening a little towards her as she smiled into his eyes.

Playing the game turned out to be more arousing than even he could have imagined. Who was dancing with the devil now? Devil Woman was an apt description of the siren in his arms. Sofia managed to be both sensual and tasteful as she moved in time to the music, leaving no one in any doubt—apart from him—that they were completely reconciled. More couples joined them on the floor and were courteous enough to allow them a degree of privacy.

'When did you learn to be such a good actress?' he murmured, his mouth very close to her ear.

'Am I acting?'

It wasn't just her voice that trembled now, her body quivered against his like a doe at bay with a rutting stag in the immediate vicinity. 'I hope you are,' he dismissed, pressing home his advantage. 'I know I am.'

'And I thought you were a gentleman,' she told him

in the softest, most pleasing voice, 'but now I know you're just a prince.'

'Ouch!' He barked a laugh at the punchline. 'Not all princes are the same, and please remember this is just for show.'

'Hmm, I noticed,' she commented.

Why was he surprised when she brushed her body against his? Hadn't he touched Sofia intimately and left her hanging?

'Is this just an act?' she whispered, no doubt referring to his rapidly expanding erection.

'No act,' he assured her. 'You are an extremely provocative woman.'

Her black eyes sparkled with challenge. 'As you are an extremely provocative man. Shall we keep on dancing, or cause comment by standing here in the middle of the floor?'

Couples were revolving around them like spokes around the hub of a wheel. 'Forgive me,' he said dryly. 'I had quite forgotten the need to dance.'

'*I* distracted you?' she asked with a sceptical lift of one brow.

'You…surprise me,' was the most he was prepared to admit.

'So you're allowed to touch, but I'm not?'

'You must follow your instinct,' he advised as they swirled in time to the ironically carefree strains of a Viennese waltz.

'That might get me into trouble,' she said, pushing her lips down as if that didn't worry her too much.

'Past experience suggests you can handle it,' he countered, 'though I've noticed that you can say one thing while your body responds quite differently. I'd love to know what's really going on in your head.'

'Like you, I'm trying to give the impression that everything is rosy between us,' she assured him. 'There's nothing to be gained by the charities we support if rumour suggests we're at each other's throats.'

'Friction between us might draw even more crowds,' he observed.

'Better to leave your guests with an air of mystery, to add intrigue to what they've seen tonight, don't you think?' she asked as phones were pointed in their direction.

The fact they fitted together perfectly was enough for him for now. Sofia's clean wildflower scent beguiled his senses, while her hair felt like silk as it brushed against the hand he had lodged in the small of her back. Her breath was a cool, minty draught that made the urge to plunder her mouth rise like madness inside him—which would be a sensation too far for his guests. As a man gossip didn't faze him, but as a prince he was forced to curb his natural instincts. It was enough to give the impression that all was well between him and Sofia, so as far as onlookers were concerned he had forgiven her and all was well.

'Don't you like the music?' Sofia probed as they danced on.

'Why do you say that?'

'You seem preoccupied.'

Remembering to smile for the sake of the watching guests, he conceded, 'I am preoccupied.'

'Is it anything I can help with? Have I made things awkward for you?' she added as he huffed a short laugh.

'You?' he queried.

'Okay, I get it. This is an act, and you'd prefer it if I said nothing at all.'

'No. Please speak,' he encouraged. 'Conversation between us will reinforce the impression that we like each other.'

'When nothing could be further from the truth?' she suggested.

He knew better than to answer that. 'Don't overdo it,' he warned as Sofia gave a cynical laugh. 'A happy expression on your face is enough, though you could try to relax a little more.'

'You make that so easy,' she responded sarcastically as the orchestra segued into another popular Viennese melody. 'At least the conductor thinks you're enjoying yourself.'

'My master of music can't be expected to read my mind.'

They danced on until a question occurred to him. 'Do you have enough material for your next article?'

Forgetting the act they were supposed to be playing, Sofia pulled back with a gasp of surprise. 'I'm here because you invited me to the party.'

'A necessary evil to avoid offending your brothers,' he said bluntly.

'How gracious you are,' she murmured beneath her breath, growing stiff and unyielding in his arms.

He was pleased to see she managed to smile, as if there was nothing she would rather be doing than dancing with him. Sensibly, he maintained a distance between them, and throughout the dance there was an expression of enjoyment on his face. It wasn't all hard work. Forced to bring Sofia close in order to avoid collisions on a packed dance floor meant intimate contact with the soft contours of her body was inevitable.

Sofia was a good dancer. Fit and supple, she moved instinctively to the music. The gown she had chosen to wear was of such a fine fabric it did little to conceal her form. Her hand was tiny in his, but her grip was firm. He had one hand lodged in the small of her back so he could feel her trembling. Careful not to adjust his fingers by as much as a millimetre, he took her around the floor. There would be no subtle messages between him and Sofia tonight.

'That must have been torture for you,' she observed when they finally stopped dancing.

'I've known worse.'

'Will you join me in the garden?' she surprised him by asking as they approached the French doors.

She was looking across the room to where guests were spilling out onto the balcony to enjoy the still balmy evening. The romantic setting in a lovely garden, beneath a black velvet sky peppered with stars and lit by the light of a silvery moon, was surely unparalleled. And would therefore be completely wasted on a couple like them. 'Why?' he asked suspiciously.

'Why not?' she countered. 'How are we supposed to become effective team members if you and I remain at daggers drawn? And,' she added, glancing around, 'people are still watching us, and I think that walking outside for a breath of fresh air after dancing is the most natural thing to do.'

She was right in that a fragrant breeze was drifting in from the gardens, but he'd done his duty and felt no urge to do more.

'Please,' Sofia whispered, putting a hand on his arm. 'I'd like the chance to start making things right between us.'

'Another new approach?' he suggested cynically.

Her cheeks flushed red, as she no doubt remembered them kissing earlier. 'It's important to break this deadlock between us,' she insisted. 'We're going to be working together.'

'To heal that gulf would take more than a moon-lit stroll,' he informed her, and with a curt bow he left Sofia to enter the garden on her own.

CHAPTER FIVE

SHE MIGHT HAVE known Cesar would reject her olive branch. He'd made up his mind that she was guilty. Dancing together had been nothing but a necessary evil, as far as the Prince was concerned. While for her it had been thrilling. At least his guests had seemed convinced the trouble between them was over. Wasn't that all that mattered?

Apart from the fact that he had left every part of her tingling with the memory of his touch?

She had the rest of the evening to fret over going too far. Trust took time to establish, and she'd waded in with her hobnailed boots. And was so quickly lost, she reflected with a glance at her brothers. The rift between them made her desperately sad. The article had done more harm than she could mend in a single night, and she longed to make things right.

That opportunity might come at Cesar's training camp, which was where they were heading next. She might have felt more confident about that if Cesar hadn't ignored her for the rest of the evening. Deciding to sleep on the problem, she took her leave of the Queen and kissed Princess Olivia on both cheeks. She was fast coming to see Olivia as a kindred spirit.

'Sleep well, my dear,' the Queen said kindly. 'And, please, don't be a stranger.'

As they exchanged warm glances Sofia found it hard to imagine that such a poised and beautiful woman as the Queen could fall into the clutches of a conman. According to the press, that was exactly what had happened. Stricken by grief after the death of her husband, Queen Julia had searched for company online, but what had appeared to be the concern of a handsome stranger had turned out to be nothing more than a wicked plot to seize the throne. Evil always seemed to strike when a victim was at their lowest ebb. Sofia felt a great wave of sympathy wash over her as she said goodnight to the Queen.

'And remember,' Olivia said as Sofia turned to go, 'if you're still hungry Cesar's kitchens are open twenty-four seven to accommodate his huge appetite.'

Sofia didn't want to consider Cesar's appetite, huge or otherwise, but she thanked the Princess warmly, and felt lighter at the thought that the seeds of friendship really were growing between them.

First she went to her sumptuous suite of rooms to draw a great steadying breath. The suite overlooked a lake beyond the palace gardens, and had been designed to imbue a guest with a feeling of relaxation.

Most guests, Sofia's reflected. Her mind was churning with unanswered questions. And that made her hungry. Untying the laces on her dress, she allowed the glorious fabric to drift to the floor. Seeing herself in the free-standing mirror in just a flimsy thong and bra, with her hair flowing free and a coronet of fresh flowers on her head, she decided with a wry smile that she was only short of a waterfall to act the part of water nymph, with perhaps a rugged stranger riding by—one who felt compelled to rein in his horse to take a closer look.

Quickly followed by a team of brothers with towels and sarcastic remarks.

So much for daydreams!

She took a quick shower and then changed into jeans and a casual top before exploring downstairs in the hope of finding the kitchen. Guests were milling about when she came down the sweeping mahogany staircase. No one would be in a hurry to bring such a successful evening to a close, she guessed as the orchestra struck up a fresh tune.

There would be snacks at dawn, her brothers had informed her with relish. Big men with big appetites, goodness knew where her brothers were now. Cesar's *palazzo* had become a hotbed of passion, judging by the number of couples entwined in the shadows of the great hall. Not for this Acosta, Sofia reflected wryly as she followed a waiter through some grand double doors. She was hungry for food and nothing more.

Until she saw Cesar, stripped off to a pair of jogging pants and a form-fitting top, with his wild black hair only partially tamed by a red bandana.

'The party over for you too,' he said as he took a bite out of a king-sized burger. 'Hungry?' he enquired.

'What about your guests?' she asked, speaking on autopilot while she tried to get over the shock of seeing him dressed down and casual while the elegant party was still in full swing.

'It's the host's prerogative to take a break if he wants.' His shoulders eased in a careless shrug. 'My guests can join me down here if they like, though I doubt they're missing me. Burger smell good?' he said as she stared at him. 'I can recommend it.'

'Coming right up,' the young chef on duty offered with a smile.

'I don't want to put you to any trouble,' Sofia insisted.

'No trouble,' the young man insisted. 'Onions?'

'When in Rome…' She glanced at Cesar.

'I think she's saying, yes, please,' Cesar interrupted.

'Sorry. Yes, please,' she echoed, with an apologetic grin for the chef.

Cesar remained lounging back against the wall. 'Are you sure you don't mind my being here?' This was his *palazzo*, his kitchen, his chef.

'Be my guest,' he invited. 'But I forgot,' he added, 'you are my guest.'

'And most grateful for your hospitality.'

'Don't overdo it, Sofia,' Cesar warned with dry amusement.

Making peace with this man wouldn't be easy, but when had she ever embraced easy?

'Take the rest of the night off,' Cesar told the chef. 'Others can take your place. You've put in some long hours today. I appreciate it,' he added as the young chef handed over Sofia's burger.

'That was nice of you,' she commented as they munched.

'You could try not to sound quite so surprised.'

'You're as bad as my brothers!' she exclaimed as Cesar stole the rest of her bun from her plate.

'Worse,' he assured her.

She hummed agreement. 'I remember a time when you were imperious.'

'Never with my staff, though I do remember one incident when I had to deal with an infuriating tomboy on an *estancia* deep in Spain.'

Her jaw dropped. 'So you admit it?'

'On that one occasion? Yes. You were a pest.'

'And you were an imperious prince, taking up space in my stable.'

'You never had a sense of what was good for you.'

'Maybe because what's good for me has never been uppermost in my mind.'

'Does that bring us back to the article?' Cesar suggested with a long sideways look.

She sighed. 'That was a mistake. I should have known. I'm no good being at anything but what I am.'

'Clearly,' Cesar agreed. 'Though there's not much you're afraid of, is there?'

Wrong. She was desperately afraid of losing her brothers' trust, and her own self-belief, if she couldn't clear her name. Losing Cesar's regard would be yet another blow.

'Let's take that stroll in the garden,' he said when they'd rinsed their hands and cleared their plates away.

This was a pivotal moment when her life could change for better or worse, but at least they were talking.

Inviting Sofia into the garden only proved that damping down his feelings where Signorina Acosta was concerned wasn't as easy as he had supposed. He should refuse to have anything more to do with her, but like a wood nymph beckoning him ever deeper into the thicket of her life Sofia was irresistible.

When he'd suggested the walk, Sofia's surprise had betrayed the fact that she hadn't believed he'd want to spend time with her. When her gaze darkened and her cheeks flushed pink, he knew her answer would be yes. The electricity was sparking between them again. He'd worked out in the gym then showered and changed after leaving the banquet, with Sofia a constant in his mind.

And now, with her long hair still damp from the shower, and silky corkscrews of baby hair arranged like a filmy crown around her brow, she was beautiful. She'd washed off her make-up but not the smudge of chocolate on her neck. The urge to lick it off was overwhelming.

'Snacking on treats in your bedroom?' he guessed. In area, at least, she found temptation irresistible. All his guests were supplied with everything they might need, including ingredients for a midnight feast.

'How do you know?' she demanded, frowning.

'Elementary, my dear Watson. You have chocolate on your neck.'

She relaxed enough to smile. 'Aren't you concerned that your guests might see you in the garden dressed like this, and wonder what you're up to in the garden with me?'

'My guests have everything they could possibly need, and I'm sure they're quite capable of amusing themselves without my assistance.'

'I'm sure they are,' she agreed, 'but—'

'But what?' he interrupted. 'Don't you trust yourself alone with me in the garden?'

She hummed and gave him a look.

'You find me irresistible?' he proposed.

'Do I?'

'Don't worry, I'll keep a tight rein on you.'

'That might work,' she agreed huskily, on what sounded like a dry throat.

'As you so rightly say,' he pointed out as they moved off, 'we're going to be together, so we might as well clear the air.'

Was there anywhere on earth more beautiful than

Cesar's Roman garden? Lit by moonlight, marble stat-
ues stood in silent repose like elegant ghosts from ancient times that at any moment might step down from
their pedestals to join them. Beyond the vast expanse of
garden the lights of Rome sparkled like precious gems.
Floral fragrances teased her senses, lending a soothing
quality to the setting they had chosen to have this talk
that was at odds with the tension between them. But
when a band was stretched tight it had to snap at some
point. She was acutely aware of Cesar at her side. For
some reason, she was drawn to the now deserted pavilion. The door was unlocked and yielded easily. She
walked in, and Cesar followed.

'This is our chance to talk,' she said.

Cesar closed the door behind them. Leaning back
against it, he stared at her. 'Is this what you want?'

It took a single step in either direction to answer his
question. She stepped forward.

Cesar dipped his head and brushed her lips with his.
'You'd better not take advantage of me,' she whispered.

'I'd say the shoe was on the other foot.'

But he made the next move, moving in for a gentle,
lingering kiss, and as he teased the seam of her lips
apart, an overwhelming surge of hunger consumed her.

The moment was right. Reaching up, she linked her
hands behind his neck.

Looping her hair around her fist, Cesar drew her
head back. 'I've always loved chocolate.'

'It must have melted in my hand,' she admitted between whimpers of pleasure.

'I don't care how it got there,' he assured her, lavish-
ing kisses on her neck, her chin, her cheeks, and finally
her lips. 'Only that I get to lick it off.'

Her answer was to press her body against his. Leaning into him, she parted her lips, inviting the invasion of his tongue.

Cesar unleashed a tiger inside her. The fact that she was inexperienced, and definitely playing with fire, meant nothing to her now. All she could think of was keeping him close so he deepened the kiss. Their bodies acted independently, seeking each other greedily and fiercely, while throaty sounds of pleasure flew from her lips.

'I think you want this,' Cesar observed as he teased her with more and more kisses.

'You think?' she whispered as she began to undress him.

There was a moment's pause when they stared at each other as if for the first time, and then clothes were flying everywhere.

Cesar was even more beautiful than she had imagined, though in a harsh and rugged way. With a lazy smile, he mapped her breasts, delivering exquisite pleasure that left her incapable of speech. Sounds of encouragement flew from her throat when he tormented her nipples into tight buds of sensation.

'You have magnificent breasts,' Cesar commented matter-of-factly.

'I'm glad you approve.'

He laughed in a way that made sensation travel from her breasts to the sweet spot between her legs. 'Your nipples are so responsive—like the rest of you, I'm guessing?'

'You wouldn't be wrong,' she admitted.

Cesar's voice was a seduction in itself, and made her hungry for more. Naked skin to naked skin was all she could think about. Instinct said Cesar would pleasure her as no one else could.

Swinging her into his arms, he carried her across to a well-padded banquette. But seduction was not on his mind. 'You wanted to talk to me?' he prompted.

Cesar's swift change of pace was a reminder to keep her wits about her, or this opportunity to talk would be wasted. Having proved he could seduce her with little or no effort at all, Cesar had put that one aside in favour of interrogation.

'I don't have all night,' he said, confirming this.

'I apologise for the article, but there was a very good reason for it.'

'What reason could there possibly be?' His voice was cool, his expression unyielding. 'Did you expect me to seduce you and then forget what you'd done? Is that why you agreed to come with me into the garden?'

'That was never my intention.' Her voice was heated, and she had wanted a civilised talk. Why could they never meet without passion of getting in the way? 'I was just grateful to have an opportunity to talk to you. Please believe me when I tell you that everything is not as it seems.'

'So you didn't write the article, as you didn't kiss me just now?'

'If you only knew the truth,' she protested.

'How I'd love to know the truth, but as you show no sign of sharing your version of it any time soon—'

'My version of it?' she exclaimed. 'And now you're leaving?'

'Why should I stay?' Cesar demanded from the door.

'Please, I—'

'You what?' he said coldly.

'Please listen to me,' she begged softly. 'I needed that money for my retreat.'

'Which I already knew. I thought you had some-thing new to say.'

'I was invited to submit an article to a well-known newspaper.'

'A scandal sheet,' Cesar derided. 'And that's not news to me.'

'Read by millions,' she countered firmly.

He dismissed this with an indifferent gesture.

'That means it paid well,' she explained. 'I don't expect you to understand what it feels like to be short of money.'

'Oh, really?' Cesar demanded cuttingly. 'That only shows how little you know me.'

And how would she ever learn, when Cesar was no-toriously reserved about his past? 'I can't pretend to have suffered as a child,' she admitted, 'Which was why it was so hard for Xander when our parents were killed. We had an idyllic childhood, and you think that's going to go on for ever. I never imagined it could end so abruptly.'

'Yet you suffered this loss, and went on to discard the principles your parents must have instilled in you. How could you do that, Sofia, just to raise money? I find it hard to believe that, with the Acosta name be-hind you, banks didn't flock to help. Or was it glory you were seeking? To see your name in print at any cost?'

'The banks had already helped as much as they were prepared to. I'd reached my limit,' she explained. 'I thought it would be easy to write an article with mass appeal—no details, no scandal, just a taste of the glam-our that follows you and my brothers around. I didn't see any harm in it—'

'Until it was too late?' Cesar interrupted. 'By which time you had banked the money.' He held up his hand when she started to explain. 'For the sake of the charities we must move past that. Including you in the team will swell the crowds. They'll come to see how things have worked out between us, so we'll put on an act as we have done tonight. It shouldn't be so difficult. We've had our dress rehearsal, but don't ever mistake good manners for forgiveness. Do I make myself clear?'

'Perfectly.'

'Then I'll bid you goodnight.'

The ringing silence inside the pavilion seemed to last long after Cesar had gone. They were no closer to understanding each other than they had been at the start of the evening, but she had exposed how she felt about Cesar, only for him to turn and walk away.

CHAPTER SIX

TEAM LOBOS AND their associated staff left Rome for Cesar's breeding and training ranch in the far north west of Italy the day after the banquet. There were no unnecessary frills in this residence, though everything was of the highest quality. The facility was entirely dedicated to the well-being of the horses. As well as countless other animals, Cesar allowed as a pack of his favourite dogs circled his legs, looking for fuss and for treats. He didn't disappoint them. Kneeling down so he was at their level, he lavished affection on his most loyal friends.

'You still have some admirers, I see…'

His hackles rose at the sound of Sofia's voice. She was like a cork that never stayed down for long.

'Ready for battle?'

This was the far more welcome voice of Sofia's brother Dante. 'Dante!'

He sprang up and they embraced fiercely. The other Spanish Acosta brothers took their turns. Fearless, and loyal to a fault, it was a shame their sister failed to share the same brand of loyalty.

He stood back. 'You all know my sister Olivia…' Olivia raised a laugh as she gave a mock bow. 'And Jess, Dante's wife.' At his prompt, an attractive redhead joined Cesar and Dante in the centre of the arena. 'Jess is also a top-flight physiotherapist and trainer, and I know we're all going to enjoy her punishing exercises.'

Jess acknowledged the chorus of catcalls with a lop-sided grin. 'Thank you for the glowing recommendation, but we have to win the tournament before I believe your praise. Until then, all I can promise is hard, relentless training.' She waited for the comic groans to die down before revealing, 'I'll be working in tandem with another person here… Sofia…?'

As Sofia stepped forward, Cesar ground his teeth. What the hell?

'What is the meaning of this?' he demanded.

'The meaning?' Jess enquired, laughing, no doubt thinking he was joking. 'I don't know anyone better than Sofia for building team spirit. I've seen her work with her brothers, don't forget. And Sofia's organisational skills are second to none.' Jess looked at him with surprise when he failed to stifle a scoffing huff. 'That's why her retreat is such a success,' Jess continued doggedly, with a piercing look at him. 'Anyone who has experienced Sofia's retreat can tell you the benefits. They learn to live life to the full again, and they learn to trust.'

'Excellent,' he bit out. He'd heard enough of the nonsense. Only the calming presence of Dante at his side, and the grimly set faces of those of Sofia's brothers who didn't care to hear her praised went some way to soothing his frayed temper. 'We're relying on you, Jess,' he emphasised, 'for our training regime in the run-up to the matches.'

In his peripheral vision he saw Sofia stiffen but Jess continued, undaunted. 'Without complete trust between team members you can ride the best ponies in the world and field the fittest, sharpest players, but if there isn't proper communication between each member of the team—the kind of communication that doesn't need anyone to shout for the ball, or make it clear that their horse is tiring, because your fellow players know exactly where you are, how you stand, and who best to shoot the ball to—your play will never be as dynamic or as fluid as it needs to be.'

Jess talked good sense, but he still failed to see what part Sofia had to play in this. 'I invited you to become a member of this team for the duration of the charity matches,' he murmured in Sofia's ear, 'but I don't recall hiring you to help with training.'

'You didn't have to hire me,' she informed him pleasantly. 'I'm here because Jess asked me to help her, which I'm more than willing to do.'

The irony was that as Sofia didn't work for him, he couldn't fire her, even if he wanted to. No wonder he preferred binding contracts where anyone who failed to meet the mark could be let go without a fuss.

Sofia began to address the group as cool as you like. 'We're lucky to have this chance to practise together. I know how busy you all are. Knowing your team members inside out, so you're aware of their strengths and weaknesses, as well as how they play the game, will give us the advantage we need.'

He was rocked back on his heels by the sight of two women taking centre stage, as if he were a newcomer to the game. 'That's enough talking,' he decreed with a closing gesture. 'This is nothing we don't know. We're professionals. We adapt. And now we work.'

Jess worked them hard. Truthfully, Sofia was finding it hard to keep up with Cesar and her brothers, but there was no way she going to let the side down. Olivia and Jess were as determined as she was to prove their worth to the team. Jess managed to make training fun. Galloping at full stretch, leaning over the side of her pony to snatch up a can that appeared to have invisible legs was something Sofia hadn't done since she was a child. No one fell off, though noisy hilarity and catcalls released a lot of the initial tension. By the time that morning's session was over, Sofia could do little more than slide down the side of her pony in exhaustion. But neither could she remember enjoying herself so much in a long time.

'Can I help you with that?'

She turned to see Cesar lounging back against the wall, watching her. Removing tack from a spirited pony was normally a straightforward operation, but today the bridle seemed to weigh a ton and her mount was overly keen to be turned out into the field.

'You look as if your knees are about to buckle,' Cesar remarked as she almost lost her footing.

'I can manage, thank you.'

'But you don't have to,' he pointed out, and taking the saddle out of her arms he led the way to the tack room where the others in the team were waiting. 'I've arranged entertainment for later,' he announced when everything was safely stowed away.

'So long as it doesn't involve moving,' Olivia groaned. 'I don't need *entertainment*. I need a long, hot bath.'

'You can have both,' Cesar promised.

Olivia grunted disbelievingly but Jess exclaimed, 'Wonderful!' as she linked arms with her husband.

Infected by Jess's enthusiasm, Sofia smiled too. 'If I don't fall asleep in the bath, I'll be there,' she promised.

'I'll save you a place,' Cesar offered, surprising everyone, not least himself, Sofia suspected when she caught the brief flash of surprise on his face.

If she'd hoped for something more—a glimmer of warmth in his eyes, for instance—she was disappointed. There was nothing in Cesar's expression when he looked her way but the same coolness and suspicion.

He sluiced down in the yard. Everyone else had retired to their rooms to rest, clean up and prepare for the evening ahead. His grooms had taken charge of the ponies, but he chose to check everything twice. The ponies had worked as hard if not harder than their riders, and also deserved a reward.

Raking his hair back, he slung his top over his still-damp shoulders and entered the state-of-the-art building where his beloved animals were kept. He prided himself on the fact that this accommodation was as good as that of his guests.

'Sofia?' He might have known.

'Cesar!' She seemed equally shocked. 'I was just checking the ponies were settled for the night,' she explained.

'I'd have put a top on if I'd known you were here.'

She angled her chin to stare at him boldly. 'Would you?'

Silence fell as they stared at each other. In fairness, Sofia had worked as hard as anyone and yet here she was, tending to the horses when she could have been indulging in a long, hot bath.

Must she moisten her lips like that?

He held her stare. 'Don't you want to rest before the evening entertainment? "Freshen up"?' he suggested.

She grinned. 'Was that a hint?'

He ignored the comment. 'In honour of your family I've brought over a group of flamenco dancers from Andalucía.'

'That was very nice of you. Just don't let my brothers sing,' she warned with a slanting smile.

It was almost nothing, perhaps a brief window into another side of Sofia: a fun side, a family side, a care-free side of a woman he hadn't seen so far.

'Best leave singing to the professionals,' she said.

'How about you?' he asked. 'It's your tradition. Will you dance?'

'Flamenco?' she exclaimed. 'You just try and stop me.'

He had no intention of doing so, he mused as Sofia struck a pose. She looked so beautiful—alluring beyond belief. The sight of her wreaked havoc on his groin. 'To-night promises to be one to remember.'

'For all the right reasons, I hope?' she countered.

He stared into her eyes. She pleased and infuriated him in equal measure. How could she appear so frank and open after everything she'd done? If he judged Sofia by right here, right now, he'd say she was a free spirit who loved nothing more than to ride hard and live to help others. What had happened to change that? Surely she couldn't have turned into a self-serving schemer overnight?

She shrugged when he didn't answer and ended on a flippant note. 'I'll try hard not to disappoint you,' she promised with one last flashing glance.

He watched as she walked away. What was she playing at now? Sofia Acosta was as sharp as a bag of monkeys, and twice as resourceful. She was determined to keep her retreat afloat, and had already shown she would stop at nothing to do that.

Yet still he wanted her.

Why not? he mused as he watched as Sofia met his sister Olivia halfway across the yard and fell into conversation with her. Both women were beautiful, and as spirited as his most challenging mare. With a back view as impressive as her front, he loved the way Sofia strode out. He loved the sway in her shapely body. Not for the first time, he thought her perfect. Would he sleep with the enemy? Why not? But first he must unravel the enigma that was Sofia Acosta. In spite of everything that had gone before, he wanted to know her both in and out of bed.

Nope. She hadn't packed a party dress suitable for a flamenco party. All she had in her zip-up case were numerous pairs of jodhpurs and jeans in varying stages of disrepair, a stack of clean tops, two spare pairs of PJs, toiletries and comfortable underwear that could in no way be described as glamorous. This was a training camp after all. Not that it was a typical training camp. Everything was high quality and practical, but the suite of rooms Sofia had been directed to, for instance, contained enough tech to satisfy even her brothers. There was also every muscle-easing balm and potion known to man in the bathroom, which she intended to take full and luxurious advantage of. A separate room was devoted to massage, and there was a sauna, as well as a steam room and an ice bath. The latter she was determined to swerve.

She chose bubbles.

The bath was huge. The warm water was plentiful, and the selection of fragrances mind-blowing. She could happily have remained soaking all night, without the prospect of a party. Would Cesar be relaxed in an informal setting or would he still be cool and unread-able? Numerous images flashed through her mind, but for this one night she was going to forget the damning article and have fun.

Which meant sorting out an outfit for the party.

No problem, Sofia reflected as she towelled down. She had a tongue in her head and an exuberant group of *gitanos* had arrived from the mountains of Andalucía to entertain them. She could hear them in the courtyard now. There was a possibility they might have heard of her mother. Keeping the tradition of flamenco alive re-quired a tight-knit if widespread community.

It had been on a night similar to this that Sofia's aristocratic Acosta father had met his future wife. So-fia's mother had danced for him and, according to her father, the firelight had not been able to compete with the fire in her mother's eyes. It remained to be seen if tonight would be a damp squib for Sofia, or whether the traditional music and dance would thrill everyone with its upbeat message.

Sofia was welcomed into the *gitanos'* fold like a long-lost sister, daughter, friend. She was deeply touched by how many women clustered around to help her pick out a gown. Cesar had housed the performers in some of the most luxurious accommodation so there was plenty of room for all the women and Sofia to gather, and plenty of room to prepare properly, which was fortu-nate as Sofia's hair alone took a good deal of taming and grooming before it could be confined in the se-vere style worn by all the women. The last touch was an ornate comb for her hair, decorated with sparkling paste jewels, which held a flowing black lace mantilla in place. There was only one problem, in that Sofia's new friends seemed to think that she would be one of the star performers tonight. 'Your mother's talent was legendary,' the head dancer told her. 'You can't refuse.'

Neither would she. 'Of course I'll dance,' she agreed with a flutter of nerves.

She tried out a few steps, and it was a relief to find that the childhood lessons from her mother had not deserted her.

'And you must use a fan,' one of the older women insisted. 'The language of the fan is universal.'

And dangerous, Sofia reflected as she stared at the glorious bright red fan the woman wanted her to use. Flamenco was a sensual dance that ebbed and flowed as smoothly as silk, with rhythmic stamps to punctuate the dancer's movements. This built tension and excitement, while a fan allowed grace and style to soften the repeated clatter of heels on wood. But a fan must always be used with discretion, Sofia remembered her mother telling her, as it increased the charm of the dancer's spell.

She was taken aback when she caught sight of herself in a mirror, and thanked the women who'd helped her profusely. 'I can't believe the transformation!' she exclaimed, as she took in the sight of her hourglass figure in a tight-fitting black and white dress. With its frills and ruffles—which she never, ever wore normally—the costume made her feel like a different person, one who was bold and who never suffered from doubt.

What would her brothers make of seeing her on stage? Whatever their differences, she was confident they'd cheer her on. She was an Acosta. They were family, and it was this deep and abiding love that would always protect her. Her brothers might think she had abused that love, and she could only hope that one day they would forgive her.

And Cesar? What would he think when he saw her on stage?

When he entered the room her stomach clenched with nerves at the thought of performing in front of him.

CHAPTER SEVEN

'I'VE COME TO make sure you all have everything you need,' he said, taking in Sofia's much-changed appearance with interest. 'If there's anything more I can do for you,' he added, 'please let me know.'

The soft whir of the spurs on her fan as she opened it drew his attention. 'I didn't expect to find you here. Are you performing tonight? I have to say the costume suits you.'

'This is all thanks to my new friends,' she explained as the women who had helped her watched on. 'My mother's people,' she explained, remembering how her mother had told her to take compliments gracefully and always be proud of who she was. Composing her features into something less wistful, she raised her chin and said, 'Thank you.'

'So I will see you dance tonight,' Cesar concluded.

'You will,' she confirmed, thinking him so rampantly male it would be hard to concentrate on anything while he was watching. But behind that compelling persona she saw genuine interest fire in his eyes. This was a chance to make her mother proud, and her brothers too. She couldn't influence Cesar. His thoughts were up to him.

She was surprised when he waited behind to escort her. 'Will you allow me?' he asked.

'Do I have a choice?' she teased.

He linked her arm through his. 'None,' he confirmed.

The party was being held outside, where a huge bon-fire lit up the night. The stage was set at a safe dis-tance in front of it, backlighting the performers with soaring flames. A backdrop of mountains and a sound-scape of owls could lead some to think this a romantic setting. Not Sofia, who had so much to prove, though it was certainly rare to have a flamenco performance in this part of Italy, with Apennine wolves howling in the background, as if they agreed that she'd better not mess this up.

'Did you organise the wolf chorus especially for Team Lobos?' Dante enquired with amusement as he and Jess came over to greet Cesar and Sofia.

'My friends never disappoint me,' Cesar confirmed dryly. 'They are no doubt as curious and as excited as we are, especially as we're so close to their mountain home.'

It was an elemental setting, Sofia realised as she looked around, and as such was the perfect setting for Cesar.

'Are you dancing tonight?' Dante asked, taking in her costume.

'That's the price I have to pay for borrowing one of these fabulous dresses,' she admitted, 'though I hope I can remember the steps our mother taught me.'

'You will,' Dante said confidently.

She had to now.

'No one persuades Sofia to do anything she doesn't

want to do,' Cesar commented, which earned him a look and a shrug from Dante. 'Enjoy the party,' he added.

Just how much she would enjoy the party remained to be seen.

There must have been something in the air that night, or maybe it was the fabulous red fan, casting its promised spell. Surrounded by her mother's people, Sofia felt able to express herself fully and freely, perhaps for the first time since she'd lost her mother. Tears rolled unchecked down her cheeks at one point while she danced, for all the things they could no longer share, and when the final chord sounded and the main dancer came on stage, she took Sofia in her arms to whisper, 'Your mother would be very proud of you. And remember that as we cry when we lose someone, we live on in their honour to laugh and make love, and live fully again.'

And then the crowd went wild, and called for an encore.

There comes a point at the end of an impassioned flamenco solo when the dancer, having expended every last drop of emotion, cries out, *'Duende!'* and drops to the floor. He was waiting at the side ready to give his congratulatory speech once Sofia had finished dancing when that moment occurred. Sofia struck her final pose, and then allowed her limbs to soften and her face to relax as she sank to the ground.

'Duende!'

The audience rewarded Sofia with rapturous applause. Duende perfectly expressed the heightened emotions he'd witnessed on stage, and he was cheering with the rest. There couldn't be a single person present she hadn't touched in some way.

Sofia was an extraordinary performer. The story

she'd told through the medium of dance was one that everyone could relate to at some point. The mask she showed to the world had dropped away, leaving Sofia totally exposed and vulnerable. He might have had every reason to mistrust her in the past, but what he'd seen made him want to re-evaluate what he knew of.

'Congratulations!' he exclaimed as he raised her to her feet.

'I have my mother to thank.' Her eyes were shining with happy memories as she looked back into the past. 'My mother believed in the power of dance, saying music is a power for good.'

'Your mother was right, and you certainly convinced everyone here,' he admitted as he led her forward to take another bow. 'You surprised me tonight,' he confessed once they were out of the spotlight.

'Well, we don't know that much about each other, do we, Cesar?' she said as she lifted her chin to search his eyes. 'All we know is what we see now, and what rumour suggests is fact. Who knows how many more surprises are in store?'

'Just don't write another article,' he cautioned with a lift of his brow.

Her face fell, making him wish he hadn't said it. Couldn't he even allow her to enjoy this moment of triumph?

'I promise I won't,' she said in all seriousness.

'Forget it,' he rapped, angry with himself for being so crass. 'Take your applause. You've earned it.'

He left Sofia with her newly won admirers, most of whom were young dancers dressed in traditional costume, all wanting autographs and selfies with Sofia.

'I'll be with your brothers if you need me.' He jerked his chin towards the crowded bar area, feeling vaguely discomfited as he accepted he could have handled this better.

'I felt like a fraud,' Sofia told him some time later when she had returned to his side.'

'I don't know why,' he said as he drew her away from the boisterous crowd to find a quieter spot.

'I haven't done anything like this in years,' she admitted. 'Not since I was a little girl, in fact.'

'Then perhaps you should do more,' he suggested.

'I'll bring you up on stage next time,' she threatened.

'You may regret that.'

'I'm prepared to chance it,' she shot back.

'Well, now...'

'Now?' she pressed.

'I must get back to the rest of my guests. If you will excuse me?'

'Of course,' she said faintly. And was that regret?

Sofia barely had chance to speak to Cesar for the next part of the night. It was a great party, so many people to talk to. Her brothers were swept up in a good-natured crowd, relaxing and enjoying themselves, and it felt so good to Sofia to relax and unwind. Escape the web of intrigue into which she'd inadvertently become embroiled when she'd written that article. Doing nothing more complicated than talking and laughing and dancing, she couldn't have enjoyed herself more—or so she thought until Cesar stepped forward to make a short speech.

'We've had a wonderful night of entertainment, for which I'm immensely grateful,' he declared. 'And now it's time for everyone to enjoy themselves, performers and guests alike. So I invite you to party, but not too hard because tomorrow the real work on match fitness begins.'

The usual chorus of groans greeted this statement, though it didn't seem to stop anyone enjoying the party.

'But before we start training again,' Cesar added, 'I'm claiming my right to dance with the star performer.'

Me? The thought of Cesar's body enfolding hers, and without the need for pretence this time, made Sofia's heart riot. She had to remind herself that this was just an innocent dance, and when it finished she'd return to her quarters, take a shower and go to bed.

Who was she kidding?

Difficult questions could wait until later.

Her body melted from the inside out when Cesar took her into his arms. Heat fizzed through her veins, bringing everything into sharp focus. Her awareness level soared. They fitted so well together, which didn't make sense when Cesar was twice her size. But it was a fact, she realised as he led and she followed. 'Don't get used to shepherding me around the floor,' she warned with amusement born of nerves.

'I don't notice too much resistance,' he remarked. 'You're an excellent dancer, and I enjoy using my body.'

Her senses were in freefall now Cesar's rampantly male body was aligned with hers. The urge to move and rub herself against him was constant—one she knew she had to resist.

'Relax,' he murmured, drawing her closer still. 'Or stop dancing. It's your choice. We're not acting now so there's no need to pretend, if you don't want to.'

He was giving her an out she didn't want. Up to now her hand had remained unmoving in his, while her body was as unresponsive as she could make it, but the thought of leaving Cesar and walking away forced her fingers to ease in his as she consciously relaxed her shoulders. Cesar responded by linking their fingers, which she found both intimate and exciting. His other hand was lodged in the small of her back, his fingers resting on the topmost swell of her buttocks.

Waves of want flooded her. They were so close they shared the same breath, the same air, but was this sensible or would it leave her with more unanswered questions? 'We've got training tomorrow,' she reminded them both. 'I should be thinking about bed.' The insistent rhythmic strum of guitars called her a liar. She wanted nothing more than to stay and dance with Cesar.

Releasing her as the music reached a crescendo and finally stopped, Cesar stepped back. 'I'll see you back to the house.'

'You can't leave your guests,' she pointed out.

'I doubt anyone will even notice that I've gone,' Cesar insisted as he steered her away.

So speaks the man who has no idea of the effect he has on people, Sofia reflected as she noticed how many of their fellow dancers glanced at Cesar as they left the improvised dance floor. His type of machismo could electrify a room. 'I don't need you to take me back,' she insisted, avoiding his gaze. She glanced at the last place she'd seen her brothers. They would normally take her back, but they weren't even looking her way.

'Just tell me what you want,' Cesar prompted.

His grip on her wrist might be gentle but the look in Cesar's eyes was not at all safe. What did she want? What was he offering? To be alone with him? The connection between them fired as they stared at each other.

Just for one night. That's all it would be.

They didn't make it as far as the ranch house or even

the guest quarters. The hay barn loomed. The building was in darkness when they arrived. Before she could lift the latch, Cesar had swung her round, and with his arms bracketing either side of her face he kissed her hungrily and she kissed him back.

'No,' he rapped as her body enthusiastically took the lead. 'Not here. Not with you dressed like this. '

He was right. The mantilla she was wearing was held in place by a large, ornate hair comb, and the flamenco dress fitted her like a second skin.

Sweeping her into his arms, Cesar shouldered the door and carried her inside the shaded interior where the air was warm and fragrant, and countless dust motes danced on moonbeams. There was nothing to compare with the scent of stacked hay, unless it was the scent of Cesar, Sofia concluded as he set her down gently on a sweet-smelling bed of clean hay.

'You should never tie your hair back,' he said as he removed the comb and mantilla with dextrous skill. 'There should be a law against it.'

She couldn't believe how carefully he rearranged her severely drawn-back hair, finger-combing it until it hung in its usual tumbling disorder. Was this a man she could confide in, or was she fooling herself again? History showed her to be woefully lacking when it came to good judgement.

She needn't have worried. With the removal of her clothes tension between them gradually relaxed and in its place came playful intimacy. Nothing that had happened in the past seemed relevant. Only this moment mattered. Until he hit a sweet spot on her neck.

'You're like a highly strung pony, always ready to bolt,' Cesar observed huskily.

'Where would I bolt to?'

'Back to the party?' he suggested.

'In my underwear?'

'What remains of it,' he commented with amusement. 'What am I going to do with you, Sofia Acosta?'

'Didn't you bring your clipboard?'

Cesar stared at her for a moment then laughed. 'Tell me what you want,' he insisted.

Her heart was thumping. The menu was tempting. Cesar was dressed in low-slung, snug-fitting jeans that displayed more than a few tantalising inches of hard, toned flesh. No wonder her body was responding by aching and yearning.

She didn't move when he settled himself over her, braced on muscular arms.

Where to start?

'Kiss me?' she suggested.

CHAPTER EIGHT

SHE COULD NEVER have predicted what a simple request to kiss her would entail. Starting with her feet, Cesar kissed the soles, her ankles, her calves and finally her thighs, until she thought she would go mad with waiting. Locking stares, he moved past her thighs. If the attention he'd given the rest of her legs was anything to go by...

A soft cry escaped her lips when he murmured, 'Look at me.'

Staring into his eyes was the most erotic experience of her life. It was as if Cesar could see through her to every thought and feeling she had. When he found her and cupped her, she almost lost control, but his touch was so light, too light, and she wanted more. Covering his hand with hers, she demanded more. It wasn't a question of boldness now but more a lifesaver like the air she breathed. It only took a moment and she was lost.

'Greedy,' Cesar murmured as she bucked uncontrollably in the throes of a most powerful release. Unable to control her cries of pleasure, she could only respond by instinct, grateful that he used one hand to palm her buttocks and hold her in place, while he extended her pleasure with his other hand.

'More?' he queried with low, husky, sexy amusement

when she was quiet again. Her answer was to reach for the waistband of his jeans. Dealing with the belt first, she ripped it out of its loops and tossed it aside. Next came the zipper, but Cesar took over and dealt with that with efficient speed.

'I need you to do something for me now,' he said.

'Anything,' she offered fiercely.

'Your task is to do nothing at all. Your only goal is to float and feel.'

As he spoke, Cesar removed her bra, only pausing to lavish attention on her breasts before removing her tiny thong. Stripping off his jeans, he moved over her.

Moving between her legs, he teased her with the tip of his erection. But just when she was sure she was ready, he drew back. Resting her legs wide on his shoulders, he pressed her back onto the hay. 'Remember what I told you?'

A ragged sigh escaped her as Cesar dipped his head. After that first release it was a surprise to discover how easily he could make her needy again. She fell quickly, screaming into ecstasy, and the drowning waves of pleasure went on and on. 'How do you do that?' she asked when she had the breath to do so.

Laughing softly, Cesar cupped her buttocks to raise her to his mouth.

He took her gently because Sofia was inexperienced. It rested on him to set the pace. Left to herself she would scramble all over him, and it would be done in moments. He wanted more for her than that. Delay was the servant of pleasure, and Sofia was like a flower unfurling, a process that should never be rushed.

Giving her more, and then a little more still, while she clung to him, her eyes telling him everything he needed to know. She was apprehensive but eager. She wanted him, wanted this, but wasn't quite sure if she could handle it, handle him. He was so big and she was so small. He could practically see these thoughts flashing through her mind. To help ease her concerns, he spoke soft words of encouragement in his own tongue, until gradually she relaxed enough for her hands to stop gripping him like vices. They would soon close on him again when she urged him on to give her the greatest pleasure of all.

When she rested her arms above her head in an attitude of complete trust, he knew she was ready. Protecting them both, he enclosed her wrists in one big fist and cupped her buttocks with his other hand to guide her onto him. Nudging her thighs apart, he sank a little deeper, and then a little deeper still.

'Relax… *Rilassati, tesoro… Non aver paura. Non ti farei mai del male…* Don't be frightened. I would never hurt you.'

'I'm not frightened,' she assured him, though her breathing was hectic and her voice was unsteady, which told him the exactly opposite.

Easing Sofia's fear was paramount. Releasing her wrists, he made sure she made the transition from tension and concern to hunger and need within the space of a few well-judged strokes.

'Ah, yes, yes!' she exclaimed, and, exactly as he had anticipated, she reached for his buttocks to urge him on.

He rested deep, and waited to allow Sofia to become used to the new sensation. Then he gently massaged her by rotating his hips. That was her flash point. She lost control immediately, falling with excited screams of pleasure as she experienced the new and hugely increased sensation of release while he filled her. Her inner muscles attempted to suck him dry, but he had control to spare when it came to Sofia.

'*Non ancora, il mio piccolo micio*—not yet, my little wildcat,' he insisted, holding her still as she battled to bring him release.

'When? You have to! It's amazing,' she insisted on a great exhalation of breath. 'I mean, I realise that you know that, but—'

'But?' he queried with amusement as he began to move again.

'Don't expect me to speak now,' she protested on a ragged breath.

'I don't. I expect you only to—'

'Float and feel,' she remembered, heaving another great sigh of pleasure as he moved faster, the finish of each stroke a little firmer each time.

When she fell again he laughed softly against her hair. She took an age to come down. 'You are the greediest person I've ever known.'

'I don't want to know about *others*,' she assured him with all the old fire.

'What others?' he demanded, lifting his head to stare her in the eyes. 'There is only one Sofia.'

Wasn't that the truth? Sofia accepted as reality raised its ugly head—or in this case multiple beautiful heads, all perfectly coiffed and exquisitely made up, as befitted the women in the life of one of the world's most eligible bachelors.

So why was Cesar with her? Was this revenge? Was he proving a point? She hoped not, because for her this was so much more. It was an exercise in trust.

Searching Cesar's eyes, she found what looked like genuine concern, but she didn't want his pity. She'd had enough of being petted by her brothers as if she were their favourite puppy, only to be kicked out without a chance to explain her misguided actions. She longed for a man who treated her as his equal, and who would expect her to account for what she'd done. A man who would listen and maybe understand. She wanted to believe that man was Cesar, and was forced to remind herself that sex was second nature to Cesar, like eating or breathing.

'You will sleep with me tonight,' he decreed.

She stared up with surprise. 'I'll sleep in my own bed,' she stated. 'We both have to work first thing.'

A smile tugged at one corner of his mouth. 'Are you saying that if you stay with me no work will be done?'

'Not the right type of work,' she said as she reached for her clothes.

Capturing her hands in his, Cesar nuzzled her neck, her mouth, her cheeks with his sharp stubble, until she couldn't bring herself to leave. She wanted to stay with him, so they could grow closer in every way there was.

There was a rustle of foil, and then he turned her so her back was to his chest. 'I promise you'll sleep tonight,' he murmured, the sexy smile in his voice, encouraging her, as before, to lose control.

Had she really chosen her bed over his? Had that encounter in the hay barn really happened?

Determined to cling to reason, she reasoned that Cesar had made no attempt to prevent her leaving. He took his pleasure where he found it—no strings, no consequences, and she was a fool if she read anything more into it than that. But reason wasn't enough to stop her hurting and wanting, or longing for a different type of closeness with Cesar. Leaning back against her bedroom door, eyes tightly shut and with her body still singing with remembered pleasure, she could only rail silently against yet another missed opportunity for them to talk.

Had Cesar been looking for conversation?

She hadn't exactly been talkative herself. If things had been different, if the regime they'd embarked on in preparation for the matches hadn't been so demanding...

If only, if only, if only. But would you have stated your case and taken the consequences, whatever they might be?

If there was a major fallout between them, it would impact the whole team, and with the charity matches coming up fast none of them needed more ripples right now.

So you're burying it? What about the plan to thwart your blackmailer?

Grinding her teeth, as if that would shut out her inner critic, she determined to keep a tight rein on her emotions, and only tell Cesar the whole story when launching preventative measures against the blackmailer would have minimum impact on anyone else.

What about all those people you're supposed to be protecting? The people at your retreat, your brothers, Cesar?

A soft yelp of desperation escaped her throat. Her retreat was full to capacity with vulnerable people. She'd been looking for ways to open another—

And now?

Pulling away from the door, she headed out.

She found Cesar in the deserted kitchen, drinking coffee and demolishing a pizza. 'I'm sorry to disturb you.'

'You're not.'

The flatness of his statement pinned her to the spot. There was no warmth in his eyes and no recollection of remembered pleasure, as far as she could tell. Cesar had sated one of his needs and now he was sating another…with pizza.

So retreat or advance. Your choice.

She moved deeper into the room. 'I'm not here for the reason you suppose.'

'And what is that?'

Holding his black stare was a challenge she met gladly, though there was no hint of the generous lover Cesar had been only a short time before.

'What am I thinking?' he pressed.

'That I've changed my mind about spending the night with you?'

A few long seconds passed, during which Cesar drank more coffee and ate more pizza. 'Why would you do that?' he asked, his sharp gaze suspicious. 'The little I know about you says you only do what you want to do, when you want to do it.'

The sudden realisation that Cesar thought her as coldblooded as him came as an unpleasant shock, but what else could he think after reading the article she had supposedly written?

The one thing she must not do was risk turning this into a confrontation. She needed help, and couldn't be too proud to ask him. 'I need to talk to you—really talk to you,' she explained. 'Now would be good, if that's okay with you? It's important, Cesar,' she stressed when he shrugged.

'Have you finally decided to apologise for the article?' he suggested with a keen, sideways look.

'I can explain how it came about, and was then changed without my knowledge before it went to print.'

'That's some story. You want me to believe you're an innocent dupe,' he suggested. 'Forgive me if I find that hard to believe.'

'Cesar, please—'

'You must excuse me.' He pushed away from the counter. 'I'm heading off to bed. I suggest you do the same. As you mentioned before, we have training to-morrow.'

She stared at the door long after Cesar had closed it behind him. Explaining her actions wouldn't be easy. Cesar wasn't easy. But what in life was? She would just have to find another way.

He couldn't forgive her, and had only firmed his resolve. Everything about Sofia fired him up—to anger, to pas-sion, to disgust. She might be the first member of the team to arrive each morning for training, and the last to dismount when each day's demanding session was over, but she hadn't needed to write that article, and had clearly given no thought to the harm it would do.

It was still possible to enjoy her. They enjoyed each other. That was something separate. It was a simple arrangement between them, with no demands beyond those of mutual pleasure on either side.

The next day's training went well, though he'd had a sleepless night. Judging by the dark circles around her eyes, Sofia hadn't slept well either. Each time their stares clashed, electricity fired between them. It was only a matter of time before he had her again. Primal hunger needed an outlet. She knew that as well as he. As dutiful about training as Sofia undoubtedly was, she was also a hot-blooded woman and the thought of sinking deep into her exquisite warmth provided him with the most delicious torture throughout a satisfyingly testing day.

He was alone in the stables when she found him after training. The topic she chose to open with was not what he had expected. 'You want to talk about the article?' he queried, pulling his head back with surprise.

'And this time have you listen,' she insisted.

He raised a brow.

'Sorry. That sounded harsh.'

Sofia taking an unusual tack shouldn't surprise him, but the fact that her heated glances had either meant nothing or he'd imagined them, which was unlikely, irritated him. Continuing to check his pony's legs, he waited to hear what she had to say.

She joined him in the stall, where there was no sound apart from his mount contentedly munching. Their teammates were already refuelling in the ranch house, so they were alone.

'I want to explain. I have to,' she insisted. 'I can't stand this tension between us. And what's the point of waiting for the right time when the right time never comes?' She caught hold of his elbow when he stood up to go. 'Cesar—'

He pinned her with a cold glance. 'Well? What do you want to say to me?'

As they stared at each other something changed in her eyes. Her body softened, and the words she had been about to say froze on her lips. 'No,' she whispered huskily, keeping eye contact.

'Yes,' he argued softly. He'd never had a problem in recognising or responding to the needs of his body.

'We must talk,' she insisted in a breathy whisper.

Her eyes were black, her lips were swollen, and her

breathing was growing increasingly rapid. 'All you need to say is yes,' he insisted in the same low tone.

She was instantly in the moment when he found her with his hand. Her heat reached him through her breeches. 'This is what you need,' he explained as his fingers went to work. But she hadn't finished with surprises yet.

'This is what we both need,' she insisted, eyes blazing a challenge into his.

When she was done, she sank against him, spent. She'd used him. That was okay with him. Kissing her, he undressed her. She saw to the button at the top of his jeans. Wrapping her hands around him, she smiled and voiced her pleasure, as if he had provided her with all the delights of the world in one jutting member.

Having protected them both, he thrust forward. They exclaimed with relief. After a moment or two of basking in sensation, he lifted her, so she could lock her legs around his waist while he pounded into her. From there it was a crazy, furious ride towards the goal they were both seeking, and when they reached it, it was stunning in its ferocity for both of them.

'Again?' he suggested as Sofia groaned and writhed in his arms, biting her fingers into his muscles.

Her answer was to work her hips greedily against his, but to his surprise this felt like more than sex, more than even he had anticipated. It was a glorious coupling, both unsettling and complicated. This was life as he wanted it.

CHAPTER NINE

FEELING LIKE THIS about Cesar resulted in clear thinking, forward planning, even sensible behaviour flying out of the window. The power of her feelings for him allowed for no modification or delay but, as always, once they reached the summit there was only one way down. Uncertainty beckoned.

They dressed quickly. She covered the evidence of outrageously good sex with a fast smoothing of her hair and a few deep, steadying breaths. Cesar made no adjustments. His hair remained as wild as ever, while his breathing had remained steady throughout. For him, sex was an exercise, probably not entirely dissimilar in his mind from the body-stretching workout they undertook on horseback in the ring. And now exercise time was over, and he was ready to move on.

That was how much it had meant to him.

Her mind was made up. There could be no more self-indulgence. Incredible sex with someone who was starting to mean far too much to her was a luxury she couldn't afford. She had to find a way to curb want and replace it with enough confidence to make Cesar hear the truth.

She left first, striding ahead of him to the ranch house. She cared about the people there, and those currently staying in her retreat must be kept safe. Her feelings had to be put aside.

Loading her tray at the counter, she joined her brothers and Jess at a long table in the centre of the comfortably furnished wood-panelled room. There was a moment of readjustment by those of her brothers who weren't remotely on Sofia's side. Raffa and Xander exchanged glances before carrying on with their meal, heads down. They'd always been so easy together, and now she felt like an unwelcome stranger. Yes, they'd always teased her. That's what brothers did. But deep down they were there for her. Not any more, thanks to her supposed betrayal of them, and Cesar. She had to mend that rift before it became too wide to bridge.

Jess and Olivia were the only ones to greet her with genuine warmth, perhaps sensing there was more to Sofia's story than they knew. When Cesar had collected his food and joined them, there was another discernible rustle of interest around the table, but everyone was too cool to comment. He soon put them at ease with easy banter, culminating in, 'I'll take any seat.' Which just happened to be thigh to thigh with Sofia.

It was hard to breathe. How hard would it be to fall in love with him? She covered her concerns with a grin as she turned to Jess. 'Work us harder tomorrow.' Exhaustion might help. Something had to.

Jess winked, as if she understood everything. 'Don't worry, I intend to,' she promised.

'Good.' Cesar was the only one at the table who responded. Pushing his chair back, he stood up. 'We'll all benefit from another good workout tomorrow.' He glanced at Sofia. 'I'm going to take a sluice down in the yard.'

Sofia flicked a quick glance at Jess. It felt good to

have an ally. She had no idea how much Jess knew, but she could feel her sympathy coming in waves across the table.

Was she expected to join him? Sofia wondered when Cesar paused at the door. Turning away, she continued her chat with Jess. They had a lot to talk about. They both had to put up with her brothers.

Her gaze strayed out of window. Cesar was tipping well water over his head. She clenched and unfurled her fingers, remembering how he'd felt beneath her hands.

Droplets of water went flying from his thick black hair when he shook his head like an angry wolf. His torso was gleaming and wet. How was she supposed to feel nothing for this man?

'Sofia?'

She turned to face Jess. 'I'm sorry… Forgive me. I was distracted.'

Jess grinned. 'Who wouldn't be? Anyway, I was just saying, prepare to be exhausted tomorrow. There's less than a month to go before the first match. These might be exhibition matches, but you know as well as I do that when your brothers and Cesar are playing against a rival like Nero Caracas, there's no such thing as a friendly game.'

Jess wasn't exaggerating. Nero and his team Assassin were their closest rivals. 'Work us hard. Give us every advantage you can. The rest is up to fate, and how we play on the day.'

Placing her hand over Sofia's, Jess gave it a squeeze as she whispered discreetly, 'I know how worried you are, but you don't need to worry about Cesar. He's overcome mountains before, and knows how to handle himself. Concentrate on looking after yourself.'

'Thank you.' *For being my friend* didn't need to be said.

Sofia glanced through the window at Cesar. Another lonely night beckoned, and then a new day with all that that entailed.

'Need a leg-up?'

She looked around to see Cesar standing behind her. Feelings swamped her.

'No, thanks. I can manage.'

'Please yourself.' With a shrug, he sprang into the saddle and cantered into the arena.

Jess placed Sofia behind Cesar in the line, which taunted Sofia with the sight of a back view as good as his front. Powerful and unyielding, Cesar's mighty shoulders and straight spine could have been a metaphor for the way he lived.

Her heart clenched at the thought of any harm coming to him during the matches. They would be rough, they would be hard; neither side would give way without a fight. And then there was the blackmailer she had to deal with, which was like coping with a virus, sneaky and unpredictable, working in the shadows to bring a victim down—

'Sofia, are you with us?' Jess was calling from across the ring. 'Change direction now!'

Sofia wheeled her pony around just in time to avoid a collision with Xander, who blasted her with a derisive look as he cantered past.

In the unlikely event that Cesar spares the time to actually hold a conversation with you, how likely is it that he'll jump at the chance to help you with your blackmailer?

She had to hope pretty high. Like her brothers, Cesar was a man of principle—

'Sofia!' Jess rode up alongside. 'Do you need to take a break?'

'No. Sorry. I'm on it.'

'I hope so. Carelessness leads to accidents at this level of training.'

'It won't happen again, Jess.'

Just as she would never, *ever* write another article. Now all she had to do was persuade Cesar of that, and that the original article had been so heavily doctored she'd hardly recognised it.

Well, that should be easy, she reflected as Cesar gave her a black look for reckless riding.

Easy or not, it had to be done.

Her chance came at the end of the afternoon session when everyone left to freshen up. Sofia's legs felt like wood. She couldn't remember working so hard on a horse, and for the first time in her memory she stumbled when she dismounted.

Cesar was at her side in an instant, steadying her with one hand firmly lodged beneath her arm. 'Too much for you? You made a bit of a mess of today's training. Maybe don't ask Jess to make things harder tomorrow?' he suggested dryly. 'Was there any particular reason behind your request to make things hard for you?'

She chose to ignore that question. 'Training's hard for all of us. I can take it.'

Cesar gave her a critical look. 'Can you?'

Ignoring that too, she focused on the one thing that mattered. 'I have to talk to you—and I mean talk. To clear the air,' she explained when Cesar remained silent.

'It will take more than a chat to do that.' He was already turning away. 'Barbecue this evening,' he announced.

'Cesar, please,' she insisted, grabbing a moment

alone as soon as he'd finished spelling out the details. 'We can't go on like this, not if we hope to play well as a team.'

He stared at her hand on his arm. She stood back. Good enough for sex, she wasn't good enough for Cesar to engage in conversation apparently. Now she was mad. Which was unfortunate timing, as the stable hands had arrived to take charge of the ponies.

'If only you were so caring about your human counterparts,' Cesar observed, holding the door for her to pass through as they left the building.

She always spelled out her pony's preferences, and mentioned any worries she might have about the animal's condition after hard training.

Her heart lurched as their hands brushed. How was she ever going to concentrate when that was all it took? She had to. She must. She couldn't lose her brother, and she couldn't lose Cesar. 'There's something you need to know.'

'Sounds intriguing.' He speared her with a stare until it was hard to believe she had any secrets left.

'Can we talk now?'

He shrugged. 'I can spare you five minutes.'

She'd take it. 'Thanks.'

'Follow me—'

'No.' She shook her head. 'I need you to follow me.'

Without looking back to see if Cesar was following, she led the way to what had quickly become Sofia's favourite place on Cesar's ranch. It was a secluded spot by the river, where she could read and think, not that she got much spare time to do either. Her destination was a woodland grove where she could sit, sheltered by a copse of trees. It was an idyllic spot on the banks of a fast-flowing river, but it wasn't easy to reach, which was half of its attraction. Few made the effort, so it was completely private. Brambles on the ground threatened to trip unwary visitors, but for someone brought up in the country like Sofia, who was accustomed to trekking over difficult ground, it was a hidden treasure.

She could hear Cesar's long strides behind her. He had to hear her out, then he could send her home if he wanted to. Either way, she had to make a stand.

'My mother used to being me here,' Cesar revealed when they stood on the banks of the fast-flowing river. 'It was part of my introduction to a brighter world, she'd tell me. A world where things are clean, and clear, if you remain still and allow yourself to hear.'

Would he? Would he allow himself to hear? With all her heart, she hoped he would.

'When I was older, I'd come here on my own to think.'

'Did it help?' she asked, wanting to open this window onto Cesar's early life wide.

'Five minutes,' he reminded her, closing off. 'So you'd better be fast. What do you want to talk to me about?'

If that was the way he was going to play it, she'd be just as blunt. 'I'm being blackmailed.'

Obviously shocked, Cesar recovered fast. 'Go on,' he prompted.

'I signed up to write a light, fluffy piece for a fee I could plough into my retreat. At the time I had no idea Howard Blake was such an unscrupulous man, or that he would seize the opportunity to take my material and doctor it beyond all recognition. Now he's threatening to publish more articles under my name. I'm guessing they won't do you or my brothers any favours. I don't know why he's got it in for you. I do know my reputation will be ruined, but that's nothing in comparison to losing the love and trust of my brothers, and causing you more harm. If I could wind back the clock, and change things, I would, but…'

Cesar was staring out across the stream in silence. 'Did you hear me?'

'Every word.' he assured her.

She couldn't believe how calm he was, though alert like a wolf on point.

'Your five minutes are up.'

There was no warmth in his voice as he swung around to head back up the bank. 'But—'

'I promised you five minutes,' he said, briefly turning. 'You've had that and more.'

'But, please, I—'

'Don't,' Cesar warned quietly. 'How could the chance to see your by-line above an article in a national newspaper prove such a lure you were prepared to throw your brothers under a bus and me along with them?'

'Weren't you listening? It wasn't like that. Those weren't my words.'

'So you say. What I read was invented scandal. Maybe you dressed up the facts until they provided outrageous amounts of click bait with no basis of truth. How do I know? How can I be sure of you, Sofia? The dates on which your accusations were based were entirely accurate, but the events you wrote about never happened.'

'Because I didn't write them!' she exploded, growing increasingly frustrated. 'Believe me, Cesar. Have I ever given you cause to doubt me before?'

'How well did I know you before?' he countered.

'Do you seriously believe I would hurt those I love—

or, almost worse, those vulnerable individuals recovering at my retreat? If you think so little of me, I'm wasting my time.'

'Maybe you are,' he agreed.

'I need help,' she admitted grimly as she clambered up the bank to join him. 'What started out as what I thought was a normal relationship between an enthusiastic amateur journalist and a newspaper mogul quickly turned sour. If Blake can do that to me and get away with it, how many more people are at risk? He has to be stopped, and I can't do this on my own.'

There was a silence she thought would never end, and then Cesar said the words she had hoped and prayed he would. 'This is not something you can handle on your own,' he agreed. 'I know Blake from our schooldays together. We attended the same boarding school. He was the class bully, picking on younger boys with no one to defend them.'

'So you defended them,' she said.

A grim smile firmed Cesar's lips as he thought back. 'It was a full-time occupation.'

'And one he never forgave you for,' she guessed.

Cesar nodded briefly. 'Blake was the type to bear grudges. I always suspected him of being behind the swindler who tried to steal the throne by cosying up to my mother. There have been numerous attacks over the years.'

'Of which I'm just the latest?'

'Don't beat yourself up,' Cesar said, to her surprise. 'You couldn't know how devious he was, or how he would use you to get at me.'

Hope surged through her. 'So you believe me?'

'I'm giving you the benefit of the doubt,' Cesar prevaricated.

'I handed him ammunition on a plate.'

'To help your retreat.'

'Yes.' Still reeling from the thought that Cesar might believe her, and that he might help after all, she asked the obvious question. 'Why have you never hit back at him before?'

'Make myself as small as him?' Cesar shook his head. 'There are other, more efficient ways to deal with a bully like Blake, subtle ways that will keep him in a moral cage.'

CHAPTER TEN

CURIOUS TO HEAR MORE, Sofia continued with her explanation. 'To start with, it seemed as if fate had dropped an opportunity into my hand. 'Writing "a piece of fluff" for the features page was how Lord Blake put it. It seemed such a good opportunity to bring in much-needed money to support the expansion of my retreat.'

'Easy money?' Cesar challenged. 'There's no such thing. You should have been suspicious right away.'

'It's easy to be wise in retrospect,' Sofia argued, 'but when you've spent months casting about for ways to keep things running, you're open to any idea that seems remotely feasible.'

'Writing an article exposing the antics of the super-rich seemed feasible to you?'

'That wasn't how I phrased it. There was no mention of "super-rich". I wrote about humorous incidents that happened on the world tour. None of them were scandalous or libellous. I certainly didn't depict you as an "elitist degenerate", which was one of the descriptions used. What I wrote made you and my brothers seem approachable. It was supposed to make people laugh, not cause trouble.'

'Blake couldn't have doctored the piece without your ready supply of facts,' Cesar pointed out.

'But that's just it. Some of those facts I didn't even know. How could I? I don't have access to your diary. So now do you see why I need your help?'

As Cesar's thoughtful gaze rested on her face, she felt a great sense of weariness at her seemingly endless attempts to try to explain what had happened. Why wouldn't he take her at her word? She'd never knowingly told a lie, and had believed that as soon as she opened up, Cesar would believe her.

It didn't take much for weariness to turn into anger. Staring at Cesar's back as he made his way home was the final straw. Catching up, she stood grim-faced in his way. 'At least have the courtesy to let me know what you think.'

Lifting her aside, he moved on.

'I expect a fair hearing, and all I get is ignored? How do you expect anyone to stop Howard Blake if you turn your back and walk away?'

'I'm not ignoring you, but this is not the time,' he said, striding on.

'Not the time?' She caught up. 'What do you mean? What else is going on?'

At least he stopped walking.

'You're the only person I know who wields as much power as Howard Blake,' she pressed. 'Maybe more. Definitely more. If anyone can stop him, you can. Cesar, if your back was to the wall, wouldn't you do anything to make things right?'

'I've never been in that position.'

'I'm glad, but please have sympathy for those who aren't so lucky. I have to believe you can stop Blake hurting anyone else.'

She was puzzled when he didn't answer. 'Is there something you're not telling me?'

'It was a very different situation. A member of my family was under attack.'

Lifting her chin, she braced herself and ignored the sting. 'Family loyalty is paramount to me too, which is why I would never intentionally hurt my brothers. Blake will dig and dig until he finds something to use. He has to be stopped. You must be thinking I've got a cheek, asking you for help, but who else can I turn to?'

'Your brothers?' Cesar suggested in a dead tone.

'I've always wanted to stand on my own two feet. I caused this problem, so it's up to me to sort it out.'

'But you're asking for my help,' he pointed out impatiently. 'I don't see the difference.'

'You have a certain reputation when it comes to dealing with difficult people. Didn't you mention subtlety? I'm calling on your expertise.'

'Save your flattery.'

'I'll stop at nothing to prevent Howard Blake causing any more trouble. If I involve my brothers and they bring in the weight of the Acosta lawyers, this could run and run, doing more harm than good. I'm trying to avoid that.'

'You must have a record of the original article on your computer to prove that it was changed?'

'Conveniently, my computer was stolen when burglars targeted my home.'

'Stolen from your retreat?'

'Yes.'

'Do you vet the people you allow in? Your brothers tell me there's very little security.'

'That was the whole point. I wanted people to feel free, not trapped.'

'Oh, Sofia, Sofia.' Cesar gave her a long, considering look. 'I'm beginning to think that you tried to do your best—'

'If you're going to be patronising—'

'Stop,' he commanded.

She tensed at the touch of his hand on her arm.

'Sometimes a warm heart can put you at a disadvantage.'

Cesar's tone was gentle, but she had no intention of being treated like a child. Bringing Howard Blake down would take both of them equally.

Giving herself a moment, she refocused her mind. This wasn't about pride or personal considerations, but getting a job done. 'How did you stop him last time?' she asked briskly, turning to stare Cesar in the eyes.

'Money talks?' He sounded faintly amused, as if he had accepted both her stand and the fact that massive wealth could be useful in a number of ways. 'My last run-in with Blake involved a member of my family, someone else with a kind heart, falling into Blake's clutches. It was necessary to step in to protect that family member.'

'Your mother?' Sofia guessed.

Cesar was too protective and too discreet to answer her question, both of which counted in his favour.

'Howard Blake was silenced, and that's all you need to know. He got to keep his publishing empire in a deal that suited us both.'

It was hard to imagine Blake, a man who had bullied and hectored *her*, turning over meekly, though coming up against Cesar would be daunting, she imagined, even for a man as unscrupulous as Howard Blake. Her brother Xander had once referred to Cesar as being the most resourceful and determined individual he'd ever met, adding that Cesar always protected those who needed him. 'I never thought I was Blake's first target, and I'm sure I won't be the last. I'm strong enough to take the consequences, but what about the next person he picks on?'

'So what's your plan?'

'From what you've told me, and from personal experience, we know Blake can't stop himself targeting those weaker than himself. It's like an addiction. You've already dealt with him successfully, and I'm lucky to have you onside. I do have you onside?' She went on before Cesar had a chance to answer. 'We can't hang his future targets out to dry. We can't turn our backs. We have to stop him. Someone has to bring him to account.'

'You?' Cesar interrupted with a cynical lift of his brow.

'I can't do this without your help,' she said honestly.

'So you propose co-operation between us?'

'Is that so bad?'

Sofia's voice was quiet and intense. Her stare remained fixed on his face. How could he remain unsympathetic when Blake had targeted both his mother and his sister? His mother had taken a lover, a conman planted by Blake, he now thought, and there was a sex tape featuring Olivia. These were Blake's weapons of choice. Rage roared inside him as he recognised Sofia as an equally attractive target for a bully. Desperate to keep the retreat that meant so much to her going at any cost, she was exactly the type of victim Howard Blake loved to prey on. Sofia must have been a prized victim, giving Blake direct access to the Acosta brothers and his old enemy Cesar. How he must have gloated, thinking he could send them all down like a line of dominoes.

'Cesar?'

Fury must have been written on his face. Most would

shrink from it, but not Sofia. She stood to confront him and barred his way. 'We'll call him out,' she said fiercely.

He raised a brow. 'How do you propose to do that?'

'We'll set a trap. We'll feed him false information and then expose it as a lie.'

'He'll see that coming a mile off,' he reflected out loud. 'The confrontation has to be face to face. So I'll deal with him.' He held up his hand when she started to argue. 'I don't want you anywhere near him. This is something I will handle alone.'

Even as he was speaking, an idea was niggling at his brain. There was no time to waste. He had investigations to make. 'Is that it?'

Sofia reached out a hand as if to stop him, but then she withdrew it and lowered her gaze in a way that made her seem suddenly fragile. 'You go on,' she said. 'I'd like to stay here for a while.'

'Be back before dark. Remember the Apennine wolves. They roam freely in the forest.'

'I won't forget. I can look after myself. Remember?'

She stared up, her eyes luminous and unblinking. He didn't move. He couldn't move. How could he leave her alone in the forest? The light was fading, and there was more than one wolf on the prowl. Sofia had made a dangerous enemy in Howard Blake, and Cesar would take no chances. 'You're coming with me so I know that you're safe.'

'A few minutes ago you'd have liked to throw me in the stream,' she commented with amusement.

'Never,' he assured her. 'I'd only have to jump in and save you.'

'I'd save myself,' she insisted, lifting her chin.

'And how would you do that?'

'I'd do it somehow,' she assured him stubbornly.

Somehow wouldn't help her with Howard Blake. 'I do need you to do something for me,' he revealed as they started to walk back.

'Tell me.'

'The best way to show Blake he can't hurt you, let alone destroy your brothers and me, as he seems to think he can, is by making sure we win those matches and raise more money than even Howard Blake can dream of for our charities.'

'You're cutting me out,' she said with affront, having read the subtext behind his words. 'You can't do this alone. Cesar—what are you going to do?'

'It's better that you don't know. That no one knows.'

'Don't you trust me?'

She was hurt when he didn't answer right away, but his mind was made up. Keeping Sofia safe, saving her brothers and even a country from the spite of Howard Blake, was more important than explanations. 'Be the best you can be,' he advised. 'That's your revenge when it comes to Howard Blake.'

There were tears in her eyes, he realised when he turned to look at Sofia. She had guts but a tender under-belly, reminding him that emotions did matter, whether he liked it or not. 'Don't worry about Blake. I'll deal with him, so he never hurts anyone else. And when this is over,' he added in an attempt to turn her mind from the dark side to something lighter, 'I'll commission a portrait of the winning team.'

For a moment he thought his offer had missed the mark. In fairness, contemplating the evil of a man like Blake then switching to the prospect of the quiet con-templation involved when Sofia picked up her brush and paints was quite a stretch, but one Sofia had to make if she was ever to sleep easily again.

He should have known she was equal to the task.

'The winning team had better not be Nero Caracas and the Assassins,' she said, smiling in a way that touched him somewhere deep. 'I don't have enough black paint.'

It had been good to walk back to the ranch house with Cesar with some ease at last between them. It made her hopeful that other things could change for the better.

But now, back in her room, without the beauty of the countryside surrounding her, she had started to worry again—primarily about Cesar. His promise to 'handle things'. What did that mean? If Cesar could deal with Howard Blake help without putting himself at risk, that was one thing, but she had never intended him to do this on his own.

Getting ready for dinner involved showering before changing into clean jeans and a casual top for the promised barbecue. Staring at her reflection in the mirror above the sink, she craved the chance for them to continue getting to know each other outside sex. They'd made a small start down by the river, but would he take things further? It took two to form a relationship, and Cesar's wishes were one thing determination alone couldn't influence.

Cesar hosted the barbecue. He got on so well with her brothers. Jess and Olivia came straight over to welcome her. 'Okay?' Jess asked. 'Nothing aching too much?'

Only my heart, she thought, smiling. 'I'm fine.'

Olivia came up with some startling news. 'I've seen the looks that pass between you and my brother. Jess and I have been talking, and you don't need to tell us that Howard Blake set you up. Jess knows everything about my run-in with Blake, so if you need allies, look no further.'

'Thank you.'

'Take my advice,' Olivia continued. 'First find the mole.'

'The mole?' Sofia frowned.

'Someone filmed me secretly. I don't know if you heard about the tape?' Olivia pressed. 'Anyway, it was explicit,' she continued, sparing Sofia the need to answer, 'and somehow it found its way to Howard Blake. That someone is almost certainly the same person who supplied the dates and details you couldn't. Someone helped Blake doctor that article. I know it wasn't you, and it most certainly wasn't me.'

An unseen enemy was one to fear the most. Fear tightened around Sofia's heart. She drew a deep breath, and pushed it aside. 'Do you have any suspects in mind?'

'I do,' Olivia confirmed, 'but I can't prove anything yet. We'll speak again,' she promised.

Sofia's mind was spinning as Olivia moved away. Cesar's sister had left her with more questions than answers. Cesar's bottomless resources would open many doors, but now Sofia wished she hadn't asked him for help. The thought of putting Cesar in danger was the worst nightmare imaginable. She had to put things right. Quite how she was going to do that, she had no idea yet. Olivia only proved that caution must be her watchword.

'I thought it was me you wanted to talk to, not my sister,' Cesar remarked dryly as he loaded Sofia's plate with food.

'Steady. Am I not allowed to speak to your sister?

No more food,' she insisted, laughing as he continued to stack it on her plate. 'You're not feeding my brothers.'

'I'll take your plate to the table,' he offered.

Everyone else was seated by the time they arrived. Sofia sat on a bench facing her brothers, while Cesar straddled the end of it, so he was facing her.

'Olivia is a hothead,' he informed her. 'Don't believe everything she says.'

'Even if what Olivia says makes sense?' Sofia queried.

Cesar shrugged. 'Just don't allow her to draw you into one of her ill-thought-out schemes.'

'What makes you think I don't have schemes of my own?'

'If you do, I must insist you run them past me first.'

She almost choked on her burger. Chugging down a glass of water, she shook her head. 'I can't believe you sometimes. You mentioned co-operation? I get that. Putting safeguards in place is only sensible, but to defer to you on every decision I make?'

'I'm trying to keep you safe, Sofia.'

'And I'm trying to keep you safe,' she reminded him. Glancing around, she tried to work out who the mole might be. Each group was an island separate from the rest, but could any of them be guilty of betraying Cesar's trust? It seemed unlikely.

'I have a lot of things to put right and I don't expect you, or anyone else, to do that for me,' she stated firmly. 'I may not have your seemingly limitless resources, but neither am I incapable.'

'Or as experienced as me at dealing with sharks like Howard Blake,' Cesar pointed out.

'I'm a fast learner.'

'Fast learners listen to advice.'

Sitting back, she closed her eyes briefly. 'Do you have any idea how annoying you can be?'

Cesar flashed a quick and, oh, so welcome smile. 'Some.'

'Well, just forget I said anything. I shouldn't have asked you for help.'

'That's a matter of opinion. Howard Blake is a slippery character.'

'All the more reason to stop him.'

'But not on your own.' Cesar articulated each word in a low, fierce tone.

With a laugh she pushed her plate away. 'Anyone would think you care.'

'I do care,' Cesar insisted, surprising her, but just as happy surprise leapt onto her face he added, 'I'm not looking for more tangles to unpick before the match. The clock is ticking. None of us can afford to be distracted. You expected something more?' he enquired, when she couldn't hide her shock.

Recovering fast, she said coolly, 'Why would I?'

'We can't talk here,' Cesar said, frowning. 'It's too noisy. My study...' He stood.

She'd seen his study. Desk. Floor. Rug. Hard chairs. Easy chairs. Inviting sofas. All options open. But to persuade Cesar not to do anything that might put him danger, was this the best chance she'd get?

CHAPTER ELEVEN

LEAVING THE TABLE, she joined Cesar as they walked the short distance to the ranch house. Once inside they went straight to Cesar's study, where he directed her to an easy chair. He remained standing with his hip propped against the desk. 'So talk,' he invited.

'I've got nothing new to say. I just don't want you doing anything on my behalf that puts you in danger.'

'How much of your own money have you put into your retreat?'

'Every penny. And I mortgaged the property,' she admitted. 'I had to so I could take on more people.'

Cesar's look grew cynical. 'Were you planning to write more articles to fund this expansion?'

'No! Of course not! How can you even think that?'

'I'm curious as to how you intended to support yourself going forward.'

'I thought selling my paintings might help.' That sounded so lame now. How did she know anyone would buy them? So far she'd had a commission from her brother and the sniff of a promise from Cesar. That wouldn't be enough to support her retreat.

'How much do you need?' Cesar asked bluntly.

'I don't want a loan,' she said. 'I'll find the money.'

'You have a money tree?'

'I'll listen to any suggestions you care to make, but I won't sit on my hands while you go into battle on my behalf.'

'It's time to accept that you can't carry the world on your shoulders. I'm sure your brothers would be only too eager to help you if you didn't push them away.'

'I haven't pushed them away. It takes them all their time to speak to me.'

There was silence for a while and then Cesar reflected, 'I guess it must have been hard as a teenager in a household of over-protective brothers.'

'You have no idea,' she agreed, relaxing enough to smile as she thought back.

'I think I do,' Cesar argued. 'My sister was left without a father, and when my mother recovered from her grief she was…distracted, shall we say? I was in the Special Forces, and it was only when Olivia alerted me to trouble—and, believe me, Olivia seeks help from no one—that I left the army to save the throne from an unscrupulous man. So I'm not exactly out of practice when it comes to dealing with problems. I'd go as far as to say I'm your best hope.'

Maybe her only hope. 'Okay, but we do this together or not at all.'

'Too many chiefs,' Cesar cautioned.'

'You're not suggesting I leave it all to you?'

'It's not a suggestion,' he assured her.

'Not my way either,' she said, firming her jaw.

Cesar went to stare out of the window. 'My mother grieved long and hard for my father,' he said without turning around. 'Years passed and then she took a lover. Howard Blake's press were all over it. I was still in the army when the palace made an announcement that this man from nowhere, no history, no relatives, no obvious experience to make him a suitable candidate to support the Queen in her duties, planned to join her on the throne.'

'As your mother's equal?' Sofia asked with surprise. 'I didn't realise it went that far.' The throne should rightfully pass to Cesar, and she could only imagine how he must have felt, or how delicately he'd had to handle the situation without upsetting his mother, who must have been very vulnerable at the time. That, as well as protecting Olivia from a scandal, made her wonder if Cesar ever spared a thought for himself.

'What's your plan?' he asked as he swung around.

She didn't want to talk about herself, or what *she* was going to do. She wanted to talk about Cesar so she could try to understand this deep and complex man. In short order, Cesar had lost his father, found himself head of a prominent family, and been thrown into the turmoil of fixing his mother and sister's lives. He could only do that by pushing his feelings aside. Joining the Special Forces might have given the wild youth an anchor, but he'd been forced to give that up. Cesar's recent life seemed to have been one of constant sacrifice, and now she was throwing up yet another hurdle.

She understood his mother's reasons. Grief could throw anyone off kilter. Sofia had always tried to live up to what she believed were her dead parents' expectations of her, but this time, like the Queen, she'd gone too far. If she'd called a halt when she'd built a small retreat with limited places, none of this would have happened. But so many had applied to go there. How could she choose who could stay and who to turn away?

'So what next, Sofia?'

Cesar was waiting for her answer. He had the world

on his shoulders already, and now he expected her to load him down with more.

'Sofia?' he pressed.

'I plan to turn my fledgling investigative skills on Howard Blake,' she revealed.

'Hoping he has an Achilles heel?' Cesar guessed.

'I have to hope so,' she confessed. 'But it's more than that. I want to understand his jealousy towards you and the way he'll stop at nothing to destroy you, even using me.'

'I can't argue with that,' Cesar admitted. 'I've thought the same thing myself.'

'So we do agree on something?' she said wryly, hoping she was right.

When Cesar didn't answer, she decided it was time for bed. Getting up from her chair, she said, 'If I do find out anything else that might be helpful, I'll let you know.'

'You do that,' Cesar agreed. 'Goodnight, Sofia.'

'Goodnight.'

He didn't call her back or come after her. And, of course, she was glad about that.

Was she?

The sound of the door closing behind Sofia rang in Cesar's ears for some time. Not that she was angry, or even disappointed he hadn't pulled a rabbit out of a hat to show her when it came to his plans for Howard Blake. When he did decide what to do, he'd be the only one with that information. It was safer that way.

External influences hadn't made Sofia leave in such a hurry, he concluded, but the pull between them had done the damage. They'd shared a look. She'd moistened her lips. Her cheeks had flushed pink and her breathing quickened, but instead of taking things further he'd made it clear that wasn't going to happen, at which point she'd left the room. Sex was the answer to a lot of things, but not this.

Exhaling a long, steady breath, he sat back. What was this woman doing to him? When things looked as if they might become complicated by feelings, he always pulled back. Capable of feeling the deepest emotion, he also knew how to hide it well, thanks to understanding the cost of love. He had idolised his father, the strongest and noblest of men, but still found it hard to accept that a fall from a horse during training could have brought such a well-lived life to a sudden and unalterable end.

He and his father were the same in that they solved problems and found solutions. His father's tragic death was the first time Cesar had been faced by a catastrophe he could neither change nor soften. The end of one way of living and the beginning of another, quite different life had been brutal. One minute his father had been laughing and joking, poised and confident as he'd cantered around the arena, and the next his horse had stumbled, throwing him over its head. And that was it. The end. Over. Never to move, breathe, speak, or offer loving advice again.

Everything had changed on that day. His mother had been hysterical, his sister numb with shock. From a confident, hard-living youth, home on furlough from the army, he had been catapulted into a world where caring for people was more important than crowns. Stability for family and country had become his guiding light from that moment on, just as personal feelings had become a complete and utter irrelevance. All that mattered had been putting things back on an even keel.

The bombshell of the King's death had spread a

shroud of fear across the citizens of Ardente Sestieri as people had wondered what would come next. Prince Cesar, the wild youth whose exploits had entertained them, was surely not fit to be King? Cesar's lifestyle hadn't mattered to his people when his father had been alive, but for such a solid and reliable presence on the throne to be replaced by someone unknown had taken a lot a lot of living down. The trust he'd won since then could be lost in a heartbeat.

At one point he'd wondered how his mother would survive the loss of his father. They had been two sides of the same coin. How would that one, lonely side of the coin weather the wear and tear of ruling, with only one face, one opinion, one decision-maker to hold the reins, with no one to advise, curb or recommend? His mother had needed him to step up, and he'd answered her call gladly. With her so-called suitor dismissed, the Queen would rule alone with Cesar as her chief advisor. Nothing must stand in the way of that.

It was in everyone's interest to bring Howard Blake to account. But there was another reason. Sofia had shown him her vulnerable side. He couldn't walk away from that. This was a time to keep her close. He had to, if he was to keep her safe.

What other reason could there be?

Pushing his chair back, he left his study to track her down.

He found her in the empty stable where she had gone to sort out her thoughts. Whatever else was going on in her life, animals always soothed her. Cesar lost no time in delivering his broadside. 'I can't let you approach Howard Blake on your own. I won't allow it!'

Brain and body moved as one for Cesar, and he was

in front of her in a heartbeat. Scrambling to her feet, she faced him down. 'Cesar—'

'Yes, Cesar!' he cut across her. 'Who the hell else do you think would chase you down to stop you walking blindfold into danger?'

He really cared? She could see the concern in his eyes. How did she feel about that? Thrilled. Surprised. And also keenly aware that Cesar's concern could stand in the way of her setting things right.

'I'm glad you came,' she said, quickly marshalling her thoughts. 'I wanted to let you know what I've done so far.'

'What you've done?' Far from this enticing him to back off, Cesar's expression was thunderous. 'Without telling me first?'

'My plans are still in the very early stages,' she explained in what she hoped was a soothing tone. 'I won't need an army or strong-arm tactics—'

'Just tell me what you've done,' Cesar bit out.

'I just made a call.'

'Who did you call?' She'd never seen him like this. She could only describe it as anguished. 'Tell me what you've done, Sofia. I hope you haven't put yourself in danger?'

'I called a woman who lives at my retreat, the same woman who passed on the original request from Howard Blake for me to write an article. I trusted her. Dante always says I trust everyone too quickly. Now I must face the possibility that Dante's right, and this woman and Howard might be in league.'

Cesar frowned. 'But how would she know the dates in my diary?'

'Maybe there's more than one conspirator,' Sofia allowed. 'Howard Blake's pockets are deep enough to hire an army of moles. All I offer is a haven until people are ready to face the world again, while he offers a lot of money. Who could blame her if she was tempted?'

'I could,' Cesar said coldly. 'You're far too soft, Sofia.'

'I'm not soft at all,' she argued, 'but I do know what it's like to feel you've no control over your life, and to wonder and fear what's coming next. Seizing back even a little bit of control in those circumstances feels good.'

Cesar dismissed this with an impatient huff. 'You credit the person who quite possibly betrayed you with finer feelings than they deserve. If you have a suspect you should let me follow it up. I have the resources,' he pointed out. 'And whatever our differences, I would never allow someone to harm you and get away with it.'

'But you have enough to do.' Having asked Cesar for help, she was having second thoughts. He did have enough to do, and she had only made things harder.

'You don't know what you're up against,' he said with an impatient gesture.

'But I do, and I also have a theory as to why this is escalating. Jealousy,' she declared. 'I know it makes no sense when Blake's as rich as Croesus, but for some people even too much is never enough.'

Cesar didn't argue, but holding his stare for any length of time was never a good idea. Her body was always ready to seize the smallest cue, and this was not the right time to do that. This felt like the first time they'd ever talked, really talked, and both of them had listened. Surely that was something worth preserving and treasuring? All she'd wanted had been to build the connection between them and hopefully watch it turn into something deeper and more meaningful. Yes, her body burned to feel his touch again, nothing had changed where that was concerned, but now her heart yearned for company.

'You will not do this on your own. Understood?'

Cesar's instruction jolted her out of gentler thoughts. 'Don't forget I survived a house full of brothers,' she reminded him.

'Howard Blake is nothing like your brothers, and I shouldn't need to tell you that.'

'You don't,' she said, 'but if you think I'm going to sit on my butt, doing nothing, you're wrong. You have a country to consider, as well as a mother and sister to protect. Your duty lies there. I got into this mess, and now I'm going to get out of it.'

'I won't release you from your training,' Cesar told her with a closing gesture of his hands.

He wasn't used to being countermanded, let alone be taken out of the game, but Sofia was in no mood to give ground. 'You can't stop me,' she said. 'We're here because we choose to be here, not because you commanded our attendance. All of us are successful in our own right—some more successful than others,' she conceded with a shrug, 'but seriously, Cesar, you can leave this to me.'

'Seriously, Sofia,' he mocked with venom, 'that will never happen, so put it out of your mind.'

He swung her round so fast the air was sucked from her lungs. The time for calm reason had gone. 'Do you seriously think I'll allow you to risk your life? Don't you realise there's a kingdom at stake and that's what he's after? Blake tried once with my mother, dangling a gigolo in front of her. Do you think he'd care what happens to you? You'll be collateral damage—just another counter for Blake to play and discard when it suits him. I won't allow you to do that—for your sake, and for the sake of everyone who cares about you. Your life is worth nothing to Howard Blake. *Nothing!* Don't you get it?'

Cesar's face was very close. His eyes scorched hers. She'd never seen so much passion in one man. Perhaps because Cesar never showed emotion it seemed all the greater now. Whatever it was she felt, it was not the urge to pull away or even to stand on tiptoe to give him a kiss—*definitely not that*. What she felt, deep down, through every fibre of her being was the urge to reassure him. Cesar had been through enough. 'I'm not your responsibility, and I promise I won't get hurt. I'll be back to play in the matches before you know it. And we'll win—in every way there is,' she added with icy resolve.

He couldn't believe what he was hearing, and frankly he'd had enough. Sofia appeared convinced that fairy-tales could come true and that good would prevail over evil. She refused to see the danger. Whatever he said fell would fall on deaf ears. Fortunately, he'd cut his teeth on an equally wilful sister so he was in familiar territory. 'I'll bar you from leaving the kingdom if I have to. I'm not joking, Sofia.'

But the sterner his tone, the brighter grew the gleam of amusement in Sofia's eyes. 'What's wrong with you?' he demanded. But he knew. He'd seen the same thing on the battlefield. In a hazardous situation humour often showed itself, as if to thumb its nose at danger. That was the case here. Sofia thought she knew the person she was dealing with, but he really knew.

'Whatever it takes,' he warned as he took hold of her arms. His mouth was so close to hers now they shared the same breath, the same air. Her eyes held challenge, and however much he glowered back she smiled at him, until the laugh she'd been smothering broke free. 'You think this is funny?' he demanded. 'Or are you addicted to playing with fire?'

Her expression changed. Her eyes filled with an expression he rejected, not need or passion—compassion. 'Stop looking at me like that,' he warned.

'Someone should,' she said coolly.

'What are you talking about?' Letting her go, he stood back.

'It must be lonely in your ivory tower. I was hoping I could pay a visit and get to know you.'

'Isn't that what we've been doing?'

She slowly shook her head. 'So far you've lectured me and I've listened, but now I'm going to tell you what I'm doing next.'

'You think?' he scoffed.

When reason failed, his instinct took over.

CHAPTER TWELVE

As Cesar drove his mouth down on hers, she knew that if there hadn't been so much pent-up longing inside her she would have... *What? Pushed him away?*

Not a chance. Caring and hunger mixed in one fiercely compassionate need to be close to him. Pulling his head back, he stared down and smiled. 'Must you always choose a stable for your amorous encounters?'

'I didn't invite you to join me,' she countered, challenge firing in her eyes.

'Didn't you?' Cesar queried as he smoothly dispensed with her clothes. He was in even more of a hurry than she was, and she was desperate for release. Every part of her ached for him and rejoiced when he lifted her so she could lock her legs around his waist. Breath escaped her lungs in a long-drawn-out sigh as he plunged deep.

'Excellent,' Cesar growled, throwing his head back in ecstasy as he slammed her against the wall.

Ripping his top out of the waistband of his jeans, she rested her face against his hard, warm chest and made a comment of her own.

'Your wish is my command,' Cesar informed her, losing no time before thrusting her screaming and bucking with pleasure into the abyss.

Grinding her fingers into his buttocks, she urged him on.

'Good?' he asked much, much later when she was quiet again.

She smiled up. 'What do you think?'

'Once is never enough?'

She laughed. Cesar had made her greedy. 'I swear, if you stop now, tease me, or make me wait, I'll—'

'You'll what?' he demanded in a low growl.

Nuzzling her neck, he whispered encouragement in his own language, which stole what little control she had left. 'Yes! *Yes!*' she begged, as breath shot out of her when Cesar plunged deep.

One powerful release stormed into the next. Rotating his hips made her more sensitive that she could ever have believed. Speech was impossible. Breathing was hard. Fractured shrieks of enjoyment was the best she could manage, while Cesar made sure he held her where he wanted her.

'I can't hold on,' she wailed at one point.

'You're not supposed to,' he said as he encouraged her to work her hips to the same greedy rhythm as his. 'Wildcat!' he approved when she dug her fingers into his shoulders.

'Faster! Harder!' Would she ever get enough?

The next climax came out of nowhere. She was powerless to resist. It was bigger, and far sweeter in its intensity than anything that had gone before. It seemed like for ever before the pleasure waves subsided, and when they did she was as helpless as a kitten, resting limp in Cesar's arms.

'Don't tell me I've finally exhausted you,' he remarked wryly as he lowered her carefully to the floor.

'I doubt you could ever do that,' she admitted, feeling warm and safe as he wrapped her in his arms and dipped his head to brush tender kisses against her mouth. 'But was that just to calm me, so I'll do anything you say?'

'Calm?' he queried. 'Are you in a different realm from me?'

'Answer my question.'

He held out his hands…the same hands that had held her safe and pleasured her until she could think of nothing else. 'What more do you want me to say, Sofia?'

'Reassurance that I haven't fallen for some sort of charm offensive,' she said bluntly.

'Surely you're not that insecure.'

Who knew what they were until they were tested? she wondered. Since getting together with Cesar everything mattered so much to her, too much maybe.

'Just tell me this didn't happen because you threatened you'd do whatever it took to bring me into line?'

'I have needs, just like you,' he dismissed.

'That's not an answer. Is that all it is?'

'Should there be more?'

Holding her breath, she closed her eyes briefly. Cesar could shut himself off completely whenever she tried to get close. What gave her the belief that she could break through his impregnable shell?

'Of course there's more,' he stated as he raised her chin to stare into her eyes. His hands remained resting on her shoulders. She was unused to tenderness. Her brothers' idea of affection involved a not-so-gentle pat, and it had been a long time since she'd felt the loving touch of her parents. Cesar had caught her unawares, and now it was too late to hide the tears in her eyes.

He seemed puzzled. 'Is it so hard to believe that someone outside your immediate family cares what happens to you?' he asked. 'Or that a man wants you as fiercely as I do?'

'At least you're honest,' she said as she pushed a smile through her tears.

'Always,' Cesar promised, but within a moment he was back to his unemotional self. 'Come on, it's time to go.'

Face facts. Apart from the mind-blowing sex, she didn't know him that well.

How could he prove to a woman as strong and yet as fragile as Sofia that he meant her no harm?

By doing something together that didn't involve sex.

Thanking his inner voice with a silent two-word curse, he returned his attention to Sofia.

'Something wrong?' she asked as he pressed his lips down in thought.

He was only surprised at the unexpected interruption from an inner voice that had lain quietly dormant for years. Maybe nothing had happened in that time that had required it to speak up, the thought occurred to him. 'Do you play chess?'

'Chess?' Looking at him as if he'd gone mad, Sofia smoothed her hair, which required plucking quite a bit of hay out of it. 'Yes, I play chess,' she confirmed. 'Is that relevant?'

He shrugged. 'I don't see why not. We could go back to the ranch house, grab some food and a couple of beers, then engage in the age-old game of strategy. I find it clears the mind.'

'And you think it might help me?' she asked, curbing a smile.

'I don't see why not. It always helps me to focus and think clearly.'

'Something I need?' she suggested.

'Something civilised,' he confirmed,

'Civilised?' Sofia exclaimed on a laugh. 'When I play chess with my brothers it's like all-out war. If they even come close to losing, there's always a possibility they might upend the board and storm out.'

His lips tugged with amusement as he pictured the scene. 'Sounds reasonable.'

'Not to me,' Sofia assured him good-humouredly. 'But if you promise to behave, I'm happy to give you a game.'

'Come with me,' he invited.

There was a chessboard in his study. The room was quiet and warm. He sat on one side of the chess table and Sofia sat on the other. He set out the pieces. 'Ready?'

'Are *you* ready?' she challenged, dark eyes blazing with a competitive light.

'Are you sure it isn't you who upends the board if you lose? Just checking,' he soothed when she shot him one of her looks.

Doing something together that didn't involve sex turned out to be harder than expected. Sofia was a smart and merciless chess player. He knew the moment she asked to play the black pieces that she'd go for fool's mate.

Foiling her plan, he sat back.

'Okay,' she conceded, viewing the board through narrowed eyes. 'You got me.'

'Not yet,' he admitted. 'But I will.'

Maybe it was the heat they had created between them, or the recent memory of what had happened in the stable, but he was finding it increasingly hard to concentrate. Had she intentionally picked up the bishop and stroked it? After touching the piece, should he commit her to that move?

To hell with chess! His groin had tightened to the point of pain.

Having completed her move, Sofia tapped her fingers on the table.

'Would you like to use a timer for each move?' he asked.

'No.' She angled her head to study him. 'I like it when you take your time.'

'Be careful what you wish for.'

'Oh, I am,' she assured him in a tone that led him to wonder at what point Sofia had decided that moistening her lips with the tip of her tongue might be a good idea.

'Are you deliberately trying to distract me?'

'What makes you say that?' Her eyes widened in an expression of pure innocence. When she closed them again, perhaps to hide her amusement, he noticed how a fringe of black lashes cast a crescent shadow on the perfectly carved line of her cheekbone. Dragging his gaze away, he focused on the game. Too late, as it happened.

'Check,' she said crisply.

Leaving his seat, he turned away from the board to rub a hand across the back of his neck in an attitude of abject defeat. He allowed Sofia to bask in her triumph for all of two seconds and then, smiling faintly, he turned back.

Confident of triumph, Sofia was studying him when she should have been continuing to study the pieces. Leaning over, he moved his queen. 'Checkmate,' he said softly.

Sofia made a sound of disgust. 'Who's the fool now?' she exclaimed. 'Well played,' she offered sportingly.

'Do you want to play another game?'

'Best of three?' she suggested.

'I suggest we play something else.'

Electricity flashed between them. No words were needed. Linking their fingers, he led her through the silent house. They mounted the stairs to his bedroom—or, more accurately, they almost reached the first landing. Pausing to kiss her was his downfall—their downfall. One kiss led to another and then they were fighting to rid themselves of clothes.

'I promise myself that one day I'm going to have you in bed,' he growled as she reached for him.

'Pillows? Covers? The whole nine yards?' she suggested.

'Depend on it.'

He took her to the hilt in a single thrust. There was no finesse about this mating. It was wild and fierce, and deliciously intense. As if the more they gorged on each other, the more they needed. One question remained. Would they regain reason in time to continue with everyday life? It didn't seem likely right now. Their lives were complex. His was eaten up by duty and responsibility, while hers was eaten up by concern for others.

Did she ever lavish time on herself?

'Again!' she insisted.

'Hey,' he soothed. 'Remember what I said? Next time in bed.'

This was true intimacy, Sofia mused contentedly as she lay replete in Cesar's arms on his enormous bed. Had there ever been a more unselfish lover? She doubted it. Cesar was sleeping. She should be too. They had training in the morning. Or, rather, he did.

Slipping out of bed, she ran to the shower, freshened up, and then dressed while she was still half-damp. Speed was of the essence. But she couldn't leave without imprinting every moonlit inch of Cesar on her mind.

Naked he was glorious. Clothed he was glorious. Sleeping he was beautiful and strong. There was no tension on his face now, no weight of the world resting on his shoulders. She felt a quite ridiculous urge to go back over to the bed to pull the covers over him and give him one last kiss. Until the next time, she promised herself. This wasn't goodbye, it was just a temporary break. She wouldn't risk waking him. She'd do anything to protect him. And she would.

Stopping by Cesar's study, she quickly scribbled a note. She'd be back in time for the match and would spend every spare minute she had in training. She didn't expect to have many spare minutes, but she didn't want Jess or the team worrying about her fitness level.

Turning at the front door, she gazed around the hall and up the staircase, then back into Cesar's study, all the different places where they'd made love and grown closer.

They had grown closer. Cesar was slowly changing from the cold individual she'd first met into a man who gave her everything she needed. Cold was no longer a word she could associate with him. Cesar was hot and funny and caring. They hadn't exactly shared words of love, but silent communication could be more effective than words. Actions certainly were, and action was in her immediate future.

Closing the front door noiselessly behind her, she drew on the closeness that had grown between them to buoy her up and convince her that this was the right thing to do. There had been many moments of trust between them and, whatever happened next, she would never forget this time with Cesar.

She'd called a cab to take her to the airport so she could fly home to Spain. When she arrived back at her retreat, she'd root out the truth. Someone had to be liaising with Howard Blake. If she couldn't uncover the truth in Spain, she'd fly to London and confront Blake at his office.

Tears stung her eyes at the thought of parting from Cesar, but she had a mission to complete before they'd meet again.

The cab she'd requested was waiting at the gate. She turned to look at the sleeping house one last time before climbing into the back of it. A few lights were beginning to show in the windows of the ranch house as people woke up, though the sun had only now crept over the horizon. Dawn was breaking on a new day. Cesar would wake to find her gone. 'Forgive me,' she whispered.

CHAPTER THIRTEEN

THE AIR RANG blue with curses, leaving no one in any doubt that Prince Cesar of Ardente Sestieri was beyond furious.

'Understandable, Your Royal Highness,' Dom placated as he bent to remove the newspaper from Cesar's desk.

'*Leave it!*' Cesar thundered. 'My apologies,' he added grimly. 'This is not your fault.'

With a brief nod of acknowledgement at a rare climbdown by the Prince, Dom made himself scarce at the back of the room.

And still his presence continued to irritate Cesar. Maybe it was Dom's excessively obsequious behaviour lately. Royalty had staff. That was a given. Trusted staff were party to every aspect of Cesar's life. It was a boon he never took for granted, though right now he wished himself back in the army where he could trust his comrades with his life, and where he could take out his frustration on a daily basis with mind-and body-stretching exercises, without anyone knowing what he was thinking.

'The article is…upsetting,' Dom ventured from the shadows.

'You think that piece of garbage upset me?' he asked his aide with incredulity.

Snatching up the tabloid, he flung it down again in disgust. He'd skim-read the article that claimed to have been written by Sofia Acosta. In her spare time, presumably, which he happened to know had been non-existent. Blake had gone too far this time. But where the hell was she? It was Sofia's absence that was sending him into a rage. Concern for her that made his blood boil. The article was nothing more than a scurrilous piece of filth that he refused to dignify with a comment.

Why had she left without telling him where she was going? Why hadn't she woken him?

'It's hard to believe Signorina Acosta would write something like this,' Dom murmured at a level where he had to strain to hear him.

'Impossible,' he snapped.

Where was his control? What had happened to regal manners? All the niceties of life had deserted him around the same time as Sofia. As for the article, the author, whoever that might be, had gone for the jugular this time, crediting Cesar with a harem of imaginary lovers to rival the seraglio of Genghis Khan. It would take around three lifetimes for him to satisfy so many women. And, no, he refused to give it a try.

Whoever had written the article had stepped well over the line, insinuating that his relationship with Sofia was nothing more than a ruse planned by Sofia to ensnare him. She would never write such trash. The florid tone employed in the article was enough to clear her of guilt. No, this had come from the pen of some evil fantasist with a grudge and expensive tastes. The claims were so ridiculous they suggested that whoever was behind the plot to discredit him was fast becoming desperate.

'File a flight plan to Spain,' he instructed Dom. 'I'm leaving today.'

'In the middle of training?' Dom enquired with surprise.

'I'll be back before you know it.' The man was really starting to annoy him. Dom had never questioned Cesar's decisions before.

'But the newspaper owner lives in Mayfair,' Dom pointed out, staring at him keenly.

'He's next on my list.'

'May I ask who's first?'

'No,' he said flatly. He'd had enough of Dom's intrusive change of manner. 'You may not.'

'Okay. Hand it over,' Sofia demanded as she took in the scene in the ranch house kitchen.

Cesar's aide, Domenico de Sufriente, was seated at the table, pounding his laptop, and leapt up guiltily when she walked into the room. He must have been confident she was on her way home. In fact, the cab ride to the airport had been long enough to figure out that there was another possible leak for Sofia to investigate, and that it was much closer to home.

Drawing himself up with affront, Dom pursed his mouth 'Hand over what, may I ask?'

'Your laptop,' Sofia said briskly.

'I beg your pardon?' Straightening his tie, Cesar's equerry laughed, and it was a mean, sarcastic little laugh, Sofia registered. 'I don't think so,' he sneered.

As he was standing, she took her chance to glance at the screen. 'Howard Blake?' she queried, heart pounding as her suspicions were confirmed. 'You're sending an email to Howard Blake?' She pretended incomprehension. 'What on earth for? What can you possibly have to say to him? Were you perhaps warning him that I was on my way?'

'Is it customary where you come from to read people's mail?' he enquired cuttingly.

'I don't think I've ever done so before,' she admitted, 'and if you've nothing to hide, I can't see why you're making such a fuss.'

'Why should I have anything to hide?' Dom asked defensively as he slammed the lid of his laptop down. 'Your imagination has got the better of you. Personally, I'm surprised you've got the nerve to come back after the trash you've written about Prince Cesar.'

'Those were not my words, as you well know.' Dom's reddening cheeks suggested she'd caught him out. 'I wrote one article, which was changed completely. I'm not a career journalist. I'm a rider and a painter and a—'

'Philanthropist?' Dom suggested with an evil snigger, as if no one had any right to be kind to people, least of all Sofia.

'If you're referring to my retreat, it helps those who need it, and that's all I care about. You can deride it all you like, but you won't destroy it. I won't allow you to.'

'You think I'd waste my energy on destroying your pathetic little retreat?'

Judging by his expression, the only thing Dom would like to destroy was Sofia, she realised, feeling the first ice-cold frisson of fear.

Only fools don't feel fear, her brothers had told her, and Dom's small black eyes had turned as hard as marble. This was the other side of the smooth courtier's coin. It showed a man eaten up by jealousy for a prince who was twice the man he was, and for his Queen, who was vulnerable and kind, and now, incredible though it might seem to her, Sofia. 'I know you did it,' she said calmly.

'Did what?' Dom demanded in a disdainful tone.

'You're the only person who could possibly know the details that appeared to back up those scurrilous comments in the article. You're the only person with access to Prince Cesar's diary. You know all the dates and the events he attends. I ran through everyone else it could possibly be in my head on my way to the airport, and realised that no one else knows as much about the Prince's diary as you.'

A look of triumph sprang onto Dom's face. 'Are you admitting the details are true?'

'I'm not admitting anything. I'm saying you embroidered the facts to suit you and your master, Howard Blake, and I'm accusing you of colluding with Blake to introduce a suitor for the Queen's hand into court when Her Majesty was at her lowest ebb. You, above everyone, knows everything about the royal family, and how best to hurt them.'

Dom stiffened. She'd made a lucky guess but, having shown her hand, she was now in danger. Her brothers were out riding, and there was no sign of the SUV Cesar used on the ranch. He must have gone out somewhere, and there was no doubt that Dom, like his master Howard Blake, would stop at nothing to complete his mission of destroying everyone she loved. And she was alone with him in a kitchen full of potential weapons.

Contrary to popular belief, men could multi-task. On his way to the airport, speakers in his muscle car read out his texts. There was nothing from Sofia. While he was confirming that, he was calling up his security team on a second, secure line. The first thing he'd done on waking and finding Sofia gone had been to ask his team, comprised entirely of ex-Special Forces, to institute a full-scale search for Sofia to make sure she was safe. Whatever had pulled her out of bed that morning had to be serious. Sofia was a serious-minded woman.

When she wasn't wild and abandoned in his arms.

He got an update from his team leader and smiled faintly. Nothing about Sofia could surprise him. 'This has only just happened?' he confirmed as he slowed the car.

His next call was to the airport, where his jet was ready and waiting. 'I won't be needing it,' he told his people.

His last call was to check the facts. He was a meticulous man.

An impersonal voice on the other end of the line informed him that the aircraft due to take Sofia home to Spain would board in around an hour, though as yet there was no sign of a Señorita Acosta on the checked-in passenger list.

Burning rubber, he screeched into a tyre-flaying U-turn and headed back the way he'd come. The road was straight and empty. He was driving a car with a top speed of over two hundred miles an hour. It would be rude to ignore the vehicle's potential.

As fast as it was, he still had time to think. If Sofia did something unusual, there was a good reason behind it. She'd slept in his arms. That was unusual. How had that made her feel? It had made him feel too much, which in itself was unusual. She'd trusted him, and that had touched him. What grabbed at his heart now and twisted it in knots was that whoever had their claws into Sofia wasn't ready to let go. And that put her in danger.

Howard Blake was another matter. He'd been dealt

with. Cesar was not just meticulous, once he'd made up his mind he moved fast. He couldn't wait to tell Sofia that a cast-iron, signed and sealed document from Cesar's lawyers had landed in his inbox a couple of hours ago. His legal team had been working through the night to draw up a contract that would secure the financial future of Sofia's retreat for as long as it existed, thanks to an unbreakable trust that had been set up by none other than Howard Blake. Under Cesar's instructions.

To make doubly sure Blake's teeth were pulled, Cesar had purchased his newspaper empire, so Sofia was free to paint and ride to her heart's content, as well as help as many of those who needed her arm around their shoulder as she could.

The journey home was exasperating as possibility and probability jostled for position in his mind. Had Sofia read the second newspaper article yet? Would she laugh or cry when she did? His brain refused to stop whirring. Was she having second thoughts about sleeping with him? Not that much sleep had been involved. Was that why she'd left his bed? If she'd never reached the airport, but had returned to the *estancia* because she had guessed, as he had, that the trouble lay right there, then she could be in danger. Concern hit him like a punch in the gut. He put his car to the test. Two hundred miles an hour was not only achievable, but vital in this situation.

The black beast didn't let him down. The car did all but take flight.

'What are you going to do about this discovery of yours?' Dom sneered at Sofia as they faced each other in the kitchen. 'Do you plan to tell Cesar? Do you really think he'll believe you, after this second article?

He might pretend not to believe you wrote it, but does he really know? Won't he doubt your honesty?'

With each question asked Dom moved a step closer. Sofia was backing up. They had almost reached the door. She planned to take her chances and escape as soon as she reached it. 'Of course I read the article on my phone,' she confirmed—anything to keep him talking. 'It was full of accusations, and insinuations about events supposedly taking place at the training camp.'

The lies had churned her stomach. With Sofia's byline at the top of the piece, it had made her relationship with Cesar read like a sting, calculated to trap him and prove him unworthy of the throne. If he believed those lies Cesar would cut her out of his life with surgical precision. Her brothers would never speak to her again. Funding would dry up for her retreat. It would have to close, leaving those she cared for with nowhere to go. She'd be a pariah, but that was nothing compared to the effect the damning article could have on a man who was brave and strong and principled, and who led by example, a prince who would one day be King. 'Where is Cesar?' she queried, heart clenching with lurid possibility. 'What have you done with him?'

'Me?' Dom touched his crisp, tailor-made shirt just short of where his heart should be. And then he lunged for her.

Dom's hand around her neck was removed so fast Sofia had no idea what had happened. One minute she was fighting a murderous opponent, and the next Dom was flat out on the kitchen floor with Cesar looming over him.

'Cesar!' It felt as if she'd shrieked his name but it sounded like a croak. He was at her side in an instant with his arm around her shoulders, bringing her so

close in a clasp of relief that she could hardly breathe.
'Help—'

He released her in an instant and, holding her at
arm's length, he stared down with relief, as well as
something warmer and deeper. 'The conventional
phrase, I believe, is, "Thank you".'

'When have we ever been conventional?' she managed hoarsely as she clutched her throat and coughed.
'But thank you.'

'Stop thanking me,' Cesar commanded in the softest whisper she'd ever heard. 'You landed a good blow
there, making things easy for me, or why was that monster grabbing his crotch with one hand while attempting to strangle you with the other? If he'd had both his
hands free—'

'But he didn't,' she soothed. 'And, anyway, you laid
him out.' She'd checked.

'I've always been a bit of a scrapper,' she admitted.
'Four brothers?'

'I should have been here.' Cesar was in no mood for
humour. Summoning his security team, he told them
to remove the prisoner and lock him up.

'You got here as soon as you could,' Sofia argued.
'You came looking for me. That's all that matters.'

'I had to,' Cesar reflected grimly. 'I know you well
enough to be confident you wouldn't leave the house
without good reason. When I worked out what that
reason could be, I knew I had to find you fast or you'd
take things into your own hands. Are you sure you're
okay?'

The look in his eyes touched her somewhere deep.
'I'm fine.' She stood back as two military types dressed
in black entered the room.

'We have a lot to talk about,' he said.

'You read the article.' She knew he must have and felt a flutter of alarm.

'Of course,' Cesar confirmed.

'How did you know to find me here?'

'How do we know anything?' He frowned. 'Intuition? The assembly of known facts into a recognisable picture?'

Now the initial shock was over, her knees had turned to jelly. Cesar's steadying hand beneath her arm was more than welcome. It was one thing to be at the peak of physical fitness, and another to be attacked by someone who meant her harm, Sofia had discovered. She might have accepted that Dom was not the silky courtier he appeared, but his vicious lunge for her throat had really shocked her.

They went into Cesar's library. It was a cosy, reassuring room, with wood-panelled walls and comfortable seating.

'Take a seat on the sofa,' he invited. Crossing the room to a well-stocked bar, he poured a generous slug of fine brandy into a crystal glass. 'Here. Drink this...'

'I don't—'

'You do,' he insisted. 'And then we'll talk.'

She sipped and put the glass down, only then realising that the newspaper with its damning article— the same article that someone had *kindly* sent to her to make sure she didn't miss it—was lying open on the low table between them.

Closing her eyes, she exhaled shakily. 'How can I ever—'

'Don't.' Cesar raised his hand, palm flat. 'Let's get one thing straight. This is not your writing, not your fault, and nothing to do with you.'

'Without me, the campaign to discredit you wouldn't

have got started,' she argued. Picking up the newspaper, she scanned the article she'd already read as if hoping it would somehow change into something she could read without feeling sick to the stomach that anyone could write such trash.

Cesar shrugged off her comment. 'Blake would have found someone else to do his dirty work.'

Breath shuddered out of her. She didn't want to be let off the hook so easily. 'The article appears under my name and will seem totally plausible to anyone who reads it. My brothers will read it and they can only think I'm betraying you again.'

'Then I'll set them straight, though I believe you're worrying unnecessarily. Do you really think they don't know what's been going on between us?'

What is going on between us? she wondered in the few seconds it took for Cesar to supply an answer to his own question but not to hers. 'I've known your brothers a long time—too long for them not to have picked up the vibes between me and their only sister. They're probably laughing their heads off right now as they read this garbage over the breakfast table.'

'Thanks. I'd rather not think about that, not when this could be so serious for you.'

'Believe me, I'm not taking it lightly,' Cesar assured her.

'And then there's your mother and sister. What will they think? This is so unfair, especially when it's clearly untrue.'

Maybe she had expected Cesar to argue this point, and say that there was something between them and that it was so deep that it transcended cheap gossip, but he remained silent, while she couldn't seem to stop words pouring from her mouth.

'All this rubbish about secret liaisons between us, and the things we do—' Her cheeks blazed red. 'With my by-line at the top of the article, it makes it seem I set you up.'

'But we know you didn't.'

'Of course I didn't, but this article is dangerous for you. You can't take it lightly.'

'I haven't,' Cesar assured her.

His eyes were cool and calculating. She knew instinctively that he would be reviewing plans he'd already made. Why didn't he share those plans with her? This cut right to the heart of why she wanted more from their relationship.

Her pulse jagged as Cesar shifted position, but it was only to ease his massive shoulders in a careless shrug. 'So everyone knows,' he observed, lips pressing down. 'What of it? Does it embarrass you to be linked to a prince? Or would you rather not be linked to me?'

'That's not it at all,' she protested, shaking her head with frustration.

'Then how about this?' He pinned her with his black stare. 'What if that prince asked you to marry him? Would you be mortified? Or relieved?'

'Relieved?' she asked incredulously. In her fantasies perhaps! 'I'd be horrified.'

Cesar's eyes narrowed. 'Should I be insulted?'

He didn't look insulted. Hand pressed to his chest, and with his black eyes scorching her face into an even hotter shade of red, Cesar appeared to be amused.

'I take it you're joking?' she said on a dry throat.

'Am I?'

Cesar managed to imbue those two words with so much heat and promise her body went wild. Her mind, however, was by now firmly back on track. 'If I were a drinker I'd ask for another brandy. I could never be princess material. You need someone—'

'What?' Cesar queried. 'Someone like me, do you mean, from a rarefied background raised on a diet of riches and privilege, while you were a raggedy tomboy, dragged up in a stable? It may surprise you to know I was an urchin, filthy and starving, plucked off the streets of Rome after being abandoned by my birth mother. I have a wonderful woman to call my mother, and to thank for hunting me down. The Queen saved me. It's as simple as that.'

Nothing about Cesar was ever simple, Sofia reflected, though she kept silent as he talked on. 'The Queen is the only real mother I've ever known. Her heart was big enough to make a home for the bastard son of her handmaid and the King, and she went on to bring me up as her own.'

For once Sofia was lost for words. Cesar had never opened up about his past. However bad things got between them, the fact that he had chosen her to confide in meant a lot. 'I had no idea,' she said softly.

'About so many things,' Cesar confirmed, 'such as you can trust me with your life. Which brings me to repeat my question: Will you marry me?'

'I have to understand why you're asking me first,' she admitted.

'What is there to understand?'

'I understand why you bottle up your emotions, Cesar. To be abandoned at such a young age was bound to have repercussions—'

'I don't want to talk about me. I want to talk about you,' he insisted.

'By not talking about how you feel inside, you're letting the past win.'

'The past is the past. I've treated you badly.'

'And now I deserve a reward?' she asked, frowning.

'You're not one of my horses.'

'I'm glad you realise it.' A smile crept through.

'We're making progress?' he suggested.

'If you can express your feelings…'

'I do feel lots of things—especially when it comes to you. I feel lust, passion, frustration, tenderness…but most of all I feel an overwhelming certainty that I can't share my life with anyone but you. I love you, Sofia, with all my heart, my soul, and my body too. Marry me and let me keep you safe for ever.'

'You love me?' she whispered.

'How can you doubt it?'

Her head was spinning. She didn't have an answer right away. There was so much to take in that her heart felt as if it was in a vice. She'd barely recovered from the shock of Dom's attack, and then there had been the shame of seeing yet another newspaper article written in her name. Now she was faced with Cesar's bomb-shell proposal of marriage. 'I've said it before. I'm just not princess material, let alone queen.'

'Which is precisely why I think you'll be the most marvellous addition to the royal family,' Cesar insisted. 'You're what my people deserve—someone who will genuinely care for them and who's prepared to get their hands dirty. Not forgetting you'll have to put up with me.'

She searched Cesar's eyes for some hint of humour and found none. The past half an hour had brought about great change. Cesar had found her, saved her, and they'd confirmed the treachery of his aide. What was she wait-ing for? For the doubt demons to leave? Life was full of uncertainty. How you dealt with it was what mattered.

The one thing you could not, must not do was to turn your back and walk away from the chance of happiness. 'Is this a serious proposal of marriage?'

'I would never joke about something so important,' Cesar promised with a steady look.

'But there's been no lead up, no hint of what you were thinking, no preparation—'

'For life?' he asked gently. 'How much preparation do you need? Seems to me you've been doing pretty well up to this point, and I believe this is the perfect solution to silence the critics following any fallout from the article. The Playboy Prince is ready to settle down—'

Just when she was ready to believe he could change and grow in the emotional sense, he slashed her belief into tiny pieces.'

'There's no point in dragging things out,' he said.

Life drained out of her but she was a fighter, which meant refusing to give up, especially when that meant giving up the man she loved. She wasn't going to let him go without a fight. 'What about tracing a possible path for our future first?' she asked crisply. 'What about describing your vision of the path we'll be walking down together. Or is this marriage just another business deal for you? Maybe it's a way for you to get your people onside. After all, everyone loves a royal wedding.'

Cesar looked shocked.

Grief, hurt and shame collided inside her. Receiving the proposal she'd dreamed of all her life in what amounted to bullet points was unbearable. She didn't need to be told that she wasn't a likely choice of bride for Prince Cesar of Ardente Sestieri, but to be made to feel that she was nothing more than a convenient solution for Cesar hurt like hell.

And then he made it worse.

CHAPTER FOURTEEN

'I AM A brutally honest man,' Cesar conceded with a grudging grin, 'but I'll admit that what I'm thinking doesn't come out the way I intend.'

'I get that, but it's what you're feeling too that needs expressing,' Sofia observed, 'and not just clinical thoughts when it comes to something as precious as marriage. What I don't want is for you to say something you don't mean.'

'But I do mean it,' he insisted with a hard stare. 'Every word.'

'With eyes as hard as flint?' she said, breaking up inside. 'Please, don't lie to me, Cesar. I don't understand how you can love me so much that you want to spend the rest of your life with me when I'll never be princess material.'

'That's the very reason I want to marry you. Haven't I told you that before?'

'Why can't you stop pretending that the marriage you propose is anything more than a convenient solution?'

'What do you want me to say, Sofia? I thought this was what you wanted.'

Tears sprang to her eyes. 'A marriage proposal that sounds more like a business deal?' she asked incredulously.

'Don't do this to me.' Cesar pulled back when she

longed for him to move forward. 'I'm trying to be fair,' he insisted.

'So your future plans include a quirky horse-riding artist, said to have written defamatory articles about you? No smoke without fire,' she reminded him grimly. 'Does that sound like the perfect royal match to you? Will your countrymen go for it? Will the Queen stand and cheer when you tell Her Majesty our news?'

'Please, be calm,' Cesar insisted in a way that made her madder still. 'I've told you about my past so you know I'm not obvious prince material. Yet, here I am, not so very different from you. I wouldn't be asking you such a vital question if I thought you were a typical princess, spoiled, indulged, entitled, but none of those words describe you, Sofia.'

'No. I'm just the mug who fell in love with you,' she admitted, when she could finally draw an easy breath.

'You love me?'

'Of course I do!' she exclaimed heatedly.

'A fact that makes our marriage even more likely to succeed,' Cesar declared, without returning the compliment. 'So now we've got that sorted out, I'll give you a list of things to do in the lead up to our wedding.'

'No clipboard?' she asked heatedly. 'Don't tell me you forgot to bring it with you?'

Cesar appeared to be genuinely surprised. 'I'm sorry you think marriage to me such a dreadful prospect.'

Feelings erupted inside her. She wanted to go to him and hold him close, kiss him and drive the ghosts of the past away. Surely he could see that marriage between them was impossible. 'It's not a terrible prospect,' she protested. 'It's impractical. It wouldn't work. I've told you I love you—to which you showed no reaction at all. It's as if you don't value my love. '

'Nothing could be further from the truth,' he insisted. 'And I'd like to know what you base your conclusions on. I've made it plain from the outset that I'm not too grand for you. In fact, you come from a far more stable background. There must be another reason for your refusal. What is it, Sofia? What's holding you back?'

'I can't be with such an emotionless man. If this proposal of marriage is just a duty for you it wouldn't be honest of me to accept. I'd be selling your people short. We both would. They deserve more than a reluctant princess and a cold-hearted prince.'

'Cold-hearted?' Cesar queried frowning. 'Haven't I made it clear that you can have anything you want?'

'But I don't want material things. I want honesty, truth and love. Where are your feelings, Cesar? Where are you hiding them? Why can't you express them? Or do you think it's weak to show emotion?'

'Of course not.' He was growing heated now. 'I have deep feelings for my people, my family, and especially for you. What do you want me to say, Sofia? I know what I want. Marry me. Give me the chance to make you happy. You've nothing to fear from me. You're free to leave this marriage if you're unhappy, and of course that would be with a pension for life.'

That was the worst thing he could have said. Hope died inside her. It was as if her heart had shrunk until it resembled a walnut, shrivelled and dry.

'Haven't you listened to a word I've said?' she asked quietly. 'I don't want or need a pension for life. You make it sound as if I'm to be rewarded for deceiving your people.'

'I would never deceive my people,' Cesar protested, incredulous.

'With a grand royal wedding and a smiling bride?'

she suggested. 'What would you call it? When I get married it will be for love, not for what I can get out of it. The era for business-like marriage mergers is long past!'

'But you'll be safe with me,' Cesar insisted, as if he couldn't believe what she'd said. 'I've bought up Howard Blake's empire so he'll never trouble you again. My former equerry Dom is currently in custody and will be judged by the highest court in the land. I intend to live my life protecting you and my people in every way I can. If you have even a gram of the renowned Acosta honour, surely you'll support me in this?'

'By marrying a man who cannot share his true feelings with me?'

It was tragic to think Cesar did have feelings, deep feelings, but he was incapable of expressing them in a way her heart could accept. In that, she supposed when she thought about it, they were both guilty.

'I'm sorry I've got no pretty words for you,' he said at last. 'That's just not who I am. Rest assured, I have no intention of forcing you to do anything you don't want to do. I'm relying on your good sense to get you through this.'

'You make it sound as if I must survive some unpleasant illness that can be dosed with a spoonful of sugar. I want so much more out of marriage than that. Love dies if it's all one-sided, and I couldn't bear—'

'To be abandoned again?' he suggested gently.

She took a moment to refocus, as he added, 'Losing your parents has left a gaping wound, and it's important for you to know that I understand. It will take time to prove I can help you heal, but I need the chance to do that.'

A tsunami of emotion threatened to overwhelm her. She had no doubt now that Cesar was sincere. Marrying him was a dream that could so easily become reality. All she had to do was say yes. But she wanted the best for Cesar too. He was a king amongst men, strong and principled, sincere, and she'd never find anyone like him again. Her heart yearned for nothing more than to twin with his. She truly couldn't fault him. And, of course, she loved him with all her heart.

'Maybe I could have said things better,' he conceded in the silence, 'but I'm not an orator, and I didn't plan to win your heart with words. I can see now that I've rushed things, but once I see a goal I go for it. There's been no time to woo you as you deserve, but I'll try to make it up to you. Most importantly, I'll care for you and keep you safe. Anything you need for the wedding can be ordered online,' he added, frowning as he compiled his mental list. 'If you need people to help you to prepare, call them now and put them on standby. Transport will be arranged for everyone who attends the ceremony. Make that clear to anyone you invite—'

'Cesar!' Her shout stopped him in his tracks. 'There can be no wedding. Have you listened to me at all?'

'The ceremony can take place in one week's time on my private island of Isla Ardente,' he said, unwittingly supplying the answer to her question.

'You're making plans for an event I have no intention of attending,' she pointed out.

'But that's the neatest way,' he insisted. 'When we're married we'll draw even bigger crowds to the charity matches. You'll need a ring, of course,' the man she loved with all her heart added, frowning, 'So why don't you browse the internet and choose something you'd like?'

For a moment the plastic rings that came in Christmas crackers flashed into her head. They would be perfect for a sham wedding.

'Better still, leave it to me!' he exclaimed, 'I have contacts at all the top jewellers—'

'Of course you do!' she interrupted. Doubt crept into the mix as she imagined all the expensive trinkets Cesar must have purchased over the years.

'There's no real urgency for an engagement ring' he added thoughtfully, 'though I expect you'd like something to show off at some point—'

'Show off?' she burst out.

'Whatever you like,' Cesar countered, with a smile that proved he was oblivious to her mounting frustration. 'Though we'll concentrate on finding a wedding band for now. We can sort out more jewellery later—'

'Stop this,' she exploded. 'Is this what your proposal boils down to? A sparkly stone and a pair of handcuffs disguised as a wedding band? Believe me, I'm not that desperate to get married. I'd sooner wed a walrus and feast on sea cucumbers than marry a man who opens his wallet without opening his heart.'

'But you want me,' Cesar stated flatly.

'If you're asking whether I like having sex with you, why not say so? I do. You're an amazing lover. Would I like to have more sex with you? Yes, of course, but having sex is very different from planning to spend the rest of your life with someone.' It hurt to even think those words, let alone say them. Being intimate with Cesar had meant *everything* to her. She'd given herself completely, freely, trustingly and lovingly, but had it meant the same to him?

'Perhaps you see things differently,' he suggested.

'I see you clearly.' She drew on every bit of control she had to keep her voice steady and her eyes direct. 'The unexpressed feelings you have are possibilities waiting to happen. You get angry when you can't express yourself, but I don't need flowery words any more than I need expensive gifts. I just want you to be honest with me—with both of us.'

Cesar frowned. 'Are you frustrating my plans?'

'There you go again,' she said with a hint of desperation in her voice. 'We should be getting married because we want nothing more than to be together. Not because it suits your agenda. Open your heart, Cesar. Let me know how you truly feel.'

'But we could save a country together.'

'As well your reputation,' she observed shrewdly.

'Not to mention yours,' Cesar countered. 'Just tell me what you want. Name your price.'

'Name my price?' she repeated in a strangled whisper.

'Clumsy words,' he admitted, raking his hair with frustration. 'I told you I'm no good with words.'

But the damage had been done.

'This marriage will lift the mood of my people—'

'You can't even call it *our* marriage,' she burst out, unable to keep silent any longer.

'It would instantly make a mockery of the article,' Cesar continued as if she hadn't spoken. 'Despite what the writer suggests, there was no seedy liaison between us at the training camp but an unfolding love story that will now have a beautiful ending.'

'Is that what you truly believe?' she asked. Hope pushed its way through the tangle of weeds like a green shoot.

Only to be trampled on.

'I've told you to name your price, Sofia, so please tell me what you would like to make this marriage happen. Please, appreciate that this is a difficult situation for both of us and time is short.'

She shook her head sadly. 'Not for you. You seem

to have it all worked out. Would you like my bank details for a money transfer or will you pay me in pieces of silver?'

'Stop it,' Cesar advised calmly. 'If you think about this logically, you'll come to agree that nothing could be more uplifting for my people than a wedding between us.'

How could they be so far apart? She hid an agony of disillusionment behind another question. 'Have you discussed this with my brothers?'

'I thought you were old enough to make your own decision.'

'As I thought you experienced enough in the ways of the world to know what's right,' she fired back. 'What you're proposing is a marriage of convenience—convenient for you, that is.'

'All I want is for you to be happy and safe.'

'You have a strange way of showing it.'

'Do I?' Cesar asked, seeming perplexed.

'Asking me to be your wife surely requires me to say yes before arrangements can be made? A little more thought and preparation generally goes into these things than the advice to "Browse the Internet".'

Cesar raked his hair. 'But you can have anything you want.'

'*Things* don't matter.' She waited, and then waited some more while Cesar stared at her as if she was speaking a foreign language. 'I give up,' she said at last. 'Seduction might be your forte, but when it comes to wooing a woman you have zero idea. It takes more than a vault full of priceless jewels to build trust, and more than pomp and ceremony to impress me. If you had suggested a small, informal barefoot wedding on the beach of your private island, with just a band of twine around my finger and some fresh flowers in my hair—'

'Done! That's an excellent idea.'

'What?' She stared at Cesar in horror.

'I'll get my team on it right away, and then I'll present my beautiful bride to our people at a formal blessing in the cathedral in the capital sometime later.'

'Best find yourself a bride first,' Sofia advised before she left the room.

Well, that went well. Cesar paced up and down, frowning, long after Sofia had slammed the door and disappeared. Her final words had been like a well-aimed blow to the chin, but instead of knocking him out they had knocked him into a different mind-set. He'd been so preoccupied, facing the threat to him and Sofia, that he had instinctively moved into leading and planning mode, which on this occasion had involved a wedding ceremony, when Sofia had needed proper reassurance that he loved her before, not after, a proposal of marriage.

He had assumed she would realise that his offer was heartfelt, but now he realised she'd thought it a ruse to distract his people from the latest gossip. The thought of marriage to Sofia had struck him like a bombshell, mainly because marrying anyone else was unthinkable. That nightmare was only exceeded by the thought of Sofia marrying someone else. He loved her with all his heart, he realised now, but had he left it too late?

Years back, when he'd been in the army and his comrades had been getting married one by one, he had envied them for the love they shared, and for the company they could look forward to with someone who loved them unreservedly. Marriage had once seemed an elusive possibility for the so-called Playboy Prince, but he had longed for nothing more than to settle down and build a family…if only he knew how.

Sofia had made that achievable. She was no spoiled, milksop princess, staring haughtily down her nose at his people while acting as everyone's friend. He wanted a real woman with real character, someone who would take him to task, and here she was, but had he messed up the best chance he'd ever have?

He had to find a way around this. He wanted Sofia to be his wife, not to smooth over the cracks of the article or because it made sense but because he adored her and he wanted her in every way there was. It was hard to express his feelings, but if he kept on trying, maybe he'd get better at it. He had to or he'd lose her for good. And there would never be another Sofia.

Time was short, and the task ahead of him was not just demanding, but would normally take months to complete. How long did it take to woo a woman? He had no idea. It had never been necessary in the past. He prided himself on being a meticulous organiser, but where this was concerned he was in the dark. How long would it take to convince Sofia she could trust him completely when he was starting his campaign from such a low base?

Happiest when he was doing something, he called a meeting for everyone to attend the following morning before training. Until then, guessing Sofia had had enough of his 'bulldozing ways', as she'd called them, he keep himself busy riding, working out, swimming, reading, sparring in the gym with her brothers—anything but risk speaking to Sofia before he was ready. He was good at planning and hopeless at wooing, but when it came to winning Sofia's heart, he was on a mission to succeed.

CHAPTER FIFTEEN

PUNISHING HER PILLOW for the lack of anything else to thump, she sobbed like a baby and railed against fate. How could a man who had risen like a phoenix from the ashes of his childhood, with a brain to rival Einstein's and personal success that exceeded most people's, be so dense as to imagine that a pretty ring and the promise of riches could find their way to her heart?

She didn't want that with Cesar. She wanted new paints, a puppy and a kitten, and a bridle for her horse. She wanted time together to laugh and be silly, and plan a future that didn't involve self-interest and what she had to gain. There was so much she wanted to do, and all she needed was the chance to get out there and do it. The idea of extending her retreat to encompass an entire country, where no one felt left out or forgotten, would be a dream come true. And, yes, she was a bit of a dreamer, but wouldn't Cesar be the perfect counterbalance to that?

She was glad when the phone rang. Maybe that would shake her out of this noisy, messy pity party. 'Hello?'

'Sofia?'

Her heart stopped beating.

'Cesar here.'

As if she didn't know, as if her entire body, mind and soul hadn't recognised that deep, husky voice the moment he'd spoken. A quick analysis of his tone said this was an exploratory call to judge her mood, as she was attempting to judge his.

'Are you all right? Sofia? Say something.'

'I'm fine.' She sniffed. 'A bit of a cold coming on, that's all.'

'Good. I've called a meeting tomorrow morning before training to give the official line on the latest article. I trust you will attend?'

She was confused and not a little angry. '*Your* official line?'

'Yes.'

'Don't I have a say in this?'

'I'll speak first, and then open the floor to questions.'

'Cesar…' She hesitated, frowning. 'Do you ever listen to yourself?'

'You mean playback when I've been interviewed? Sometimes—'

'No. I mean right now,' she informed him. 'If you could only come down from Planet Exalted and speak to me as an equal.'

'I do,' he protested.

'Good, because I'd like to stand at your side and give my own version of events, if that's okay with you?'

There was heavy silence for a good few moments and then he said stiffly. 'If that would make you happy.'

'It would.'

Perhaps she should be angry with Cesar but she had grown up with four brilliant brothers—brilliant in the sense of their keen, ever-seeking minds, and brilliant because they were so good to her—but they often saw no further than their noses, especially where matters of the heart were involved. 'What time tomorrow?'

Cesar gave a time. She thanked him and promised

to be there. Putting the phone down, she went to stare at her reflection in the mirror. Very nice if red eyes and runny noses were your thing. Not such a good look for a woman who was about to buckle on her armour to fight for the heart of a man she couldn't bring herself to let go. Never mind what Cesar could do for her. What could she do for him?

He felt like a child on Christmas Day waking early to check that everything was as it should be when the moment came when gifts could be opened in a shower of discarded paper and laughter. A run, a ride, a workout in the gym, and a swim before his shower, and he was ready for what would be a very different day.

Dressed in riding gear, he greeted Sofia's brothers in the arena. Sofia was already there, with his favourite mutt Bran at her heels. He took it as a sign. The hound viewed him with his big, intelligent brown eyes, assessing his mood as Cesar was assessing Sofia's.

'Good boy, Bran,' he soothed as the dog trotted over to him. He dug out some treats.

'Well?' Sofia's youngest and wildest brother Xander demanded, snapping a whip impatiently against his boots. 'You called this meeting. What do the two of you want to talk about? We've got training to do.'

'Cesar has asked me to marry him.'

Sofia's voice carried clear and strong in the vaulted space. A good few seconds of deafening silence passed before Sofia's older brother Raffa commented, 'He must have enjoyed your article.'

'I can do without your sarcasm, Raffa,' she scolded.

Her brother shrugged.

The only four men in the world who could possibly, in a concerted effort, take Cesar down were staring at him as if his remaining time on earth would be short. That didn't bother him. What did concern him was Sofia's blood-drained face. She was standing in front of them at her most vulnerable. He lost no time reassuring her.

'I'm here to ask you, Sofia's brothers, to do me the honour of allowing me to ask for your sister's hand in marriage.' Pretty words could trip off his tongue when he was desperate. 'I want to do everything properly,' he explained with a long look at Sofia. 'And in case you're wondering, I've already asked Sofia to marry me and she said no. My timing was out, but I'll make that right.'

'If Sofia said no, that's an end of it,' Xander insisted, slashing a whip impatiently against his booted calf.

'No.' Sofia held up her hand as she stepped forward. 'At least do Cesar the courtesy of listening to him—as I shall.'

'So talk,' Xander growled.

'Have you engineered this proposal to spare you the accusations in the latest article?' Raffa demanded suspiciously.

'Of course not.' He could state that with a clear conscience. 'If there had never been an article, I would want to marry Sofia. For me, there's no one like her. No one remotely close. And I love her.' He had to hope he wasn't too late. 'Humble pie is not a dish I eat with any frequency,' he admitted with a self-deprecating shrug, 'but this is different, this is for Sofia, and I'll grovel if that's what it takes.'

'My sister has brought you to your knees?' Dante suggested, failing to hide his amusement.

'She did,' he confirmed. 'I've promised myself to listen and act in future, rather than the other way around. I think we all know that your sister had nothing to do with those articles. My equerry, Domenico, is the culprit, and has been dealt with, while his master Howard Blake will be funding Sofia's retreat, as well as any future retreats she cares to open, out of his substantial bank account.'

'How on earth did you get him to agree to that?' Xander remarked with a glance at his brothers.

'I bought his company with a binding agreement that ensures Blake signs away part of those funds to Sofia's retreats each year. So now all that remains is your answer...'

'Sofia?' Dante asked.

Not realising what he had arranged with Blake, Sofia appeared shocked numb, and could only nod her head briefly. 'You did this for me?' she managed finally.

'Useless with words, better with actions,' he confirmed with a smile.

'I can't believe what you've done!' she exclaimed.

'But it pleases you?' he confirmed.

'Securing the future of my work? Of course. I can't thank you enough.'

'Okay, you two,' Dante interrupted, holding up his hand as he prepared to mount his pony. 'Let's call a halt to this. We've got training to do. As I understand it, Cesar is asking our permission to court Sofia with the intention of making an honest woman of her—a princess, in fact. We can hardly deny him that opportunity.'

Sofia's brothers agreed with a knowing laugh. When they finally quietened down, Xander said, 'Have you ever asked permission to do anything in your life, Cesar?'

'Never,' he admitted bluntly. 'But this is different. This is Sofia.' And these were men of honour that he was proud to call friends.

'Are you sure you know what you're taking on?' Raffa asked with amusement.

'I've got some idea, but I'll take her in spite of her faults.' This ended in a chorus of good-natured catcalls, and then he added, 'Because I love her with all my heart.'

'Should we start the training now?' Sofia suggested, a warm note in her voice as she winked at Jess and gave him a lingering smile.

Suitor-in-training would be an accurate description for him. How good it felt. Triumph surged through him as he sprang into the saddle and wheeled his hot-wired pony around.

By the end of that day's training Sofia was mentally and physically exhausted. It had been almost impossible to keep her mind on training after Cesar's impassioned declaration. She kept glancing at him as if to make sure this new, improved Cesar wasn't a figment of her imagination. Nope. He seemed pretty real to her. Her brothers said nothing more about it, and it was a thrill to feel much of their camaraderie returning. Cesar saying she was innocent was enough to convince them. She couldn't thank him enough for that. She'd take brotherly love any day over a flashy diamond ring.

When the session ended, Cesar dismounted first. Handing his reins to a groom, he insisted on helping her down. 'You've worked so hard your legs will buckle under you.'

'My legs will obey my commands,' she insisted, stubbornly as usual.

Wrong. Her legs did not obey. They buckled. Cesar's hand steadied her, but he made no move to crowd her or do any more than set her firmly on her feet.

'See you at supper,' he said.

So much for romance, she reflected wryly, wondering how and when Cesar's idea of wooing would actually show itself.

Before cleaning up for the evening ahead, she went to check on the ponies. Bran trotted along at her heels. She stopped at one of the stalls where a pony belonging to Cesar was receiving attention. Glad of something to take her mind off Cesar, she sent the groom away to enjoy her supper and set about applying the poultice herself. Soft words and the cooling relief soon had the pony's ears pricked again.

'Problem?'

'Cesar!' She wheeled around at the sound of his voice. 'No. She'll be fine for the match if you rest her tomorrow.'

'I guess we're all feeling the strain of Jess's training,' he observed.

Sofia was feeling the strain of something. She smiled faintly. Cesar didn't appear to be any the worse for wear as he rested back against the wall of the stall. In fact, he had never looked more startlingly dynamic, with his deep tan, close-fitting breeches and plain dark polo shirt. His thick black hair was all messed up and catching on his stubble, while his eyes, his lips—everything about him... He was so hot it felt like being hit by an electric charge. She dropped her gaze, only for it to land on well-worn leather riding boots hugging hard-muscled calves. Swallowing deeply, she looked away to concentrate on the pony. 'See you in the ranch house when I've finished here—'

'Change of plan,' he announced, pulling away from the wall. 'I'm cooking tonight.'

'You're...?'

'You can close your mouth now,' he said, his lips curving in a grin. 'My mother the Queen taught me some campfire specials.'

'That seems unlikely.'

'My mother is a very surprising woman.'

'I don't doubt it.' There was something shining in Cesar's eyes—a warmth she hadn't seen before, and affection. And was that hope that she'd agree to his suggestion? A campfire supper was a small thing, but it marked a big step forward in their relationship. She wanted nothing more than to be close to him, normal with him, and what better way than singeing sausages over a campfire? Did she really mean that much to him? He couldn't have been more forthright when he spoke to her brothers,

'See you around eight o'clock—lower field,' he instructed.

She smiled inwardly at his tone of voice. Some things never changed.

Give him a chance, her inner voice insisted.

'Lower field?' she queried. That was one she hadn't heard of.

'Anyone will tell you where to find me. Don't be late.'

'I won't,' she promised softly.

Sofia rode out to meet him, by which time he'd lit a fire and their meal was cooking, though the most important ingredient had just arrived.

'Cesar!' she exclaimed as she dismounted. 'What have you done?'

'Brought an easel and paints along to join us. I thought you might be missing your painting, and there's nothing more beautiful than sunset at the river. I thought you could sketch an outline, and maybe finish the painting before you leave for Isla Ardente. That way you can hang the painting anywhere you choose—here, or in my house on the island.'

'You mean you'd seriously hang my painting in your ranch house?'

His lips pressed down as he pretended to consider this. 'If it's any good.' And when she cuffed him, he added, 'It could be your ranch house if you agree to become my wife.' She stared at the easel and paints, and then at him. 'Do I get a second chance to make this right?'

'Nothing could make me happier...' she breathed, eyes wide, lips parted seductively '...than a reunion with my easel and paints.'

A laugh cracked out of him. *'Touché!'*

'But seriously,' she added, 'this really does make me happy. Thank you.'

She looked beautiful. Her hair was loose, wild and tangled after her ride, and her cheeks were flushed pink. She'd dressed for a picnic in casual clothes—a cotton shirt in a faded check print tucked into a pair of clean jeans.

'You didn't need to do all this. You still don't,' she said. 'Putting things back to normal with my brothers is more than enough for me. I can never thank you enough for all you've done.'

'I don't want your thanks any more than you want lavish gifts. All I want is your hand in marriage, for no better reason than I love you.'

'Nicely put,' she teased, but the smile on her face was one of pure happiness. And then she dropped a bombshell. 'Though we don't have to get married. You do know that, don't you?'

His gut clenched. 'What do you mean?'

'Just that you silenced the gossips when you exposed Howard Blake and his accomplice Dom. Your country applauds you, your mother has never doubted you, and I... I only want you to be happy.'

'Without you?' He frowned. *No. No. No.* This was supposed to be perfect. An evening together in a glorious setting, away from all distractions was their chance to put the past behind them, to discard it like an old notebook crammed full of notes that were meaningless now so they could start again on a clean sheet.

'We do have to get married,' he argued quietly, feeling as if his entire existence depended on his next few words. 'I can't live without you. I don't want to try.'

'You mean it, don't you?' she asked him softly.

'Every word,' he stated firmly. 'If you can see this as base camp, we'll start our journey here. I can't promise there won't be difficulties along the way but we'll get through them. Are you up for starting tonight? See where it takes us?'

Sofia didn't speak for the longest few seconds of his life, during which the road ahead of him loomed bleakly at the prospect that she might say no.

'I'd be honoured to accept your proposal, on the understanding that this is a true partnership.'

'Of equals,' he confirmed.

'In that case...'

'Kiss me?' he suggested.

'What's keeping you?'

The meal was singed to a cinder by the time he had answered that question. Fortunately, his chefs had left him well prepared, and Sofia declared the remaining food some of the best she had ever tasted.

'And you prepared all this yourself?' she exclaimed with approval.

He would start as he intended to continue—with the truth. 'I put my name to it,' he admitted, staring up through half-closed eyes. 'I also warmed it up, which took a certain degree of skill.'

'Save your skill for the bedroom,' Sofia scolded.

He would, but restraint was killing him.

'Please thank your chefs from me, and tell them the food was delicious.'

'Don't I get any credit?'

'For that? Or for this?'

When Sofia kissed him, he congratulated himself on not following the impulse to thoroughly ravish her. True to his vow, he'd store up that desire and would suffer a straining groin for as long as it took. But not for too long, he trusted.

A welcome distraction came when Sofia went to examine her easel and paints. Even in jeans she looked like a queen, he reflected as she walked to the riverbank. His groin tightened on cue, reminding him that where Sofia was concerned there was no such thing as too much sex. To ramp up the agony, he'd chosen a setting that was perfect for lazy lovemaking. The grass was lush and deep, and it would be soft and fragrant beneath then. The night breeze would cool them— *Dio!* He wanted her. Now he knew the true meaning of agony.

'Are these artists' materials really mine?' she asked, turning to greet him as he joined her at the easel.

'They're all yours',' he confirmed, thinking how beautiful she looked with the last rays of the sun bathing her in a cloud of light. Looping his hands loosely around her waist, he encouraged, 'Go to it. I can't wait to see what you come up with.'

'I know what you've come up with,' she scolded. 'And this is only our first date.'

'But I can kiss you,' he said, starting by kissing her neck.

'You can,' she agreed. Her voice trembled with a throb of excitement so her next words were unexpected, 'But that's all you can do,' she insisted.

Unseen, he ground his teeth until he was sure they would shatter.

They cantered back together. Wind in her hair and Cesar at her side, she had never been happier. Her lips were bruised from his kisses, though the frustration of holding back from progressing those kisses was pure torture. And now the idea of marrying a prince, and therefore becoming a princess, was niggling at her. Cesar's life was so very different from hers. No way was she regal material. Born a tomboy, she was happiest and most relaxed at an easel or in the saddle. Cesar was rich and she was poor, having invested every penny of her inheritance in the retreat.

'You're very quiet,' he commented as they slowed their horses on the approach to the yard.

'Happily contented,' she said as she dismounted. That wasn't strictly true. She wanted Cesar's arms around her and his naked body, warm and demanding, against hers.

Springing down from the saddle, he led their horses to the stable. 'I'll see them settled down and then I'm going to bed. I suggest you do the same. Remember, we've got training in the morning.'

She didn't want to sleep alone, and had expected Cesar to change his mind about wooing her 'properly', she realised now. 'I hadn't forgotten, but thank you,' she called to him on a dry throat.

With one last, brief sideways glance Cesar raised an amused brow and walked away.

CHAPTER SIXTEEN

THIS WAS KILLING HIM. Taking things slowly did not suit him. Cesar ground his teeth as he led their horses back into the stable complex. Having not only read the menu but having tasted it, holding back where Sofia was concerned was up there with the hardest things he'd ever had to do. Hard being a word he wanted to expunge from his mind right now.

Taking things slowly was the sensible thing to do, he persuaded himself as he removed his horse's tack. In Sofia's case, it was the only way. But that didn't mean he had to like it or that it was going to be easy. He had never held back, whether in the army, business, polo or anything else, but having promised to court Sofia as she deserved—when what he wanted was to throw her over his shoulder, carry her off to bed and make love to her until her legs refused to hold her up—he would stick to the original plan. But if there was one thing this experience had taught him it was that celibacy was massively overrated.

She couldn't sleep that night. Things were so bad she had actually left her bedroom door open a crack in the hope that Cesar might find his way in. No such luck. Thin strands of lilac light were already pushing their way through the curtains. Everyone would be up soon, and there was no sign of him. Not even a text.

Scrambling out of bed, she took a quick shower and got dressed, ready for the morning training session. Leaving her room, she crept down the corridor. Everyone was still asleep. Her next stop was the ranch house. Running across the yard, she entered the main house through the back door with the key they'd all been given in case they felt hungry when the cookhouse was closed. Setting to, she made pancakes, something she was rather good at, if she did say so herself. Loading a tray with coffee and freshly squeezed juice, she loaded it with pancakes for two and went to say a proper thank you to Cesar.

Backing into his bedroom, she put the tray down on the nightstand by his bedside. His pillows looked as if they'd been punched into oblivion and his covers were in a knot. There was no sign of Cesar but she could hear the shower running. Her throat dried with anticipation. Would he stride out of the bathroom naked, fully clothed, or would he have a towel looped around his waist?

'Sofia!'

Naked.

Okay.

Securing her wide-eyed gaze to his, as if to prevent that gaze from straying, he reached for a robe, handily tossed onto a nearby chair, and shrugged it on.

Too late. Her gaze had already strayed. Her breath quickened and her lips parted. 'Pancakes?'

'I could do with something to eat,' Cesar confirmed, though she thought she detected a wicked smile on his wicked mouth. And was his robe left unfastened on purpose?

'You'll catch cold.'

'Not a chance,' he said, padding purposefully in her direction. Rather than reaching for the food she had prepared, or pouring a cup of coffee, he reached for her. Cupping her face in his hands, he whispered, 'You look so beautiful this morning. And what a thoughtful thing to do.'

She could have drowned in those eyes. She still might.

Bringing her close, Cesar kissed her good morning.

His kisses were like incendiary devices to her senses. Closing her eyes, she dragged deep on the heady mix of soap and warm, clean man. If she could have this for the rest of her life, she would be the happiest woman on the face of the earth.

'Coffee?'

She realised Cesar was speaking to her. 'I made the breakfast for you,' she insisted. 'It's nothing much, just another thank-you for the easel and paints, and the delicious picnic last night.'

'I have a confession to make.'

'You do?' Apprehension gripped her. She should have known this was too good to be true.

'If we're going to make this work, we have to be honest with each other. Correct?'

'Correct,' she agreed tensely.

Cesar's burning gaze lit with humour. 'I want you, and it isn't in my nature to wait.'

Laughter drove her tension away, and then their fingers brushed as she accepted the cup of coffee he'd poured. How was it she'd never noticed before how seductive the brush of a hand could be? 'Pancakes first?' she suggested.

Cesar laughed. 'Seriously?'

'Of course seriously,' she insisted, trembling with excitement inside. 'Do they look that bad?'

'They look absolutely delicious. Do your worst,' he encouraged.

Oh. She forced herself to brighten. 'Sugar?' she asked with a smile.

Cesar's answer was to yank her close enough to drown in his eyes. 'We're going to be very late for training,' he promised. But then he gently disentangled himself and started eating pancakes.

The result was a frustrating day. Sex helped to wipe her mind clear of doubt, Sofia realised, reeling with exhaustion by the time training ended. Doubt had been her constant companion since losing her parents, and it was back full force now. What if Cesar's proposal was only to prove to her brothers that his intentions were honourable? Once they left this training camp hothouse behind, and life returned to normal, would Cesar come to realise that he didn't love her after all?

The temptation to confront him with these concerns battled with her desire to squeeze every last drop of happiness out of their time together. Remembering how Cesar had touched her face so tenderly last night didn't help, and only made her realise how much she'd miss him if Cesar came his senses and realised that marrying her would be wrong. Tears stung her eyes as she walked back to the stable. Thank goodness Jess had pushed them hard. She'd had less time to think. But now—

'Hey, you!'

Cesar's call stopped Sofia in her tracks halfway across the stable yard. He was tossing a bucket of ice-cold water from the well over his impossibly magnificent half-naked self. She closed her eyes to that, and to him, or she tried to.

'Where are you rushing off to?' he asked with a frown, staring at the large, zip-up bag she was carrying. It contained all her loose possessions from the tack room. She was on her way to add it to the stack of luggage in her room.

'Hey, yourself.' Her face burned with guilt at having been caught out. She should have told Cesar before arranging her journey home, but once she'd realised the best thing to do was to give them both space, she had rushed through the arrangements, knowing that if she stopped to think too much about it, she'd never go through with her plan. She'd confided in Jess and had promised she'd be back in time for the match. Jess clearly didn't agree with what she was doing but had enough sense to keep those thoughts to herself, confining herself to comments on Sofia's fitness, saying that if she kept up her training back home in Spain, Sofia would be more than ready for the match.

'I couldn't get an internet connection in my room,' she told Cesar now, 'so I'm off to the cookhouse to see if I can sort out something there.' She was a terrible liar, and he knew it.

'Internet?' he probed. 'Why don't you use mine at the ranch house?'

'I never thought of that.'

'Really?' He quirked a disbelieving brow.

If she stayed another hour her heart would shatter. However Cesar dressed it up, a marriage of convenience would never work between them. Her heart would break before their union had a chance.

'You seem preoccupied, Sofia.'

'No.' She shook her head.

'Wistful, then.'

'Memories can do that,' she admitted.

'Live in the moment and be happy.' Cesar spread his arms wide as if to welcome her into his world. 'Don't look so worried. What you see is what you get.'

Which was not just a prince, she thought as he stared down. Cesar was a deeply principled man who wielded great power and wealth. His destiny was preordained. She'd been lucky enough to cross his path briefly, but that was all. There could never be anything more between them. She had to help Cesar to see that he must forget the idea of marrying her, and if that meant leaving him so that in time he forgot her, then that was what she would do.

Love involved sacrifice sometimes, and this was one of those times. The threat of scandal was already fading, its roots stamped out. The press had new headlines. The people of Ardente Sestieri were confident in their prince. It was just Sofia who was out of step. But the one thing she owed him above everything else was honesty. 'Is there somewhere we can talk?'

'No,' he grated out, surprising her with the harshness in his tone. 'There is not. And you're not leaving me,' he stated firmly. 'I won't let those demons from the past destroy you. You have to be brave to love completely, and I know you can.'

'Cesar—please… You don't understand. I can't do this to you. I have to leave. It's for the best.'

'Whose best? Yours?'

She lifted the bag. He took it from her. She wrestled it back. 'I'm going home. You can't stop me. I should have told you before, but—'

'There wasn't time?' he suggested. 'Forgive me, Sofia, but where is your loyalty now?'

'I won't let the team down. I'll be back for the match. We both need time to cool down and think, and then you'll see that I'm right.'

'Oh, will I?' Cesar challenged fiercely. 'When are you going to stop running, Sofia? You can't escape your parents' death, no matter how far or how fast you run.'

'What?' The bag dropped from her hands. 'Is that what you think this is about?'

'I don't think, I know it is,' Cesar assured her. 'How do I know? Because my emotions have been strangled for years. I resented you to begin with for the way I saw myself reflected in the way that you behave—the self-inflicted isolation, the determination to help others at whatever cost to yourself, the overwhelming urge to win, to race, to exhaust yourself—and it still doesn't blot out the pain.

'It doesn't work, Sofia! Because when you've finally run yourself into the ground and lie down on your bed at night the pain's still there. And it will be with you until you deal with it.'

Sofia seemed to visibly shrink in front of him. 'How do you do that?' she asked him in a small voice.

'You learn coping strategies. You remember the good times as well as the bad. I'm still a work in progress,' he admitted. 'But we can fix this together. I won't lose you now.'

'You can't stop me leaving.'

'True.' Sofia was ready to be hurt some more, he realised as her dark eyes searched his. 'I would never stop you with force,' he assured her, his voice full of understanding. 'You have to decide you want to stay, just as you have to move forward instead of constantly looking back. You can do it,' he said gently, 'because now you're not on your own, you have me.'

She exhaled on a faint smile. 'How do you know all this?'

'Because I still have pain here.' He pressed a hand against his heart. 'I just hide it better than you.'

Taking hold of Sofia's shoulders in a loving grip, he brought her to face him. 'I know how you feel because I've spent most of my life hiding my feelings. When my father was killed, when I lost comrades in the forces, and when my mother took up with a man who only ever meant her harm and I felt I'd lost her too, I hurt like hell, but I've become an expert over the years when it comes to hiding my true thoughts.' He frowned. 'I can't do that with you, Sofia. Stay with me, and I promise I'll make you happy, and we'll work through this together.'

She wanted to stay with Cesar more than anything, but if she agreed to marry him, what would happen when the training camp ended and the matches were over, and she was no longer outstanding in any way? She'd be plain Sofia Acosta again—a great rider, with some small skill in painting pictures and a retreat to run. She wasn't suited to royal life.

Cesar needed someone with style and panache, who could sit beside him, exuding elegance and grace, and who would behave properly at all times. Not some country bumpkin with grime under her nails and dog hair and slobber on her clothes. 'I'm just not suitable.'

'For what?'

Cesar's eyes had a wicked glint, and his mouth was tugging up at one corner in the way she loved. 'Don't do this,' she warned.

'Do what?'

'Seduce me with a look. Make me change my mind—' She broke off, seeing her brothers with Olivia and Jess crossing the yard. Let off the hook, she yelled, 'Hello!'

'Come on, Sofia,' Cesar insisted, reclaiming her attention. 'You're only allowed so much time to bury your head in the sand and pretend this isn't the best thing that has ever happened to either of us.'

Come on, Sofia, her inner voice echoed. *Prince or not, Cesar is the best thing that ever happened to you.*

'Dump that bag in the barn,' he suggested. 'Join everyone in the cookhouse. You must be hungry after training.'

Was she giving Cesar another chance or herself? Sofia wondered as they headed off to the cookhouse together.

For the first time he could remember, no one teased them when he and Sofia finally sat down in the cookhouse to eat their meal.

'Okay?' He took hold of her hand in full sight of everyone present and brought it to his lips. There was a moment of complete stillness, but no one commented, and after a moment or two the buzz of conversation started up again. He wouldn't have cared whether or not they were accepted as a couple, but it felt good to have the acknowledgement of those closest to them that he was taking his wooing plans forward.

'Getting there,' Sofia whispered back with an intimate smile. 'You've given me something to think about,' she admitted. 'A lot to think about, in fact.'

'Like another date night?' he suggested.

'Only if it comes with pizza and a bottle of beer.'

'I can sort that,' he confirmed. 'Whatever your heart desires.'

'My heart isn't as sophisticated as yours'—

'No doubts,' he interrupted. 'We're in this together, remember?'

She thought about this for all of two seconds before adding chocolate ice cream to her list of requirements for their second date.

'Deal.' He held out his hand across the table to shake hers. And never wanted to let go.

Now they got catcalls. 'Find a room,' one of Sofia's brothers bellowed.

They shut him out. The amused glance they shared said it all. Sofia couldn't have been happier to be teased by her brothers. When'd she first arrived at the training camp the relationship between Sofia and her brothers had been strained, to put it mildly, but now she was elated to find it back to normal. They should expect more of this, he accepted wryly as they rose as one from the table. Fingers linked, they walked out of the cookhouse without a backward glance.

CHAPTER SEVENTEEN

THE FACT THAT chocolate and pizza could taste so good on a dish called Sofia would bring a smile to his face for the rest of his life. Date night had started innocently enough with Sofia cutting pizza into slices while he wedged lime into bottles of beer. They talked, relaxed, laughed, and talked some more.

But the more they laughed, the more sexual tension soared between them. Fingers brushed, eyes met, gazes steadied, lingered, until something had to give. Drawing Sofia into his arms, he meshed his fingers through her hair and kissed her as tenderly as if this was the first time they'd touched.

'Why are you always so impatient?' he growled against her mouth when she moved her body seductively against his.

'Have you looked in a mirror recently?'

'So you only want me for my body?'

'We can start with that,' she teased. 'But actually,' she added, turning serious, 'I want all of you, every bit of you, even the bits you didn't know you had. I want to hold your secrets in my heart and laugh with you as we've laughed tonight. I want to grow old with you.'

'You don't want to know all my secrets,' he assured her.

'Yes, I do,' she argued in a whisper, 'but you'll tell

me in your own time. There are things you don't know about me, and a lot I don't know about you, but we can find out together. And sorry to ask but do you think we could stop talking now?'

'You are a shameless hussy.'

'Thank goodness you made me that way.'

'As you're naked in my kitchen, I guess it would be rude to ignore—'

'Ice cream?' she interrupted. 'But I don't have a dish.'

'Won't you catch cold?'

'Not if you warm me. Lick it off...'

'I intend to.'

From there it was a rough and tumble that saw them end up on the floor, with pizza scattered everywhere and rapidly melting ice cream coating parts of them urgently needing attention.

'It's in my hair,' Sofia laughingly complained at one point.

Swiping ice cream from his chin, he ordered, 'Stop complaining.'

'Everything's an opportunity for you,' she scolded between shrieks of hysterical pleasure.

Rolling Sofia onto her back, he loomed over her. 'Sofia Acosta, I'm asking you again, and again, and again, will you marry me?'

'Must I repeat my answer?'

'Do you want more pleasure or not?'

'Why ask when you know my answer?'

'Because last time I didn't ask, I instructed, and I'm trying to mend my ways.'

'By proposing while I'm covered in ice cream, lying naked on your kitchen table?'

'I can't think of a better time, can you?'

They stared into each other's eyes, and then Sofia's

mouth began to twitch. Once she started laughing, she couldn't stop.

'I'll go down on bended knee later,' he promised.

'I'll hold you to that,' she warned as he silenced her with a kiss.

It was a long time later, after an extremely lengthy shower, that they finally made it to his bed. 'I just want you to be sure,' Sofia told him as he drew her into his arms. 'Marriage is such a huge step for you.'

'And for you, as it is for anyone,' he argued. 'I can't pretend we won't live in the spotlight, but it's up to us to make time for each other.'

'And our family,' she whispered against his mouth.

'The balancing act won't be easy,' he agreed. 'Serving our country in the full glare of publicity while maintaining a happy family life will be a challenge, but as we both thrive on challenge I don't see a problem. We'll be stronger together than we are apart.'

'You make a good case, Prince Cesar,' Sofia teased tenderly.

'I'm fighting for a woman who is worth the world to me. If you had left me, I would have regretted it for the rest of my life—and I've got too much living to do to waste time on regret.'

Sofia's eyes searched his with concern. 'A huge royal wedding with a cathedral full of people we don't even know?'

'What about that wedding on the beach you talked about?'

'You can't. You're a prince.'

'I can do anything I want to do,' he assured Sofia. 'We can have a grand ceremony in the cathedral to celebrate the birth of the first of our many children or a formal blessing in the months after our marriage. Our countrymen are romantics at heart—they're Italian,' he reminded her. 'And we won't sell them short. We'll share our lives—good and bad—so they have an insight into the human side of our royal partnership. I know my people's generosity of spirit well enough to be confident that they will applaud our decision to have a simple beachside wedding, for no other reason than it means so much to us.'

'Saying our own words in our own way, rather than repeating words written by someone who doesn't even know us,' Sofia reflected out loud. Her eyes brightened as she saw the possibility of change for the better opening out in front of them both.

'Exactly.'

'You'd do this for me?'

'I'd do anything for you,' he confirmed. 'I'm saying I love you in every way I know. I'll always respect royal traditions, but we can still do things our way, a new way, and if a wedding on the beach is what you want, a wedding on the beach is what you shall have.'

'I can't think of anything I want more than to be your wife, to stand alongside you, whatever the future brings. I love you so much,' Sofia whispered, staring up into his eyes.

The first charity polo match was brought forward. The crowd was vast. The game was fierce. Sofia and Olivia proved indispensable members of the winning team, which was naturally Team Lobos. They defeated the infamous Argentinian Team Assassin, led by past world champion Nero Caracas, by seven goals to six. Any other result would have been unacceptable, Sofia's fiercest brother Xander told Cesar without a flicker of expression on his tough, unforgiving face.

To allow the cheering fans to see many of the world's top players in action, both sides swapped different players for each chukka, so there was a huge crowd of players and their families in the cookhouse afterwards, where warm camaraderie prevailed. What had happened on the pitch stayed on the pitch, and all that mattered now were the huge sums of money raised for their favourite charities. It was the perfect time to make an announcement.

Tapping a champagne bottle, Cesar grabbed everyone's attention. As silence fell, he announced, 'Sofia and I are getting married.'

'Does Sofia know?' demanded Nero Caracas, Cesar's arch-rival and great friend, to a chorus of raucous cheers.

'She does,' Sofia shouted, coming to Cesar's side to link her arm through his. 'And you're all invited to our wedding on the beach on the beautiful island of Isla Ardente.'

Isla Ardente. Paradise on earth. That was Sofia's first impression of Cesar's private island, and it only improved in her eyes as she walked barefoot down the firm sugar-sand beach to join her life with his.

Cesar had dressed simply in a loose-fitting white linen shirt that was striking against his tan. He had completed the ensemble with delightfully fine linen trousers in a dusky shade of taupe that would slip off as easily as he'd put them on. These things were important when you spent most of your life in tight-fitting breeches.

Sofia was wearing the wedding gown they'd chosen together. It was also flimsy and easy to remove. A dream of a dress, it was an unadorned slip of ankle-length ivory silk that moulded her body with loving attention to detail. She wore her hair down with a coronet of fresh flowers, picked that morning in the palace gardens, secured around her forehead with a floating rose-pink ribbon. Instead of a bouquet, she carried her wedding gift from Cesar. The puppy was his hound Bran's prettiest daughter. So Cesar hadn't quite kept to the rules when it came to this marriage, any more than she had.

Jess was waiting as she reached his side to take the puppy from her. Linking fingers with Sofia, Cesar brought her hand to his lips. Dipping his head, he murmured, 'I love you... How beautiful you are.' And then his lips brushed her neck, her mouth. 'I can't wait to get you alone—'

The celebrant cleared his throat abruptly, which made the unruly guests laugh, but even the minister was smiling; everyone was in the same euphoric mood.

'I do,' Sofia confirmed as the surf rustled and lapped over her naked feet.

'Time and tide wait for no man, not even a prince,' Cesar explained with a dark smile for Sofia as a groom brought up his great black stallion.

Swinging into the saddle, he lifted Sofia into his arms, and to the cheers of their guests they galloped away for some vital private time before the wedding feast began.

EPILOGUE

'WE'VE COME A long way, *piccola amata*.'

'A very long way,' Sofia agreed, smiling as she snuggled closer to Cesar. How she loved this intimacy between them. Most of all she loved the happy family they had created amidst the pomp and duty of royal life.

Currently they were staring down with the same astonished adoration they had experienced when their twins had been born three years ago. Their latest beloved newborn was a baby girl called Thea, after Sofia's mother. Thea was sister to Nico and Tino, their three-year-old sons. The boys were currently nestled on the bed alongside them, admiring the new addition to their family.

'I bought you something,' Cesar remembered, delving into the pocket of his jeans.

'Cesar, no,' Sofia protested as he brought out a night-blue velvet jewel case. She gazed lovingly at their children. 'You've given me everything I need already.'

She could never have predicted how happy they would be. The people of Ardente Sestieri celebrated their Prince's tight family unit at an annual celebration in the castle gardens each year. This year Cesar and Sofia would share the joy of a new baby with their people, and not just with a series of photographs taken by Cesar but with new portraits of the children painted by Sofia, just as soon as she was back at her easel.

The polo matches continued to raise vast sums for charity, while Sofia's retreat had developed into a world-wide charitable foundation with outreach services, and Cesar was popularly acclaimed as the most charitable and caring Prince in his country's history.

'Aren't you going to open it?' her loving husband prompted. 'The boys are waiting. We love you so much, and Nico and Tino helped me choose the gift.'

'I'll love it whatever it is,' Sofia assured them, but Tino and Nico were more interested in their baby sister curling her tiny fists around their fingers.

'Another warrior woman,' Cesar groaned.

Sofia gasped on opening the jewel box. He helped her to remove the most beautiful diamond necklace from its snug velvet nest.

She had become accustomed to wearing the price-less, heavy and opulent gems of state. Always conscious of their history, she felt humbled wearing them, but this was a different jewel, because this was a gift from Cesar's heart.

The fine gold chain held three pure blue-white diamond hearts. 'With room for more,' Cesar pointed out.

'Do you really think these three will give us the chance to add to our family?'

'You can depend on it,' he promised.

Staring into the darkly seductive eyes of a man she trusted and loved more than anything else on earth, she believed him.

* * * * *

AFTER THE
BILLIONAIRE'S
WEDDING VOWS...

LUCY MONROE

For the love of my life.

Because you have made more than thirty years
together feel like it will never be long enough,
because when we hit bumps you launched your own
bid and it was so worth working our way
back to bliss.

I love you so very much and I always, always will!

CHAPTER ONE

GREEK BILLIONAIRE AND societal icon Alexandros Kristalakis stepped into the hall, having wrapped up an international call with one of his business interests in America, unsurprised to find his wife waiting.

Unlike early in their marriage, Pollyanna was always punctual now.

Never late anymore, but neither was she spontaneous. Exuberant expressions of affection had disappeared along with her spontaneity. He'd believed, at first, that was the result of being pregnant the first time around, a difficult period for her emotionally and physically. But giving birth and early motherhood had not seen a reversion to the old habits he'd enjoyed so much.

He could not complain. Pollyanna had worked too hard to adjust to her new lifestyle as the wife of a billionaire Greek from an old and established family.

Coming from a far more relaxed background and a family that had none of the societal expectations of his own and the very different American culture, she'd naturally found it a challenge. But not a challenge his amazing and resilient wife could not meet.

Despite speaking almost no Greek to begin with, she had attended the necessary social functions and lent her newfound position to the support of worthy causes. With her naturally open nature and warm personality, she'd won over his friends and acquaintances, making a place for herself in Athens society not reliant wholly on her role as his wife.

Six months pregnant with their second child, the leggy brunette was more beautiful than the day they married.

Even if nowadays her warm personality was muted by a dignity more fitting to the name Anna his mother insisted she be called, rather than the more common Polly she used go by.

Her designer gown in the ice blue that had become known as her signature color clung to breasts that had grown at least a cup size since conception and fell in an elegant drape over her baby bump. His child growing inside his wife.

It gave him a sense of pride not even his most ruthlessly executed business deal ever had.

He gave her an openly appreciative look. "You look beautiful, *yineka mou*."

"That's what you pay the exorbitant fees to the stylists for." She didn't smile, or meet his eyes with her crystalline blue gaze.

She hardly ever did anymore. With him.

Other people still got the benefit of her warm nature, but he got the elegant wife who never spoke out of turn or reacted without thought. Except in the bedroom. There, she was still the passionate being he had known he could not live without.

He'd known she was something special the first time they went to bed together.

So he had asked her to marry him, instead of one of the many proper Greek heiresses his mother had been throwing at him since uni days.

And she had said yes. Of course she had. Why wouldn't she?

He had been able to give Pollyanna a lifestyle she couldn't even have dreamed of.

Nevertheless it wasn't the expensive designer gown or glittering diamonds she'd opted to wear for the weekly family dinner, or even the silky chestnut hair swept up in an elegant twist, but the way she glowed with her pregnancy that had prompted his compliment.

Even looking a little tired, as she did now, she still took his breath away. "It is all you," he assured her.

She gave him a barely there tilt of her lips, clearly unimpressed by his praise.

She used to smile when he told her how beautiful she was to him, her expression open and full of delight at his appreciation. He did not know what had changed in that regard, but something had.

Just as somewhere along the way he'd lost the privilege of using the term *agape mou*. Oh, she never told him not to call her his love. She didn't do that anymore, make demands, or argue. She just winced every time he used the words, so he'd stopped doing it. She didn't seem to mind *yineka mou*, referring to her as his wife, his woman seemed acceptable. So, he found himself using that instead.

They made the helicopter trip to his childhood home in silence, which was not unexpected. Unless they wore headsets, hearing one another above the sound of the rotors was impossible without shouting. There had been a time she would have curled into his side, and they would have communicated with their eyes, if not their bodies. He did not remember the last time she'd offered that kind of open affection outside the bedroom.

Married friends had warned him that things changed naturally as a marriage settled into life's routines. He'd thought his would be immune, but even being wrong did not make him regret making this woman his wife.

Their ride from the helipad on top of the Kristalakis Building to the home where he'd grown up in the northern Athens suburb of Ekali went without incident and they arrived spot on time. Of course.

His mother greeted them both with the traditional kiss to both cheeks, though she showed respect for Pollyanna's makeup by kissing the air. Pollyanna returned the gesture, her expression perfectly contained. Not like the hothead he'd first married, who'd had a terrible time not showing the antipathy she'd developed for his mother on her expressive features.

Those features were never anything but serene now.
Except in bed.

In bed, Pollyanna still showed all the passion she ever
had, with one exception. She never reached for him first.

He didn't recall when that changed, wasn't sure he would
have noticed right away. Why should he? She always responded so beautifully to him when he initiated intimacy,
but at some point he had become aware that she did not
turn to him in the night. She did not reach across the bed
to touch. She never kissed him with great enthusiasm and
little concern for where they were as she'd used to do.

He'd accepted that kind of exuberance couldn't last in
marriage. Her lack of enthusiasm was only in initiation, not
the act, so he had nothing to complain about.

So, why did he still feel the loss so deeply?

"I see you're still making use of the stylist I suggested,"
his mother said to Pollyanna, in what should have been approval. So why did her words sound like a criticism?

Or was it that telltale wince that was barely there and
then gone from his wife's lovely face?

"As you see," Pollyanna said in quiet self-deprecation.

Corrina, his new sister-in-law, who was usually all sun-
shine and smiles, was frowning at his mother, her expression not at all approving. "Polly doesn't need a stylist. Her
natural style is perfect as it is."

His mother drew herself up in obvious affront, probably as much at the gentle rebuke as Corrina's use of Polly,
which his mother thought far too common and had refused
to use from their first meeting. Everyone called her Anna
now, even him.

Though sometimes in bed, he still chanted Polly, when
he was climaxing. The name he'd first come to know her by.

Alexandros looked to his brother, expecting him to sub-
tly rein his wife in.

But Petros was smiling at Corrina in nothing less than
approval. "As always, you are quite right, *agape mou*. She

has never needed the stylists my brother insists on paying for."

The look Corrina gave Petros was nothing short of adoration. There was something about that look that bothered Alexandros, but he could not put his finger on what it was. It was a good thing that his newly married sister-in-law looked at her husband like he was a superhero. That was as it should be.

So why did Alexandros get a strange, unpleasant feeling every time he noticed it? He looked sideways at his own wife. She was not returning his regard.

No surprise there. She never looked at him unless good manners dictated she do so. She stood now, removed from the conversation like a statue in a museum.

"I do not expect to be taken to task in my own home," his mother said in freezing tones.

That didn't seem to impact Corrina at all.

Petros, on the other hand, wasn't so calm. Displeasure turned his expression dark and he snapped, "Giving Polly a compliment is not taking you to task. My wife is allowed to have a different opinion from you, and if you are not mature enough to accept that, perhaps we need to rethink these family dinners."

"Petros, how dare you talk to me that way?" their mother demanded, sounding utterly shocked.

"Oh, Mama, don't take on so," their younger, and unashamedly spoiled sister butted in. "You know how protective Petros is of his beloved wife. It's the way of the Kristalakis male. You remember how Papa used to be?"

As always, mention of her dead spouse brought a fragile smile to his mother's face, and she unbent enough to nod. "I suppose, but still, Petros, I am your mother."

His mother had fallen apart after his father's death. After losing both her parents only a year prior, he maybe should have expected her broken response to further loss. But he hadn't, and things had gotten very bad before Alexandros had taken action.

For a time, he had worried they would lose her to grief. They nearly had. She'd stopped bathing, stopped going out. In desperation, he had booked her into a luxury rest facility.

It had worked and she'd returned to the villa more herself, but Alexandros never forgot those dark days and how fragile of spirit his mother was under her society *grande dame* facade.

"And Corrina is my wife."

There could be no doubt in that room which woman came first in Petros's estimation. His mother looked furious again, and Stacia glared at their brother. "No one is denying that. We all love Corrina." Then Stacia shook her head, put an arm around her mother and said, "You can't be angry you raised him to be so much like Papa."

"No, I suppose not."

Stacia smiled. "Corrina and Anna are the luckiest women alive, being married to Kristalakis men. I'm sure no one will ever measure up for me. They are the most protective and considerate men on the planet. Right, Anna?"

Alexandros was surprised when his sister tried to bring his wife into the conversation. Even after five years, Stacia hadn't warmed up completely to his American bride. But he was shocked stupid by Anna's response.

"I wouldn't know, Stacia. I never knew your father." Pollyanna moved to take a seat in one of the armchairs, precluding him sitting beside her. She didn't use to do that either. Another barely there wince worried him. Was she having pain in her back and pelvis again with this pregnancy? "But Alexandros has never been the protective and considerate husband to me that Petros is to Corrina."

The words were so shocking that for a moment, his usually facile brain froze in trying to understand them. She had not just said that his brother was a better husband than him.

Pollyanna's reply to his sister had been incomprehensible enough, but the tone in which she said it even more so. His wife did not sound angry. She did not even sound resigned. Pollyanna sounded like she simply didn't care that *he*, Alexandros Theos Kristalakis, did not measure up to his younger brother in the husband stakes.

Worse was yet to come as he took in the reactions of his family.

Stacia managed to look both offended and *satisfied* at the same time. His mother's expression showed offence and concern, but it was Corrina's reaction that struck him like a blow to his ego. She looked at Pollyanna with undisguised pity. And his brother?

Petros wasn't looking at Pollyanna at all; he was looking at Alexandros, and his expression was equal parts anger and disappointment.

It was not the type of look Alexandros was accustomed to receiving from *any* member of his family, but especially his younger brother.

Alexandros had a realization so stunning, it nearly took him out at the knees. His brother and his brother's wife thought *he* was a poor husband. Even more staggering, the flat tone of his wife, the absolute belief that tone imbued to her own words said she thought the same thing.

A discussion he'd had with his brother before Petros's marriage to Corrina came back to Alexandros now.

Alexandros gave his brother, Petros, a stern glance over the coffee they shared after a productive meeting with their top-level executives. "Is it really so much to ask that you put your honeymoon off for one week so you can attend this gala? You know how important it is to our mother."

"Yes." Petros's glare was more than stern; it showed a stubborn resolve Alexandros was not used to his brother turning on him. "If you think I'm making the same choices in my marriage you've made in yours, then you are wrong. I know Mama had a hard time after Papa died, but her feelings are *not* more important than the woman I have chosen to spend the rest of my life with. I will never put her desires ahead of Corrina's."

"Family requires sacrifice. We balance the needs of our wives with those of the rest of our family." It hadn't been easy for Alexandros to watch his mother and wife jockey for position in his life.

But ultimately he'd never doubted Polly's ability to hold her own and stand up for herself when it mattered.

There was no humor in Petros's laugh. "You mean like you balance *your* wife's needs against that of our mother and sister?"

"Precisely."

"No thank you. I would like my wife to still be in love with me five years from now."

"What the hell is that supposed to mean?"

"It means that I am not putting off my honeymoon to make our mother happy."

At the time, Alexandros had dismissed the dramatic implication of his brother's words. But they came back to haunt the eldest brother now.

Had Pollyanna stopped loving Alexandros? She still responded to him in bed like a woman in love. Or a woman in lust. But love? It wasn't an emotion he'd been particularly worried about when they first got together. He'd called her *agape mou* but had rarely told her he loved her, and she'd never pressed for declarations of that nature. Not even when he proposed.

He'd taken that as more proof of how well suited they were.

Alexandros had said the words the first time when their daughter was born, and had given her an eternity ring to remind her of the sentiment when he did not say it.

Looking back, he realized she'd responded in kind but not with the kind of enthusiasm she'd said the words in the beginning. And he could not remember the last time *she'd* told *him* she loved him.

He thought, that like him, she realized they did not need the words.

"How can you say something like that?" his mother was saying with ringing censure.

Pollyanna tilted her head, like trying to understand the question. "Surely there is no reason for me to lie? There cannot be a single person in this room that harbors any illusions in regard to my place of priority in Alexandros's life."

She spoke like she meant what she said, like she couldn't understand *why* his mother had taken offence, why Alexandros might take offence. Then as if she had not said anything inflammatory at all, she turned to Petros and asked, "Have you and Corrina decided to stay in the Athens apartment for now?"

And his brother answered, pulling his wife into the discussion. Apparently, they were going to stay in the apartment. That was another difference between Petros and Alexandros.

His younger brother had moved into one of two penthouse apartments at the top of the Kristalakis Building when he graduated university and took up his first position in the family business.

He and Corrina had opted for her to move in there with him after their wedding, rather than back into the more spacious family home Alexandros had not moved out of until he bought the country villa he and Pollyanna lived in now.

Generations of their family had lived in the huge luxury villa together since his second great-grandfather had bought it for his new wife.

"But won't that be limiting once you start your family?" his mother asked.

Petros shrugged. "We're in no hurry to have babies, but when we do, we'll decide if we want to find a house in Athens, or move to the country like Alexandros did."

"We certainly enjoy our weekends at your villa," Corrina said to Pollyanna with a smile. "Though I'm sure it's as much the company as the location."

Pollyanna returned Corrina's smile with more warmth than he'd seen all evening.

He'd noticed that his brother had not said like Alexandros *and Pollyanna* did, because she hadn't had any say in their move, had she? Alexandros had seen how unhappy his wife was living with his mother, so he'd broken with generations of family tradition and bought them a house. And had it decorated.

His mother had assured him that surprising her with the fait accompli would delight his wife, who was not exactly inclined toward interior decor.

Pollyanna had *not* reacted with rapturous delight at the news they would be living in the country and he would be commuting to work in the city.

In fact, their argument about where they were going to live was the last big dustup he could remember with his then-volatile wife. He'd thought she'd finally settled into her place as the wife of a billionaire, had accepted he had her best interests at heart.

But that settling in had come with a cost that he was only now beginning to truly appreciate.

"Alexandros did not put off having children," his mother said in clear disapproval of his brother's stance in that regard.

Corrina looked ready to say something, but then shook her head and pressed her lips firmly together.

"What were you going to say?" Alexandros asked, still reeling from the knowledge his sister-in-law pitied his wife in her choice of husbands.

"It's not important."

"This is family. You should be able to speak your mind."

The scoffing sound that came from his wife's direction was surprising only in that she'd stopped making commentary on his family a long time ago. He'd thought her attitude toward his mother and sister had changed.

Had Pollyanna simply given up on trying to get him to see her point of view?

Corrina gave him a wary look. "I was only going to point out that if pregnancy was as difficult for you as it is for your wife, you might actually have waited to have children."

"That is a ridiculous thing to say," his mother censored. "It is a woman's lot to deal with the more difficult aspects of bringing children into the world. That does not make my son selfish for expecting his wife to give him heirs."

"My *wife* did not say it made my brother selfish." Petros sounded good and furious now, not merely annoyed with their mother, but pissed enough he would leave.

Unsurprisingly, it was Alexandros's wife who stepped in to smooth the waters. She was very good at that. "I love being a mother," Pollyanna said directly to Corrina. "I knew what I was in for when I agreed to have a second child."

His wife gave a serene facsimile of her genuine smile and looked at his mother now. "I know you don't mean to criticize either Corrina or Petros for their wish to wait a while before having children."

"No, of course not," his mother agreed.

Though even Alexandros was aware her words had certainly sounded like criticism.

Petros didn't look any more convinced than Alexandros felt, but Corrina looked more relaxed.

She smiled at Pollyanna. "You're a brilliant mother."

"Thank you. Helena is the joy of my life."

There had been a time when she had claimed that he and their marriage were the joy of her life, but he couldn't remember the last time she'd said anything similar either.

Dinner was announced then, precluding any further tense discourse.

Not merely because of the change of venue but because his wife did as he realized she always did and made every effort to steer the conversation in less volatile directions. As he sat there mulling over predinner discussion, he was still aware of how many times Pollyanna did not react to what were clearly pointed barbs from his mother or his sister.

Had it always been like this and he ignored it in favor of family peace?

It was past ten o'clock when they got in the back of the limo for their ride to the helipad so they could return home.

Alexandros had been stewing all evening and barely waited for the door to shut them into seclusion before saying, "I can't believe you told my family you don't think I'm an attentive husband."

The laugh his comment startled from his wife was anything but amused. "Are you trying to claim that you are?"

"When have I ever neglected you?" he demanded in a driven tone. "Would you look at me when we're talking?"

She lifted her head, her blue eyes shadowed by fatigue not anger. "When haven't you?" she asked.

"I am not a neglectful husband."

"If you say so." She let her head fall back against the headrest and closed her eyes.

"It's not even worth arguing with me over?"

"I don't know if you've noticed, but there are very few things I find worth arguing with you over anymore, Alexandros."

When she used to argue about everything, screaming when he would not listen. She hadn't even argued over her refusal to bring their daughter to the family dinners.

Pollyanna had simply pointed out in a very reasonable tone that since Helena was usually in bed by the time they ate, keeping her up was not conducive to the baby's well-being. She'd added that Athena and Stacia were welcome to visit during little Helena's awake hours.

She hadn't mentioned his brother because Petros had made an effort to spend time with his sister-in-law and then his niece from the very beginning, the only person in Alexandros's family who had accepted Pollyanna's joining the family without any reservations. He and Corrina now came to Villa Liakada to visit once a week, frequently opting to stay the weekend and fly back into Athens on Sunday evening with Alexandros and Polly for the family dinner.

Petros and Corrina had made their visit midweek this time around however.

Though their daughter, Helena, was now three, she was still too young to be kept up. Alexandros and Pollyanna had yet to revisit the issue.

"Why didn't you ever suggest that my mother change our family gatherings to the midday meal so our daughter could be included?" he asked.

"Why would I? I have no sway with your mother. She's not my family." The last was said with absolute certainty.

But it was not true. His mother *was* her family. Only clearly, Pollyanna did not see it that way. Had Pollyanna refused to accept the connection, as he had always assumed, or did that lack lay at his mother's door?

Had he made too many concessions to his mother because of her emotional fragility and too many demands of his wife because of the strength he knew she possessed?

Emotional self-analysis was not something he was comfortable with, but he was beginning to see that so much he had taken for granted was not as he believed it to be.

"Did you expect me to make the suggestion?" he asked her, trying to understand a relationship he had thought he had figured out perfectly.

"No."

"Why not?"

"Did you make it?" she asked wearily.

"No." He had never even thought of changing a long-standing tradition until just that moment and was a little ashamed of that fact.

Not only would his daughter have gotten to spend more

time with her *yia-yia*, but the more casual setting of lunch would have been easier on his wife. Though she'd never said so.

"Then?" she prompted, with little interest lacing her tone.

Having no answer and not even sure why he'd brought it up, he admitted, "I don't like you telling my brother he's a better husband than me."

"I would never presume to comment on how good a husband your brother is."

"You said he was more attentive and considerate than I am."

"If those are the traits by which you measure good or bad, you might take issue, but we both know you don't."

"What is that supposed to mean?" he demanded, noticing as if from outside himself that his voice was rising.

She didn't seem to care he was practically shouting, not bothering to open her eyes or look at him again. "If you wanted to be attentive, you would be. If you wanted to be protective, you would be. If you wanted to be considerate, you would be." She stopped, thought. "Maybe. Being considerate means noticing how the decisions you make affect others, and I think you're really bad at that."

"I make decisions that affect thousands of people all the time."

"Yes."

"And you don't think I care how they are affected?"

"No."

Just that. No. Not a reason why or a maybe. Just *no* and he knew she meant it.

She had no idea that he did his best to maximize jobs and keep people employed in jobs they *wanted*, even if it couldn't always be in the same company, or even country. And she assumed those kinds of considerations never made it past his ruthless need to also maximize profits.

"I can be considerate," he informed her, wondering how she'd missed his efforts in their marriage.

Had he really got it so wrong? For *five* years?

"To your mother, maybe," Pollyanna acknowledged without missing a beat. "But even as much as you spoil Stacia, I wouldn't say you are particularly considerate of her feelings or desires when they conflict with what you want or the way you think things should be done."

"Is this another argument where you lament the fact I won't always take your part against my mother?" Even as he asked the question, he tried to remember the last time they had had that disagreement and knew it was years past.

"No. I wasn't aware we were arguing at all." She sighed, still not opening her eyes. "Is there a reason for this conversation? Only I'm really tired."

"I forgot. I'm not worth arguing with."

"Alexandros, what exactly do you want me to say here?"

"That I'm not a bad husband," he blasted her.

Finally. Finally, her head snapped round, her eyes opening to flash at him with anger he remembered but had not seen in too long.

"Alexandros, I am six months pregnant and the mother of a very active toddler. Even without all the committees you insist I chair or participate in, I would be exhausted. Not just tired. Exhausted." And suddenly she looked it, her usual vibrancy so muted as to almost be extinguished.

She placed her hand protectively over her baby bump. "I am making new life inside me and I still suffer from nausea. It hurts to sit in any but the most comfortable chairs, hurts to walk and stand. Just like with my last pregnancy. But still you *insist* I suffer through a stylist's ministrations so I can attend these unpleasant family dinners, which require an uncomfortable fifty-minute helicopter ride each way."

"I did not realize it was such a struggle for you." But he should have.

Damn it. He should have.

"Of course you didn't, and if you had? You would not have cared. Never once, in our entire five years of marriage, have you *ever* made a decision with my happiness, or even my well-being at the forefront of your mind. A bad husband? No, you're not a bad husband. You're a *terrible* husband."

In receipt of those indictments, he was shocked stupid and silent for several long moments.

"If I'm so awful, why have you stayed married to me?" he asked finally, a wholly unexpected fear that one day maybe she *wouldn't* taking root inside him.

He'd realized long ago that the material benefits of being married to a billionaire were not the perks he thought they would be for her. So, what kept her married to a man she considered a total failure as a husband?

"You're just now asking yourself that?" She sighed. "We made promises before God, and I won't just ignore those promises in favor of an easy out. We also have a child together. From the moment of conception, I stopped making decisions based solely on my own happiness."

He had no doubt she spoke the truth on both counts, but those reasons for his wife staying married to him were not exactly good for his ego.

"So you'll stay married to me no matter what?" That didn't jibe with the woman he knew his wife to be under the placid facade.

"No, not no matter what."

"What would make those vows invalid?" he was driven to ask, a nameless dread telling him that he was on the thinnest ice when he hadn't even realized he'd stepped out onto the frozen lake.

"Abuse. Infidelity."

"And that is all I have going for me? I don't abuse you and I'm not unfaithful."

"Pretty much, yeah." She sighed. "And you're good in bed," she added as if forced to do so. "You are not a selfish lover."

Just selfish in every other way.

He had no words to respond to that statement.

CHAPTER TWO

THEY HAD ARRIVED at the helipad, and for the first time ever, Alexandros was relieved to have a confrontation interrupted because he literally did not know where to go from here.

He watched his wife scoot to get out of the car and really noticed for the first time just how tired she was. Why hadn't he noticed before? Those bruises under her eyes had been there before they left the house. The way she moved more slowly than normal—that had been there too.

He cursed and then reached in to lift her out into his arms and carried her to the helicopter. She didn't fight him. In fact, she gave him the biggest shock in an evening of shocks when she relaxed into him and simply let him take her weight.

Was it a sign that on some primal level she still trusted him? Or was she simply *that* exhausted?

When they got into the helicopter, he shrugged out of his dinner jacket and then pulled her into his arms, putting it around her like a blanket. Again, she didn't fight him, but relaxed into him, falling asleep almost immediately.

Okay. *That* exhausted.

She did not wake on the flight home, nor when he lifted her from the helicopter and carried her inside.

When he reached their bedroom, Alexandros undressed his wife for the first time since meeting her *without* plans to have sex. Not that the sight of her body didn't turn him on. It *always* turned him on, but he wasn't such a monster he couldn't see how much she needed her rest.

No matter what she chose to believe, he did care about her well-being. Of course he did. She was his wife. And though he rarely said the words, he loved her.

He carefully removed the pins from her hair and fetched

makeup wipes from their en suite in order to do what he'd never done before. He gently removed all traces of the makeup he knew she did not like to wear.

So, why did she wear it?

Because he'd made it clear he expected her to look the part of the wife of Alexandros Kristalakis, one of the most powerful men in Greece, if not the world.

He'd thought he was helping her fit into a world she had no experience of, but he couldn't help wondering how much help his advice couched as demands had really been.

Alexandros might be singularly obtuse to her feelings like she accused him, but he'd noticed that while she did the charity work he insisted was part of being his wife, she chose to support charities that his mother did not. His wife had put the power of his purse behind children's charities and those that served the marginalized, charities that did not have the cachet of those his mother supported.

In five years, his wife had built her own circle of friends and interests, and while those circles might overlap his and that of his influential family, they were not encompassed by them. Were in fact, he realized, as far removed from them as she could get without removing herself completely from his sphere of influence.

He finished preparing his wife for bed and then slid her lovely, pregnant body under the sheet and summer-weight duvet. She didn't shift until he joined her in the bed, forgoing the call to China he'd meant to make. He put his arm over her and tugged her close, the feeling that he was on the verge of having her ripped right from his arms too strong to ignore.

"Andros," she whispered against his chest in her sleep.

He went rigid at the name he hadn't heard in years, not even during lovemaking. Then without even considering it, he was turning and facing her, gently shaking her shoulder. "Why don't you call me Andros anymore?"

"Andros was the man I fell in love with," she said in a voice that sounded more asleep than awake.

"And who is Alexandros?"

"The man I married." She made a snuffling sound and turned in her sleep. Away from him.

Alexandros wrapped his body around his wife, his entire perception of his life going through a painful metamorphosis.

Polly woke warm and relaxed, feeling better than she had all week despite the way the night before had ended.

She had no memory of undressing or taking off her makeup the night before, but she slept naked, the way her husband liked her, with no day-old mascara clumped on her lashes when she blinked her eyes open.

Polly was alone in the bed. Nothing new about that, but the single yellow rose on her husband's pillow was.

She picked it up and automatically brought it to her nose to sniff as she read the note he'd left with the flower on her pillow.

Good morning, *agape mou*.

Nothing life altering in those four words, except it was the first time in their relationship that Alexandros had written a personal note to her. He didn't do cards for holidays or anniversaries, or even her birthday. He did big, extravagant gifts that touched her less than a simple card would have done. Money was easy for Alexandros.

Sentiment would have been harder.

He did texts and sometimes phone calls, but since she stopped replying immediately or picking up the phone every time his number showed, those instances had become less common.

She went to find her daughter, knowing the little girl would be up soon if Helena was not already. They breakfasted together like they usually did, Polly answering her precocious three-year-old's many and often unexpected questions. Today's topic was pandas, culminating in an altogether to be expected request to visit the zoo.

The thought of walking the long pathways at the zoo with a rambunctious toddler did not appeal, but they could take the nursery maid with them, so Polly said, "Maybe, darling, but not today."

"Okay, Mommy."

Polly's phone buzzed with a text and she checked it, startled when it was Alexandros inquiring how she was feeling.

She shot off a quick reply—Fine—and went back to talking the merits of different habitats at the zoo with her daughter.

A second text buzzed seconds later.

Do not say you are fine when you are not. Are you still exhausted?

She stared down at the phone in consternation. Since when was she not supposed to say she was fine when she wasn't? Alexandros didn't do drama. He didn't do anything that interfered with his well-ordered, fully business-oriented life.

Why are you asking? Is there something you want to add to my schedule?

That was the only thing she could think would have prompted the unprecedented text. But then why hadn't he contacted her social secretary? She'd hired Beryl the first year of their marriage, when Polly had realized that she needed a buffer between herself and the in-laws from hell. And that chances were, her husband was never going to be that buffer.

From an old elite Athens family that had fallen on hard times, Beryl was the perfect person to arrange social occasions with Alexandros's family and the rest of Athens society. Her efficiency also made it possible for Polly to fulfill her responsibilities as the wife of a billionaire and still be the kind of mom she'd always determined to be.

She sent another quick text off to Alexandros.

Just text Beryl. She has my calendar.

Which of course Alexandros knew, but Polly was thrown for a loop and reacting.

Her phone rang and she was surprised to see it was Alexandros.

"Hello."

"I'm not trying put more on your schedule, *yineka mou*. I was simply trying to find out if you are feeling any better this morning. You were well and truly exhausted last night."

"I'm pregnant. It comes with the territory."

"But having to get dressed up to attend an unpleasant weekly family dinner doesn't help, does it?"

Was he expecting her to apologize for saying that? She wasn't going to. If he didn't like the truth, he should not ask for it. Or better yet, he should make a different truth.

But she'd given up on that happening when she was pregnant with Helena.

"I will be home for lunch," he said into the silence between them.

"Why?" she asked in surprise.

"To see my wife and daughter."

She didn't say, *But you just saw me last night*, because though that was true, their daughter would be thrilled to see her beloved papa.

"We'll see you then. Only if you want me to wait lunch for you, that's fine, but Helena goes down for her nap at one o'clock."

If he was expecting their daughter to skip her nap to play happy families, Polly was going to have to rearrange their schedule if she didn't want to deal with a super cranky toddler for the rest of the day.

"I will be there by noon."

"All right."

The sound of a helicopter landing at five minutes to twelve brought Polly's attention up from the plans Beryl had given her to go over for an upcoming fundraiser. Helena was coloring at her little desk beside her mother's in the room Polly had appropriated for her use after moving into the mansion.

Besides the nursery, it was the only room that had any stamp of Polly's personality and preference for comfort and warm colors in it. The rest of the mansion they called a home looked like a high-end modern hotel. Even their bedroom felt like she should be calling for a late checkout on the rare occasions she slept in.

"That will be Papa. Shall we go meet him?" Polly put her hand out to her daughter.

"Papa is here?" Helena squealed, jumping to her feet.

Alexandros was crossing the lawn from the helipad when they got outside, a big smile on his face for his daughter. Helena pulled away from Polly and ran to him, her papa lifting the little girl and giving her a hug and kiss while listening with rapt attention to her baby chatter.

The sight of the super virile man holding the little girl made Polly's heart clench like it always did. This man might not be the husband she'd dreamed of, but he was *it* for her.

If she could have stopped loving him, she would have. But she'd learned that shutting off her emotions was a lot harder than pretending for the sake of her pride that she didn't have any.

Alexandros had wanted to know the night before why she had stayed married to him, and she'd withheld the most relevant answer. She had fallen head over heels in love with him five and a half years ago.

And she still loved him. He wasn't perfect, but there was so much about him to love.

It came out over lunch that Helena wanted to go to the zoo, but instead of looking at Polly like he expected her to tell him when that was going to happen, Alexandros gave her a worried frown. "Wouldn't that be taxing for you right now?"

She wanted to snap that everything was taxing for her in that minute, but Polly didn't do waspish comments anymore. She'd grown up. Or so she told herself.

So she shrugged instead. "I can hardly expect our daughter's life to go on hold simply because her mom is pregnant."

"If we had a nanny, she could take her."

It was an old argument. Polly had refused to hire a full-time nanny, preferring instead to have two different nursery maids working different shifts. Dora, a middle-aged widow, was on hand from six in the morning until two in the afternoon. And Hero, a local girl who had been attending online university while helping her parents on their farm, covered the hours from six to midnight.

Both had rooms in the mansion, and Polly was sure Hero found her studies much more manageable than she had as a farm laborer, especially as Helena was usually asleep by eight.

And neither woman had primary responsibility for *Polly's* child. Polly was and always would be a hands-on, dedicated mom. "Dora could take her, come to that," she told her husband. "But I'm Helena's mom. Our outings together are important."

"And when you are feeling better, you will be able to go on them again," he said, his tone oh, so reasonable.

"If this pregnancy is like my last one, my discomfort isn't going anywhere."

"Call it what it is, pain. And since I realized you were suffering from it again, I've researched possible remedies."

"I am not taking painkillers." They'd had that discussion when she was pregnant with Helena, and Polly had thought he'd agreed with her.

"Naturally not, but have you considered chiropractic and acupuncture? I have the name of a reputable clinic staffed by two doctors that have only rave reviews from their patients."

"You want me to try alternative medicine? *You* do?" Mr. Conservative, only the Greek way is the best way, and only the really rich Greek way of doing things met even that mark?

"It is not alternative medicine. It is perfectly valid holistic medicine. Thousands of years of success cannot be discounted as merely alternative."

"Who are you and what have you done with Alexandros Kristalakis?"

He laughed, the sound booming and masculine and altogether alluring.

But she hadn't been joking. She really didn't understand what was going on. "How did you even think to look for that clinic?"

"I told you, I did some research."

"Because you realized I was in pain?"

"I wish I had realized sooner, or that you had told me."

"But why would I tell you?" she asked in honest bewilderment.

Anytime she'd complained during her first pregnancy, he either asked his mother to advise Polly, which had never been a pleasant experience, or he'd quoted some lowering thing his mother had said. To this day, Polly herself wasn't sure if Athena said the things she did to undermine Polly, or because she really believed them.

Athena was of a different generation, not to mention a completely different socioeconomic background.

The worst had been when Alexandros had fallen back

on his standby that women had been enduring the inconveniences of pregnancies since the beginning of time. He always couched it with how strong and resilient Polly was, so of course she would be fine.

Only she hadn't been fine. First, she'd be nauseated to the point of throwing up several times a day, all day long for the first four months. Then a month of relative bliss and then the pain in her pelvic floor had started, followed quickly by lower back pain and finally pain in both hips had stacked on top of that for her final month with a return of her nausea.

This time around, the nausea had clung on past the fourth month, but she was no longer throwing up, so that was an improvement.

He stared at her like she was the one being incomprehensible, but when had her husband ever invited her to share her complaints with him? He was a dynamic workaholic who powered through lack of sleep and physical infirmity with a strength of will that used to intimidate her.

Because she'd felt the need to be worthy of that kind of dynamism. She didn't anymore.

Polly accepted that while that was who her husband was, it was not her.

And she accepted the fact that he expected those around him to deal with their own challenges. So, she did, even if she gave herself more of a break than he ever would have done.

Or tried to anyway, within the parameters of her job description.

Socially conscious wife to Alexandros Kristalakis.

"Perhaps because if you had told me, I would have made changes sooner."

Change would be a fine thing. "What changes?" she asked anyway, wondering what he considered concessions made to her condition.

"I have informed my mother and sister that until further

notice, our once a week family get-togethers will happen here and they will be lunches, not dinners."

"What? Why?" Did she *want* to host the family meals? Wouldn't that just give Athena, and more likely Stacia, even more reasons to criticize Polly?

But she could not deny that a lunchtime get-together would be much easier for Polly to manage from both a physical and schedule perspective.

"It is a change that should have happened when you first got pregnant. I forget that other people do better with more sleep than I get, and my pregnant wife should be getting even more sleep than her usual." He gave her a self-deprecating smile that sort of took her breath away.

Her husband did not *do* self-deprecating.

"You don't believe that. You don't believe in giving in to infirmity."

His smile slid away to be replaced by an expression that almost looked hurt. "Am I really that arrogant? That lacking in compassion?"

"Yes," she answered immediately and without a shred of desire to lie.

His strong features showed consternation. "I am sorry you believe that, but trust me when I tell you that your pain and discomfort *do* affect me."

"Since when?"

"Always."

"But before..." She let her voice trail off, not sure it was worth getting into.

His handsome mouth firmed. "Not worth discussing?" he asked silkily. "But I will answer your implied question. The last time you were pregnant, I was in the middle of a takeover bid from a conglomerate that wanted my flagship company. I was not as focused on you as I should have been, which was why I asked for my mother's help."

Polly didn't mask her expression fast enough to hide what she thought of his mother's *help*.

He smiled ruefully. "Just so. I accept that she was not the comfort to you I thought she would be."

Appreciative of that insight, belated though it might be, Polly went back to what else he'd revealed. "But surely no takeover bid could have been any real threat."

"One thing you will learn in business. No matter how big you are? Someone is always bigger, if only temporarily. I'd made some risky moves, not realizing they were waiting for just such an opportunity. I was too focused on business, and when you told me the difficulties you were having with your pregnancy, my mother assured me you were fine. It was all very normal. Your doctor confirmed that."

"It was normal, if not easy for me to deal with." And she'd really wanted his support, not his mother's repressively traditional advice.

"I really thought Mama would help you through the difficulties of pregnancy while I worked seven days a week to keep my business."

"Your mother *help me*?" Polly asked in disbelief, even as she appreciated he hadn't just ignored her for business as usual. And he'd believed she was okay because maybe that was what he needed to believe while his attention was directed elsewhere.

It put her last pregnancy in a different light, but it didn't appreciably change how she saw her husband's attitude to her. Because whatever the cause, even pregnant, Polly had not been anything like his primary concern.

"I did not appreciate how old-fashioned her views on pregnancy were," he acknowledged with unexpected candor.

Even oblique criticism of his mother was not something she was used to from Alexandros.

He was very protective of the older woman. He'd once shared how close to losing her he'd felt he'd come after the unexpected death of his father.

The Kristalakis patriarch had only died a little over a year before she and Alexandros met. She'd wondered sometimes if that was what had driven Alexandros's uncharacteristic impromptu marriage proposal.

"Or how much she *enjoyed* my discomfort."

He frowned. "I'm sure that is not true."

And with that, they reached the end of any honest dialogue about his mother and her attitude toward Polly.

Polly didn't bother to argue her viewpoint. She'd learned there was no advantage to it. He didn't hear criticism of his precious mother.

And honestly? Polly wasn't sure Athena *had* enjoyed her pain. It had seemed like it though, all mixed up with Athena's and Stacia's efforts to undermine Polly's place in Alexandros's life.

Regardless, Polly would not allow a few unexpected moments of understanding on his part lull her into thinking Alexandros had changed in any significant way.

This refrain, in different guises, was an old one. Athena Kristalakis had been furious with her son marrying an American nobody instead of one of the beautiful Greek socialites she'd been pushing at him for years.

Under the pretext of friendship, Athena had drawn proverbial blood over and over again in her campaign to send her unwanted daughter-in-law packing. She and her daughter Stacia had done their best to make Polly feel like the outsider she was, making sure those in their circle treated her with the same disdain they did.

Athena had even changed Polly's first name! Calling her Anna, without asking for Polly's approval. Which she would *not* have given.

Anna was *not* Polly's name and she never thought of herself that way. However, as time went on, Polly had allowed her *Anna* persona to develop. The Anna facade stood between her and any real interaction with her detractors, and most of the time, even with her husband anymore.

"Your silence does not signify agreement," he said as if just figuring that fact out.

"No, it does not." It never had.

"It is your way of telling me you can't be bothered to argue any longer."

"Maybe." She was reeling.

He'd gone from stone dense to insightful literally overnight, and Polly didn't know how she felt about that.

"I think my mother has almost as much ground to make up with you as I do."

Suddenly, Polly had her own insight.

Her husband was terribly competitive. And last night she had inadvertently triggered his need to prove he was the better husband between himself and his younger brother.

News flash—that would require something Alexandros simply could not give her.

His love.

"I'm beginning to realize just how often you use silence as its own answer," he said in a tone she found difficult to interpret.

"You used to tell me off all the time for disagreeing with you so often."

"Be careful what you wish for—isn't that how the saying goes?"

"Are you saying you *want* me to argue with you?" She didn't buy it. Not for a single second.

"I want you to think it's worth it."

"It's a goal to shoot for," she said with more facetiousness than she usually allowed herself with him.

His sardonic look said he recognized it. "You have an appointment with the chiropractor and acupuncturist the day after tomorrow," he said, changing the subject away from confrontation like he never did. "I would have arranged it for tomorrow, but you've already got your appointment with your OB."

"Wednesday? But I have committee meetings in Athens. Did you forget I was going to fly in on the helicopter with you?" Beryl had arranged it, as she always did when Polly needed to get into city.

Polly would come home in a car with a driver, usually after sharing lunch with her busy husband. It was one of those treats she looked forward to. Adult time during the day with Alexandros.

"There will be no more uncomfortable helicopter rides into Athens for the duration of your pregnancy." His tone said this was not one of those occasions he wanted her to think it was worth arguing with him.

Too bad! "But my charity work!" Work he'd insisted she had to do in order to fulfill her responsibilities as his wife.

"Can be done by someone else."

Like *her* efforts had no intrinsic value because she was the one making them? Thank you so much, husband! "What if there is no one else?"

"We will hire Beryl an assistant and she will take your place in committees, etc. After working for you so long, she knows your stand on things, what you would want to involve yourself in and what you would not." He reached across the table and took her hand. "Listen to me, *pethi mou*. You are too valuable to me to allow you to continue putting your health at risk. And while the work you do on behalf of children at risk and the marginalized is incredibly important, it is not more important to me than *you* are."

He was saying all the right things, but she wasn't believing them.

She couldn't afford to let herself go down that road again, where she thought he loved her, valued her and had married her for anything other than the untrammeled lust he felt for her body.

"While Beryl is invaluable to me, *she* is not the wife of a billionaire."

"But she has your ear, which means she influences your donation and spokesperson power. It will suffice for this season of your life."

Season? Did he mean beyond delivery of their second child? "I assume you've already spoken to Beryl about this change in her duties." He might make it sound like he'd just thought of hiring her social secretary an assistant, but Polly wasn't that naive.

Alexandros did not wait to act.

His hand squeezed hers. "Naturally, you are right. You know me well."

But did he know her? "Didn't you think that maybe you should have discussed some of these changes with me before you made them?"

"I saw a problem and I sought to fix it. What is wrong with that?"

"The problem is mine to fix."

"Only you weren't fixing it. You were running yourself ragged doing all the same old stuff."

She couldn't deny that. Polly had her own measure of pride and hadn't wanted to admit she wasn't physically up to the same schedule she'd always kept. "If you've hired a nanny behind my back, we are going to have some serious words," she warned him.

"It would almost be worth it to see you engaged enough to actually argue with me, but that is not something I would do."

"You *want* me angry with you?" she asked. This was the second time he'd alluded to wanting that and she was trying to understand *why* suddenly he wanted her to revert to how she'd used to be.

Willing to argue every time she didn't agree with his autocratic view of the world. Angry with him more often than she'd ever wanted to be.

Because she kept expecting him to treat her like he loved her.

She didn't have those expectations any longer.

"No." Which did not surprise her. "I want you *real* with me, and I'm only just now realizing how long it has been since I saw the real Pollyanna. Only in the same way I have realized that there are an honored few that already do."

"What do you mean?"

"My brother. His new wife. The few you call friend and not acquaintance."

He'd left off her family, but maybe that was because he realized bringing them up would only point out how differently her parents and siblings treated Polly to how his own mother and sister did. "None of them call me Anna."

And at its most basic level, that was the dividing line.

"So, all I have to do is call you Pollyanna to get back into the charmed circle?" he asked in that seductive tone he usually reserved for the bedroom.

Heat climbing her cheeks at her body's instant reaction to it, she said, "I don't know what circle you're talking about."

But she did. He meant the people she trusted, including those few she'd learned she could rely on since moving to Greece.

Her husband, she had learned *not* to trust.

"Yes, you do."

"Yes, I do," she admitted.

"I call you Anna."

"Yes."

"You do not like it."

"It is not my name."

"It is a nickname."

"That your mother finds more acceptable than my real name. Yes, I know."

"You have never asked me to call you Pollyanna instead."

She shook her head. Was he rewriting history now? "That is not true."

He stared at her, his mouth open to refute her words, but then he must have remembered. Because he went oddly pale. "You told me Anna was not your name and you would prefer if I would not use it."

"But your mother had made it clear how very lowbrow she found my real name."

"So, I called you Anna around her."

"Not just around her."

He winced in acknowledgment. "I slipped once too often and realized I needed to use it all the time, for consistency."

The other option of course would have been for him to *never* use it. For consistency. And because Polly had made it clear that was what she wanted. But then, when had Polly's wants, or even needs, ever trumped his mother's? Never, that was when.

Their daughter demanded her father's attention right then, and Polly was grateful for it. She was done with this weird walk down memory lane.

No one could change the path their marriage had taken, because she'd realized way too late that she'd married a man programmed to hurt her.

Because, despite a few claims to the contrary, usually when she'd done something that made him really happy, like giving birth, he did not love her.

No man who loved her would treat her the way that Alexandros had since their marriage and her move to Greece. The very fact he'd insisted on moving into his family home, one they had had to share with the two wicked witches, showed just how little her feelings had mattered to him.

He knew from the beginning that Athena had wanted him to marry an entirely different type of woman. It had taken Polly longer to see the contempt behind the smile.

Even so, Alexandros would be *so* annoyed if he knew she thought of his mother and sister in those terms.

But Polly's thoughts were her own and even her *had to be in charge* husband could not police them.

They put their daughter down for her nap together, and Polly enjoyed the family togetherness so much, moisture burned the back of her eyes.

"Are you all right?" he asked as they left their daughter's bedroom together.

"I'm fine." She didn't consider that two-word answer deception.

She simply said what he expected to hear.

Suddenly she found herself in his arms and being carried past the staircase that would have taken them back downstairs, down the hall and to *their* bedroom.

"It's the middle of the day, Alexandros!"

"When has that ever stopped me?"

It was true that some weekends they utilized the time during their daughter's naps to enjoy marital intimacy, but since he was never home during the day during the week, and not always on the weekends, it was something very new.

"Don't you have to get back to the office?" she asked in wonder as he laid her down on their bed, his expression harsh with need that hadn't been there a moment ago.

Or maybe it had been and she just hadn't let herself notice it.

"The office can wait." He removed his jacket and tie in rapid succession, his nimble fingers already working the buttons of his shirt open.

She gasped, her shock was so great at that unprecedented statement.

CHAPTER THREE

ALEXANDROS IMPATIENTLY TUGGED his shirt over his head with only the cuffs and a few buttons undone. Shock turned to passion as the body she loved touching so much was revealed to her hungry gaze.

He unhooked his leather belt and didn't even bother taking it from the loops as he usually did before undoing his slacks to push them down his hips.

"They're going to get wrinkled like that."

"Do you care?" he asked lazily.

She shook her head, her gaze glued to his now-naked body.

"I love the way you look at me. In the bedroom." There was something strange in his expression she couldn't read though. Like something about what he'd said bothered him.

Polly leaned up on her elbows, confident in this, as she was in no other area of their relationship. In this area, there could be no denying they were entirely simpatico.

While she no longer believed he loved her, the joining of their bodies was *still* making love because of her feelings for him. And she did believe he felt affection for her.

It wasn't all the amazing sexual compatibility they'd shared since the first time they touched.

"You do it for me," she said cheekily but with a heated look she knew he wouldn't misinterpret.

"Tease me at your own peril," he warned.

But she wasn't worried. Polly reached down to tug at her dress, as if she was going to pull it off.

He leaped. Like literally leaped and took hold of her wrists. "No. That's mine."

"What is yours?" she taunted.

"Undressing you."

"I undress myself all the time."

"Not when I'm there to do it for you."

And that was true. Even when sex wasn't in the offing, her husband considered it his privilege to take her clothes off if he was around to do it. Whether it was to get ready for bed or to change for dinner didn't matter. He got a big charge out of it.

This time though, sex was definitely in the offing. It spiced the air around them, making it heavy with the mutual desire that had not dimmed in five years of marriage.

His sex rigid with need, he crossed the carpet to their bed. When he reached Polly, her husband tugged her to her feet and turned her around so he could slide the zip down on her dress, revealing curves that were exaggerated by pregnancy. He took his time peeling her dress down her arms and sliding it ever so slowly down her body.

"Now, who is teasing, Alexandros?" she asked, her tone breathy with desire.

"Your husband."

"You are that." She'd never denied it, for good or ill.

"And I always will be," he said with more force than finesse before cupping her breasts. "No one else will ever touch you like this."

"You're feeling possessive."

"Because you are mine."

"And you are mine," she reminded him. "We have matching wedding bands."

His hot mouth landed against the side of her throat, sending her thoughts splintering. Alexandros knew all her hot spots and seemed intent on visiting each one.

Somehow, she found herself naked on the bed, his head between her legs, his mouth driving her pleasure higher and higher. Two fingers pressed inside of her, rubbing against that inner bundle of nerves that made her scream with need.

She wanted him inside her. "Alexandros! Now!"

But instead of moving up her body, he suckled at her clitoris, and she came with a long scream she couldn't have held back with the best will in the world. He nursed her through aftershocks of pleasure until she was nearly sobbing with the pleasure that was not abating.

Only then did he shift up her body and press his hardness into the wet, slick, swollen opening of her body.

He pressed inside her, stretching her, filling her, giving her more and more pleasure. His initial thrusts were long and slow, and she could feel a second climax build impossibly fast.

This time when she came, he was with her, his own hoarse shout blending with her cries.

Afterward, he pulled her close, his body wrapped around hers completely.

She rubbed her head against his chest and kissed his hard muscle. "This is nice."

"Better than nice."

"Mind blowing."

"Better."

She yawned. "Mmm. I shouldn't be tired. I slept in this morning."

"But you are pregnant. You need your rest."

"If you say so."

"I do."

She didn't know how long he cuddled her, but she was dozing when he slid from the bed. "I need to shower and get back to Athens."

"Work waits for no man," she mumbled.

He laughed. "Perhaps not, but it waited this afternoon for my woman."

She smiled at him, reveling in the truth of that statement.

Polly fell asleep to the sound of him showering in the en suite, waking hours later to discover he'd given strict instructions for her not to be disturbed. Beryl had fielded calls, and Dora had agreed to remain overseeing Helena until Hero showed up. All organized by Polly's billionaire tycoon before he flew back to Athens.

Polly barely had time to make it to share dinner with their daughter, unsurprised when she got the message from the housekeeper that Alexandros had been held up in Athens and wouldn't be joining them. Helena asked, but wasn't upset when told her papa would see her to tuck her in later.

And he made it back in time to do so, so neither was Polly.

The next morning, Polly stopped in stunned silence when she realized her husband was sitting at the breakfast table with Beryl and Helena.

"I stayed to go to your obstetrician appointment with you." He sounded like he expected a medal for that.

"You said you didn't have time."

"When did I say that?"

"When I was pregnant with Helena."

"Things were different then."

"The takeover thing?" she asked.

He nodded, color scoring the masculine angles of his face. He didn't like thinking about that time any more than she did, if for very different reasons.

"Should I point out that I'm six months pregnant?"

"Things change."

Or he realized his brother would have been attending these appointments with Corrina from the beginning. Once again, he was competing in the husband stakes.

But since she'd always craved having him by her side for the doctor appointments, she simply said, "Okay."

He gave her a look she couldn't read, not that she tried very hard to do so. She was too busy getting her own suddenly chaotic thoughts into some kind of order.

She and Beryl went over her schedule for the day, and Polly realized Alexandros had meant business when he said he thought she was doing too much. He'd given Beryl instructions already to cancel things or go in Polly's place.

Polly didn't argue because, honestly? She was so tired today, she'd found it hard to get out of bed.

That wasn't unusual with this pregnancy, but she fought on, trying for normal.

Her OB's eyes widened and then narrowed when she realized that Polly's husband was with her.

They'd met only once before. When Polly had given birth to Helena. And it had not been a mutual admiration society then. Dr. Hope had been less than impressed when the father-to-be hadn't shown up until the final few minutes, having come after receiving the call he'd asked for.

One of the bodyguards, who was keeping tabs on what was happening in the birthing suite had let Alexandros know when it was time for Polly to start pushing.

Polly hadn't been alone though.

Alexandros had made it possible for her parents to come over from the States to stay the last two weeks of Polly's pregnancy. Her mom had been with her every minute and her dad in and out of her room during Polly's long labor.

Her father had returned to his job a week after Helena's birth, but her mom had remained another month. All at Alexandros's request, she reminded herself.

Considering how often her OB had suggested Polly cut back on her schedule, she probably should have expected Dr. Hope to tell Alexandros off for how tired Polly was, how she was clearly not being taken care of like she needed.

But the litany of reminders of how many ways in which Polly did *not* get the TLC she so desperately craved from her husband came as an unwelcome shock.

And in a wholly unexpected moment of out of control emotion, Polly ranted, "I don't know why everyone has to rub in the fact that my husband doesn't care enough about me to take even the most rudimentary care! Don't you think I know that? I'm doing the best I can."

Only maybe she wasn't. Maybe Polly needed to take

a step back from her pride and let some of Alexandros's money do what he wasn't ever going to. Take care of her.

Dr. Hope looked pained. "I know *you* are, Polly." She cast a very pointed look at Alexandros.

"I do not think she was saying these things to rub it in as you say, *yineka mou*. She was saying them to me, to tell me what a selfish louse I've been, so maybe if enough people say it, I will *listen*."

"You're not a louse." Though sometimes she thought of him as a rat. Was that any different?

Polly turned her head away, because looking at her husband hurt right then, and she'd thought she'd come to terms with the limitations of their relationship. But he was rewriting the rules and she just didn't know why.

The rest of the visit went better with Alexandros asking all the questions any concerned husband and second time father-to-be might do. Dr. Hope unbent enough to answer every question patiently and without further condemnation.

Polly waited until they were in the car, the privacy window closed between them and the driver to ask, "Why are you being so nice to me? I just don't understand."

Then she had such a horrible, terrible thought, she couldn't breathe for a few seconds. The one area of her marriage she'd never worried about, was suddenly in doubt. The one thing she thought they got right. Maybe wasn't right anymore.

She didn't know why she'd never worried about it before. Maybe because he'd always been such an attentive lover. Maybe because he'd told her he abhorred infidelity and she had believed him. Maybe because she simply had never been able to imagine him as a cliché... The powerful tycoon philanderer.

But right now, with him acting so strangely, with her hormones and emotions all over the place from her pregnancy... Polly did wonder.

Sitting up straight, her body rigid with stress, she accused, "You've taken a pillow friend. That's what you Greek tycoons call them, isn't it? You've got a mistress and you don't want me to divorce you when I find out!"

"No." He looked like he wanted to laugh, but then seemed to all of a sudden realize she was very serious and how bad that was for their marriage. "No! Polly, you are the only woman I have touched intimately since our first date."

"Can I believe you?"

"Have I ever lied to you?"

"Yes." Pain of an entirely different kind racked her pregnant body. "Your sister warned me, but I thought she was talking nonsense. Trying to hurt me like she found such sport back when I used to let her get to me."

Alexandros could not believe what he was hearing. "I have failed spectacularly in the husband stakes, but I have *never* lied to you."

He could not even deal with what she was saying about how Stacia had treated her because the fact his wife did not trust him was instantly, glaringly obvious. This was not hormonal raving. Pollyanna did not believe him.

"You have," she disagreed.

"When?"

"When you asked me to marry you. You said you would do anything you had to to make me happy."

And clearly in her mind, he hadn't. "I thought giving you anything you wanted would make you happy."

"But you don't. Not the things that matter."

And finally, after five years, he might be starting to understand the distinction. "I'm working on it."

"But you lied then. You lied when you said you loved me."

"I did not lie. I just didn't understand what I needed to do to keep those words true. And I do love you."

She laughed like that was a great joke, only she didn't sound happy about it.

"You are my wife, by *my* choice. I am not lying." The words sounded hollow to his own ears as he realized just how stopped up the ears were they were falling on.

"A man does not treat a woman the way you've treated me when he's in love with her." Pollyanna sounded so certain in her own mind, so sure of her interpretation of the years of their marriage he knew denial would be useless.

He said it anyway. "A man too focused on his business and keeping peace within his extended family does."

A man still grieving the loss of his father and afraid of how close he'd come to losing his mother. Despite how much he wanted to fix what was broken, those words would not leave his lips. Alexandros had never been an emotionally vulnerable person.

It was not his nature.

It was not how his bigger-than-life father had taught him to be.

Unimpressed with the words he had managed to utter, Pollyanna shrugged, turning her head away, and he knew the words again had fallen on deaf ears.

Or maybe they had been the wrong ones.

"I will change," he promised. Had already started changing, but he didn't expect her to trust that.

"Not on my account."

"Naturally on your account, but on mine too. I want what we had in the beginning."

"It's dead."

He didn't believe that, but clearly he hadn't just failed, he'd destroyed the fragile bonds of trust between them. All right. Okay. He'd taken over businesses that looked like they could never be revived. Some of those companies were his biggest earners now.

Let the rescue bid for his marriage commence.

* * *

When they were going over her schedule during breakfast on Wednesday, without another unexpected turn-up of Alexandros, Beryl told Polly not to worry about preparing for travel to her appointments with the doctors that Alexandros had set up.

Apparently, he had arranged for the appointments to take place at the mansion. There was already a massage table in the room off their personal gym, used by both her and Alexandros's personal trainers.

She wondered if Alexandros knew that Polly had stopped seeing her personal trainer the second month of her current pregnancy.

And then reminded herself she didn't care. Polly did what she had to in order to keep the peace, but no more. She'd built a life for herself in Greece that resembled the life he expected her to lead, but was not actually that life.

Except for a very superficial resemblance.

She was on charity committees, but not the flavor of the month, only the ones that really resonated with her. Most did not have the wherewithal to throw the glittery balls her mother and sister-in-law were so fond of. She'd made friends from those charities, not others from Alexandros's set, but normal people who cared enough to *sacrifice* time and money for causes they believed in.

Polly wore designer clothes and used a car and driver like Alexandros insisted. But she donated from her wardrobe twice yearly to charity auctions and only bought exactly what she would need for each season. Her walk-in closet never getting more than half-full. Her driver was a retired veteran with a disability that still allowed him to drive, but not a lot else to earn a living. Her car was the same one bought for her use the first year she married Alexandros.

Alexandros arranged for a new car for her every other

year and she donated them for the use of the directors of the charities she knew needed them most.

Polly attended only the functions with her husband that she could not get out of and never gave up dinnertime with her daughter. She didn't fight about it; she simply didn't show up, and her husband had learned that time with their daughter was sacrosanct to Polly.

She wasn't unhappy. She loved being a mom. Loved her husband even if she knew he did not really love her. She *did* believe he was faithful. That moment in the car had been all pregnancy hormones, but he'd taken her seriously and that in itself had been a novel experience.

It had also cemented the belief she already had that he would not take a mistress.

No matter what Stacia said, Alexandros Kristalakis was not the type to keep a pillow friend.

He never broke his word on purpose. She didn't trust him, not because she thought he lied to get what he wanted but because he lied without meaning to, and that was in her view even more dangerous.

Polly knew that she and Helena were important to him, if not of utmost importance.

It was more than a lot of women had.

Maybe not all that Polly had wanted, or even believed she had when she agreed to marry the Greek tycoon, but not a bad life.

She looked across the table at her daughter and smiled. No, not a bad life at all.

Polly and Helena were in their saltwater pool, playing before lunch, when the sound of an arriving helicopter sent Polly's gaze winging upward.

It was Alexandros's helicopter, but she was sure he wasn't on it. It must be the transportation he'd arranged for the doctors. Her appointments weren't for another two hours though. Perhaps they needed time to set up?

She could have cut her time in the water with her daughter short, but there was a housekeeper to meet them and make sure they had what they needed.

Going back to the game intended to increase her daughter's comfort with putting her face under the water for swimming, Polly dismissed the arriving helicopter from her mind.

"Now, that is a beautiful sight." Humor and masculine appreciation filled her husband's voice.

Startled into immobility, Polly stared at the apparition standing on the pool deck. "Alexandros! What are you doing here?"

At the same time as she spoke, her daughter realized who was there and tried to leap away from her mother and toward her father, arms outstretched. "Papa!"

Six feet four inches of sartorial masculine gorgeousness leaned toward his daughter like the effect of salt water on his suit was of no concern.

Swooping Helena up as a maid strategically wrapped a towel around the little girl, he gave Polly a slashing grin. "I'm having lunch with my two favorite females and then working the rest of the day from home."

Like a landed fish, Polly stood there her mouth opening and closing, but with no words making their way past her lips. What was he doing here? His favorite females? Really?

"Not if your mom and sister are in the running." Polly snapped her mouth shut so hard, her teeth clicked.

She had not meant to say that. Hadn't made a comment like that since before Helena's birth. Not after he'd told her that the world did not revolve around her, that Polly would have to get over her *unnatural* jealousy of his family if their marriage was going to work.

Instead of getting angry as he used to do, her husband gave her another heart-stopping smile. "There is no competition, *yineka mou*. You are my wife and Helena is my daughter. No one is more important to me."

"Since when?"

But he just smiled again, shook his head and said, "Are you getting out? I thought Helena needed lunch so she could nap."

"She does, of course. We were only playing for ten more minutes."

"By all means, stay in the water. I like the view."

She looked down at her pregnancy-distended belly in the simple, but bright one-piece Polly had purchased for swimming in her final months before their baby's birth. What was there about this view for him to like? In *that* way? Because he was giving her a look over their daughter's shoulder that sent sensations she preferred to keep confined to their nights in bed together zinging through her body.

Regardless, the opportunity to swim a few laps without having to watch her daughter was all too appealing. Polly spent as much time in the pool as she could because it relieved the pressure in both her lower back and pelvis.

"If you're sure you're okay with her?" she asked him.

"Of course."

She didn't ask again, just turned and took a standing dive into the water, pushing for the other end of the pool.

Reveling in the freedom to swim unencumbered, Polly did a few leisurely laps before climbing out of the pool and grabbing a towel. She could have stayed in longer, but she couldn't stay away from the sweet tableau of father—suit jacket and tie now missing—and daughter—wearing her little terry cover-up—talking earnestly on one of the loungers closest to the pool edge.

Polly hated breaking it up, but she had to, or the sweet little girl would turn into a hungry, tired little terror. "Time to get dressed for lunch, poppet."

"But Mama…" Helena whined.

And Polly knew that tone. Definitely time for lunch and then nap.

"Come. Dora will help you dress while I help Mama."

"You're going to help me get dressed?" Polly asked delicately.

The heated look that came her way made her really wish they didn't have plans to eat with their daughter in a matter of minutes. *"Ne."*

Alexandros carried Helena inside and up the stairs, handing her off to Dora when they reached the landing and putting his arm around Polly to walk her to their bedroom.

"Why did you come home again today?" she asked breathlessly as they stepped inside the sanctuary.

He turned her around to face him. "Because I wanted to." Then he kissed her and she forgot the question and everything else. Just that quickly.

It was always like this. Polly could not resist the physical temptation of her husband. Not for a kiss, or for more. She never had been able to. Even more, she could not resist the emotional connection she felt to him during times of physical intimacy.

She knew it didn't go both ways or he could not spend as much time traveling as he did.

Because if it was up to Polly she would never have willingly spent a single night away from him.

He pulled her still-damp body right against him, letting her feel how quickly he had responded to the kiss. His hardness pressed against her and she wanted nothing more than to move to the bed so she could explore the hard male body she found such delight in.

Clever masculine fingers were peeling her swimsuit down her arms, exposing her breasts. Already beaded nipples tightened nearly painfully as the air brushed cool against wet skin.

He cursed before cupping her. "You are so beautiful."

"Pregnant," she said wryly. "Fat."

"Ypérochos, énkyos, dikos mou."

When they'd first married, she hadn't spoken any Greek, but she'd taken pains to learn. Because now she lived in

Greece and it made communication easier, but mostly? Because he used Greek in bed and she'd wanted to know if he was saying he loved her. He didn't, but he did say stuff like this and it went straight to her heart.

Gorgeous. Pregnant. Mine.

"Yours." She had no problem admitting a truth she'd never been able to hide.

"Dikos mou. Gia pánta."

Forever? Yes, she supposed she was, but she didn't say it. "We have to get dressed," she said with real regret.

"I need to get *un*dressed and you need a shower," he corrected.

But she shook her head. "I'll have to shower after lunch. We're going to be late to the table as it is."

"We can phone down. Dora can see to Helena's lunch, *yineka mou.*"

"No. Our daughter is expecting us." Helena saw less of her father because of her sleep schedule than Polly saw of her husband. "It wouldn't be fair to her."

"And what of us? Is it fair to eat lunch when we want each other so much?"

"Didn't you once tell me that anticipation made it all the better?" He'd been talking about the nights they had to spend apart, when they both missed their physical intimacy. "If we're fast, we can share a shower after lunch and before my appointments."

"We will take as long as we need *after* lunch with our daughter."

And presumably the doctors could wait on the billionaire and his wife. Polly simply shook her head again. She could argue polite behavior after lunch too.

Helena was excitable over lunch, showing off for her papa and pushing to stay up and play rather than take her nap. "But I not tired, Mama."

"You need your rest, poppet."

"But Papa will be gone when I wakes up." Helena burst into floods of tears.

Before Polly could pull her cumbersome body to her feet to go around the table to comfort her daughter, Alexandros had said a not very nice word beneath his breath and leaped to his feet. He pulled their daughter into his arms and promised in both Greek and English that he *would* be there when she woke from her nap.

Helena's sobs only increased and Alexandros looked at Polly, his expression stunned.

"I don't know why she's crying like this," Polly admitted, hating that helpless feeling that was such a normal part of parenting.

Their daughter kept chanting *Mama*, but when Polly got up and came around the table to take her, she clung to Alexandros with all the strength in her little body.

"Come now, *agape mou*. This crying is not productive. Tell us what is wrong."

Polly covered the smile on her mouth at the business speak leveled at their three-year-old, but it was all she could do not to laugh.

"I don't want prod-i-vive," their daughter wailed.

That was it. Polly bust out laughing, and both father and daughter gave her matching looks of outrage. The wails stopped though.

She tried to get control of herself, but the giggles kept coming.

"Why is Mama laughing? I was crying." Oh, Helena sounded so offended by that turn of events.

"I do not know why she is laughing any more than I know why you were crying," the great Alexandros Kristalakis admitted in a driven tone.

CHAPTER FOUR

HELENA'S FACE CRUMPLED, but she didn't start crying again. "Why you here, Papa?"

"Because he wants to be," Polly forced out between her inappropriate but cleansing humor.

The tension that had been building throughout lunch—and she wasn't even sure why—was gone.

"You sound very sure." The sarcasm was thick in her husband's tone.

But Polly just shrugged, finally getting her laughter under control and returning to her seat. If she didn't sound too confident it was because she herself had no clue why her husband was there for lunch for the second day in a row, with the unprecedented promise to work from home for the rest of the day, when he had never come home early in five years of marriage.

Alexandros frowned at Polly, but assured their daughter. "Yes. I want to be."

"Is Mama sick?" Helena asked her father fearfully.

"No, remember, I explained, honey? Mommy is just making your baby brother in her tummy. I'm not sick."

"But Papa is here."

"Yes." Polly didn't know what that had to do with her being sick.

"Lunch is for Mama and dinner is for Papa."

Polly tilted her head to the side. "But, Helena, your father is here during lunch on the weekends. Sometimes."

Alexandros winced at the *sometimes*. "I will be here more. I miss you and your mama, *koritsi mou*."

That was news to Polly. And she wasn't sure she believed it.

Their daughter looked no more convinced. "Faire's mama got sick and her papa had to take care of her."

"Who is Faire?" Alexandros asked, in what she thought was focus on the wrong thing entirely.

"One of your daughter's friends from playgroup," Polly answered before meeting her daughter's shimmering eyes. "I'm not sick, sweetheart. I promise."

"But Papa is here during the day. He's not here for the daytimes. He comes for bedtime. You are here during the daytimes. I don't want you to go away, Mama!" her daughter wailed, and then burst into tears all over again.

Alexandros placed Helena on Polly's diminished six-months-pregnant lap and then dropped to his knees so he could put his arms around them both. "No one is going anywhere. Mama is not sick," he said, adding his promises to Polly's, assuring their daughter that everything was all right and he was never going to let anything happen to her mama.

It took a while, but they got Helena settled down for her nap. In bed between Polly and Alexandros. It was not the first time they'd shared a family cuddle, but those times were rare. Polly couldn't even miss the intimacy she and Alexandros had been planning, because the moment was so special.

Besides, she needed her rest too and didn't fight her eyes closing. "Wake me in time for the doctor appointments," she instructed her husband, who was no doubt going to take off and start working as soon as she fell asleep.

Only he was lying beside her when she woke, their daughter still asleep between them.

Feeling more refreshed than she had upon waking that morning, Polly smiled at him. "You're still here."

"The fact that my being in the vicinity is such a shock for both you and our daughter does not speak well of my presence in either of your lives."

Polly had no experience with her husband in self-examination mode. She wanted to comfort him, but his words were no less than the truth.

"No denials?" he asked, his expression troubled.

"Your business and family have always come first."

"You two are my family."

"Of course, but—"

"There is no but. You and Helena are the only family I could not live without. Don't you know that?"

"Um, no, not really." And just because he said the words didn't make them true. Even if he believed them, because his actions had said otherwise. Over and over again.

"And you do not believe me now," he said, showing that he was still in that disturbingly insightful mood.

"Not really, no." There was no point lying. He'd know, and besides, dishonesty wasn't her style. Except when she told him she was fine when she wasn't, and she had her reasons—maybe even conditioning—for doing that.

"Watch this space." With that, he climbed off the bed coming around to help her up. "Come on, *agape mou*. Time for your appointments, chiropractic first."

More surprises awaited her as he insisted on attending both appointments with her, asking first the chiropractor and then the acupuncturist if there were things they could do to help her with the pain and nausea. Both doctors suggested weekly visits along with herbs and naturopathic solutions that would not impact her pregnancy negatively.

Alexandros only left when the acupuncturist explained that her treatment would be most efficacious if Polly spent time in peaceful contemplation with the acupuncture needles in place. She'd been shocked she had not even felt them going in and that they caused no discomfort at all as she lay, comfortably supported by pillows on the massage therapy table.

Soft piano music played in the background, the herbs the acupuncturist had used to further stimulate the flow of her energy giving off a soothing scent.

An hour later, Polly sat in a lounger by the pool, sipping water and watching her husband encourage their daughter to work on her swimming tech... for the first time in weeks, Polly ... risk that happy condition.

So, when her daughter asked Polly ... maced but went to stand anyway.

However, Alexandros waved her back o... "Relax, *agape mou*. You can swim with us and... doctor said you needed to drink your water."

"All right." She relaxed back, wondering *if* there would be another day, as she took another sip of water under his watchful gaze.

Even on the weekends, time together as a family in the pool didn't usually happen. That was something that she and Helena shared during the day, during the week. Like so many things.

That weekend, they hosted their first family luncheon. Petros and Corrina arrived with Athena and Stacia in the helicopter but reached the house ahead of the two women.

"You look lovely and fresh today, Polly," Petros complimented after giving her a buss on both cheeks. "Where is my niece?"

"I put her down for an early nap, so she would be at her best when your mother and sister arrive." Polly turned to Corrina and hugged her. "I think married life is agreeing with you. You look wonderful."

Corrina was dressed in casual summer elegance, but it was the happy glow about the Greek heiress who had gone to school in England that brought a smile to Polly's own features.

"And you don't look nearly so tired as the last time I saw you. How are you feeling?"

"Really well. I've had a second session with the chiropractor, and both he and the acupuncturist are coming back in a couple of days."

...grinned. "I'm still gobsmacked that Alexandros ...ged all that."

"Would my brother not do whatever was in his power to make sure you were as comfortable as possible if you were pregnant with his child?" Alexandros asked chidingly, showing he'd been listening even if it had looked like he was busy greeting his brother.

Corrina blushed, giving Polly a *caught* look. She smiled charmingly up at Alexandros. "Of course, but holistic medicine? Really?"

"It's been working for people for millennia."

"Well, of course…" Corrina let her voice trail off, clearly not sure what to say.

"It's working for me now." Polly laid her hand on Alexandros's arm. "I feel better than I have since getting pregnant."

He stilled and then slid his own arm around her waist in a jerky movement that was unlike his usual graceful self, pulling her so close, her entire side pressed into him.

She gasped, impacted by the touch far more than she should be. Pregnancy hormones.

As if he knew she was feeling things she shouldn't be in company, he turned her to face him and slashed a knowing smile down at her. "Feeling all right, *pethi mou*?"

Swallowing, she nodded.

He leaned his head down as if he was going to kiss her. In front of his brother!

But he frowned instead when his mother's voice came from the doorway to the drawing room.

"Stop pawing your wife in that common manner, and come greet your mother, Alexandros," Athena demanded imperiously. "I was surprised no one was outside waiting to greet our arrival."

The animation drained right out of his wife and she shifted, as if trying to step away from Alexandros.

But he had no intention of letting her go. "Not just yet," he said to her.

"What? But…" Pollyanna stared up at him, like he'd grown two heads. "Your mother wants you."

"And I want a kiss." He didn't wait for his wife to answer, but lowered his head and claimed her mouth.

With purpose. He wanted the life back, and in this, she always gave him spark.

For the count of three full seconds, Pollyanna did not respond at all, but then she relaxed against him and returned his kiss.

"Really, Alexandros, kissing your pregnant wife in company."

Pollyanna went stiff at his sister's snide tone, and Alexandros allowed her to step back when she pressed against his chest, pulling her head away from his. Ignoring both his mother and his sister for the moment, he cupped Pollyanna's cheek. "I find you irresistible, *agape mou*, but I'll keep. Did you want to go get Helena?"

Pollyanna nodded, her expression a cross between confusion and wary happiness.

He turned to face his sister and spoke before Pollyanna had a chance to leave the room. "I will kiss my *beautiful* wife where I like and in whatever company I find myself. Acting like a jealous cat because you don't have someone interested in doing the same with you only makes you look petty."

He flicked a glance over his shoulder and noticed that Pollyanna had a spring in her step as she crossed the drawing room that was rarely there in his mother and/or sister's company.

"How can you say something like that to me?" Stacia demanded, wounded eyes filling with tears.

Five years ago? He would have fallen for it and jumped in to apologize and promise she was still his number one girl. They'd both been grieving the loss of their dear papa, and he'd felt his new role as head of the family keenly.

Alexandros had grown older and hopefully wiser. He now realized that playing into his baby sister's need to be center of attention had done damage to his marriage and the way his wife perceived him. And he didn't think he'd done Stacia any favors either.

"I can say it because it is true. Keep a civil tongue in your head when you are here or you won't be invited back."

"You don't mean that," Stacia yelped. "You wouldn't exclude me from the family."

"I should have excluded you from socializing with my wife a long time ago." And how he was only realizing that in this moment did not speak well of his intelligence. "You are on notice. Take heed, or you will find more than just your social life curtailed in relation to me."

"What are you saying?" Stacia asked, her voice pitching.

"That you are old enough to find a job, if not a career, and your allowance is now on the bubble. A bubble that will burst if your behavior does not remarkably improve."

"I do not know what that wife of yours has been saying to you, Alexandros," his mother butted in. "But Stacia is your sister and calling her a jealous cat for being uncomfortable with an inappropriate public display of affection is not what I expect from you."

"There is nothing inappropriate about kissing my wife," he told his mother curtly. "And I stand by my warning." He gave Stacia a look. "Heed it."

His mother's mouth pursed with disapproval. "Your father left you head of the family and your sister is your responsibility."

For once, he didn't overlay the expression on her face with his own fear of her emotional fragility and saw his mother's attitude for what it was. Damaging to his wife.

And that would no longer be tolerated.

His mother had grieved the loss of his father, but just

like all of them, she'd grown stronger and more able to deal
with her pain.

Now was the time to let her know she didn't get to visit
her disappointment that he had not married a Greek social-
ite on his wife. Ever again.

"One. Let's be clear. My wife hasn't said anything. Two.
My sister is an adult, not a child. Three. If you want to take
care of her monetary extravagances out of your own income,
no one is stopping you."

"How dare you talk to me like this? You still have not
even bothered greeting me. I raised you with more manners."

He walked forward and kissed both his mother's cheeks,
then stepped back. *"Kalimera."*

"That is better."

He looked down at her, letting her see his expression
was not a happy one. "Good. Now, make sure your daughter stays polite and we will all be happy."

Helena came running into the room, making a beeline
for Petros. "Uncle Petros, Uncle Petros!"

His brother swung the toddler up and asked how her
nap was.

Helena shrugged, the movement so like something he
would do that, not for the first time, Alexandros thought his
wife had her hands full raising a child so like *him.*

"I slept," Helena informed her uncle.

"Would you like to say hello to your *yia-yia*?"

Helena tightened her hold on Petros, but nodded. Her
usual vibrancy dimmed some, just as his wife's did, as his
daughter looked at the older woman.

Why? He'd watched Helena interact with his mother. She
was not afraid of her *yia-yia*, but she also wasn't enamored
of her. And this was not normal for a Greek grandmother
and her granddaughter, especially not his family. Alexandros could remember himself, his brother and their sister
adoring their grandparents.

Helena should be thrilled to see her doting *yia-yia*.

Was it possible that Helena's relationship with her *yia-yia* had been impacted by his mother's less than approving attitude toward the little girl's beloved mom?

His daughter gave her grandmother a kiss of greeting on each cheek, accepting the same in return, but made no move to leave her favored uncle's arms to offer any further affectionate overtures. And Petros did not offer the child over either.

Neither did his mother reach for Helena.

In the past, he would have explained this response as a result of his wife's attitude toward his mother, and as such would have had a talk with his wife, expecting her to *fix* it. But recent insights had made him less quick to jump to that as the solution.

He would watch the way his mother, and his sister, interacted with his daughter.

And over the course of the next hours, he noticed things he had never noticed before.

Not only in the way his mother and sister related to his daughter, but in the very established patterns of their behavior toward his wife.

Even after the very serious warning he'd given his sister, she poked at Pollyanna, though admittedly without ever crossing the line to actual rudeness. Many of her comments had more than one meaning so she could claim easy deniability in the intent to offend.

"I don't understand why we couldn't keep dinners as they were. It's tradition. If Anna isn't up to joining us, surely you could have come on your own," Stacia said to him as they all relaxed on the terrace with after-luncheon drinks.

Pollyanna, though dressed as elegantly for lunch as the other women, played on the lawn with their daughter, Petros and Corrina joining them for a game of croquet that Alexandros realized he regretted not being a part of.

Every time it was Helena's turn to swing the mallet

nearly as tall as she was, Petros stepped in to help her. On Helena's first turn, Pollyanna had moved as if to help, but Petros had said something and done so. No doubt realizing a pregnant woman didn't need to be bending over a toddler trying to navigate the mallet swing.

And Alexandros realized he wanted to be there, his arms around his daughter, playing with his family.

"She is my wife, which makes Pollyanna part of this family. Excluding her from family dinners because of her pregnancy, of all things, seems to defeat the purpose, don't you think?" They were Greek. They were Kristalakis. Family was paramount.

How did his sister think it was even acceptable to ask such a question?

His father would turn in his grave if he knew the attitude Stacia had toward the mother of the family's first grandchild of this generation.

"Your father started the tradition of family dinners on Sunday when I expressed a desire to have a set time for our family to be together, no matter what business the week might include," his mother said wistfully. "It is not so easy to give up something that makes me feel like he is still with us."

A week ago, Alexandros would have given in immediately to the subtle guilt trip, but he was on a rescue bid for *his* marriage and his parents' traditions could not supersede what was best for him and his wife.

Stacia and his mother wore twin expressions of expectation as they looked at him. Like they had no doubt his mother's words would change his mind about the new order of things.

"You and the rest of the family are still welcome to have your Sunday evening dinners, but I am a married man with a child and I should have stopped attending when Helena was born. Naturally, my wife and child should come first for me, should always have come first."

"You and your wife do not need to live in each other's pockets," his mother chided gently.

"Is that what you told my father? Only I remember you being very adamant that he spend those Sunday evenings with us, even if he was too busy the rest of the week."

His mother said nothing, her expression startled. Like she hadn't expected him to argue.

"Or are you implying that my wife and my daughter should be less important to me than you and our family were to my father?" he asked, beginning to realize the answer to that question was not always what he had assumed it was.

Alexandros had always believed that his mother respected his marriage and role as a father because of the expectations she had placed on his own father. Because family was *everything*.

But then, had he treated his wife and daughter like they were everything to him?

He wasn't sure he wanted to acknowledge the true answer to that question either.

"Of course I am not implying that," his mother said, but with a lack of conviction even Alexandros at his most blind could not have missed.

"Why didn't you ever suggest a change to our family dinners so you could see your granddaughter on a weekly basis?" he asked his mother.

"I already told you, I found our Sunday dinners a sentimental gathering I did not want to do without."

"Not even if it meant seeing your only grandchild?"

"Your wife could have arranged to bring the baby to visit," Stacia said with clear criticism.

"Surely it would have been easier for you to visit here," Alexandros said to his mother. "You were the one who suggested I move my pregnant wife out of the busy crowds of Athens."

He'd agreed because he'd thought that moving his wife

out of the family home would circumvent the tension that existed between his mother and his wife.

Pollyanna had not reacted as he'd expected her to, accusing him of wanting to exile her to the country, of isolating her from the friends she'd managed to make despite the best efforts of his mother and sister in undermining her place in Athens society.

He'd dismissed the arguments as the result of pregnancy hormones and made it clear he would not tolerate her ongoing, and unnecessary, jealousy of his mother and sister.

Pollyanna was his wife.

There had been no need for her to be jealous of his family.

Or so he had believed.

"I still expected your wife to make the effort to share her daughter with us."

"Which she does." Once a month Pollyanna took Helena on the two-hour car ride to have tea with her grandmother. Alexandros did his best to join them when his schedule permitted.

Which admittedly wasn't as often as he now realized it should have been.

"So, why did we have to change family dinners?" Stacia asked, whining in a way that had been annoying when she was a teen and in adult woman was entirely unpleasant.

"We changed family dinners because if you want to share the time with me *and* my family, you will do so here and during the afternoon," Alexandros said implacably.

Neither his mother, nor his sister looked pleased by that response.

Had they always been this difficult?

Or had his policy of giving in to them to keep the peace blinded him to how intransigent and selfish both women could be?

Deciding he'd spent enough time discussing a situation that was not going to change, he stood up and excused himself so he could join the croquet players. Swooping in to scoop his daughter up, he swung her up in the air, loving her joy-filled laughter.

Polly smiled at the way her daughter responded to attention from her father.

Helena adored her papa and Alexandros was a very hands-on dad when he was around. She was really glad to see that having his mother and sister here for lunch did not mean he would ignore his daughter for them.

Weekends were the only time Helena really got to play with her beloved papa, and Polly would have hated to see some of those hours lost because of the change to the Kristalakis once a week family gathering.

On Helena's next turn it was Alexandros who knelt beside his daughter, coaching her on the use of the mallet to tap the ball.

"I see how it is," Petros teased. "You saw Helena was winning and decided to horn in on the spoils of her victory."

"We are an unbeatable team, aren't we *koritsi mou*?" Alexandros asked his daughter.

Helena grinned up at her papa and then her uncle. "We're going to beat you, Uncle Petros."

Polly grinned at her daughter's arrogance, so like her father's. If anyone wondered how she still loved her husband after five years of marriage that had opened her eyes to how unimportant she was to him, all they had to do was look at Helena. How could Polly not love the man who had given her such a beautiful daughter?

More viscerally, how could Polly not love the man who was so like the child that she adored with every fiber of her being?

She saw the best of her husband in her daughter every day.

"Oh-ho, I see how it is. Now that your papa is here to play on your team, Uncle Petros is chopped liver."

Helena's tiny little face screwed up in disgust. "I do not like liver, Uncle Petros." She shivered dramatically and adorably, and looked up at Corrina. "It's yucky."

Corrina laughed. "You're right about that, Helena."

"Liver is good for you." His mother's voice from just behind Polly told her that the wicked witches of the west had joined them on the lawn.

Polly moved so she was on the other side of Petros without even thinking before she did it. When she could, she avoided even proximity with her mother or sister-in-law.

Alexandros whispered something into his daughter's ear that made Helena laugh and then they took their turn, neither one responding to his mother's quelling pronouncement.

"I hope you do not allow your daughter to dictate the food served her because she finds it *yucky*," Athena said to Polly with that superior tone she liked to take. "A child cannot be allowed to determine what is best for her."

"My daughter's diet is balanced and varied," Polly replied mildly.

"It was not as if *you* had anything to say about what we ate as children, Mama. That was entirely the nanny's purview."

Had those words come from Petros, Polly would only have been slightly surprised, but the fact her husband had made the comment that could be taken as standing up for *her* was downright shocking.

Her mother-in-law looked every bit as astonished as Polly felt. "Alexandros, naturally, your nanny acted on my instruction."

"If you say so, but no one of any intelligence would question the care my wife takes of our daughter. She is an exemplary mother in every aspect of that role."

Warmth burgeoned in Polly's chest, pleasure at that unequivocal vote of confidence from her husband filling her to bursting.

"I'm sure I wasn't questioning her mothering skills," Athena said repressively.

"I don't want to play anymore," Helena said from the circle of her father's arms.

"Why not?" he asked her.

"It's not fun now."

Out of the mouths of babes. Athena joined them and sucked the fun right out of the game, but Polly honestly didn't think her mother-in-law meant to do it. She was just so used to taking digs at Polly, she didn't realize the damage she was doing to her relationship with her granddaughter.

Polly had seen how Athena wanted to have a warmer relationship with Helena, but seemed incapable of understanding how to make that happen.

"Why don't we get out your Match the Cards game? Your *yia-yia* likes to play that with you," Polly suggested to her daughter. Then she turned a conciliatory smile on her husband. "She's probably getting tired."

But Alexandros frowned at his mother. "I do not think that is the problem."

Athena's expression showed vulnerable confusion, and Polly couldn't help feeling sorry for the older woman. So many of her machinations had led to final outcomes that were not to the widow's liking.

A doted-on heiress and then spoiled wife, Athena was used to getting what she wanted from the people in her life.

It had taken a while for both Polly and Athena to realize that Athena's attempt at excluding Polly from her social circle had backfired on her.

Polly had sought friendship with like-minded people, building the only kind of relationships she knew how. Real and based on shared ideas and attitudes. Those types of relationships engendered loyalty, both from her and the people she shared them with.

So, when Polly avoided social situations that would put her in proximity to Alexandros's mother or sister, her new friends noticed. And they stopped inviting those two women to whatever the event was if they wanted Polly to come.

She didn't join committees or charities which Athena or Stacia were attached to, and the same happened.

Athena had once accused her of doing it on purpose, but Polly hadn't. She wasn't petty.

No matter how her mother-in-law or sister-in-law had treated her, she had not set out to exclude them. However, by avoiding as many occasions as possible where she had to deal with being sniped at and undermined, it had happened inevitably. And honestly? It had made her life more pleasant.

But it had not been on purpose.

No more than this cooler relationship between her daughter and her *yia-yia* had been. Polly wanted Athena to enjoy the same pleasure of time spent with Helena as Polly's mom did.

But despite the fact that Polly's family only saw Helena a few times a year, the toddler adored them in a way she did *not* her *yia-yia* and Theia Stacia.

Because children might not understand the why, but they still picked up on the tension between the adults around them.

Polly was Helena's person. She was the one grown-up that Helena had trusted since infancy to always be there, to soothe, to play, to care for her.

Over time the fact that Athena made no effort to hide her disdain for her daughter-in-law in her granddaughter's presence, that attitude eventually affected the amount of trust Helena gave Athena and how much pleasure she found in her *yia-yia*'s company.

Still, Polly did what she could to facilitate the relationship because ultimately, her daughter deserved it.

Polly put her hand to her lower back, rubbing a little. "I'm tired, even if our daughter isn't. I wouldn't mind watching you all play." Though she felt much better since her chiropractic appointment, playing croquet had maybe not been her best choice.

She did not expect what happened next. How could she?

But Alexandros passed their daughter over to Petros and then swept Polly up into his arms. "Of course you are tired. What were you doing playing croquet in your condition?"

Avoiding his mother and his sister.

"I'm pregnant, not an invalid," she said as millennia of women no doubt had been saying before her to their macho, overprotective spouses.

Not that she would have ever described Alexandros as overprotective before, but apparently this pregnancy was bringing out his more basic nature.

"Papa is carrying Mommy," her daughter pronounced in shocked delight and then let loose a peal of laughter.

Polly found herself smiling at her daughter's clear amusement and noticed that Alexandros was smiling as well. He looked down at her, and their gazes caught, his smile turning sensual, hers growing intimate.

"Watch where you are going, brother, or you are going to trip and drop your pregnant wife." Petros's voice was laced with overt amusement.

Alexandros stopped, giving Polly a heart-stopping look. "He is right, but I find looking away from you a challenge."

"I could always walk on my own," she teased, when she had not felt like teasing him in a very long time.

His arms tightened around her. "No chance."

"You've grown very protective all of a sudden," she said just a little breathlessly.

"I have always wanted to protect you."

She winced and looked away. What was she supposed to say to that? He'd done a rotten job practically from the beginning, and for a man who prided himself on always getting it right, that had always said something to her. Something very negative about any chance that the man she married had really loved her and not just her body.

He cursed under his breath. A really basic word he *never* said in her presence much less his mother's.

Polly's gaze flew back to her husband's face.

"I failed utterly. That is becoming clear to me."

She shrugged. He had.

"Keep watching this space, *agape mou*. Failure is *not* in my nature."

CHAPTER FIVE

No. AND BEING compared unfavorably to his younger brother in the husband stakes was not something Alexandros would take lying down.

Polly wasn't going to complain. Even if his reasons weren't the ones she wanted, her husband was finally treating her like she was important, and that was something she'd always wanted.

She'd built a life since her marriage without the need to have that desire filled, but it had always been there.

He carried her onto the terrace and settled her on a lounge chair, bringing her a glass of juice before sitting down at the nearby table to play the matching card game with his daughter, his mother, Petros and Corrina.

Uninterested in the child's entertainment, Stacia went inside with a comment about how hard her phone was to read outside.

Why her sister-in-law needed to be on her phone during what was supposed to be Kristalakis family time, Polly did not know, but she did not mind at all that the young woman wasn't expecting Polly to entertain her.

Polly found herself dozing, the sound of her daughter's and husband's voices a pleasant buzz in the background of her mind.

She surfaced from her doze to a conversation between her mother-in-law and husband.

"It is obvious she needs more rest than she is getting," Athena said with a concern Polly could not help doubting.

What was her mother-in-law up to?

"I think Anna is rather frail physically," Athena added.

Polly frowned. She was not frail, never had been.

"She is fine. A nap does not indicate frailty," her husband assured his mother.

"I do not know. Perhaps, and this is not something I like to talk about, but you should make sure she is getting a *full* night's rest rather than keeping her up."

Polly woke fully then, so furious she could barely breathe.

Her mother-in-law was trying to drive a wedge between Polly and Alexandros in the one area of their marriage that Polly felt confident of his full attention. The bedroom.

Polly sat up and turned so her feet were on the tile and she was facing to the two people standing near her. "Where is Helena?"

"Petros and Corrina took her inside. She wanted to watch one of her movies."

Polly knew exactly which one. Helena found the animated story about the Scottish princess who fought for the right to make her own choices obsessively fascinating. Honestly, Polly loved the movie too and didn't care that it wasn't one of the most recent children's offerings.

However, right now she wasn't thinking about princesses. She had her own wicked witch to deal with.

"Alexandros?"

"Yes, *yineka mou*?" He put his hand out to help her up.

She let him lift her, though standing in her flat sandals did not put her anywhere near eye to eye with her six-foot-four-inch husband.

Tilting her head back, she gave him a gimlet stare. "I know that there have been many times you've taken your mother's opinion of what *I* need over mine."

He inclined his head, his handsome mouth firming into a line.

"If you do that in this instance, I will not be responsible for my actions," she warned him.

"This instance?" he asked, while his mother gasped in clear outrage.

"The sex thing. You will not stop having sex with me on her say-so. Do you understand me?" Even her doctor had offered that as long as it was comfortable for Polly, sex was fine.

His eyes widened in obvious shock that she would approach the topic so bluntly.

His mother was saying something about not needing to talk about something that intimate in mixed company.

Polly glared at her mother-in-law, for once doing nothing to hide her anger with the older woman. "Then perhaps you should not have brought it up to my husband. Something that is so very much not *any* of your business."

"I was only trying to look out for your well-being," Athena claimed.

"No, you were trying to drive another wedge between your son and his wife, and I warn you, I have tolerated your interference for the last time in my marriage." Where the words came from, Polly didn't know.

But she meant them. And the look she gave her husband said it wasn't just his warnings that people had better take heed to.

Yes, she'd stopped and eavesdropped outside the drawing room while texting Hero to please bring Helena downstairs.

Athena did a very good impression of a woman mortally offended. "How can you speak to me like that?"

That was a good question. When was the last time Polly had even tried to stand up to the mother-in-law from hell? Before they'd moved to this house, before the birth of her daughter. Once Polly had realized just how little positive motivation lay behind Athena's machinations and how incredibly blind to that truth Alexandros was, Polly had shifted to oblique maneuvers to avoid rather than confront what she saw as something that could not be changed.

So why confront now?

Was it that *watch this space* from her husband that had felt so much like a promise?

Or was it simply that Polly was fed up?

"I have said what I needed to say to both of you." Polly encompassed both her husband and her mother-in-law with a look that Helena could have told them meant Mommy wasn't joking around here.

Then Polly turned to go inside and find the rest of their guests.

Stacia was pacing restlessly outside the drawing room from which the sounds of the movie could be heard. "Oh, Polly, there you are. Is my mother ready to go?"

"I do not know."

"Well, I am. This coming to the country once a week is so inconvenient. I do not know why you had to go and convince Alexandros to change *our* family's traditional weekly get-together." Stacia gave Polly a less than pleasant look.

Polly just shook her head. "Alexandros already told you. The change was his idea, but you know something, Stacia? I'm just wondering, when are you going to stop sniping at me? Your brother and I are married, we are staying married and acting like a spiteful cat all the time isn't going to change that."

"He deserves better than you, and he only stayed married to you because of Helena."

"I didn't even get pregnant with Helena until after we'd been married a year. I don't know how you worked that one out."

"He was going to leave you. The move to this house was just the first step, but then you had Helena and he couldn't leave. A Greek man doesn't leave his children."

"An honorable Greek man does not leave his wife, or his children," Alexandros inserted into the conversation. "I have no idea where you got the idea that us moving to this house was in some way an indication I was finished with my marriage."

Polly met her mother-in-law's cool gaze. "I bet I can guess."

It was Alexandros's turn to shake his head. "This entire conversation is distasteful to me, and after my warning earlier I wonder, Stacia, how you thought you would get away with staging it."

"I don't think she can help herself," Polly offered. "Sniping at me has become so ingrained in her behavior, I don't think she knows how to react to me like an equal."

Alexandros made a sound of disgust. "That is not acceptable to me."

"You never cared before. I don't understand why you're acting like the fact your wife and I don't like each other matters to you now." Stacia's petulant attitude wasn't going to do her any favors with the man who was already angry.

Didn't his sister realize that?

He turned to Athena. "It is time you and Stacia left. Next week, do not bring her with you. She is no longer welcome in my home and I have paid the last installment of her allowance that she will receive from me."

"You can't do that!" Stacia screeched. "You're the head of this family. I am your responsibility."

"And if you ever manage to find someone willing to marry a shrew, I will pay for the wedding, but I'm done financially supporting a woman who treats my wife with such a lack of respect."

"I'll sue you!" she shouted.

"On what grounds?"

"Father left the company to you so you could take care of the rest of us."

"Father left each of us, including our mother, monetary assets as well as shares in the company. The fact that you ran through the lump sum you were awarded already is not my problem. The fact you cannot access your shares or the income from them until you are thirty is something you have to take up with your trustees."

"Of which you are one!"

"And not one who is going to argue for early dispersal," he said with freezing calm.

"Oh, for heaven's sake, Stacia, you are twenty-six years old, you have a university degree. Get a job," Polly told her sister-in-law.

"Just because your family is happy to grub for a living, doesn't mean I'm going to stoop to doing so," Stacia seethed. She glared at her brother. "I will sue you. You just wait."

"You will not cause that kind of scandal, Stacia." Athena only despised one thing more than her daughter-in-law. Scandal. "Your brother gave you clear warning, and now you are paying the price for not listening. Perhaps if you apologized *politely* to Anna, Alexandros would see clear to continuing your allowance."

Polly bit her lip, because she had no doubt that an apology would not cut it.

Once Alexandros got to a certain point, he was immovable. Unfortunately for Stacia, she had not realized that he'd reached that place before he'd issued the warning before lunch.

"I'm very sorry if something I said might have offended you," Stacia said to Polly with one of the volte-faces Polly had grown accustomed to over the years.

Stacia could be in the middle of a spite-filled rant at Polly and turn up all smiles as soon as Alexandros was within hearing distance.

"You offended *me*," Alexandros made clear. "Your words were meant to *hurt* my wife and your apology is not accepted. It is time for you to leave."

Both Stacia and Athena objected then, but Alexandros would not be moved. Petros came out, closing the door to the drawing room behind him. "What is going on? You are making so much noise, I could hear you over the movie."

Polly went toward the door, needing to make sure Helena wasn't upset by the altercation in the hall, but Petros put his hand up to stop her. "She's fine, totally enthralled by her warrior princess and singing along. How does she know *all* the words?"

"She's got her father's memory." And Helena had seen the movie multiple times.

With Polly. She could sing all the words too and would rather be doing that right now than arguing with Athena and Stacia. Not that Polly was arguing at all. She'd just been trying get calmer heads to prevail. No such luck though.

Alexandros was in pure head-of-the-family, my-word-is-law mode and his mother and sister, unused to him telling them no about anything were in screeching, this-can't-be-happening mode.

Athena and Stacia tripped all over each other to tell Petros what was happening, both women somehow managing to make it sound like Polly had started it all, when in fact she had started nothing. Alexandros took immediate exception to the implications and the argument raged again.

Polly looked longingly at the closed door.

At one point, Athena said, "If you ban Stacia from family lunches I will not feel I can come either."

"You will have to do as you think best," Alexandros replied without hesitation, shocking everyone, including Polly.

She stared at her husband, feeling like he'd been taken over by aliens. Since when did he do or say anything that would upset his mother? Okay, today. But it had been a first.

Not fulfill the family tradition of the weekly get-together? That was simply not possible.

"Alexandros—" Petros started, his tone conciliatory.

But Polly's furious husband cut in before his brother could say anything more. "What, Petros? Would you allow either of them to speak to, or about, your wife the way they've been with Pollyanna?"

Petros's mouth snapped shut and then he shook his head decisively. "No, I would not."

"Corrina is everything a wife should be," Stacia said with umbrage. "She's beautiful, has been educated at the best schools. She's Greek, from a good family and she has her own fortune."

"While I am none of those things and come from a middle-class American family," Polly said with no shame. Because she was not and never had been embarrassed about her upbringing.

Her parents were good people. Her siblings were amazing, and not one of them would ever treat someone the way Stacia and Athena had since the first day Polly had stepped foot in Greece.

Polly had been all set to be the best daughter-in-law she could. She'd had all the sympathy in the world for a woman who had lost so many important people in her own life in too few years, but Athena had not wanted an American upstart as part of her family. And she'd made sure Polly knew it.

Stacia's jealousy and spite had only added to Polly's discomfort.

"You are beautiful. You are educated," Alexandros said to her now. "You are American, but have adapted amazingly well to living in my home country and I don't need you to have a fortune to know that mine has never been much of a draw to you."

Polly's eyes filled with tears. Darn pregnancy hormones. "I just wanted you."

"And I only wanted you. I don't need a wife with a pedigree. I need *you*."

She'd always had something that outstripped a pedigree for him. Her body. He could not resist her and the feeling was mutual. It might not be the love she'd believed she'd had when she got married, but it wasn't anything to dismiss either. The kind of passion they shared was rare and very precious.

Both her sisters were deeply in love with their husbands and loved in return, but both had shared with Polly that their sex lives were adequate. While hers? Was spectacular. And she didn't dismiss that as nothing of importance.

"I need you too," she said in a wobbly voice.

He jerked his head, like her words had touched a live wire inside him. Then he pulled Polly into his arms and against his chest. "Petros, please escort Mama and Stacia out to the helicopter."

Simply ignoring his mother's and sister's continued protests, Alexandros guided Polly into the drawing room, settling them both on the sofa with their daughter and even contriving to sing along to some of the songs with Polly and Helena.

As if the big argument had not happened.

Polly paused just inside the drawing room. "You might consider giving them a break."

"What?" He stared down at her like she was the one who was acting out of character.

"Your mom and sister are used to getting their way. Maybe give them a chance to adjust to the new family normal before you ban them from family lunch and stop giving your sister an allowance."

"You told her to get a job," he reminded her.

"Honestly? It would do her good, but I think you could ease into it. Give her a month to find something she's willing to lower herself to do. You know?"

"I'll think about it."

"And your mom?"

"Made her own choice about not coming for the family luncheon."

Polly couldn't deny that. "But if she changes her mind?"

"I will welcome her to my home as always."

Petros and Corrina stayed the night, flying back into Athens with Alexandros the next morning.

Polly found her more relaxed schedule a lot more pleasant than she'd expected it to be, and she loved having as much time as she wanted to play with Helena.

When her daughter went down for her nap after lunch,

Polly relaxed with a book. She didn't remember the last time she'd been able to read just because she wanted to.

Curled up in her favorite lounge chair in her room, she was surprised when the door opened.

Beryl was attending a meeting on Polly's behest and Dora had already left for the day. Of course, any one of the other servants could have decided they needed to talk to Polly about something, but she was rarely interrupted when she was in her sanctuary.

She looked up, waiting to see who needed her and was startled at the sight of her husband.

"I didn't hear the helicopter." Had he told her he was coming home early?

She didn't remember him doing so.

He looked at the book in her hand. "When you are lost in a book, a bomb could go off and I am not sure you would notice."

"I haven't gotten to really enjoy a good read in so long, I guess I forgot." She cast a quick glance at the baby monitor, relieved to see the lights indicated her daughter was still sleeping. "I'll have to rethink reading while Helena is napping if I didn't hear the helicopter."

"I'm sure our daughter's voice would penetrate. Your mother instincts are too strong for it not to." Alexandros looked around the room like he'd never been in there before. Maybe he never had.

It was her sanctuary, but she never came to this room in the evenings when he was home.

"You've put your mark on this room."

"I redecorated it when I did the nursery."

"You never said."

"You never said I couldn't."

"Of course you could. This is your home. You could redecorate the entire villa if you wanted to."

She shrugged. "I spend my time in here and in the nursery. I don't need to redecorate anywhere else."

"That my wife, who spends more time here than any-where else, restricts her living to a few hundred square feet of thousands does not speak well of your comfort in your home."

He was just now noticing? But she smiled. "I use the pool. And the dining room of course, and the breakfast nook." She preferred the smaller sunny room, even if the decor was just as generically modern as the rest. "And the terrace. Helena and I spend a lot of time on the terrace." She'd had a play structure installed at one end for her daughter and her daughter's friends to use when she hosted the playgroup.

"I noticed you don't use the media room for watching movies with Helena."

"It's too much. We've used it to host a movie afternoon for her playgroup." The parents had been impressed, but the littles hadn't found the theater style seating as comfortable as piles of pillows on the floor of the still admittedly for-mal drawing room.

Instead of looking happier at her list of the places in the villa that Polly and Helena used, her husband's face took on a pained expression. "It's your home. You should feel comfortable *everywhere.*"

"Childproofing rooms that were decorated with a then childless billionaire in mind hardly seems worth it when Helena and I are perfectly content to use the areas best suited to her needs."

"I never considered the childproofing aspect." He frowned. "You said it was decorated with me in mind, not you."

"Obviously." Polly would never have gone for all the marble and neutral shades. And knowing she was pregnant, though not having shared the news yet at the time with him, she would never have put so many expensive objets d'art on display where tiny fingers could reach them.

He winced. "It is your home," he reiterated. "It should reflect your taste."

"That is not what you said when we moved in." He'd been livid she hadn't appreciated his effort in hiring a popular interior design firm to do the entire house at great cost.

"Perhaps I've learned something in three years."

She shrugged. "It doesn't matter anymore." She'd gotten used to living in a mansion that felt like a high-end hotel.

"The existence of this room says otherwise."

"I wanted a place that felt like home."

"And the other ten thousand square feet of the villa?"

"Feels like one of Zephyr and Neo's hotels." The property developer duo didn't socialize as much as others in their position. Both were firm family men with lovely wives that had befriended Polly her first year in Greece.

The friendship had come as a double-edged sword. Polly loved spending time with the Stamos and Nikos families, but seeing the devoted husbands and fathers that both Zephyr and Neo made was hard when her own billionaire didn't seem to get how to manage that feat.

She couldn't just dismiss his neglect and business-oriented priorities as the necessary challenges of a man in his position when she saw others who handled their family lives differently.

Even now she clung to the consolation that Zephyr and Neo had a very different background from Alexandros, and neither had a snooty family to pacify.

Displeasure creased Alexandros's handsome features. "In other words, transitory."

She'd never thought of it that way, but maybe he was right. "Maybe."

"Our marriage is not temporary."

"Your mother and sister both wish otherwise," Polly acknowledged wryly.

It was something she would have not have said even before yesterday, but he had stood up for her in a way he never had and she felt some of the confidence she'd had early in their marriage returning.

The grim set of his lips said he got her point. "I should have set them straight about the way they treat you a long time ago."

"If you had, it's probable that the schism that happened yesterday wouldn't have." Polly might have understood some of Alexandros's attitude in the beginning of their marriage when his family was still mired in grief, but that didn't change the truth. "They both got used to saying whatever they wanted to, and about, me. Neither took you seriously when you warned Stacia to watch her tongue yesterday."

"But you did?" he asked.

She had, as shocking as she'd found his late in the game championship of his wife. "I know that look you get when you will not be moved, and you had it."

"And yet my mother and sister, who have known me since my birth and hers respectively, did not recognize this look?"

"Maybe they've never seen it before. Your usual policy with them is to give them what they want." He'd once told her he expected peace on the domestic front.

And he'd shown her that the way he ensured it was to give his mother what she wanted *like a good son*, and to spoil his sister because that was what everyone in that family expected of him toward Stacia.

"While depriving my wife of the support she should expect from me." He did not sound impressed by that concept.

She wasn't either, but she'd learned to live with it. "No comment."

"You used to tell me I spoiled them."

"You did." And he'd had his reasons, but yes, definitely spoiled.

"And yet, no matter how I provided for you materially, *you* never felt spoiled by me."

"I needed different things from you." Time. Attention. His willingness to stand by her side in a family confrontation.

"Needed past tense?" he asked.

"I learned to find contentment with what I had."

He said an ugly word, and suddenly she realized he was seethingly angry.

"You're furious," she said, feeling fragile and not even sure why.

"Ne."

Yes, she translated.

Polly bit her lip. "With me?"

Suddenly his face changed completely, and he pulled her into his arms without warning. "With myself. With my mother and my sister, who should have made you welcome, but instead did much to guarantee you found life here as my wife difficult. But mostly with myself, *agape mou*, mostly with myself."

He kissed her then, his lips gentle and completely at odds with the emotion pouring off of him.

She responded, as she always did, allowing her body to melt into his, parting her lips for the tender caress of his tongue. They kissed for long minutes, the only sound in the room their shared breathing and their daughter's sleeping snuffles over the monitor.

Finally, he pulled back and made a point of looking around her sanctuary. "I like it in here."

"I do too."

"I would like it if you brought this warmth into the rest of our home."

"Would you?" She didn't remind him again that he'd changed his tune.

Because the fact he had? Was something good.

"Not immediately and not all in one go." He brushed a barely there kiss across her lips. "I do not want you exhausted by another project when we've worked to take others off your plate."

"We?" she asked delicately.

"Okay, I made some unilateral decisions, but you looked relaxed and pink with health when I arrived. I do not think that can be seen as anything but a positive."

Believing positive reinforcement might work as well with the father as with the daughter, she gave him a warm, approving smile. "I have enjoyed my more relaxed schedule."

"Do you *like* the charity work?" he asked for the first time ever.

"You mean my job as your wife?" Because that's what it was.

Once they'd gotten married and moved her into the family home, he had laid out a whole set of expectations for how she was going to live her life that she had not anticipated.

"Is that how you see it?"

"What else? You even give performance reviews," she teased.

But it was true. Especially when they were first married, he'd make sure to take time to talk about what he felt she was getting right and what he thought she could improve on in her public role as his wife. Unfortunately, she'd discovered that public role took a lot more of her private time than she'd ever wanted it to.

In the beginning, she would have been happier if she could have gotten a job in her field, but his mother had thrown a fit at the idea of Polly working as a *menial laborer*, which is how she considered Polly's formerly demanding career as a pastry chef. Later, Polly would have preferred more uninterrupted time to dedicate to being Helena's mom.

"No, I do not think I have ever considered your role as my wife in the light of a job before." And his tone said he didn't like seeing it that way either. "As to what you call performance reviews, I was only trying to help you find your way in a very different world to the one you left behind."

"It never occurred to you that it would have been a lot easier to find my way if I had been allowed to maintain what I could from my life in America."

"What do you mean?"

"If I had been able to get a job as a pastry chef, I would have made friends more quickly and with workmates." She pulled away from him and walked over to look out the window. "I know those weren't the people you *wanted* me to make friends with, but I wasn't raised in your rarified atmosphere and it would have been a lot easier for me to have some friends who understood my middle-class outlook on life."

"I thought that in the long run you would settle in better if you made relationships in that 'rarified world' as you call it where you were now living."

She spun back to face him. "Then why dump me in the back of beyond, taking me away from the friends I had managed to connect with?"

"I thought you would be happier in the country. You were raised in rural Upstate New York."

"With you gone during the week and living in this great honking hotel?" she asked with disbelief. "No wonder your mom and sister considered the move the beginning of the end of our marriage."

Only no one had counted on Polly turning up pregnant. It wasn't as if she and Alexandros had been trying for a baby. They'd agreed they wanted to wait at least two years before they started trying, and Polly had grave misgivings about having a baby with him by the end of the first year of their marriage.

But she'd gotten the flu and her pills had been rendered ineffective. Not that she, or he, had realized it. Not until she'd started losing her breakfast.

"I do not know where Stacia got the idea that my buying this house was an indication that I saw our marriage as anything but permanent."

Polly twisted her lips at how he ignored the truth of her comment as he had so often in the past. "Probably a combination of believing what she wanted to and the fact that for almost the first year after we moved here, you spent most of your work week in the Athens apartment and only came home on the weekends."

And those had been shortened from Saturday afternoon to before dawn on Monday morning, when he'd fly out again. Polly had no intention of glossing over the reality of what her marriage had been like then.

Even *she* had wondered if he had intended the move as a way to make her a smaller player in his life, if not a prelude to the dissolution of their marriage.

"I was fighting the takeover and then working like hell to make sure it could never happen again." Frustration laced his voice. "Everything my father and his father and grandfather before him had built was resting on my shoulders, but also the livelihood of tens of thousands of employees."

CHAPTER SIX

HE'D BEEN DOING the best he could for his family.

Polly could see now that was how Alexandros had seen it. And honestly? She could not dismiss all those employees and their lives as being unimportant. He'd hurt her, but he hadn't done it on purpose, and he hadn't ignored her just to make another few million.

Moving her to the back of beyond and acting like he was doing her a favor? That was something else. Something maybe they still needed to work out between them.

Because she had missed the country, and she'd told him so, but she hadn't expected that to result in being moved away from the friends she still missed, or the opportunities to cook in the soup kitchens that had offended her mother-in-law so much, or the easier access to *him*.

"But Stacia didn't know that." Neither had Polly, if it came right down to it. "She and your mother took your behavior to mean that you'd lost interest in our marriage. It's natural they came to the conclusion that you only stayed married to me because I was pregnant with Helena."

"But you know that is not true."

Polly didn't answer right away. Because she *had* believed that.

Just as she'd felt trapped in a marriage that was nothing like what she'd expected or wanted it to be, she'd assumed he was equally trapped by her pregnancy. If Polly ever had considered divorce in that first year, those thoughts were stopped cold by the discovery she carried his child.

She'd owed her daughter the best form of stability she could give her.

Polly had always believed Alexandros had felt the same.

He stared at her, like reading her thoughts on her face.

Maybe he was. Even her own mother told Polly she wore her heart on her sleeve.

Unless she was channeling her Anna persona, but that crutch had been harder to lean on lately.

With a curse, Alexandros strode across the room and swept Polly into his arms. Then he sat down on the love seat where Polly liked to give Helena a cuddle while she read to her daughter. This time it was Polly sitting on Alexandros's hard thighs, his arms steel bands around her. Like he was afraid she'd disappear if he let go.

She dismissed the fanciful thought, and said, "I think me getting pregnant with Helena was a wake-up call for both of us."

She'd realized her marriage was something she had to make work. And he'd... Well, she thought he'd realized pretty much the same thing.

"My wake-up call came last weekend at my mother's home."

Polly gasped.

It was the first time he'd referred to the family villa as being his mother's home and not his as well. Even after they'd moved to the country, he referred to the family villa as home.

She was so stunned that it took a few seconds for the rest of what he said to sink in. And she almost smiled. Almost. Because it hurt a little. That she'd been right. That believing he wasn't measuring up to his own brother as a husband had sparked the amazing transformation in Alexandros's viewpoint toward his marriage and Polly.

"Nothing to say?"

"Not a lot, no." She had realized she had to make their marriage work, even if it meant changing her own expectations, when she was pregnant the first time.

Regardless of whether or not his ego had prompted it, Alexandros had come to something of the same conclusion a week ago.

"Better late than never?" she tried.

He grimaced. "You consider your role of my wife as a *job*?" he asked, proving he was still stuck on that point.

"What would you call it when I have a list of duties to perform that have nothing to do with our personal relationship? When I have a set of expectations for how I must spend my days?" The bitterness in her own voice surprised her.

But he'd opened this Pandora's box in their marriage.

She'd shut the lid tight on her personal dreams and expectations when she realized that no matter how much she fought him, she *was* trapped in a marriage that wasn't anything like she'd thought it would be. That whatever else her husband felt for her, it wasn't love and that no matter what, their unborn child deserved a stable and content homelife.

"I…" He let his voice trail off, without a ready response.

If she could believe it. And she found that very difficult. He was never without a ready response.

"So, you *don't* like the charity work?" he asked finally.

"It's not that black-and-white."

"Isn't it?"

"Do you like spending time with me and Helena?"

"You know I do."

"So, sell off your company and spend all your time with us."

He stared at her in nothing less than abject horror. "You don't mean that."

"It's not that black-and-white, is it?"

He sighed. "I suppose not." For Alexandros?

That was quite the climbdown.

"When we talked about having children before we got married, do you remember what we said?" She looked into the espresso gaze that had so caught her that first time their eyes met and willed him to think back.

"That we both wanted you to be able to stay home with our children."

"And you promised me that I could. You said you understood that I wanted to be the mom who was home after school, that our house would be the one that our children and their friends hung out in. Even if it was a mansion." He'd used those exact words.

"You are an at-home mother." Confusion made his body tense against hers.

He had never liked not understanding. Anything.

"Am I?" Only she didn't feel like one when the charity work and social events he insisted she had to host and attend were as demanding as any full-time job. "Today I got to play as much as I wanted to with Helena. I got to help her make cookies for the first time without planning the event two weeks in advance on my calendar."

There had been a time that Polly spent time baking every day, just to relax. She'd clung to that in the first year of their marriage, but obligations on her time and her mother-in-law's attitude toward such pursuits eventually saw the end to her indulging in her passion for creating.

"In fact, it was one of the few times I've been in the kitchen with our daughter because there are so many things I want to do with her and there simply isn't enough time to do them. She spends a lot of her time with me, in here, while I work with Beryl, my attention divided."

"You do make it sound like a full-time job, but you must understand. This is how I was raised. I grew up with a mother who kept such social obligations as a matter of course." And a grandmother before that.

She knew it was ingrained in him to see life a certain way by his family, by his history, by his culture and by his own personal experience. That didn't make it any easier for Polly to live the life he expected of her.

"Your mother never held any other job, and she relies a lot more heavily on her personal staff than I ever had," Polly pointed out.

"Because you believe that if a job is worth doing, it is worth doing right."

"And personally." Polly wasn't putting her name to something she wasn't actually personally involved in, but recently she'd begun to realize that maybe her own stubbornness had pushed her to a higher level of involvement than necessary.

That wasn't an easy thing to acknowledge or admit. Because it meant that not only was some of her discontent with her life at her own instigation, but her own pride and intransigence had led her to taking time away from Helena that she hadn't needed to.

"I know that a lot of moms don't have the time they want with their children," she acknowledged to him, for now not addressing her inner revelations. Not ready to share the burden of blame when *so* much rested on his attitudes and expectations. Still, she added, "I try very hard to remember that my life is easy in comparison to other women's."

"Because you are rich."

"Because my husband is a billionaire."

"What is mine is yours." He said it like he believed it.

But again she thought it was a matter of him believing something in the abstract, but his actions showing a deeper conviction toward something else.

"Not according to the prenup. And honestly? If that were true, you would not have bought this house without my input." Could he finally understand that had been taking his tendency toward control one giant step too far?

"That was a mistake."

Again, shock rendered her nearly mute, but she managed to force out, "Was it?"

"You are my wife." He cupped her cheek, his hand warm against her skin. "I should never have made the decision to move us out of Athens without your agreement."

Polly was kind of stunned he was admitting it finally. "I didn't want to live with your mother and sister any longer." Even though, at first, she'd been okay with it.

He'd explained how the villa had been their family home for generations. How his mother had begged them to make their home there rather than him moving out. In the light of Athena's recent losses, Polly's heart had been moved to agree.

And she'd moved into the villa, believing she could help heal the family's grief only to learn that nothing she said or did was going to endear her to Athena or Stacia.

"But when you bought Villa Liakada, I'd made friends in Athens, built a life for myself. You took it all away."

"And thought I was doing you a favor in the process," he said with a self-deprecating twist to his handsome lips.

"Yes."

"I hurt you."

Many times. "Yes."

He winced, his own expression revealing a vulnerability she wasn't sure she could believe. "I have always wanted you to be happy in our marriage."

"I've found contentment."

He leaned down, pressing his forehead to hers. "Damned by faint praise."

"It could be worse," she admitted, whispering because she felt like there was a fragile bubble of intimacy around them she did not want to break.

"I could be a philandering abuser," he said with pure self-derision she had never seen him point at himself. "Believe it, or not, but I need to be something better in your life than that."

Suddenly that bubble was suffocating, and she couldn't stand being in his arms, held like something precious when so many times she had not mattered to him at all.

She pushed against him, but he resisted.

"Let me go, please." She needed to breathe.

He released her, his expression one she did not want to try to interpret right then.

She stood and moved to where her book sat on the table by the chair she'd been in earlier. Needing something to do, she slotted it back into the bookshelf. "I think we married too quickly, without really realizing what the other person wanted."

She didn't claim they were both too young, because Polly had been twenty-seven and Alexandros had been thirty-two.

They'd met when he was in the States. She'd done the desserts for a meeting he attended, and somehow the middle-class pastry chef had bumped into the billionaire.

That first meeting had been electric, and she hadn't even hesitated when he'd asked her to dine with him the following evening. She'd fallen for him hook, line and sinker. And she'd thought the tsunami of emotions had been two-sided.

Six weeks later, they were engaged and he was headed to Asia for more business talks. They saw almost nothing of each other in the three months leading up to the wedding, but she'd thought their phone calls, texts and emails had built a foundation she could rely on.

She met her mother-in-law at the wedding rehearsal.

Athena had been reserved, but not overtly hostile. She'd worn black, claiming she was still in mourning for her deceased husband. Since he had died only a little over a year previous, Polly had believed.

Since then, she'd had cause to wonder that color choice for the mother of the groom.

Their month-long honeymoon had been bliss, but then her real life as the wife of an old-money Greek billionaire began. And it had not been anything like a fairy tale.

Polly stood there, staring at the spines of the books she hadn't had time to read and wondered where they went from here?

Alexandros clearly wanted to improve their marriage.

She didn't know if she could trust him enough to open herself to trying.

"If you had it to do again, would you have married me?" he asked her, having come up behind her without her realizing.

He laid his hands on her shoulders, turning her around

so their gazes met. His was filled with a nameless emotion. Hers, she knew, would be wary.

Because she felt wary.

She stifled a sigh. "That's a pointless question. We *did* get married. We did have a daughter. We do have a son on the way."

"I wasn't there to learn the sex of either of my children." It sounded like he really regretted that.

"I told you."

"*Ne.* You told me. The first time with a sweet little pink cupcake that tasted like ambrosia and stopped my heart with the knowledge you were carrying my daughter."

But for their son, she'd texted. We're having a boy. The joy-filled phone call had gone to her mother and the special cupcake? She'd made for Helena.

Her daughter had squealed and insisted on sitting down right then to draw a picture to put on her baby brother's nursery wall.

"I bought champagne for the entire office staff to celebrate that text," he said, proving their thoughts were running on similar tracks.

"And a pair of sapphire earrings for me," she said.

"No alcohol while you are pregnant."

"They're lovely earrings."

"But you would have been more touched if I'd bought a stuffie."

She shrugged. "Maybe, but I knew you wanted me to know you were happy about the baby. And that's what matters."

"I am happy about the baby. I adore Helena and cannot wait to welcome her little brother into the world."

"I'll be giving birth soon enough." In about fourteen weeks if all went to plan.

"I plan to be there for the entire labor and delivery this time," he told her.

"If you can't, I'll manage. Mom and Dad already have

plans to be here a week before the due date, and they're both staying a full month this time."

"Nevertheless, I will be there."

Polly didn't reply. She didn't want to call him a liar, but she doubted even the certainty he would be in the country when she gave birth.

He sighed. "I think I've broken too many promises to you without ever meaning to."

"I think if it had been intentional I wouldn't have stayed, but even I could tell that we just didn't see the world the same way."

"There is no reason that Beryl cannot continue on as she is now, even after the baby is born."

Polly pushed back her knee-jerk reaction of denial and considered what she really wanted, and what would be best for her and the two children she would have. "I would like that."

"Then, that's the way it will be." He stepped back, and she contrarily missed his warmth.

She moved away from the bookcase, tidying up the few things that were not in their proper place. Hope was a terrifying ember burning in her heart. Polly could not snuff it out, but the fear that it would lead to more pain down the road wouldn't go away either.

He looked around her sanctuary again, a small smile playing on his lips. "I should have begged Zephyr Nikos to convince his wife to do the decor here in the villa. Despite you comparing this place to one of their hospitality properties, you and she share a similar design aesthetic."

Polly smiled. The thought of having Piper redecorate the villa was a pipe dream, but something she would have loved.

"Would you like to move back to Athens?" Alexandros asked with every evidence of being serious.

But could he really mean it?

Most of the friends she'd made in Greece still lived in Athens, or visited there. Corrina and Petros were there, and they were her very best friends. Helena adored them and would love to see her uncle and new aunt more often.

But Polly forced herself to think beyond what would make her happy. "I'm not sure it would be fair to Helena. She's never known any other home than this one. And she has friends in her playgroup."

"The constant in her life is you, Polly. Not this house." Alexandros gave her the slashing smile that had first caught her eye. "You are an amazing mama. She will make other friends. And if I know you, you'll make sure she still gets to visit her current playmates. After all, you are the woman who makes sure our daughter sees her *yia-yia* once a month despite how my mother has treated you."

"You are a constant for her too," Polly offered, because it was true. And because maybe it needed to be said. "You are a good father."

Maybe he wasn't around as much as her father had been for Polly, but Alexandros loved his daughter very much and it showed.

"I am glad you think so. Very glad, but the truth is, *both* of you see less of me than you should because of the daily helicopter commute."

"We *would* see more of you if we lived in Athens," she acknowledged.

Not only was there the daily commute to consider, but he spent at least one night a week in Athens, which cut their family time down even more.

"We'll take as many of our staff with us as are willing to move." He was talking like it was a done deal.

Even so, as much as she might like that, she didn't see their staff traveling to Athens with them. "A lot of them have family in the area."

"I'll offer a significant moving bonus and the two-hour drive is not so onerous they can't make it to visit family."

"You would do that, so that she has continuity of homelife?" Polly asked, a little shocked at the idea they could take the staff, many of whom had become friends, with them.

"I would do that so that *you* don't have to get used to new people either."

It was true that getting used to new staff when she'd moved in here after only just adjusting to the staff at the Kristalakis family home had been very hard for a woman who had grown up doing everything for herself. Her family came to visit more often now they'd gotten used to the staff too; she didn't want them to cut down their visits again either.

"Would we find the house together?" she asked, unwilling to make another major move without input in where they ended up.

"That is important to you, doing it together?"

"I don't want to live in another hotel."

"You could pick it out."

Disappointment filled her. "You're probably too busy to take time off to house hunt with me."

She went to turn away, but he grabbed her and gently pulled her into his body again. He'd always been a physical lover, but he was so much more touchy-feely right now.

And she kind of loved it.

Not that she was admitting that one out loud. It would make her sound needy.

"Not at all," he assured her.

She didn't know what he saw on her face, but he cursed in Russian. A habit he'd developed after Helena's birth so he didn't accidentally say a word she might repeat in Greek or English.

Alexandros pressed their bodies close and groaned. "Our daughter is going to wake up any minute and Hero will not be on duty for hours yet."

Polly hid her grin at his impatience. "You'll survive."

"If you were living in my skin, you would not be so sure."

Then he went all serious again. "I want you to be happy in our next home."

"So, give me the final right of choice," she challenged.

"Done."

She let the grin take over her face. "Watch out, you'll end up in a farmhouse."

"In Athens? I am not worried, *yineka mou*."

"So, we are really moving?" she asked, disbelief more prevalent than acceptance.

"Our primary residence, yes."

"You mean we're keeping the villa?" Relief she would not have expected washed over her, but this was the house she'd brought her baby home to.

The first house that had been only hers and Alexandros's.

"That is entirely up to you, Polly. This house is in your name." He kissed her lightly. "But if I get a vote, I would like to consider keeping it. I would still like to get out of the city on occasion and think it would be good for our children as well."

She could only nod. The house was *hers*? But according to the prenuptial agreement, anything he bought for her she got to keep in the eventuality of a divorce. She'd never considered he might buy her a house that had cost several million euros.

"I think your brother and Corrina will be glad of that, too," she said for lack of anything better to say. Her mind was still melting under that knowledge that Polly owned the villa.

Alexandros's smile was warm. "You are very close to them."

"I am."

"I am glad."

Even after that closeness led to his being challenged in his perception as a husband? That was a pretty nice sentiment actually. Especially for a man as proud as her husband.

"I'm six months pregnant." It just popped out. She hadn't

been thinking of her pregnancy as a stumbling block to moving, but the truth was this pregnancy had been really hard on Polly and she wasn't sure she was up to it.

"You think this is a bad time to make the move?" he asked, like that mattered more than anything else. "You know I won't allow you to do too much. We'll have movers and professional packers. You'll only have to supervise."

She didn't mention that supervision could be very taxing, simply looked at him and asked. "Will you help?"

"In every way that I can. I promise."

She nodded. Beryl would as well, even if they had to hire her a second assistant.

Polly discovered that house hunting with her billionaire husband was nothing like she might have expected.

He hired *the* preeminent estate agents in Athens who then provided virtual walk throughs on potential properties.

She'd pictured going to look at houses together, but so far, they had both watched the videos separately and then discussed them. Usually after tucking their daughter in for the night.

They were spending more time together however because her workaholic husband had come home early again this week, twice. And he had arranged to work from home once, without a single overnight at the Athens apartment.

Helena was blossoming under the extra attention from her beloved papa. Polly was blooming too, but fear of going back to the way things had been cast a shadow over her enjoyment of her husband's increased presence.

Polly was leaning back against Alexandros's chest as they looked at potential property together on his phone. It was one she'd gotten very excited about.

"If you are that keen on this house, you could go see it with the agent tomorrow," he told her.

She felt her body tense. "I thought we were visiting the properties together."

"I cannot do it tomorrow."

"What happened to no more uncomfortable helicopter rides into Athens for me?"

"I thought you and Helena could come to the apartment for the rest of the week, perhaps longer."

They would be right across the hall from Corrina and Petros. And Alexandros's office would be an elevator ride away. Excitement coursed through Polly. "You've never invited us to the penthouse."

He used one when he stayed over, while Corrina and Petros lived in the other full-time. One floor below were a set of four apartments used by the company for business related needs, but the penthouses were gorgeous from the pictures Corrina had sent Polly on her phone after moving in.

"I've had the penthouse childproofed and a plexiglass guard added to the balcony railing, which I've had raised another two feet. Not that you'll allow Helena out there without supervision, but it's an extra measure of security for her." Tossing away his phone, he tugged her into his lap, so their gazes met. "And I never realized you needed an invitation to join me in Athens."

"I didn't?" she asked, stunned by the concept that he would have welcomed her presence and that of their daughter at any time.

"No. I realize now that I had made it seem like to you that I saw you as separate from my business life, but I don't. Everything is for and about you and Helena and our unborn son now."

"But..."

"If you want the truth, it hurt that you never came to stay, especially those times I had to spend more than a night in the city." He frowned, swallowed, looked away and then back at her, like he was making himself man up. "I thought it was just too much trouble to you to come."

"But I didn't know you wanted me there."

"When I first bought the villa, I had visions of us sharing our time between there and the apartment."

"But then I came up pregnant and was way too nauseated to travel into the city."

"When you started to feel better physically, you never brought the possibility up."

"Neither did you."

"You'd stopped being as affectionate. I thought you were going through pregnancy stuff and I didn't want to push."

"But after I had the baby?"

"That first year, she was so fragile and tiny."

"And you didn't like to think of her in the helicopter."

"You either."

"But you used it every day to commute."

"Fear can be irrational." He sighed. "When I was with you in the helicopter, I was not afraid for your safety."

She nodded, fascinated by this insight into how her husband had thought. "Then it became habit, for us *not* to come to Athens." And that explained why when she flew into Athens with him, she was always taken back to their villa via car.

"A bad one."

"Yes, a very bad one." She had to agree. "Thank you for telling me you wanted us there. It means a lot."

"I honestly did not know it had to be said." And he was clearly uncomfortable giving voice to what he might consider needs that showed him up as weak in some way.

She wanted to reward him, so she kissed him and was totally unprepared for the tsunami of passion that would unleash.

Lying naked, sweaty and so satisfied with pleasure her body was still buzzing with it, Polly snuggled into her husband's side. "That was unexpected."

He mumbled something.

With great effort, she lifted her head and looked up at him. "What did you say?"

"You kissed me." Color burnished his taut cheekbones.

"We kiss all the time." In bed. And lately, out of it as well.

"I kiss you and you respond."

But *she* didn't kiss *him*. Emotion swamped over Polly in hot and cold waves and not all of it was good. She'd withheld her naturally affectionate nature because she had no longer been sure of him.

She'd thought he hadn't even noticed. She'd been wrong.

He'd made a lot of changes and effort in the past week; maybe it was time she did too. She could kiss him, if it meant that much to him.

Smiling she snuggled back into his side, running her hand over his chest, and reveling like she used to do in the knowledge that she was the only person with free rein to touch this incredibly powerful man like this. "I still want you to go on the walk through with me."

He made a sound that could have been arousal, or it could have been contentment, but he answered. "Surely one of your parents took responsibility for most of the house hunting."

"My parents still live in the first house they bought before I was born." She sat up, but kept her hand on him. She didn't know why, just that she needed to. "I have no idea what the process of finding a home was like for them, but my sisters and brothers tromped from house to house together."

His expression turned pained, but his hand trapped hers against his skin. "And you want to do this?"

She couldn't imagine her husband having the time for something like that. "No, as long as we go *together* to view our top three, I'll be happy."

His smile was both relieved and oh, so sexy. "That I can do."

Thinking about how much time it took to find and buy a house and how hard he had to work to make that time, she looked back on his purchase of the country villa with different eyes.

"You really were trying to do something special for me when you bought this villa."

"I was, but I see now that without your input how could this house have ever become our home?"

"That's a nice thing to say."

"I'm feeling anything but nice." He moved her hand down to the evidence of his renewed desire.

She curled her fingers around the hard flesh and gave him a heated look. "I'm not feeling so nice myself right now." She squeezed the flesh in her fingers.

He groaned. "That feels very nice to me."

And then it began again, the passion between them building to slow and easy this time as he let her touch and explore in the way that gave her the most pleasure. By the time she put her mouth on him, he was shaking and swearing though.

In Greek. He was too far gone to use another language.

She loved the earthy taste of him, the way his hardness felt in her mouth. This was her man. No one else would ever get to see him like this, much less touch him with the freedom she had to do so. Their marriage was not perfect, but this part? The passion? The desire? The way they pleasured one another?

It was as out of this world as it had been the very first time.

When she knew he was on the verge of climax, when Polly herself could take no more waiting, she climbed on top of him. "My turn."

His inarticulate sound of agreement turned her on even more.

She positioned herself over his thick erection and lowered herself, gasping as his bulbous head slipped inside her tender flesh, sensitized from their first round of lovemaking.

"That's so good," he said in a guttural tone she loved.

"Yes." She pressed down until he was fully sheathed inside her and then stilled, just savoring the amazing feeling that had not gotten old through five years of marriage and two pregnancies.

"Please, *agape mou*."

"What? You want me to move?" Her tease would have been more effective if she wasn't so breathless and her hips weren't jerking in little tiny movements without any volition from her.

"Ne!"

Oh, yes. That was what she wanted. Polly began to move, rocking her hips, and rode him to first her completion and then only a moment later, his.

His hoarse shout was still ringing in her ears as she collapsed down onto his chest, so replete even her baby bump didn't make it awkward.

CHAPTER SEVEN

HELENA WAS ECSTATIC at her first helicopter ride. She pointed to everything out the window, jabbering away, unconcerned that her parents could not hear her well enough to answer.

But then Polly and Alexandros both smiled at their daughter and nodded at easy intervals.

Polly's eyes caught her husband's, and they shared a moment of understanding, their smiles turning intimate and warm for a moment out of time.

They landed on the helipad on top of the Kristalakis Building, Alexandros handing Helena to a bodyguard, while he personally helped Polly out and then leaned protectively over her body to shelter her from the wind generated by the slowing rotor blades.

The penthouse apartment he led them to wasn't anything like Polly had been expecting. Warm colors made the high-end rooms feel welcoming, and there was a chest filled with toys for Helena in the main living room as well as her perfect princess bedroom.

"How long has the apartment been set up for family?" Polly asked, looking around in wonder.

Helena made a beeline for the pretty white bookcase filled with her favorite stories and pulled out brand-new copies of the ones that had become dog-eared in her room in the villa. "Look, Mom! All my best stories!"

"I see that, sweetie."

Helena was in her element, but Polly was overwhelmed. There could be no question that Alexandros had gone to great lengths to make sure his daughter would be comfortable.

Polly turned and stared up at her husband. "How long?" she asked again.

He shrugged. "Pretty much since Helena's birth."

"But you never said."

"I was waiting for you to say you wanted to come."

"What? Why, for goodness' sake?" she demanded. "How was I supposed to know you wanted us here? That's not the way it seemed to me."

But the evidence of her eyes said something entirely different. It said that he *had* wanted her in Athens with him. "If you wanted us here, why did you move me out to the villa?"

"I did not realize that you would consider the move as a statement of intent."

"How was I supposed to take it?"

He grimaced, for once his ready brain stuck for an answer.

"You were waiting for me to say I wanted to come?" she asked in disbelief. "But I never wanted to move out of Athens in the first place. I would have thought that would have been a given."

Only very clearly, it had not.

"I thought you would be happy to move to the country. I thought your anger was over me choosing the house without your input. You'd made it clear you wanted to move out of the family home."

"But I said..." What had she said back then? She couldn't even remember now. She knew how she'd felt, but she'd been so angry, so resentful that by the time he bought the villa, she was halfway to closing her heart off from him already. "I really hated living with your mother and your sister."

"I am sorry I did not understand how bad it was for you."

She nodded. She believed him. She just wasn't sure if she could trust him. He was paying attention now, but he hadn't. Not then. Not later.

"I learned not to talk to you about the important stuff." She sighed and then made a conscious effort to go for the positive with a small smile. "But we're here now and it's a really nice place to be."

"I am glad you think so." He didn't look happy so much as relieved.

He wasn't used to being criticized. She'd figured that out early on. And Alexandros had been deeply offended when she reacted to his gift with anger instead of enthusiasm.

She let her smile grow. "It's a beautiful apartment."

"It makes me think of you."

That was worth a reward. She leaned up and kissed him. "I like that. Are you saying that all those nights you spent on your own up here, you were thinking about me?"

"What else would I think about?"

"Business?"

"Well, naturally without you and Helena around to keep me balanced, I tend to work very long hours." He said it like admitting a grave sin.

She just grinned and took him by the arm, leading him into the living room, where they could sit down together. "I would expect nothing less. That's why your family is so good for you."

"You are good for me, *agape mou*. And yes, so is our daughter and this little one." He laid his hand over her belly.

The baby kicked and she grinned. "He knows his daddy's touch."

They settled onto the spice-colored sofa together, Alexandros pulling her close into his side. Neither spoke. She was basking in the present, enjoying the knowledge that she and their daughter were not only welcome here, in the bastion she had considered an adjunct to his business, but desired.

"What are you thinking?" she finally asked him after several long, peaceful minutes.

"I am enjoying your presence here in my arms and the sound of our daughter telling herself stories in her bedroom. I dreamed of just such a moment many times."

Polly didn't remind him he should have invited her if he'd wanted her there, but she did ask in a soft teasing tone, "So what have we learned about vital communication between a husband and a wife?"

"That it *is* vital." There was no humor in her husband's voice, just conviction.

"I agree. Is there anything else you've been wanting and not telling me?" she thought to ask, though with very little expectation of a positive reply.

Billionaire tycoons weren't known for not expressing their needs, or desires.

"I want to date again."

"What?" Polly pulled away so she could see her husband's face. "What do you mean? We go out together."

"To fundraisers and social functions necessary for my business."

"Well, yes, but that *is* our social life."

"I want more."

"You do?" She found that really hard to believe.

"Your sisters have date nights with their husbands. I've heard them talking about it when they come to visit."

"They do, but they don't have social calendars anything as packed as ours," Polly acknowledged ruefully. "In fact, they've all expressed envy at the galas I get to attend."

"But those galas aren't the best way to rekindle romance."

"They could be."

"What do you mean?"

"It's not about where we go, or even what we do when we are out together. It's whether we're *together* or just attending the same function."

"Of course we are together."

"Are we?" she asked, thinking how little time they actually spent in one another's company at most of the social events they attended.

He looked down at her and stopped to think, which she appreciated. He wasn't just giving her a knee-jerk reaction. "Please explain."

"On a date, your focus is on me. My focus is on you.

The venue, the entertainment, the others around us, they are secondary, right?"

"Agreed."

"So, a gala could be a date, but only if our focus remained on each other."

"However, as it stands, you and I both end up talking to different people, socializing in different circles."

"Yes. You to advance your business interests."

"And you to make connections for your charity work."

"Some of the time. Others, I'm just catching up with friends," she informed him. "But regardless of our reasons, we are both in the habit of going our own way once we arrive at a function."

"That used to bother me about you," he informed her.

"What? You expected to me to stand by your side in silent companionships while you talked business and political interests related to your business?" she asked with a tinge of mockery.

But his serious nod stunned her. "Yes."

"Faithful Penelope, I am not," she informed him.

"So I learned. Not that you lack fidelity, but you do not see yourself as a satellite to my life."

"I'm not." What a strange thing for him to say.

"My mother was, to my father."

"But she has so many charity interests now. Are you saying she didn't when he was alive?"

"She did, but she still spent most of their evenings out in his near vicinity."

"I'm not sure how she managed that, but I'm not her."

"No, and I do not expect you to be."

"Are you sure?" Because that was something she'd often thought he did in fact expect and was destined to be disappointed by.

"Let me rephrase that," he said with one of his devastating smiles. "I have learned not to expect you to be. I have come to realize that if you were like my mother, I would have had no more interest in marrying you than the women she'd been throwing at my head since I became an adult."

Polly's own smile was tinged with mockery. "Sexual chemistry has a lot to answer for."

"Our relationship is not just sex." His dark gaze bored into hers.

"Of course not. We have a daughter together and a son on the way. We have a family."

"It has never been just sex." He sounded really offended.

"I didn't say it was?" she asked, rather than stated, because something she said had garnered this reaction.

"You said I married you because of sexual chemistry."

"Didn't you? I mean if we hadn't been so explosive in bed, I don't think you would have made the effort, considering our differences and your busy schedule."

He opened his mouth, like he was going to deny her assertion, but then he shut it with a snap. "That may be true, but I proposed because I was in love with you."

She'd thought so too, at the time, but Polly had long since realized what she'd thought was love was a mixture of genuine liking and sexual compatibility.

"I'm pretty sure that if you loved me, you wouldn't have been so content to be away from me so much. You wouldn't have expected me to do whatever your mother wanted, no matter how miserable it made me." She sighed and stood up, needing to put some physical distance between them. "I learned to accept that you like me. A lot. I know you're sexually attracted to me, more than you have ever been to another woman."

"I hear a but coming."

"But I think what you call love, I might call affection."

"And these emotions are not the same to you?"

"No."

"How are they different?"

"When you love someone, you consider their needs, their

wants, their comfort. You want to protect them and make their life better for them."

"You do not think I feel any of these things for you, harbor any of these desires?"

"So long as you are not inconvenienced, maybe."

"But if I *am* inconvenienced, you think your needs, what you want, your very comfort becomes secondary to me?"

"Until very recently, to your mother and sister as well."

"And when I tell you I love you?"

"You haven't actually said those words very much."

"But I call you *agape mou*."

"Which means *my love*, but doesn't necessarily mean you love me. It's more like calling me *darling*."

"In some instances, yes, but not between us. Not when I say it to you."

She shrugged, not willing to argue Greek semantics. When it came down to it, it was his actions that told the real story, and until very recently the story they told hadn't been a very romantic one. She wasn't sure what they said now. Guilt? Competition with his brother? Competition with himself even? Alexandros was always top marks in whatever he did.

"But you do not believe me."

Stifling another sigh, she looked at him. "Do we really need to talk about this? Only I've really been enjoying our fresh rapport and don't want it spoiled with an argument."

"Because you know it will upset me for you to acknowledge you do not believe me when I say I love you?"

"Because you don't like being wrong. Full stop. So, if we get into this and I refuse to agree that you love me, yes, you'll become upset, but worse, you'll feel the need to convince me."

"And you don't think I can," he said in dawning understanding.

She shrugged.

"*Ohi*, say what you mean."

"Fine. No I don't. Because you think if you throw enough words at it, you'll change my point of view, only it's based on five years of your actions, and those cannot be dismissed or recategorized with mere words."

"Why not? Did we both not come to realize that you had misread my actions in not inviting you to come stay in Athens with me as I misread your actions in not coming at all?"

"If you wanted a concession in a business deal, would you expect the other party to know, or would you ask for it, demand it even?" she asked, getting irritated with him for his unwillingness to let this conversation go.

Polly had accepted her husband's lack of love and found a contentment in her marriage despite it. What right had he to stir up feelings she'd settled long ago?

"My marriage is not a business deal!" He'd raised his voice, but not to scary deep, angry levels.

Even so, Polly worried Helena was going to come searching to see what had her precious papa upset.

"No, it is not, but my point is simply that the very fact you didn't ask for what you say you wanted would indicate that it wasn't that important to you."

"Not so important I might actually be afraid of your rejection?"

"You aren't afraid of anything."

"You are wrong about that, Polly. And you are wrong about what I feel for you." He stood up in one fluid movement and joined her, pulling her into his arms, his head coming down so his lips hovered right over hers. "If actions convinced you my feelings weren't as deep as they are, then actions are what is needed to change your mind. Not more words."

On that, at least, they agreed.

She didn't get the chance to say so because he kissed her and she fell into it like she always did. His mouth moved over hers even as he pressed his big body against her, the evidence of his arousal pressing into her stomach.

Flames of need flared through her core.

She wanted him. She always wanted him.

"Papa, you sure do kiss Mom a lot." Helena's little voice broke through the passionate haze surrounding Polly.

Polly went to jump back, but Alexandros stayed her with his hands. "Give me a moment," he practically pleaded.

She stilled and let her own breathing settle as she felt him will himself to calm down.

Polly turned her head to see Helena's sweet little face. "Are you finished reading your stories?"

Although Helena didn't actually read, she called it that when she told herself the stories from her books.

"I'm hungry."

"Then I'd say it is time to eat." Alexandros released Polly and stepped back, quickly angling himself away from their daughter. "Do you want to cook?" he asked Polly, "Or should we order takeaway?"

"If the fridge and pantry are stocked, I'd prefer to cook." Polly was warmed he'd thought to ask, because ordering delivery was what she knew his natural inclination would have been.

But Polly loved to cook. And he was respecting that reality right now.

"I left instructions for them to be."

"Good."

They spent the next forty-five minutes very pleasantly as a family while Polly prepared dinner after whipping up a quick snack so Helena would not grow fractious waiting.

In many ways, the next week was idyllic. Helena loved the penthouse apartment and because she had her people around her, didn't seem to miss the villa. A much more rested Polly got to take her daughter to the park, but didn't have to do a lot of chasing because the two nursery maids had accompanied them to Athens for the week.

While Hero had already agreed to make the permanent

move to Athens, and was very excited to be able to transfer to a brick-and-mortar university, Dora was still deciding if she wanted to move out of the area where her adult children continued to live.

Polly spent part of each day on the house hunt. Some days she did actual walk throughs on promising properties and others, she watched more virtual tours, narrowing down what she really wanted in their new Athens home.

She realized on about the third day in the city that she would miss the villa. Strange and unexpected as the feelings were, Polly nevertheless acknowledged she'd made friendships in the country now too. That even the villa, for all its sterility, had been her home for more than three years and she would miss it.

She brought it up to Alexandros during dinner that evening. They were eating at a Two Michelin Star restaurant while Hero watched over Helena back in the penthouse.

It was supposed to be a date night, and Polly had taken pains with her appearance, looking forward to the evening more than she wanted to admit.

"But we discussed this. You can keep the villa. No one is saying you have to sell it." Alexandros laid his hand over hers, seemingly more interested in Polly than the gourmet food in front of him.

She'd brought up her surprising—to her—ambivalence about leaving the villa. Not because she thought they had to sell it, but because it had really surprised her that she was actually a little sad about moving to Athens. More excited than sad, but still. She hadn't expected to be sad at all, and said so.

Alexandros gave her a look that went right through to her soul. "Of course you have mixed feelings. You have strong emotions and have built bonds as you are wont to do wherever you are."

"You say that like it's a good thing." Only she could remember more than one occasion when he had derided her *deeply emotional* nature as he called it.

"I have a strong suspicion that our marriage would not have lasted past the first six months if you did not feel emotions as deeply as you do. I have just cause to celebrate and be entirely grateful for that nature."

Out of nowhere her throat thickened and tears burned the back of her eyes. He was grateful for the soul-deep love that had prevented her from leaving him when she realized they might not be as well suited as their short, but intense, courtship had led her to believe.

She had cursed that same quirk of her nature more than once.

He reached across the table and took her hand, his eyes filled with affection. "Thank you for not giving up."

She shook her head, not wanting to cry. This was a date, darn it. Time to change the subject. "You talk like whether or not to keep the villa is all my decision." She winked at him. "It's a family decision surely."

And he'd said he'd like to keep the villa, so they could still spend time in the country as a family.

He shrugged. "It is your property."

"I was shocked when you told me that," she said with a smile.

She couldn't help wondering what might have been different for her over the past few years if she had known that from the beginning.

"So I noticed, though you must know your lack of knowledge of that fact surprised me." The waiter unobtrusively and silently refilled their wineglasses, before stepping away from the table.

Alexandros brushed his thumb back and forth across the palm of her hand, sending jolts of electric current through her. Such a tiny touch to elicit such a response in her body.

"How was I to know?" she asked, realizing how much

she enjoyed having her hand in his in this public setting. It felt good. Sensual, yes, but also romantic. Though she would not make the mistake of saying so.

"But I told you when we moved in."

Confused, thinking maybe she'd missed part of the conversation while focused on the effect of his hand on hers. "Told me what?"

"That I'd bought the house for you."

She thought back to that emotionally tumultuous time and tried to remember what he'd said, certain it had not been that the house was hers lock stock and barrel.

"What do you think, yineka mou? I bought it for you."

What she'd thought had not been at all charitable, and the row that had followed had been one of their worst.

"I thought you meant you bought it for me to live in." Any other interpretation had never occurred to her.

Alexandros let out a sound of frustration. "I am beginning to see that you and I have a real problem with communication."

"You think so?" she asked teasingly.

But his expression was as serious as she'd ever seen it. "If you didn't realize the villa was yours, yes, we do."

"The prenup." To her, those two words explained her belief entirely that he would not have bought such an expensive property and put it in her name.

He gave her a pained look. "The prenuptial agreement was not my way of saying I didn't see our marriage as permanent. Nor was it intended to prevent you from enjoying the gifts I wanted to give you. It was in fact, intended to protect you as much as me, if the worst happened."

"The worst?"

"Something happened that made staying married impossible." He sighed. "It wasn't a contract intended to make you think I thought that something *would* happen."

"When I first signed it, I didn't think that," she admitted. She'd been living in a dreamworld of love at first sight, where she was his forever soul mate. "But later, after things changed between us and I realized where I fit on your list of priorities, it did seem like a pretty airtight agreement to govern the eventual and maybe even *inevitable* dissolution of our marriage."

He winced when she mentioned his list of priorities, but only said. "That is the intention of a good prenup, but I saw divorce as neither eventual or inevitable." His tone held the kind of conviction she could not simply dismiss.

His honesty deserved some of her own. "Your sister and your mom were aware of the fine details of the contract and used them to poke at me whenever the occasion arose. They wanted me to realize that you didn't see me as a permanent fixture in your life."

Rage flared in his dark gaze before it banked and only sincerity remained. "But that is a lie. I married you. I consider marriage a lifetime commitment."

Which was something they *had* discussed during their whirlwind courtship. When had she started believing other people's opinions about how her husband viewed the permanence of their marriage commitment?

Probably around the same time she realized that his mother's and sister's feelings and attitudes were more important to Alexandros than Polly's were.

He let his mother literally change her name and he'd followed suit.

"This is heavy discussion for a date night," Polly said ruefully.

"I suppose dating in marriage is a little different than out of it, but I'm still hoping to get lucky later," he teased, clearly attempting to lighten the atmosphere between them.

In the mood to let him, Polly grinned back. "I think that might be arranged…but then again, I might make you wait."

His low laughter was sexy and warm.

* * *

When they left the restaurant, Alexandros surprised Polly by taking her to a swank city hotel rather than back to the penthouse.

"What are we doing here?" she asked as he helped her out of the car.

"As much as we both love our daughter, I thought we could use a night for just us." Alexandros took Polly's arm and led her inside, bypassing the large and elegant lobby. "We have a suite on the top floor."

"Helena will be sleeping by the time we get back to the penthouse," Polly pointed out.

"Yes, but if she wakes in the night, or earlier than we do, Hero will be there for her." He smiled down at Polly with devastating charm. "While I will be there for you."

"Oh, you think I might wake in the middle of the night?"

"I plan for you to be awake, whether you will have gotten any sleep is debatable."

A frisson of anticipation zinged through Polly. "I love that tone you get."

"What tone?" he asked as he led her onto the elevator and then used his keycard to access the top floor. "The one that says I want you?"

She would have answered, but he tugged Polly into his body and covered her lips with his own, the kiss claiming and intentional and everything she loved about being the focus of this man's sexual desire.

The doors of the elevator opened a moment later, but Alexandros did not pull away. He just shifted, so she was protected in the corner as he continued to kiss her.

Polly was peripherally aware of a woman's voice and a man's low chuckle, but even knowing they shared the elevator, she could not make herself break the amazing kiss. Alexandros was not one for public displays of affection, and knowing that made the way he held her and continued to move his lips against hers, even hotter.

Alexandros moved his mouth to her ear, breathing softly in her ear and sending chills through her. "Finally. We are alone."

"We are?" she asked breathlessly.

He laughed low and husky. "Didn't you notice the other couple get off a moment ago?"

"No." She turned and nibbled that spot on his neck she knew drove her husband crazy. "Maybe I should be worried you did."

"I am always aware of our surroundings when I am with you. It's my job to make sure you are protected."

CHAPTER EIGHT

"I wish you'd felt that way about your mother and sister." The words were out before she'd even thought them, old wounds too deep to ignore completely. She sighed. "I'm sorry."

He leaned back and looked down at her, his expression searching. "Why are you sorry?"

The elevator stopped and the doors opened. Polly stepped into the elegant foyer, inhaling the heady scent of jasmine as she noticed a beautiful bouquet on the marble table. "Which is our room?" she asked, indicating the four doors off the foyer.

"This way." Alexandros led her to the right and swiped his keycard to open the door.

She stepped inside, where the scent of her favorite essential oils permeating the room. Jasmine that had so delighted her when they stepped off the elevator mixed with vanilla and just the hints of orange and myrrh. It was a mix that had been prepared especially for her and that she used only in the diffuser in *her* room in the villa.

She looked around for a diffuser, but couldn't find it at first, until she realized a gorgeous clay pot glazed in deep blues and browns had mist coming from the stylized top. "Where did you get my aromatherapy mix?" she asked, a little awed.

Yes, he was a billionaire. Yes, her husband was scarily efficient, but to have gotten her scent he had to have noticed it that *one* time he'd been in *her* room.

It was the kind of attention to the tiny details in relation to her that he had shown when they first got together, but much less frequently since marriage and her move to Greece.

"I asked the housekeeper at the villa why your room smelled so perfectly like you."

Polly smiled, flattered he considered the delicious blend of scents as much *her* as she did. "That diffuser is a work of art."

"Literally. I contacted an artist you like and asked if she had anything that could be made into a diffuser."

"When did you do that?"

"Last week."

"She worked fast."

"She had the art piece. It was just a matter of installing the water chamber, etc."

"For a date night?" she asked, just a little stunned.

"For a gift. I thought using it tonight would make the gift more special."

Polly couldn't help herself, didn't even want to. She reached up and hugged him exuberantly and kissed him the same way before leaning back. "Thank you. It's lovely."

"I am glad you like it. Now, why were you sorry in the elevator?"

Polly sighed and then grimaced. "We're having such a nice date. I don't want to ruin it."

"That is the second time you have said that. Believe me when I tell you that the only thing that would ruin this date is if you were to leave."

"I'm pretty sure you wouldn't be thrilled if we didn't make love." She would not be keen on such an outcome either.

"I love your body, my dear wife, but even if you were not to share it with me tonight, I would still count myself a very lucky man to be here with you."

"You used to say stuff like that all the time." She'd noticed when he stopped.

"And you used to kiss and hug me several times a day." He had noticed when she'd stopped too.

Was it possible he'd felt something of the insecurity that had plagued her when their relationship changed?

"Hugging and kissing you isn't a hardship," she offered before doing both again.

He kept her close and deepened the kiss when she would have pulled away. Somehow she found herself sitting on a cream sofa in front of the fireplace in the sitting area, making out with her husband. He did something with one of his hands and then the fire flared to life and Polly couldn't help smiling.

"You know how much I love a fire in the evening." Not that fires were necessary but a few nights a year in the Mediterranean climate.

"I'm in all-out seduction mode, if you hadn't noticed." He said it lightly, like he was teasing, but something in his gorgeous espresso gaze said he was entirely serious.

"Let me let you in on a secret, Alexandros. When it comes to you, I'm a sure a thing."

"That is good to hear, *agape mou*, but I have learned not to take anything about my very precious wife for granted."

"You're turning into quite the romantic." And she really didn't care if that was prompted by his need to prove he was as good a, or better, husband than his brother.

His smile flashed, his entire face covered in happiness.

But before she could ask him why he seemed so happy, he kissed her again. This time, hands came into play. Dragging an inciting hand up her leg and her inner thigh, and cupping her breast with his other hand, his thumb playing over her already stiff nipple, Alexandros seemed intent on driving her insane with need before they even got their clothes off.

He teased reactions from her body like a man who had spent years studying it, like she was the specially crafted instrument and he the prodigy who would spend the rest of his life playing it.

Not a passive lover by nature, Polly gave as good as she got, touching her husband as only she was allowed to do.

That truth had never gotten old. She was way more possessive than she ever thought she would be, but in his way, Alexandros was too.

One thing she never worried about was that he would have a roving eye. Because, like hers, his possessive streak was accompanied by a bedrock of loyalty that would not be shaken.

Needing more intimacy than they could achieve with their clothes on, Polly sat up and shook her head. "Stop for a minute, Andros."

Her husband went so still, she wasn't even sure he was breathing.

"I didn't meant freeze." She laughed. "Just get your clothes off."

"The love, it is still inside you. Perhaps buried very deeply, but still there."

She wasn't having some heavy conversation in the middle of sex. Not today. "Get naked." When he still didn't move, she said, "Please."

"Say it again and I will do whatever you wish."

"Say what again?" she demanded, ready to recite the alphabet in both English and Greek if it meant getting his suit off.

"Call me Andros."

Nonplussed, she stared at him. He was serious. She wasn't sure why it was so important to him that she call him by the nickname she'd once used exclusively, but she wasn't about to say no. Not if it meant getting what she wanted.

"*Andros*, take off your clothes."

He shuddered, like she'd touched him in the very way she was longing to do. "*Ne. Ne.* Anything you want, *yineka mou.*"

He stood up and stripped out of his suit before she even got the zip undone on her dress. Lately she wasn't keen on zippers, but when she knew her evening would end with her husband, that was something different.

He loved unzipping her, and she loved how he kissed her nape and between her shoulder blades when he did.

So why was she even trying to undo the zip herself?

Because she wanted naked. Now. Only... Maybe she still wanted that little bit of pampering too.

"Could you?" She meant to turn and offer him her back but the view of his body arrested all movement on her end.

She loved the olive-toned skin that rippled over muscles honed by a strict workout regime some athletes would find it difficult to maintain. But Polly's husband never did anything by halves. He had to be the best at whatever he did.

Which meant he'd worked out his training schedule with a trainer who also served top echelon athletes.

The results were fantastic as far as Polly was concerned, both because she loved looking at her husband's amazing body but also because she knew he was taking care of his health.

Ensuring he would be with her and their children for a very long time to come.

But that amazing body that turned her on so much?

Also served as a reminder of how important it was to Alexandros to be the best. Not second, and definitely not a poor shower, especially, she thought, when compared to his brother.

"Stop," he instructed.

"Stop what?" she asked.

"Whatever you are thinking. Just stop thinking it."

A small laugh huffed out of her. He was so arrogant, thinking he could dictate even her thoughts, but in this instance? He had a point.

"I want you." She would always want him.

"I am so hungry for you I'm not going to get your dress off if we don't get that zip down now," he told her, his voice a near growl.

Shivers of desire and atavistic need skated along her every nerve ending.

Polly shifted so he could reach the zipper. Finally.

If she didn't know better, she'd think his hand trembled against her as he tugged the zip down, but there was no mistaking the sucking in of air as he exposed her back. "I would love to take time to appreciate the beauty of this sexy bit of lace holding your gorgeous breasts in, but it will have to be another time."

He undid the clasp and pulled the fabric aside before placing a kiss on her spine. But it was the kiss on her nape, the one she'd been waiting for that made her shudder with need.

"You are so perfect for me. So responsive."

"Yes." The one thing they'd always gotten right was their perfect physical response to one another.

He brushed her dress down her body, letting it pool at her hips as he slid his hands back up her torso to cup her breasts. Polly was so sensitive that she moaned at the contact. Alexandros brushed his thumbs over her turgid nipples and the sound that came out of her was far more animalistic.

"Yes, play with them, Andros!" she demanded.

"Like this?" he asked, pinching her nipples with just the right amount of pressure.

Each press of thumb to forefinger matched a pulse of pleasure in her most intimate place.

"So good!" She loved touching him, but sometimes she enjoyed him playing her body like the sexual virtuoso he was to her.

Alexandros began tugging her nipples and rolling them in between the simple moments of pressure, and pleasure built in Polly as if he was caressing her clitoris. "I'm going to come like this," she warned him, unable to believe she was so on edge.

Polly pressed her thighs together, sending sparks of ecstasy through her core, but it wasn't enough.

"Andros, please!" She wanted. She needed. She was in an agony of pleasure not quite fulfilled.

"Then, come for me, *yineka mou*. Show me what my

touch to your body does," he coaxed against her ear, hot air sending more chills of pleasure along her body.

"I…" She moaned. Words were too hard.

He pinched just a little harder on her nipples, his hard sex pressing against her back, his need clear, but he made no move to stop doing what he was doing.

"Inside!" She shifted her pelvis, seeking more touch between them. "I want you inside."

"I thought you wanted it like this," he said gutturally.

"Inside!" she demanded again.

He didn't make her beg, but lifted her so her dress could fall to the floor. Her and Alexandros's fingers tangled in the attempt to get rid of her panties, but neither laughed.

He grunted, she mewled with need and the lingerie was on the floor with her dress.

Then he lifted her, and she spread her legs, knowing what he wanted. Alexandros lowered her until his leaking sex kissed her tender flesh. She pushed down so his head pressed inside.

He let her take him at her own pace, though his body was rigid with the effort.

Finally he was in, filling her intimately as no other man ever would do, as no other woman would ever feel him. They rocked together, chasing pleasure, seeking that ultimate moment of completion.

Usually in this position, he reached around to touch that special bundle of nerves, but he continued his ministrations to her breasts and nipples. And that was all she needed.

Overwhelming pleasure spiraled inside her, built even more quickly by how his hardness caressed her G-spot.

"That's right, *agape mou*. Move on me like I am all that you need."

"You are," she gasped out, her breath coming in harsh pants.

"And *you* are all that *I* need."

The words sent her careening into the ultimate pleasure, her body convulsing around his, a shout of intimate joy coming out of her. He pressed his mouth into her neck, his movements growing jerky, and then he let out a guttural groan against her neck, his own climax making that big body under hers go rigid.

Afterward he carried her into the shower, a decadent tile enclosure easily big enough for the two of them. They washed each other, their knowledge of the other's body not making the exercise any less special or enticing.

When he lifted her and carried her dripping wet to the bed to make love again, she could only ask him to hurry.

This time, he took his time, building the pleasure between them until they were both sweaty and shaking with need. When they finally went over, she thought she'd sleep on the damp sheets and not care, she was so wrung out from pleasure.

But Alexandros ran her a bath and then joined her after calling housekeeping to come change the sheets while they were in the bath.

"Nice to be a billionaire," she slurred sleepily, lying against him in the softly scented water.

"Even nicer to be your husband." His tone was intense, like he wasn't joking.

She was too tired to figure out whatever message he was trying to give. "I'm not changing the sheets." She yawned. "Be lucky if I make it back to the bed."

"Do not worry, *yineka mou*, I will take care of you."

She patted his chest. "Nice husband."

Dozy, she didn't catch what he said.

They soaked for a while before he lifted her lax body from the water. Alexandros helped her dry before drying himself and then carrying her to the freshly made bed.

The following days were idyllic. Like she'd always dreamed her marriage would be.

Alexandros was back in the penthouse every evening

by six. They ate dinner early together as a family before he helped her put Helena to bed. He usually spent an hour or so on the computer in the evenings, but Polly understood his multibillion-dollar company demanded more than a nine-to-five effort from its head. They didn't watch movies on the sofa together, but Polly usually ended up sitting, leaning against him as she read or worked on recipe ideas in her notebook.

Alexandros had joined Polly and Helena for lunch twice, which she'd loved and so had their daughter. Polly and Alexandros had curtailed their social obligations in ways she'd never believed he would be open to.

They had only attended three high society functions, and Polly was thriving under the less demanding schedule.

She felt better than she had since getting pregnant. No longer exhausted, she reveled in the time she had to spend with her daughter, exploring the child-friendly parks and attractions of the ancient city.

Polly loved it all, but there was a little place in her heart that didn't trust this new lifestyle to last.

That same place made her put off any concrete actions looking for a house in Athens. She kept looking at videos the estate agent sent her and passing on likely candidates to Alexandros, but Polly avoided in-depth discussions about the potential properties, and while she'd gone to visit a couple, she had not asked Alexandros to join her.

She could not help wondering if they lived somewhere not quite as convenient for her husband as an elevator ride away, would she and their daughter see him nearly as much?

They had been in Athens two weeks when Alexandros brought the house hunt up as they relaxed together in the living room after putting Helena to bed together. He was on his computer, and she was continuing to catch up on her reading list, their silence companionable.

So she was startled when he asked, "Are you really finding it that difficult to find a house that will meet our needs here in Athens?"

She laid her books aside and stared at him, trying to assemble her thoughts without sounding like the untrusting wife she was. "Um, no, of course not."

"I thought you'd love that house in Palaio Psychico." He mentioned one of the properties she'd gone to view in person.

A gorgeous, newly built house with a pool that was half indoor and half outdoor, a play area already prepared for children with a climbing structure with slides and swing. The architect had designed rooms and a layout that felt comfortable. It was the best candidate so far for something Polly would consider a family home, not just a showplace.

"Your sister would have kittens if you bought me a house in the most exclusive neighborhood of Athens." Which was not an answer.

His expression said he recognized her misdirection for what it was. "Since when do you care what my sister thinks?"

"You don't like upsetting her. Or your mother," she reminded him, in case he'd forgotten.

Life had gotten very strange in past weeks.

"In case you have not noticed, I have learned my lesson in that regard."

"I, yes, I'm sure. Lesson? Why are we talking about your family?" Only she knew why. She'd brought them up.

Would Polly *ever* learn *her* lesson in this regard?

Alexandros set his computer aside and shifted Polly from her comfy spot beside him to his lap. Feelings that had nothing to do with house hunting sparked through her.

"You are babbling, *yineka mou*. Why is that, I wonder?"

She shrugged, much more interested in the feel of his hard thighs under her bottom than their current discussion.

He laughed. "Hold that thought and answer my question."

"What question?" she asked, her thought train derailing on a tide of lust.

He cursed. "You are too delectable, but we are not ignoring our relationship for sex this time."

"Isn't sex part of our relationship?" she asked as she shifted and sighed with the decadent pleasure of his nearness.

He kissed her like he couldn't help himself, the passion between them building fast. She was working on the buttons of his shirt, wanting skin, when his hand stilled hers.

"Stop," he ordered gutturally. "I mean it, Polly."

She smiled at his use of her name and not the despised Anna. "I don't want to stop."

"We'll make love."

"Of course we will." It was the one part of their marriage they got right.

She didn't realize she'd said those words aloud until he lifted her from his lap and placed her back on the sofa. "And maybe that is part of the problem, *agape mou*."

She frowned, still not always comfortable with his use of that particular endearment and more than a little unhappy about the physical distance between them he had created. She would feel rejected, but the bulge in his slacks proved he was as turned on as she was.

Only he wanted to talk.

And Polly? Really didn't. Talking wasn't all it was cracked up to be.

But the stubborn expression on his face said Alexandros wasn't letting this go.

Feeling vulnerable in a way she hadn't in a very long time with him, Polly crossed her arms over her chest and settled back against the sofa, doing her very best to give the impression of a woman who could take or leave lovemaking. "I would say it's a very good thing."

After all, if they weren't so good at the intimacy part of their marriage, she wasn't entirely sure their marriage would have survived the first year. That didn't make her feel proud, but it was a truth she could not ignore.

"It is a wonderful thing," he assured her.

"And yet you are over there." She indicated the other end of the sofa with a wave of her hand. "And I am here."

"Do not pout. This is important, I think."

"I am not pouting." Maybe.

His smile was indulgent, but the expression in his espresso gaze was serious. "Our marriage has been broken for a very long time, and I did not realize it because I am blessed with a wife who is generous and beautifully passionate in bed."

"What are you saying?"

"Why haven't you asked me to look at any of the house options here in Athens?" he asked, showing he had that trick down too.

She shrugged. "Are we in a rush to find a house?"

"You are less than three months away from giving birth. I would say so, yes."

"But we don't have to move before the baby is born."

"Why wouldn't we?"

"Maybe I like living here in the penthouse. Helena is happy here."

"She would be just as happy in a house with a garden to play in."

"We have the roof garden." It had a pool as well, and she and Helena got their daily dose of swimming just as they had at the villa. There was room for a play structure up there, but she didn't know how Alexandros would feel about changing the look from elegant showpiece to family friendly.

"You want to stay here?" he asked, surprise lacing his tone. "We could turn the guest room into a nursery, I suppose." He frowned as if in thought. "I imagined you'd prefer to have more room."

She laughed, the sound harsher than she would have expected. "Helena and I used maybe four rooms in the villa when you weren't there."

He grimaced, acknowledging a truth he'd been ignorant of until very recently. "Because it felt too much like a hotel to you."

"Yes." She sighed, deciding to be honest, even though she wasn't sure about revealing her thoughts and fears to the man she had learned not to trust, but had never stopped loving.

Whoever said there could be no love without trust didn't understand the nature of consuming love.

Of course, she'd prefer to trust her husband with her heart, but she wasn't going to stop loving him just because she couldn't.

She took a deep breath and let it out slowly. "Cards on the table?"

"That is one of those American idioms you are so fond of, isn't it?"

She rolled her eyes. And he accused her of going off on tangents. "Yes, it means—"

"That you will show me your thoughts you've been hiding. Yes I know."

"I'm not hiding anything." She sighed. "Not on purpose."

"What have you been hiding *not on purpose*?" he asked.

"Okay. First of all, you realize that this penthouse has more square footage than the house I grew up in?"

He inclined his head, waiting, she was sure for her to get to the point.

"My parents raised four children in that house."

"So, you want a smaller house?" he asked, sounding like he was trying to figure out what she was saying.

"Not per se, but this penthouse has four bedrooms. Yes, one is set up as an office that we can both use, so that's nice."

"You are rambling again."

"I'm not. I'm explaining."

"I apologize. I am listening." He made the gesture she'd taught Helena to indicate turning her listening ears on.

Polly smiled. "Good. We don't need a guest room. We can put my family up in either the corporate apartments, when they come to visit, or a hotel if you have business associates using the apartments on the next level down."

"Business associates or out-of-town employees can use a hotel in that case. Family always comes first," Alexandros declared.

"That's great. I'd rather have Mom and Dad closer when they come to stay especially."

"But you do not want a house that could accommodate this?" he asked.

"I like the penthouse. I like especially that it's so easy for you to come home to."

Understanding flared in his gorgeous gaze. "You think if we buy a house that will require any sort of commute that I will not come home as often?"

"Yes. Even Palaio Psychico would require a fifteen-minute drive in good traffic." If they moved there, her super busy tycoon husband would have no hope of popping in for lunch when his schedule had an extra hour in it.

"And that is thirty minutes more than you want to spend away from me each day?" he asked, sounding pleased rather than like he thought she was needy and demanding.

Which gave her the courage for honesty. "Closer to an hour with you coming home in congested traffic, but yes."

"And perhaps you are worried that if I have to work late into the evening, I will be tempted to stay here rather than drive to our home?" he guessed.

She shrugged. They both knew that was more probability than possibility.

"I assure you that it would never happen."

That was nice of him to say, but she had her doubts.

They must have shown on her face because he frowned. "In essence, you do not want to pick out your dream home here in Athens because you do not trust me to place a priority to spend time there with you and our children?"

He wasn't sounding so pleased now.

"You're a workaholic, Alexandros. Pretending otherwise won't change the truth."

"I explained that."

"You explained not being around for my first pregnancy. And I understand it now, even if I wish you'd been forthcoming at the time. But Alexandros, you have *always* worked long hours. Since our move to the villa, you spent at least one night *every* week here in the penthouse. Sometimes multiple nights."

"That cannot be true." Now he was giving her the look, the one that said she was too demanding and needy.

Polly pulled her defenses around her, reminding herself this was why she could no longer trust him with her love. "If you don't believe me, look at your pilot's log. It will show you the truth."

He grabbed his phone, she was sure, doing exactly that. He no doubt thought he would prove her wrong, but his expression changed to one of chagrin as he read the pilot's log.

She waited in silence for him to acknowledge the truth.

He put the phone down, his expression easily read. Her super smart, super competitive husband did not like being wrong.

"Well," she prompted.

"Not every week." He sighed. "But as good as. And I now realize I spent multiple nights here in the penthouse far more often than I should have."

She said nothing. She'd known that. She hadn't needed to read the pilot's log. Why? Because she had missed Alexandros when he was gone. Obviously, he had not been as afflicted, not even realizing how much time he spent away from her and Helena.

"Nevertheless, a fifty-minute helicopter ride is not the

same as a fifteen-minute drive," he claimed in the growing silence between them.

"But an unnecessary commute, in any case."

"We cannot do the type of entertaining expected of a man of my stature in the penthouse."

"We still have the villa. We can continue to entertain there when necessary and host the local events at the same facilities we've used in the past."

"But that was when our home was in the country. We are talking about my family living full-time in Athens."

"So, buying a house here in Athens is about your consequence?" she asked quietly, not surprised, but a little disappointed by that fact.

He stared at her. "That is not what I said."

"Isn't it?"

"Are you picking a fight?"

"Disagreeing with you is not me picking a fight, Alexandros. Neither is me asking you a legitimate question."

He surged up from the couch, anger making the lines of his gorgeous face harsh. "So once again I am the big bad billionaire?"

CHAPTER NINE

INAPPROPRIATELY, POLLY WANTED to laugh.

But he had the look of a sulky boy, and she just knew he wouldn't appreciate her saying so.

"You may be big," she teased, indicating a certain part of his anatomy with a significant look. "And there is no question you are a billionaire, but I never said you were bad."

"You did. You said I am a bad husband."

She opened her mouth to deny, but realized she *had* said that, or as good as. "You've improved loads," she offered.

"And let us not forget I perform well in the bedroom," he said angrily.

She blinked at him, not sure what to say. Alexandros was happy to go head-to-head with power players, but he'd never liked arguing with her. If she gave him an out, he always took it.

Always.

For some reason, this time, he was forcing the issue, refusing to brush uncomfortable feelings back under the carpet.

"Please remember that I want to live here so your children and I can have more time with you. This is not me saying you are a bad husband." That was absolute truth. "It is me saying I want our marriage to work. If you're serious about fixing the brokenness, then so am I."

The anger drained away, but the expression it left behind was more sad than relieved. "I must cling to that truth, I suppose."

She put her hand out, asking silently for help standing. Not that she couldn't get up on her own, but it was harder now and she wanted the physical connection.

He immediately took her hand and leaned forward to

slide a hand around her waist before smoothly pulling her to her feet.

"Thank you." She made no move to put distance between them. "Is it really so important for you to have a showcase here in Athens?"

He leaned his forehead against hers, not speaking for several seconds.

She didn't push.

"No. It is not, but the idea that you don't trust me to change…that hurts."

"I am sorry," she whispered, unable to deny the lack of trust.

"Me too."

She didn't ask what he was sorry for. Was he sorry she didn't trust him? Was he sorry he had destroyed that trust? Did it matter?

They made love that night with a tender desperation, both needing the connection of their bodies to affirm their merged lives.

The next day Polly chatted with Corrina about her desire to continue living in the penthouse apartment. "You and Petros seem more than happy living here," she pointed out.

"And I wouldn't mind staying indefinitely." Corrina paused and then shrugged. "If some changes were made to make this area more family friendly."

Polly looked around the perfectly manicured container garden on the roof, the furniture that was designed to impress business associates and even the pool that didn't have a rail on the stairs going into the shallow end for children to hold on to.

"You know your husband actually owns the Kristalakis Building, not the corporation? I asked and Petros told me." Corrina smiled at Helena's antics in the pool. "Your daughter is so sweet."

Polly smiled. "I like to think so."

Their younger nursemaid, Hero, was swimming with the three-year-old, looking like she was having as much fun in the water as the toddler.

"Anyway, the company could easily buy condos or use hotels for corporate guests, and the family could reclaim the floor below our places," Corrina suggested. "The apartments could be remodeled to accommodate the security team as well as a playroom for the children and suites for family guests."

Polly frowned at the work that would take, but was unable to dismiss the idea entirely. "That would be a pretty big undertaking."

Corrina shrugged with the insouciance of someone born to wealth. "It's not as if you'd have to put up with the mess. They wouldn't be touching our apartments. You know?"

"But…"

"And we could wait to do the remodel until after your family visits for the baby. Until then, the security team and family can use the apartments as they are."

"I like the idea of indoor play area for the children."

"The roof garden isn't exactly practical on the hottest days of summer for anything other than swimming, but we're going to have to install some shading up here. I've wanted some for a while. And that area over there would be a great spot for a play structure." Corrina indicated the center of the roof. "We don't need to get rid of the helicopter pad, just shift to the spot they land and put up a wall with a locking gate for safety's sake."

It would be the safest and easiest to oversee spot, but it would definitely change the roof to family focused rather than business impressive.

"You've been thinking about this."

"I want children someday and I don't want to move into the family house, Polly."

"But Petros would buy you your own home."

Corrina didn't look too sure about that. "Maybe. Maybe not. He's really struggling with the family schism that's happening right now."

"Is he?" Polly felt badly, knowing that schism was between *her* and her mother-and sister-in-law.

"Yes." Corrina reached out and patted Polly's arm. "Don't get that look. I mean it. This is not your fault. It is Athena's and Stacia's fault. They're both way too used to getting their way with Alexandros and Petros. Trust me, I wasn't putting up with Athena manipulating my marriage, much less that little madame, Stacia."

Not like they'd manipulated Polly's. Polly got that. Still. "You're everything Athena wanted in a daughter-in-law."

"Don't you believe it. Women like that are never happy with their daughters-in-law. They want to be the center of their sons' lives."

"No, I'm sure Athena wants both her sons to be happy. She just doesn't believe Alexandros can be happy with me." As hurtful as her mother-in-law's behavior had been for Polly, she had never felt the other woman was purely selfish.

Not like Stacia.

"More the fool her. No one else could have given Alexandros what he needed in a wife. Only a blind person would think differently."

Uncomfortable with that declaration, Polly fell back on humor. "We're very compatible in bed." She waggled her brows suggestively and both women cracked up.

"What is so funny?" Petros asked, sliding onto the seat beside his wife.

"Papa! Uncle Petros! Look how fast I swim!" Helena demanded from the pool.

"Is something wrong?" Polly asked Alexandros as he settled into a matching chair kitty-corner to Polly's.

It was midmorning, nowhere near lunchtime.

"No. Why should there be?" Alexandros's expression chided her.

Because it was work hours and he was there, with them, not in his office doing stuff to take over the business world? She didn't say that, realizing from his expectant and not altogether pleasant expression, he was just waiting for her to say something of the sort.

Not sure why he was suddenly spoiling for an argument, Polly just gave him a sugar-sweet smile. "No reason."

Her husband's dark gaze narrowed. "A meeting got canceled and I decided to spend my suddenly free hour with my family."

"Well, I'm glad you did," she said sincerely.

And that was one more reason staying here in the penthouse was a good idea. Apparently if they were close at hand, Alexandros would opt to give his family these unexpected moments rather than work.

Even if that only happened occasionally, it was worth it.

Alexandros clapped along with his brother in appreciation of Helena's swimming efforts.

"Well done, poppet," Polly said to her daughter with a big smile.

"Now that smile is genuine. What do I have to do, I wonder, to earn that kind of warm approval?" Alexandros said, his voice low and sensual. "Or do I already know?"

Polly looked over at him, realizing what he was implying at the same time as she caught that even if his brother had not heard what she'd said to cause her and Corrina's laughter, her husband had.

And while his tease had been all sexual innuendo, there had been an angry edge to it Polly did not understand.

But she got it later when they were readying for bed, and it appalled her. "You want to do what?" she demanded, making no effort to modulate her tone to something resembling calm.

"You are convinced the only place I value you is in the

bedroom. I think we should take a break from sex while we work on other aspects of our marriage."

"Whose idea was this? Have you been talking to your mother?" she demanded.

"I have in fact, but it wasn't her idea."

"I bet. She convinced you it was your idea, didn't she?" Athena had tried suggesting the no-sex thing once already, ostensibly for the sake of Polly's health during her pregnancy.

"My mother feels badly for all she has done to undermine our marriage and the ways she hurt you, even when it was entirely unintentional."

Unintentional? "Did you just imply your mother did not mean to undermine our marriage? That there was something accidental about her assurances that our marriage was a temporary aberration in your life and the prenuptial agreement was proof?" she asked in a dangerously controlled voice.

Alexandros didn't appear worried. "She misunderstood the prenuptial agreement as much as you did."

"Oh, did she? And why is that?"

He tugged at the collar on the shirt he had yet to remove in preparation for his shower before bed. "The agreement my father had her sign was materially different."

"It was?" Polly asked in a flat tone, never having considered that possibility.

"It was a different time."

"Was it?" Or had his father simply trusted his wife more than Alexandros had trusted Polly?

Another possibility sent a hollow feeling through Polly. Maybe subconsciously, Alexandros *had* considered their marriage temporary. But then Polly had gotten pregnant and their marriage became a permanent fixture in his life, one he could never admit to himself, much less anyone else that he had ever seen in a different light.

"You know, Alexandros, I'm done fighting your mother's

machinations. You want to sleep separately while we *work on* our marriage? Be my guest." She pointed to the closed door, her message clear.

"I did not say we should sleep separately."

"You said we shouldn't have sex." And if he thought that was possible while sharing a bed, he'd lost his mind.

"Well, yes." Though he wasn't sounding so confident about that little detail.

Right at that moment, Polly did not care.

She went into the closet and came out with a suit, shirt and tie for him to wear the next day. "Take these to the guest room. I'll get your underthings and you can grab your stuff from the bathroom."

"What? I'm not moving out of our bedroom."

"Yes. Yes, you are."

He took the clothes from her but shook his head. "No, that is not what I meant."

"Neither of us can sleep in the same bed without touching each other. I choose not to be teased by what I cannot have. Ergo you will be sleeping in the guest room."

"But that is not what I want."

"Tough."

He stared at her like she was the unreasonable one. She didn't care. She was just done.

"Get out, Alexandros. I need my rest." She placed her hand protectively over her stomach, not even a little ashamed to pull the pregnancy card.

She'd had two difficult pregnancies and very little in the way of accommodation for them.

She'd spent so long not giving in to her own limitations for his sake and the sake of peace between them, but she was done with that too.

For once, Polly was going to insist on what she wanted, what would be easiest for her.

His male pride and ego could go hang.

He'd promised her he wouldn't let his mother, or sister, come between them, but here he was doing just that. All the anger that Polly had tamped down for five years of marriage was sizzling through her bloodstream like lava, the volcano of her fury so close to eruption, it was all she could do not to scream.

"You said we get along in bed," he said, like that should explain everything.

"And you said you want to give that up to focus on other areas of our marriage. I guess we'll see just how good you are at doing that, won't we?" she asked with a snide tone she wasn't proud of, but neither was she shouting at him.

So, there was that.

He drew himself up like her words had firmed his resolve. "Yes, we will."

"Well, then…" She indicated the door with her hand.

He frowned. "We can still share a bed."

"No, we cannot. You want no sex. I want to sleep alone. Deal with it."

"Polly you should not take this as a rejection."

"Don't worry, that's not how I see it."

"I want to say that's good, but your tone implies it's not."

"Alexandros, I'm done talking. Please leave."

He opened his mouth but then shut it as if her words had finally registered and he had decided to respect her desires.

With a final look at her that she could not read and didn't really care to, Alexandros turned and left. He was back moments later to retrieve the pile of remaining things he'd need for the morning that she'd gathered.

She waited until he was finished in the bathroom before going inside to take her evening shower, ignoring his quiet *good-night* as he left the room.

If a few angry and pain-filled tears mixed with the water, there was no one else there to see.

Alexandros flopped to his side, missing his wife's form in the bed next to him more than he would have expected, even though this sleeping arrangement was not what he'd been angling for. After all, sleeping on his own in the penthouse wasn't something new for him. But he could not get comfortable.

He wasn't so stupid he even tried to tell himself it was the bed. He missed Polly and couldn't help feeling he might have made a huge tactical error.

The conviction that Polly believed the only thing they had between them was sex had grown day by day. She'd said it more than once.

Bed was the one place in their marriage that they got it right.

He was too much of an overachiever to accept that kind of limitation. He wanted her to trust him. To believe he loved her.

He didn't want her to think his words of love were just a mix of affection and lust like she'd said they were.

He loved her madly, deeply and forever.

No way could he accept that view.

And he was at a loss as to why she could not see the truth.

Yes, he'd made some mistakes. Loads of them if he were honest, but he'd shown her his love too. Okay, yes, they struggled with communication. Yes, she'd misunderstood some things, but enough to believe he didn't know what he meant when he told her he loved her?

It made no sense.

Alexandros had given more to Polly than he had to any woman that had come before her.

He had made her his wife. He had changed things in his life to make her happy.

Only somehow, he had failed.

And failure did not sit well with him.

He *would* prove to his wife that he loved her and didn't just lust after her. Though that emotion was strong enough.

He hadn't argued with his banishment to the guest room for two reasons.

One, his wife was angry with him, but it was the look of wounded vulnerability he could not argue with.

And two, she had been right. If he slept with her in his arms, he would have touched her. And if he touched her, his good intentions would not have stood against his physical need for her.

Maybe he needed to prove to both of them that lust was not the basis of their marriage.

He knew she thought his mother had instigated this, but Polly was wrong on that count. Every time his wife had implied their compatibility in the bedroom was their saving grace, he'd grown more and more bothered.

And determined to prove her wrong.

His mother had told him that if he wanted to fix what he had broken, he would have to sacrifice his own wants and desires.

He could not think of a bigger sacrifice than to give up sex with his wife while he proved himself to her.

But lying there in the dark, craving her touch, just wanting to hear her breathing beside him, he had to question his own wisdom.

Perhaps he could prove his love without giving up the one thing they got right.

Maybe he'd been a world-class idiot giving that one thing up when there was a very real possibility it was the *only* thing that had kept his marriage together at times.

The thought chilled him and made it no easier to sleep.

Alexandros heard his wife moving around as soon as she got up.

Though she was quiet, no doubt not wanting to wake their energetic daughter, he was aware of every rustle that indicated Pollyanna was no longer sleeping peacefully in their bed. If she had slept peacefully at all. He certainly had not.

The prospect that his request the night before had given

his wife as poor a night's rest as he'd had did not sit well with him.

Skipping his usual workout, Alexandros was even more efficient than normal with his morning ablutions, finishing his shower quickly and dressing without fuss. Alexandros left his suit jacket off until after breakfast as was his usual habit and went in search of Pollyanna.

She wasn't in their room or the kitchen as he'd expected her to be. She baked when stressed and he'd half expected to walk into controlled chaos, but the kitchen was pristine. A quick search of the apartment and their personal terrace only revealed his still-sleeping daughter in her room.

He opened the door to the foyer. No Polly.

But their security guard was in his usual place.

"My wife?" Alexandros inquired.

The guard nodded toward the ceiling. "Up on the rooftop."

"Alone?" Alexandros barked.

He tried to let Polly have as much normalcy to her life as possible, but she was the wife of a billionaire. Alone was not a word she got to indulge in.

"No, *kyrios*. Sanders is up there watching her from a distance."

Trying to give his wife the illusion of privacy. Alexandros approved.

Alexandros nodded his acknowledgment before knocking on the door of his brother's apartment. Petros was dressed to work out, as Alexandros had expected he would be. They both started their days early.

"I need you to keep an ear out for Helena while I talk to Pollyanna."

His brother didn't ask why, or suggest they talk later, just nodded his head and made his way into the other penthouse apartment. Knowing his daughter was in good hands, Alexandros headed up to the roof.

Sanders stood unobtrusively in the shadows, and Alexandros dismissed him with a quick hand gesture.

Pollyanna didn't seem to be aware of Alexandros's presence, her focus on the budding sunrise. Ensconced on the designer outdoor sectional the decorator had assured him was perfect for the space, her feet tucked under her, she held a steaming mug.

His wife had not dressed, but merely pulled a wrap on over her pajamas. It was a homey look that she made altogether too enticing.

"*Kalimera*, Pollyanna."

She looked up, no surprise evident in the smooth movement, her expression serious but lacking the suppressed fury that had been there the night before.

In that moment, he did not know if that was a good or bad thing.

"Good morning, Alexandros. I see you are ready to face your day."

He shrugged. It would never occur to him to come out onto the rooftop garden half-dressed, much less in his sleep shorts and T-shirt.

It was one of the ways they were very different. He did not have the luxury of presenting any appearance but absolute control.

He settled on the sectional as well, rather than taking one of the armchairs. "How did you sleep?"

She gave an almost smile. "You know? Surprisingly well. I was so angry you were listening to your mother about our marriage again, but suddenly I was just tired. And I slept."

He winced. That didn't sound as promising as it should have. Tired of him? Tired of trying? Tired of what?

"My mother told me that if I wanted to fix what *I* had broken, I had to be prepared to sacrifice my own wants and desires. I could imagine no greater sacrifice than to give up the physical expression of the passion between us, though I honestly believe she had no idea I was thinking about how sex seemed to paper over cracks I hadn't even known were there."

Pollyanna studied him, like she was trying to read his mind. Maybe she was. "Really? At the villa, you know what she said."

"I do, but it is very possible a woman of my mother's generation actually believes that forgoing intercourse during pregnancy is what is best." That she felt the need to offer that advice was something he still found difficult to fathom.

But then Pollyanna had not been looking in the best of health the last time he saw his mother and sister before the visit to Villa Liakada.

His wife inclined her head. Not an agreement, but not a dismissal either.

Her ability to be fair, even in the face of great provocation was something he should *never* have dismissed when she asked for his support against his mother and sister.

Alexandros had been unable to get past the *against* concept, never taking the next step to realizing how very necessary presenting a unified front had been and how very much his wife had deserved his support. Full stop.

"I told her that if I lost you because of her and Stacia, I would cut them both from my life permanently." It was very little in the way of reparation for past mistakes, but he offered it with absolute sincerity.

Surprise flared in Polly's beautiful blue eyes. "Did you mean it?"

"I did." That she even felt the need to ask increased his anger with himself.

He should never have made her doubt her importance to him or where his ultimate loyalty lay.

"I appreciate that you feel so strongly, you would say something like that, but let's not pretend. No matter what their machinations, if you lose me Alexandros, it won't be *their* fault."

Tension thrummed through Alexandros, his jaw tightening so it was hard to speak, but he managed it. "I know."

"You're the one who broke promises to me, who told me he loved me and then treated me like I didn't matter too many times to discount." She'd said things like this, back when they were first married. She'd said them with tears and she'd screamed them.

And he had not listened.

He was listening now, though his wife's voice was void of emotion.

Alexandros gritted his teeth against a sound that wanted to come out of his own aching throat, the back of his eyes burning with impossible moisture. "I am sorry."

"I wonder. Are you sorry? Do you believe you were genuinely in the wrong, or are you simply trying to prove that your brother is not a better husband than you?"

"Is that what you think this is about?" Alexandros asked, unexpected pain ripping through him.

Alexandros was not an emotional guy. He couldn't afford to be.

"Yes." That was all.

Just one word given in a flat tone from his overly emotional, voluble wife.

No overexplaining. No tears. No glaring.

He did not like this lack of emotion in her. One way she'd always been his complement was that Pollyanna could give voice to feelings he could not even admit having to himself.

"It is true. I do not like thinking you see my brother as a better husband to his wife than I am to you. I am a competitive man," he admitted, wondering for the first time in his life if perhaps that trait was not always a good thing.

Her lips twisted. "I know."

Of course she did. Pollyanna knew him well, whereas he had lost sight of who she was and needed to learn her heart all over again. "I find it far more disturbing that you would consider me a poor husband at all, if you want the truth. I'm sure you think that's very conceited of me, but you are the best wife I could ever imagine having." He still marveled at the miracle that had them meeting. "That I would not be the same for you is not something I can accept."

"That may change."

He knew she wasn't talking about him becoming her ideal of a husband. She didn't believe he wanted that role badly enough to change. She was talking about her being his perfect mate. "I assure you, it will not."

"I'm done making all the compromises," she said in a tone that warned him more was coming. "For the next little while, I think I may be done compromising at all."

"Tell me what you want, and I will see you get it." It was another promise, but she would learn this one wasn't empty.

"Even if it means I want six months to build our relationship without your mother's or sister's influence?" she asked, her voice laced with doubt in his sincerity.

CHAPTER TEN

ALEXANDROS'S KNEE-JERK REACTION was to deny such a thing. What would his father have said?

However, he'd just promised he would give his wife what she needed so they could work on their marriage.

He could make the same choices he always had in the past and expect Polly to go along with his family's norms, or he could do something different. Something that proved she mattered more than anything or anyone to him.

"You do not want to see my mother at all, even at our son's birth?" he asked, rather than reacting with his first instincts. His mother would be devastated. "What about her seeing Helena?"

"I will not allow our daughter to be hurt," Pollyanna said, as if that should be obvious.

"Then what?"

"I trust Corrina to supervise visits with your mother."

"And the birth of our son?" It was only ten weeks away, give or take.

"I don't want your mother or your sister anywhere around me during that time." The implacability in Pollyanna's manner could not be ignored. She wasn't going to move on this matter. "I don't want them visiting me, or our baby in the hospital."

"My mother will be very hurt." He wasn't going to argue with his wife, but he needed to point out the consequences of such a course of actions.

Pollyanna's wry gaze said she was fully aware. "Tell me something, Alexandros. If a company that relied on your goodwill did everything it could to undermine you in the market and talk Kristalakis Inc. down, what would you do?"

"Destroy it." He sighed, fully aware of how quickly and

unhesitatingly he had answered. "But this is family, Polly-anna, not a business rival."

"I didn't say a rival. I said a company that should be your ally, but for reasons of their own decided not to be."

He nodded, acknowledging the point.

"And I don't want to *destroy* your mother, but I do want her to stop and think about the cost of her behavior. If I had left you as she wanted, I would have raised Helena in America and this baby would never have come to be. Athena would rarely have seen her granddaughter and she never would have gotten the chance to know her grandson."

All the air whooshed out of Alexandros's body. "You are not leaving me." He swallowed back the tightness in his throat. "*Please*, do not leave me."

"I have no plans to do so, but if your mother had gotten her way, I already would have."

"She didn't believe you were the right woman for me." Alexandros had no choice but to acknowledge that.

His mother had baldly admitted as much to him when she'd come to his office to apologize.

"That implies she's had a change of heart."

"She has."

"I hope that's true, but my six-month moratorium stays. And I don't want you seeing her either."

"What? You do not mean that."

"I do."

"But Polly, my father is gone. It is my duty to look after my mother." He could not abandon the older woman entirely, no matter how angry she made him.

Which said what about the threat he'd been so sure he meant about cutting her out of his life if he lost his wife?

"Your brother can do the looking after for a while. I don't want to wonder if your actions are driven by your own feelings or hers. I want a chance to get to know each other again without poisonous whispers making things that should be beautiful ugly."

Pollyanna leaned toward him earnestly. "I believe if we are both willing to work at it, if we truly do focus on our marriage for the next six months, then maybe you'll be in a place where you won't put her feelings above mine and maybe I'll be in a place to trust you not to."

There was that word, *trust*. The one thing besides her love that Alexandros most wanted from the beautiful, vibrant woman he had married.

"Petros was very smart to move into the penthouse after marriage, wasn't he?" Alexandros asked ruefully.

He'd thought his brother had been wrong to refuse to postpone his own wedding on their mother's whim; now Alexandros realized just how wrong he'd been about so many things.

Pollyanna relaxed back against the sofa, taking a sip of her tea. "I think he learned from our mistakes."

"You mean *my* mistakes."

"No. I didn't argue moving in with your family and then it took me a while to realize your mother's and sister's behavior was intentional."

"Because you could not imagine my mother and sister trying to break us up. Your family would never do something like that." And she hadn't argued moving in because her tender heart had been moved by the losses his family had suffered and his mother's plea they all continue to live together at the villa as a family.

As generations of the Kristalakis family had done.

"No, they wouldn't. My mother? She despised my oldest sister's husband when they first married, but she never said a word against him."

"How did you know she despised him?"

"I didn't like him either, and I went to my mom for advice. She told me it didn't matter if we liked him, my sister loved him."

"But you like him now."

"I do. So does Mom."

"What changed?"

"The easy answer? He did. We did. The hard one? My sister got ovarian cancer. It's a terrifying disease that kills more women than survive it. My sister survived and a lot of that is down to how well he took care of her. He found an experimental treatment program in Canada, and even though they told him there was no room for my sister, he wouldn't take no for an answer. He got her in. That pushy certainty he was always right saved my sister's life, and I learned that he loved her as much as she loved him. Just because he wasn't touchy-feely and had a sometimes acerbic sense of humor didn't mean his emotions weren't just as engaged. Mom and I love him now."

"My mother thinks you are a saint." His mother had spent their time apart as a family doing some soul-searching of her own, and she had admitted to Alexandros she hadn't liked what she'd found.

"In six months, she can tell me that herself if she really thinks it." Again, there was no give in Pollyanna on this.

"I wouldn't lie to you."

"On purpose, no, I don't think you would."

"But unwittingly, you think I would."

"Something like that."

"What else?" he asked, more than a little worried what other "un-compromises" his wife wanted.

"I want to stay in the penthouse."

That, at least, was easy. "Done."

"Corrina thinks we can convert the corporate apartments into more usable space for visiting family, our security team and some kind of indoor playroom-slash-gym for the children."

"Whatever you want."

"I want this space to be family friendly." She indicated the rooftop garden with an all-encompassing wave.

"What does that mean?"

Pollyanna listed some things she and Corrina had brainstormed the day before.

"I will find a nearby building to move the helipad to. I would prefer a more parklike setting for our children." Which would require the entire space of the rooftop.

If they were going to live in a penthouse, his family was going to have the best that lifestyle had to offer.

"Are you sure?" Pollyanna asked, as if she really thought he'd balk at something so simple.

"You could have asked me for any of this anytime in the past five years, and I would have done it," he assured her.

"Maybe you actually believe that, but I know it's not true."

"I can prove nothing about my intentions in the past, only the present. Know those intentions are for your contentment."

"Not happiness?"

"No one person can assure another's happiness."

"I agree."

"You chose to be happy while living under the strain of a life not anything like what you'd wanted or imagined you would have with me." He understood that now. "I believe you will find it much easier to make that choice if you are genuinely content with your lot."

She took another sip of her no longer steaming tea, the scent of chamomile wafting to him. "You're probably right."

"I like to be right."

"I know." A worried expression flitted over her lovely features, but then it was gone. "I'm not going back to full-time corporate prop after the baby is born. I want time with my children."

"You seem much more relaxed with the current schedule." And it bothered him more than she would ever understand now that he understood how much she had not enjoyed her previous one. How exhausting she had found it and how she had tried so hard to be the attentive parent she wanted to be and still not let *him* down.

"I am."

"Then we will keep it."

She stilled, like she was waiting for him to take the words back. Of course, he did not.

Finally, she nodded. "I would like that."

"Corrina and Petros can do some of the socializing for the company's sake we have been doing these past five years."

"So, you won't just start going to these things without me?"

"Ohi." No, he would not. Absolutely. Did she not realize he would miss her? But he did not say so, only offered what he knew she would believe. "I too want to see my children grow."

"I'm glad." Pollyanna untucked her feet, no doubt preparing to stand. "Well, that's a good place to start, don't you think?"

"I do." He reached for her tea and took a sip, grimacing at the taste.

She smiled. "Not your favorite."

"No, but you like it."

"I do."

"And that is all that matters." He hoped she understood that he was talking about more than tea here.

"Is there anything you want to see happen?"

That she would even ask proved to him once again how committed to making their marriage work his incredible wife really was. "Your generosity of spirit humbles me. Since you are asking, date nights. I want them once a week, whether we've been to a business-related social function, or not."

"I'd like that, Alexandros." She stood, clearly assuming he was done.

But he wasn't. "I want to call you *agape mou* without you flinching, frowning, or turning your face away."

"I…" She let her voice trail off and showed she understood how important this was by really thinking about her answer. "I'll try."

He nodded. "About last night—"

"As angry as you made me, I think it's a good idea," she slotted in before he could tell her he'd been stupid to suggest such a thing.

"You do?"

She nodded.

"For six months?" If his voice rose on the word *months*, he could be forgiven.

"No. The six months is about your mother and sister only. I'm due in ten weeks and then six after that while I heal."

"That's still four months," he practically shouted.

She startled, like his raised voice had surprised her. "It was your idea."

"And it was stupid."

"No. You were right. We both used sex to paper over the cracks. I don't want those cracks becoming chasms."

He wanted to argue, but Alexandros found he could not. He had let his wife down in a very real way. If this was his penance, then he would pay it.

"You want to go shopping? With me?" Polly wasn't sure she'd heard her husband correctly.

It was just not *him*. The Alexandros Kristalakises of the world did not trail along with their wives to the shops.

His smile was all warm engaging charm. "You may have not noticed, but you are expecting our son in just over two months."

"Hard to miss." Harder to miss was that it was midmorning and her business tycoon husband was in their penthouse, not his office.

Again.

"We have no nursery for him."

They did have a nursery. At Villa Liakada. "We have

everything at the villa." She should have had the nursery furniture, the bassinet at the very least, brought to Athens.

Polly wasn't sure why she hadn't already taken care of it. The entire layette she'd put together for her son's arrival was still in there as well.

"Which we will need when we are staying there on weekends."

"Papa!" Helena came careening into the living room, Hero close in her wake. "Are you going to go swimming with us?"

"Not today, *louloudi mou*. I am taking Mama shopping."

His *little flower* made a face. Helena definitely took after her father in her lack of interest in that pastime. "Do I have to go?" the three-year-old asked suspiciously.

"*Ohi*. You will go swimming with Hero, have a lovely lunch with Aunt Corrina and then take your nap, *ne*?" They were going to have to hire a second nursemaid to replace Dora in Athens.

The older woman would keep her position on a part-time basis for when they visited the villa, but she hadn't wanted to make the move to Athens.

"I get to visit Aunt Corrina?" Helena asked excitedly.

"Most assuredly, but only if you promise to nap nicely for Hero afterward. She has schoolwork she has to do."

Polly smiled her approval at her husband remembering what to him was probably trivial, but was very important for Hero. "You're a very nice man for a billionaire business shark."

"I am glad you think so." His smile had a spark of something that sent need sparking through Polly even as their daughter promised most sincerely to take her nap nicely.

Hero and Helena, accompanied by two of the security team, left for the pool a moment later, and Polly was left alone with her confusing husband.

"You want to furnish a nursery? But you're sleeping in it." Had he forgotten that salient fact?

"I live in hope my wife will invite me back into our bed, sex or no sex," he said, his voice low and seductive, his body somehow closer than he had been only a second ago. "Until then, we can have a daybed installed in the office."

There was certainly room for one. One thing about the penthouse was that the rooms were all oversize. There was enough square footage for six bedrooms easily, but the architect had designed the apartment on a grand scale, every room oversize with lots of built-in storage.

Her husband had been overstating the case when he said they didn't have the facilities to entertain. Parties of fifty or more? Would be crowded. But their dining table could be extended to accommodate seating for ten.

When it was kept in its current formation for six, there was more than adequate space for hosting a cocktail party comfortably, even if they didn't have a banquet-size room like they did at Villa Liakada. And while it was nowhere near the size of the rooftop garden, their personal terrace was quite large and well situated to increase their entertainment space.

"I did not kick you out of our bed. It was a mutual decision, based on your suggestion, I might add." She missed him in their bed.

Of course she did, but not having sex to fall back on as a distraction tactic was forcing them both to be more forthcoming and maybe even more aware of the other's needs outside of the bedroom. She'd realized how much he enjoyed her company when it didn't lead to sex, how important it was to him to spend time together, regardless.

She liked knowing that, but also acknowledged that there had been many times in the past she had unknowingly disregarded his need for her companionship, thinking it was all about the sex.

"One I regretted almost immediately, but even so, I think it has been illuminating in a good way for both of us."

His words so closely resembled her own thoughts, Polly smiled. "I think so too."

"That does not mean I want this moratorium to last indefinitely." He said it like she might actually be thinking along those lines.

"Neither do I," Polly assured him.

"Good." He leaned down and kissed her.

Polly responded, letting her body relax into his.

Alexandros took her weight, sliding his arm around her expanded waist. When he pulled his mouth from hers, they were both breathing heavily, but there was no urgency to take things further. It felt too good just to be held, to be needed for more than her body.

That thought hit her hard. Did she think of herself that way? Had he been right that Polly had stopped believing in the romance of their relationship? That he cared for her as more than a convenient, if very compatible, bed partner?

"So, you want to go shopping?"

"I've cleared my schedule for the rest of the day."

Wow. She shifted so she could meet his eyes. "The whole day?"

"We don't have to shop the whole time," he said, sounding just the tiniest bit panicked.

Polly laughed. "We don't have to shop at all. We can order everything online."

"You don't like ordering personal things online, unless you have no choice," he said, showing a perception she would not have expected, but more than that, a consideration for her feelings that she'd learned not to expect either.

The fact her newly perceptive husband realized just how personal the nursery was to her touched Polly deeply.

"He's going to sleep in our room in the bassinet for the first few weeks," she reminded Alexandros.

"I remember Helena. I thought your mother and mine were going to come to blows over your refusal to put our newborn in the nursery at night."

"Just because she doesn't choose to voice her opinion over all her adult children's decisions, doesn't mean she can't hold her own when she needs to." It had helped that in that case, Alexandros had not sided with his mother.

Polly had told him flat out that he could move out of their bedroom if he didn't like the baby's bassinet being in there. But he'd told her he had no problem with it.

He had adored their daughter from before her birth.

"Not that she liked her bassinet at first," Polly remembered fondly. "She only slept well when you held her on your chest." The nights he'd spent in Athens away from them those first two weeks had been rough.

Helena had eventually settled into her bassinet and not needed her daddy's heartbeat in her ear to sleep.

"I remember. It was a special time."

Love for this man poured through Polly, and she smiled at him. "Yes, it was."

They shopped high-end boutiques for nursery items and additions to the baby's layette, but then Alexandros instructed their driver to take them to a store on the outskirts of Athens.

They hadn't found a crib and changing table yet, though Polly had seen a couple that would work. Just nothing that she'd fallen in love with. "Where are we going?"

"You'll see."

"I don't like surprises."

"That is not true."

She laughed. "No, it's not, but I still want to know."

"Are you hungry? Would you like lunch first?"

Her tummy rumbled, answering his question.

His laughter was rich and warm, and she couldn't help what she did next any more than she could have stopped taking her next breath.

Polly leaned over and kissed him, not rushing it. Letting

her lips move against his, loving how he returned the caress instantly but made no move to take it deeper.

Finally, she pulled back only far enough to look into his eyes. "Thank you."

"You are welcome, but why are you thanking me?"

"For taking this time, for doing it with a smile and that super sexy laugh that makes me all warm inside."

"I'm very glad to know my laughter affects you that way."

"It's more than that, it's knowing you're happy to be here."

"I am."

She didn't remind him there had been a time when he wouldn't have been. They were going forward, not staying mired in the past. "So am I."

They ate lunch on the patio of a café that served traditional Greek fare. Polly enjoyed her spanakopita very much, but kept snacking on the pistachios on the crudités plate.

She ate the last one and frowned.

"Would you like me to get you more?" Was that laughter in his voice.

Polly blushed. "I don't know why, but I've just been craving pistachios this pregnancy."

"No doubt your body needs the nutrients found in them."

"Or I just love their salty goodness."

"Or that." He laughed, but waved a waiter over and requested more for their table.

"I'm going to turn green if I keep eating these," she joked.

"Even green, I will still love you."

Polly went still, his words doing things to her heart and emotions, not all of them good, but mostly good.

"You've never been a guy who says that a lot." And she'd finally decided it meant he didn't feel the emotion like she did.

It hadn't been like that in the beginning of their relationship. She hadn't needed the words as a frequent affirmation. But that was before they meshed lives that she now realized had probably never been meant to go together.

He acknowledged her words with an indecipherable look. "I have come to see that not saying the words may have convinced you they were no longer true."

If they ever had been. "If it had just been a matter of saying it, or not saying it, I don't think I would have drawn that conclusion." Her dad adored his wife and children. However, he had never been a man to make a lot of verbal declarations. "But it isn't, is it?"

"What do you mean?" His gorgeous face revealed a confusion that might have annoyed her weeks before.

She'd thought he should *know*, but now she saw it as more endearing. He was trying.

"If you had shown me that you loved me, if I had been a priority in your life," she explained, "I don't think the lack of words would have bothered me. It might other women, I don't know. I only know myself."

"And you needed actions I did not give, so the lack of words cemented a belief inside you that I do not love you."

"Yes." It was a level of honesty they did not usually engage in.

But there was no moving forward as they'd both said they wanted to do without putting truth out there to be dealt with.

He nodded. "It is my intention to both say the words and to show you that I feel them."

She wanted that, more than was safe for her heart. "This *reconstruct our marriage* plan is a risky one, you understand that, don't you?"

"I would have said not to do it was riskier."

"But I'd settled into our marriage, found my peace with the limitations of our life. You're doing your best to convince me that we can have something different, something better. If I believe you and you let me down, I don't know if I have what it takes to find that peace again." Simply admitting that was scary for her, because it meant her future might take a turn she did not want, had never wanted, but might not be able to avoid.

"Is that why you are fighting this so hard?" he asked, as if he was finally understanding something that had bothered him.

But she didn't understand his question. "How am I fighting it?" She'd agreed to try, hadn't she? Agreed to work toward an emotional intimacy she'd blocked herself off from since before the birth of their daughter.

"You do not trust me to change."

"Well, no." But that wasn't fighting against him trying to, was it?

He winced, like he'd really hoped for a different answer. "Because you fear that if you trust me and I let you down again, it will be the end."

She laid her hands over her stomach, letting the life there give her a measure of peace. "Yes."

"And you do not want that?"

She shook her head. "We have two children together." She didn't want to bring their son into a broken home.

Alexandros nodded. "Both our daughter and our unborn son deserve the strongest family we can give them."

"And in your mind, that means having a strong marriage?" She'd thought he believed that, when they'd first dated and gotten married.

Then she'd come to believe Alexandros had very different priorities than building a strong marriage with her.

"Ne." He infused that one word of affirmation with a deep sense of feeling and commitment.

And she liked hearing it. A lot. This bid of his to save their marriage wasn't only about his need to prove he was as good a husband as his brother.

"You know, our marriage wasn't rocky." Not until he'd

started pressing her for things she no longer felt able to give. Like her trust.

"How stable could it be if you were not as happy in it as I was?"

"From my perspective, it was very stable."

"Only because you never considered the possibility that if you no longer loved your husband, you could fall in love with someone else." He said the words like even voicing the thought pained him, but it was a real worry for him.

She would never have expected him to entertain such a thought. "I would not allow a relationship to develop to the point that might happen." And she'd never fallen out of love with *him*, so it was a moot point anyway.

She was terminally afflicted.

"I believe you would not knowingly do so."

"But you think it *could* happen?" she asked, still surprised he harbored such a worry.

"I think I will never take that risk."

"Staying married is really important to you." Had it always been? Polly didn't know.

Wasn't sure it mattered. It was true now and that was what was important.

Pain flared in his espresso gaze. "It is, and I am sorry you came to believe otherwise."

"I'm not sure how much I *believed* and how much I *feared*. And once I got pregnant, well, I never even considered you'd end things between us."

"That is something at least."

"Family is important to both of us."

"Yes, but perhaps I put too much emphasis on my family of birth and not enough on the one I was making with you." It was a huge admission for a loyal Greek son and brother to make.

"If you want to visit your mom, you can. I should never have made that a condition of—" Polly paused, trying to think how to put it "—whatever this is between us."

"You are very tenderhearted."

"I just know how much it would hurt me not to talk to my mom or siblings for the next few months. And you have always adored your family. It isn't fair of me to make you choose between me and them." Even temporarily.

"Like they tried so very hard to do?"

He was admitting it? "I thought you'd convinced yourself your mom's machinations were unintentional?"

"I realize now my mother was utterly convinced our marriage could not work and that ultimately I would not be happy in it, but I do believe some of the hurt she dealt you was not on purpose. Only the result of her natural arrogance."

"Like mother like son," Polly teased.

"No doubt. You should have met my father, but I think if he had lived you would have had a very different welcome from my family."

"You think he would have liked me?" Petros liked her. He always had. Maybe their father would have too.

"He would have loved you and the way I became a better person with you in my life."

"What an incredible thing to say. You believe that?"

"I know it," Alexandros said with full sincerity. "Thousands of employees have kept their jobs over the years of our marriage because when I took over their companies, *you* were my conscience."

"Really?" He thought about her at work? That in itself was a revelation.

"Absolutely. Ask Petros if you do not believe me. My policy for dealing with mergers and takeovers took a sharp turn after our marriage."

"Why?"

"You don't remember your lectures on the importance of the individual?"

How could she forget? She'd found his willingness to listen to her take on philosophy and human interaction as heady as their sexual combustibility. "I thought you were indulging me. I didn't think you were *listening*!"

"Didn't you?"

"Maybe at first," she admitted. And she'd liked it, the possibility that she could influence someone so powerful because of his affection for her.

"I did listen and I did change." He looked at her like he wanted her to hear the unspoken message behind those words.

He was listening to her now, and he was trying to change.

Polly didn't stifle her urge to touch him as she might have done recently, but reached across the table and brushed her fingers over the back of his hand. "Noted."

Alexandros's smile was brilliant. "Good."

"I should have realized you were building walls around your heart." The lines of his face moved into a serious cast. "At first, though, I was just relieved you had stopped arguing about every little thing."

He sounded ashamed of that fact.

"You don't like being in conflict with me." Recent willingness to the contrary.

He grimaced, looking a little ashamed. "It makes me feel powerless."

How could this man ever feel powerless? "I would have said that you had all the power to bring peace between us."

"Not when I was just waiting for you to settle into our life." His wry expression acknowledged that might have been a shortsighted attitude.

But suddenly she wasn't feeling as much bonhomie as before. "You thought I'd get used to being dictated to by your mother and mocked by your sister?"

He grimaced, his shrug almost self-effacing. "That was not quite how I saw it, but yes."

"In a way, you were right. I did make my peace with our marriage," she acknowledged.

"By relegating me to a place outside your heart, I would have said even outside your intimate circle, but—"

"There was still the sex." And that sex had made him think things were fine and allowed her to pretend they were too.

He winked, a bit of his usual arrogance flashing. "Very good sex."

"Terrific sex," she teased back and then sighed as the brief flash of humor faded. It was time for more honesty. "Emotionally, you *were* outside that intimate circle."

He nodded. "You stopped trusting me with anything but your body."

Polly had no reply. They both knew it was true, but hearing the words hurt.

Both of them, if his expression was anything to go by.

"I'm not going to see my mother, or my sister, until you are ready to see them too," he announced, like he was making a major concession.

Anger gripped her and she gasped. "That's not fair."

"How?" he asked, looking genuinely confused.

Could he be that dense?

"Because I'll feel pressured to see them, so you don't suffer the loss of them in your life."

"I do not want you feeling pressured, but surely you realize my family has to mend bridges with you as well." He sounded so rational, so pragmatic.

But he was once again ignoring every need Polly expressed and putting the needs of his family ahead of her. Or at least, that's what it felt like.

Filled with unexpected fury, Polly surged to her feet and tossed her napkin on the table. "How about we see if we can even mend the broken bits between *us* before you start pressuring me into making happy families with the Kristalakis Harpies?"

Instead of being offended, or even miffed at the unflattering distinction, Alexandros threw his head back and laughed. "Harpies they might be, but they are still your family, *yineka mou*."

But Polly wasn't feeling the humor and shook her head firmly, her frown severe. "Oh, no, they are not. I married you, not your family and if I *never* want to see either your mother or your sister again, then that is my prerogative. And I'd believe you were really changing in your attitude toward me if you had come to that conclusion on your own."

She turned and headed toward the street, knowing the car would be called, if not by her husband then by security. No one wanted her wandering off.

That had been drilled into her from the beginning. And maybe just this minute she was acknowledging a certain level of resentment because of it.

When she'd first come to realize just how much her life and personal freedom had changed, Polly had told herself she had to just deal with it. She had fallen in love with a billionaire and married him. Her choice. So, she had to accept the good with the bad.

And if there seemed to be more bad than good, well, it had still been her choice.

Only it hadn't been an informed one.

How could it be? Polly had never had any experience with the kind of life the truly wealthy lived.

And Alexandros had made no effort to warn her in advance. Not of any of it. He'd expected his mother and sister to help Polly navigate her new life, but they resented the heck out of his new bride and just wanted her gone.

Polly had been so focused on him and what Alexandros made her feel, she'd never considered how much her life was going to change. That she would never again be able to wander the streets of a downtown, or go to a mall alone to shop, walk and think.

Never be able to take her children for a walk in the park without security, would have to look for hidden motives in overtures of friendship.

Wouldn't even be able to cook in her own kitchen anytime she wanted.

Once her children were old enough, they still wouldn't be able to stay with her parents for a week in the summer. Polly's mom and dad's humble home didn't have the security measures to keep her children safe.

Who was Alexandros to tell her that, on top of everything else she'd had to give up in her life as his wife, she had to claim his mean-spirited and manipulative sister and mother as *her* family?

Not in this lifetime.

Suddenly he was there, right beside her, his arm offered. "Come, let us finish our shopping."

She jerked a nod but made no move to take his arm.

The silence that reigned in the car was not the companionable silence they'd shared so often the past week. Tension thrummed between them. Polly had no desire to dispel it and ignored any efforts her husband made to do so.

CHAPTER ELEVEN

ALEXANDROS'S SURPRISE FOR Polly turned out to be a shop for a master carpenter who specialized in baby furniture.

Pushing away negative thoughts and feelings, as she'd learned to do, Polly ignored the presence of her husband and allowed herself to enjoy the beautiful handmade pieces.

She found a crib in dark wood and matching dresser with a changing mat on top. The old-world style charmed her, and she started asking the sales associate about the construction and adherence to safety guidelines.

"All my furniture meets the strictest safety guidelines because I ship internationally." The deep, pleasant masculine voice had Polly turning.

"You made all this?" she asked, with a little awe, indicating all the beautiful pieces in the showroom.

His smile was warm, and understandably proud. "I did."

"How? I mean…"

"My grandfather was a master carpenter. He had me in his shop when I was a small boy, learning to sand and oil wood."

"And you followed in his footsteps?"

The man nodded.

"That's so neat. I started baking with my grandmother and became a pastry chef."

"I am sure your grandmother was very happy to see her skills living on in you."

"As your grandfather must be."

The man's smile slipped a little. "We lost him in my teens but when I am in my shop, making furniture for the next generation, I feel his presence and know he lives through my memories."

Polly blinked back tears. "That is beautiful." She wiped

at her eyes. "Sorry, I'm that typically emotional pregnant woman."

"I think perhaps you are a sensitive soul, pregnant, or not." He went to offer her a handkerchief from his pocket.

But her husband's hand was there first, his crisp cotton square shaken out for her.

She grabbed it and dabbed at the moisture. "Thank you, Alexandros."

"*You* are Kyria Kristalakis?"

"Yes, she is my wife." Alexandros inserted himself between them, forcing the carpenter to take a step back.

Looking far from intimidated, the man winked at Polly. "Your husband is feeling protective."

Polly looked up at Alexandros, not really understanding where all this testosterone posturing was coming from. "I guess." She shrugged and looked back at the carpenter. "I would really like this nursery suite. Is it available?"

"For you, I will have it delivered this week."

Alexandros growled, the sound primal. "We can find our furniture elsewhere."

"No, we cannot," Polly informed him, enunciating each word so there could be no misunderstanding. Then she smiled at the master carpenter. "I would love if you could have it delivered this week. We're getting a little close for comfort."

"And you did not even want to go shopping today." Alexandros sounded almost petulant.

But billionaire tycoons didn't get petulant, did they?

She rolled her eyes at him. "I never said I didn't want to go shopping, I said I was surprised you did."

The shop owner laughed and, showing he had some self-preservation, asked Alexandros for the details for delivery. But then he smiled at Polly. "Do you have a bassinet?"

They'd bought one earlier that morning and she said so.

He shrugged. "Okay."

"But you have one you think my wife would like?" Alexandros asked, as if the words were being pulled from him.

"It is in the same style as the crib and dresser changing table."

"Oh…" Polly wanted to see it. She really did, but she'd already gotten one, and that would be silly. Wouldn't it?

"Show it to us," Alexandros instructed.

"Please," Polly prompted his good manners.

Her husband frowned down at her, but said it.

"She has you wrapped around her finger, doesn't she?" the master carpenter asked Alexandros as he led them across the shop and into the back room.

"She doesn't think so."

"Is she blind?"

"Sometimes."

Polly ignored them both for the gorgeous bassinet in the center of the room. "Oh, it's stunning." It had wheels, so she could move it around the penthouse as needed.

In the same old-world design as the other pieces they were buying, the beautifully stained dark wood gleamed with the love and care that had gone into making it.

"Have it delivered along with the other pieces." Alexandros took her arm to lead Polly away.

She balked at moving. "But we already have a bassinet."

"I will have it returned."

"But…"

"You want this one and I want you happy."

"It's just a bassinet."

But it wasn't. It was Alexandros telling her she didn't have to settle. Not now. Not ever?

Or was she reading too much into a simple furniture purchase?

They were back in the car, moving slowly through the packed Athens traffic when Alexandros reached out to take Polly's hand.

He squeezed it and then brought her hand to his lap, absently brushing his fingers over hers. "I am sorry, *agape mou.*"

His use of the endearment sounded very intentional.

Polly turned so she could see his expression. "Why sorry?"

He was looking at their hands together, like the sight held the answers of the universe.

"I was Cro-Magnon man in there. Isn't that what you call me?"

"On occasion."

"I don't like other men flirting with you."

"I never noticed that before." It was an inevitable reality at so many of the functions they attended together. Polly had never been particularly comfortable with the social flirting but had noticed early on that it was common.

Thank goodness her husband had never indulged. She never would have been sanguine about it.

And Polly never flirted back, but she had always been cordial.

"I never doubted before." It sounded like a hard-fought admission.

One she would not ignore. "What are you doubting now?"

"Your love. My right to it. Whether you will stay with me." His shrug was more bleak than negligent.

"Have I ever once threatened to leave?"

"No, but you said earlier that what we are doing right now, all this honesty, it is risky."

She nodded. "Okay, so that made you feel insecure?"

Polly expected him to deny it. He was too arrogant to feel insecure.

But Alexandros nodded. "*Ne.* Though, if I'm honest I haven't been feeling all that secure with you since that dinner with my family."

"The one where you decided I thought your brother was a better husband than you."

"The one where you said as much."

She was going to argue, but he'd taken her words to mean that so there was no point belaboring what she'd actually said.

"I would have thought that the knowledge I'd stayed with you despite it all would have given you more confidence. Not less."

"What man wants to believe his wife stayed with him for the sake of their child? Not this man." He spoke the last with a lot more force than she'd been expecting from his subdued demeanor.

"I didn't just stay with you because of Helena." Yes, Polly's first pregnancy had played a pivotal role in her decision to accept her life and stop beating against the walls of his indifference to her needs. But… "I loved you when I married you. I loved you when I got pregnant with Helena." She took a deep breath and went for full disclosure. "I love you now."

"Perhaps you do, but you are no longer in love with me. The stars…" He stopped, swallowed, then continued. "They are gone."

His voice came out thick with emotion.

He'd said something like that before, but he was wrong. "Alexandros, when we are at Villa Liakada there are so many stars in the sky, it is like a blanket of twinkling lights." She scooted as close as she could get to him with her seat belt. "Here in Athens, the stars are still beautiful, but there are a lot less of them."

Polly brushed her hand over her husband's bowed head. "Or are there?"

He stilled, but didn't answer.

"Just because we can't see them for the light pollution, doesn't mean they aren't there, Alexandros. Every star we can see in the country is still in the sky in the city."

"What are you trying to say to me?" he asked in a thick voice.

"Alexandros, the stars are still there."

Hot moisture splashed on the back of her hand.

Shock rendered her mute for several seconds but then another drop of moisture landed on her hand.

"Alexandros?"

"How can the stars be there?" his words came out choppy, tinged with emotion she had never heard from him before.

Even the day he'd proposed.

He'd been all arrogant certainty she'd say yes that day. And she had.

But right now? He was hurting. Hurting like she had never thought he could hurt because of her.

Polly said the only truth that mattered right then. "I love you, Andros."

A sob snaked out of her powerful husband, then he was clinging to her while his loss of composure sparked her own. They held each other, a watershed of emotion pouring over them both.

"I love you, Polly, *agape mou*. You have to believe that. I need you to believe that."

She didn't answer. She couldn't. She believed he loved her. She couldn't not, but what did that mean?

For him? For her?

Because if he'd always loved her, then what did that say about how easily he dismissed her feelings before?

"We need..." He paused like the words were too hard to find.

"What?" she prompted. "What do we need?"

"A place to talk where we will not be interrupted and where I can hold you properly."

"Another hotel suite?" she said, teasingly, trying to lighten the mood a little.

He shook his head, his demeanor entirely grave. "This discussion is too personal for any place but our home."

"Okay."

He nodded. "Okay."

He released her with one arm, but kept the other around her while he grabbed his phone and texted someone. A few minutes and several texts later, he said, "Done."

"What?"

"Petros and Corrina will keep Helena tonight."

"That's kind of them."

"Petros has an interest in us working through our problems."

"He does?" Well of course he did. Petros loved his brother and he loved Polly like a sister now too.

"Yes," Alexandros said grimly.

"Okay, well, it's still nice of them."

"It is, yes," he admitted grudgingly. "Another instance where my brother is showing his *considerate* nature."

"You can be really caring and considerate too, Andros."

"Do you think so?" He didn't sound like he believed she thought anything of the sort.

"It may have taken you five years to get there, but once you realized what your mom and sister were like with me, you put a stop to it. Once you realized I wanted to see more of you, you took steps to make that happen."

"That doesn't make me considerate. That makes me a desperate man who does not want to lose his wife."

"But you *can* be considerate."

"I've convinced Piper to redecorate the villa. She and Zephyr will be in Athens next week and she'll consult with you then on what you want."

"That really *was* thoughtful. Thank you." Though Piper designed the decor for her husband's resorts, she excelled at the type of warm and inviting decor that Polly loved.

"One instance out of how many where I ignored your preferences for expediency or taking my mother's opinions over your own about what *you* needed?"

He really had been listening, but she didn't like her super confident husband in this down spiral. He had made mistakes, but he really was doing his best to rectify them.

"Who was it who took the entire day to shop with me for nursery furniture? Who made sure I rested when I needed to?" And maybe sometimes when she didn't. "Who bought me a second bassinet because I loved it?" She winked. "Who bought that second bassinet even after the very talented furniture maker flirted with me?"

The master carpenter had said Polly had her husband wrapped around her finger. Could it be true? Now?

Were Alexandros's eyes open, and in opening them, had he become genuinely determined to see her as happy as possible?

"You had more in common with him than you do with me."

"Not possible. I have love in common with you, and that's bigger than anything else."

"You think so?"

"I'm beginning to."

His expression turned arrested. "You are."

"Yes."

The kiss they shared was beautiful and hot, and when the car stopped, the only thing Polly wanted to do when they got home was take her husband straight to bed.

Like he was reading her mind, Alexandros slammed the door to their home in the face of the security team.

By the time they reached their bedroom, neither had a stitch of clothing on and Polly's lips were swollen and hot from kissing.

Alexandros lifted her and laid her on the bed as if she was both precious and breakable.

Then he joined her, his expression so intent. "Polly. *Agape mou.*"

They reached for each other at the same time, kissing and touching. The passion between them tinged with love so recently acknowledged.

He was tender.

She was pushy.

When their bodies connected, they both stilled and savored the moment. For the first time in so long, she felt a complete emotional connection with him every bit as deep and real as the physical one.

They moved together, his hands on her body, her hands giving pleasure where she could. She screamed with her orgasm, more tears burnished his eyes with his.

After, he held her close, kissing her temple, whispering words of love in Greek and English.

The walls around Polly's heart crumbled as she accepted that he meant every single utterance. He wasn't perfect, but he was undeniably hers, and she was the one thing he would never willingly give up.

"You never have to see my mother or sister again, if you don't want to," he promised with another soft kiss.

"Is that realistic?" she couldn't help asking.

"They hurt you. They hurt us. We will make it realistic. No one will be allowed to hurt you again on my watch."

"You can't promise that."

"Can't I?"

"Well, your arrogance is back in force, I see." She smiled at her gorgeous husband, thinking more about how happy she was than what they were talking about.

That was probably why it took her a moment to take in the words he was saying.

"We can move to America and be near your family."

"What? What are you saying?"

"I have spoken to Petros, and he can take over running the company. I will take a secondary role in a new American office."

"You? Secondary?" She couldn't imagine.

"I want you happy, and you are not happy here with my family. You will be more content living near yours."

"First, I *am* happy here. Now. Adjusting to life as your wife wasn't easy. I won't pretend otherwise, but I *am* your wife and I love our life in Greece."

"You didn't love it only a few weeks ago."

"I didn't love aspects of it, but we've found compromises to make our family life the stuff of my dreams." They'd even agreed not to have a housekeeper for the penthouse, just some daily cleaning help, so Polly could cook any time she liked and take a more normalized role—for her—in her children's and husband's lives. The villa housekeeper had been very pleased to stay on in the country. "I'm so happy with the way things have been, I'm nearly sick with it."

"I could not tell."

She rested against him, finding a comfortable angle for her pregnant tummy. "I was afraid to show too much, to trust in the changes."

"You thought everything would go back to the way it was."

"Thought? No. Feared? Yes. I'm truly sorry, but yes." She *hadn't* trusted him. Not even a little. No matter how hard he'd been trying, Polly had struggled to believe the changes would be permanent.

But something had changed. Something inside her and maybe something inside him.

"And you do not fear this now?" he asked, like checking the facts.

"No. Now especially, I *know*." After his offer to give up the legacy his father had left him and move to another country, she really knew. "I know that it's worth fighting for what I need. It's worth fighting for our family."

"But it wasn't before."

"Before, I genuinely believed I wasn't that important to you." That all her fighting and arguing was just wasted energy.

"And now you believe differently?"

"You've made a lot of concessions for my happiness, things I didn't recognize as such even before your rescue bid for our marriage."

"Not enough."

"No, maybe it wasn't enough, not then. At least not for me to keep trusting you with my heart."

"But you trust me now. You told me you love me."

"And I meant it."

"As did I."

"I know."

"You believe." His smile was incandescent.

She was feeling pretty glowy herself. "Yes, I believe."

He took a deep breath, like girding himself to say something difficult. "I think you should consider us moving to America."

"There is no need. I'm not going to think about doing something that will hurt you and I never wanted to begin with."

"But—"

"No, Andros. This is our life and I *can* love this life as long as I know that the children and I are some of your top priorities. That you love me for me, not the emulation of the perfect Greek society wife your mom tried to make me into."

"I have always loved you for you, and I never wanted you to become someone different. Though I can see now that I did a poor job of helping you adjust to our life or believe that. But you and our children are my *top* priorities."

"I'll remind you of that the next time you work until midnight two days in a row."

"Not going to happen."

"It will, sometimes…but that's okay, so long as I know it will be the exception and not the rule."

"A very rare if ever exception."

He was such an overachiever, but she loved that about him, so Polly just smiled. "I bet Petros wasn't keen to take over the company."

"No, he was not, but he agreed."

"What was the stick?"

"What do you mean?"

"A carrot wouldn't have worked. There's no incentive big enough to entice your brother into your role. He's very happy being second in command."

Alexandros shrugged. "If he didn't want to take over, I was going to sell the company."

"What?" Polly sat up and stared down at her too-relaxed husband. "You can't do that. That company is your father's legacy and his father before him."

"Yes, but the legacy I want to build requires you by my side."

"I wasn't going anywhere."

"And now we know you never will, but more importantly, we know that you will be happy staying."

He got so focused when he had a goal. And now she realized she *was* his ultimate goal. "I love you so much, Andros, but sometimes you scare me."

"You have nothing to fear from me."

"No, but I think I'll have to watch out you aren't sacrificing your own happiness for mine going forward."

"I would be honored for you to watch out for my happiness."

Then they were kissing again and whispering more words of love and making promises that lovers make.

EPILOGUE

THEIR SON WAS born a week early and they named him Theodore Robert for his grandfathers.

Polly's mother and father were there and she'd relented at the last minute, calling her mother-in-law when she'd gone into labor and inviting her to the hospital.

Athena had sent Polly a very moving letter of apology beforehand. They'd spoken on the phone a few times, short conversations, but entirely void of the former veiled insults and implications Polly should be doing this, that and the other, differently.

Alexandros had started having lunch with his mother once a week, but never pressured Polly to join him.

His sister hadn't shifted her attitudes at all and therefor had no place in her brother's life. By his choice, not Polly's suggestion.

Maybe one day Stacia would grow up and think of someone else's point of view, but until then, Polly didn't have to deal with the younger woman's poisonous words.

Alexandros never dismissed Polly's opinions now, especially when it came to family life. When they disagreed, they talked. Sometimes, they argued. Heatedly. They were both passionate people. Making up was fun.

And Polly's mom remarked that her daughter was definitely more her headstrong and passionate self than she had been in a long time.

Eight weeks after the birth of their son, Alexandros took Polly on a second honeymoon. They toured the islands on a yacht big enough to accommodate their children, the nursemaids and security. But no one else.

It was a glorious trip, but Polly loved coming home because this time, the honeymoon didn't end with stepping back in Athens.

Her attentive husband continued being loving and wonderful amidst everyday life.

* * * * *

MILLS & BOON

Coming next month

PRIDE & THE ITALIAN'S PROPOSAL
Kate Hewitt

'I judge on what I see,' Fausto allowed as he captured her queen easily. She looked unfazed by the move, as if she'd expected it, although to Fausto's eye it had seemed a most inexpert choice. 'Doesn't everyone do the same?'

'Some people are more accepting than others.'

'Is that a criticism?'

'You seem cynical,' Liza allowed.

'I consider myself a realist,' Fausto returned, and she laughed, a crystal-clear sound that seemed to reverberate through him like the ringing of a bell.

'Isn't that what every cynic says?'

'And what are you? An optimist?' He imbued the word with the necessary scepticism.

'I'm a realist. I've learned to be.' For a second she looked bleak, and Fausto realised he was curious.

'And where did you learn that lesson?'

She gave him a pert look, although he still saw a shadow of that unsettling bleakness in her eyes. 'From people such as yourself.' She moved her knight—really, what was she thinking there? 'Your move.'

Fausto's gaze quickly swept the board and he moved a pawn. 'I don't think you know me well enough to have learned such a lesson,' he remarked.

'I've learned it before, and in any case I'm a quick study.' She looked up at him with glinting eyes, a coy smile flirting about her mouth. A mouth Fausto had a sudden, serious urge to kiss. The notion took him so forcefully and unexpectedly that he leaned forward a little over the game, and Liza's eyes widened in response, her breath hitching audibly as surprise flashed across her features.

For a second, no more, the very air between them felt tautened, vibrating with sexual tension and expectation. It would be so very easy to close the space between their mouths. So very easy to taste her sweetness, drink deep from that lovely, luscious well.

Of course he was not going to do no such thing. He could never consider a serious relationship with Liza Benton; she was not at all the sort of person he was expected to marry and, in any case, he'd been burned once before, when he'd been led by something so consuming and changeable as desire.

As for a cheap affair...the idea had its tempting merits, but he knew he had neither the time nor inclination to act on it. An affair would be complicated and distracting, a reminder he needed far too much in this moment.

Fausto leaned back, thankfully breaking the tension, and Liza's smile turned cat-like, surprising him. She looked so knowing, as if she'd been party to every thought in his head, which thankfully she hadn't been, and was smugly informing him of that fact.

'Checkmate,' she said softly and, jolted, Fausto stared at her blankly before glancing down at the board.

'That's impossible,' he declared as his gaze moved over the pieces and, with another jolt, he realised it wasn't. She'd put him in checkmate and he hadn't even realised his king had been under threat. He'd indifferently moved a pawn while she'd neatly spun her web. Disbelief warred with a scorching shame as well as a reluctant admiration. All the while he'd assumed she'd been playing an amateurish, inexperienced game, she'd been neatly and slyly laying a trap.

'You snookered me.'

Her eyes widened with laughing innocence. 'I did no such thing. You just assumed I wasn't a worthy opponent.' She cocked her head, her gaze turning flirtatious—unless he was imagining that? Feeling it? 'But, of course, you judge on what you see.'

The tension twanged back again, even more electric than before. Slowly, deliberately, Fausto knocked over his king to declare his defeat. The sound of the marble clattering against the board was loud in the stillness of the room, the only other sound their suddenly laboured breathing.

He had to kiss her. He would. Fausto leaned forward, his gaze turning sleepy and hooded as he fastened it on her lush mouth. Liza's eyes flared again and she drew an unsteady breath, as loud as a shout in the still, silent room. Then, slowly, deliberately, she leaned forward too, her dress pulling against her body so he could see quite perfectly the outline of her breasts.

There were only a few scant inches between their mouths, hardly any space at all. Fausto could already imagine the feel of her lips against his, the honeyed slide of them, her sweet, breathy surrender as she gave herself up to their kiss. Her eyes fluttered closed. He leaned forward another inch, and then another. Only centimetres between them now...

'Here you are!'

The door to the study flung open hard enough to bang against the wall, and Fausto and Liza sprang apart. Chaz gave them a beaming smile, his arm around a rather woebegone-looking Jenna. Fausto forced a courteous smile back, as both disappointment and a very necessary relief coursed through him.

That had been close. Far, far too close.

Continue reading
PRIDE & THE ITALIAN'S PROPOSAL
Kate Hewitt

Available next month
www.millsandboon.co.uk

COMING SOON!

We really hope you enjoyed reading this book.
If you're looking for more romance, be sure to
head to the shops when new books are
available on

Thursday 18th
February

To see which titles are coming soon, please visit

millsandboon.co.uk/nextmonth

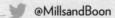

MILLS & BOON
A ROMANCE FOR EVERY READER

- **FREE** delivery direct to your door

- **EXCLUSIVE** offers every month

- **SAVE** up to 25% on pre-paid subscriptions

SUBSCRIBE AND SAVE

millsandboon.co.uk/Subscribe